Double Measure

GEORGE H. FORD is the author of *Dickens and His Readers* (N290) and is one of the editors of the *Norton Anthology of English Literature.* He is Chairman of the Department of English at the University of Rochester.

Double Measure

A Study of the Novels and Stories of

D. H. Lawrence

by George H. Ford

The Norton Library
W · W · NORTON & COMPANY · INC ·
NEW YORK

First published in the Norton Library 1969 by
arrangement with Holt, Rinehart & Winston, Inc.

PUBLISHED SIMULTANEOUSLY IN CANADA
BY GEORGE J. MCLEOD LIMITED, TORONTO

PRINTED IN THE UNITED STATES OF AMERICA

1 2 3 4 5 6 7 8 9 0

For their kind assistance in arranging permissions for quotations I wish to pay particular thanks to Miss Janet D. Crowell of Viking Press and Mr. Laurence Pollinger of Laurence Pollinger, Ltd. I am grateful to the following publishers and agents for permission to quote from books which they have published or control: to William Heinemann, Ltd. and Laurence Pollinger, Ltd. and the Estate of the late Mrs. Frieda Lawrence for passages from the writings of D. H. Lawrence including **The Collected Letters of D. H. Lawrence,* ed. H. T. Moore (1962), 2 vols.; **The Letters of D. H. Lawrence,* ed. Aldous Huxley (1932); **Phoenix* (1936); *The Tales of D. H. Lawrence,* (1934); *Assorted Articles* (1930); **Twilight in Italy* (1950); **The Lost Girl* (1955); *The White Peacock* (1955); *Getting On,* A fragment from the University of Cincinnati collection; "Prologue to *Women in Love,*" in *Texas Quarterly,* VI (Spring, 1963); and also for the following books by authors other than D. H. Lawrence: *Not I, But the Wind* (1934) and *The Memoirs and Correspondence* (1961) by Frieda Lawrence; *D. H. Lawrence* by Rebecca West (1930); *The Savage Pilgrimage* by Catherine Carswell (1932); *Lorenzo in Taos* by Mabel Dodge Luhan (1933). To Chatto and Windus, Ltd. and Random House for *The Poetry of Experience* by Robert Langbaum (1957), and to Chatto and Windus, Ltd. and New Directions for *The Poems of Wilfred Owen* (1963). To Farrar, Straus and Giroux, Inc., for *The Intelligent Heart,* by Harry T. Moore (1954). To Alfred Knopf, Inc., for Lawrence's *The Woman Who Rode Away* (1928), *The Plumed Serpent* (1951), and *The Later D. H. Lawrence* (1952). To J. B. Lippincott and Company for *Lawrence and Brett: A Friendship,* by Dorothy Brett (1933). To the Macmillan Company for *The Letters of William Butler Yeats* (1954) and *Autobiographies* (1955) by W. B. Yeats. To the Viking Press, Inc., for the American editions of the five books starred with an asterisk in the above list and also for the following works by Lawrence: *Apocalypse* (1932); *The Complete Short Stories of D. H. Lawrence,* 3 vols. (1955-61); *Etruscan Places* (1932, 1957); *Fantasia of the Unconscious* (1921, 1960); *Four Short Novels* (1965); *Kangaroo* (1923, 1960); *Love Among the Haystacks* (1933); *The Rainbow* (1915, 1961); *Sons and Lovers* (1913, 1958); *Studies in Classic American Literature* (1923, 1964); *Women in Love* (1920, 1960); *The Complete Poems of D. H. Lawrence* edited by Vivian de Sola Pinto and F. Warren Roberts; and for rights for *The Boy in the Bush* (1924, originally published by Thomas Seltzer). To the University of Wisconsin Press for *D. H. Lawrence: A Composite Biography,* edited by Edward Nehls (1957-59), 3 vols.

For Pat

Preface

Because of the availability of well-prepared lists of writings by Lawrence and about Lawrence, the present study does not include a bibliography. By way of a substitute, several of the footnotes are devoted to listing books or articles which may be of interest to anyone seeking further information, or sometimes, misinformation, on some particular problem under discussion.

As for the documentation itself, in a study frequently involving a close study of a writer's texts it is especially hard to decide where a line should be drawn. To avoid excessive distraction, I have eliminated all footnotes to quotations from Lawrence's stories and novels; my hopeful assumption is that the kind of reader who wishes to locate such passages will be able to find his way round in familiar texts. On the other hand, no one is likely to be able to find his way readily through such bewildering mazes as *Phoenix* or the volumes of letters, and here, unless the context makes the location easy to identify, a string of footnotes has been supplied. A list of abbreviations used in the notes appears on p. 225.

For a Fellowship awarded in 1959 I am grateful to the American Council of Learned Societies, and, for various travel grants, to the Taft Fund Committee of the University of Cincinnati, and to the Research Grants Committee of the University of Rochester. Some of my other colleagues have provided considerable help of a different variety, even those who made little effort to conceal a marked distaste for Lawrence and all his works. Like Anna Brangwen in the Cathedral scene in *The Rainbow,* such friends have represented for me what Lawrence calls "voices of the serpent in his Eden," and an enthusiast profits, as Will Brangwen profited, by having to listen reluctantly to those serpent voices. My friend William Strauss also served memorably to swell the serpents' chorus. Equally helpful were my students, both graduate and undergraduate, who provided another kind of sounding board for the arguments developed in this book; their zestful enjoyment of Lawrence's fiction was an invigorating stimulant. Various Lawrence scholars, including, in particular, Harry T. Moore and V. de S. Pinto, have also provided encouragement and help.

For allowing me to have access to various Lawrence manuscripts and papers, I wish to acknowledge the kindness of the following owners or custodians: the late Frieda Lawrence and the Keeper of Manuscripts of the British Museum (for the ten volumes of Koteliansky papers now deposited in the British Museum); Mr. George S. Lazarus (for manuscripts of *The White Peacock*, short stories, and other items in his outstanding private collection of Lawrence's writings); Mr. Douglas Duncan (for a corrected typescript of *Women in Love*); William S. Clark and the librarian of the University of Cincinnati (for unpublished autobiographical sketches and other documents); Warren Roberts of the Humanities Research Center of the University of Texas (for typescripts of *The Rainbow, Women in Love,* and several unpublished manuscripts relating to these novels).

There remain finally those to whom one ought to be acknowledging a debt but cannot; that is, to those critics and scholars whose investigations have been only recently published. During the long span of time in which this book was taking shape, I tried to keep up, as the phrase has it, with the scholarship and criticism. In the final stages, however, one has to cry halt and settle down to his own writing. Valuable books and articles have appeared recently, such as those by Eugene Goodheart, E. W. Tedlock, Jr., and Frank O'Connor, but I have not been able to refer to many of them or to adjust my line of argument in relation to theirs. The lag is a regrettable but seemingly unavoidable fact of life in present-day book publishing. Similar frustrations develop not only when one encounters recent studies of Lawrence himself but other less obviously related works which might have established helpful points of comparison. In my own recent experience this situation has been illustrated effectively by my stumbling belatedly upon several works by a group of French critics associated with Charles Mauron. Their approach to an author and his writings, characterized by Jean-Pierre Richard as a "méthode d'interprétation thématique," often coincides with the mode generally followed in the present study, although mine is, I suppose, more eclectic, less committed to a conviction that some one critical tool can, by itself, serve to pry open the authorial strongbox.

GHF

Rochester, New York

Contents

Contents

Part One: Figures in a [illegible]

Part Two: Two Major Novels

Part One

Figures in a Carpet

"Somehow I think we come into knowledge (unconscious) of the most vital parts of the cosmos through touching things. . . . Such a touch is the connection between the vigorous flow of two lives. Like a positive electricity, a current of creative life runs through two persons, and they are instinct with the same life force . . . when they kiss on the mouth—when they kiss as lovers do."

—Letter to Blanche Jennings, December 15, 1908

"What ails me is the absolute frustration of my primeval societal instinct. . . . I think societal instinct much deeper than sex instinct—and societal repression much more devastating. . . . I am weary even of my own individuality, and simply nauseated by other people's."

—Letter to Dr. Trigant Burrow, July 13, 1927

"The art-works which can be viewed as glorifying death-wishes cover a large field. . . . It seems to be a general rule, however, that if the effect is beautiful the lust of death is balanced by some impulse or interest which contradicts it."

—William Empson in *The Kenyon Critics*

"The art of living is based on rhythm—on give and take, ebb and flow, light and dark, life and death. By acceptance of *all* the aspects of life . . . the static, defensive life, which is what most people are cursed with, is converted into a dance . . . The real function of the dance is *metamorphosis.*"

—Henry Miller in *The Wisdom of the Heart*

1 Lawrence and Some of His Readers

In Aldous Huxley's novel, *The Virgin and the Goddess,* a dinner party of physicists and their wives is thrown into confusion when the hostess announces her opinion that all scientists ought to be "compelled" to take a "post-graduate course" in the writings of D. H. Lawrence. One suspects that the basis of her recommendation (she herself being the wife of a physicist) would differ from that of Dr. Leavis when he urged the virtues of Lawrence upon the attention of Sir Charles Snow during their celebrated controversy over the Two Cultures. And it would differ also from that of Father Tiverton when he assured us that Lawrence was an improving author for Christians.

Like the work of all major writers, Lawrence's house of fiction has many mansions, and it is the critic's first task to try to indicate which among these he proposes to explore, and to suggest also some of the assumptions underlying his own particular recommendations or assessments.

The following study also originated at a dinner party. The host, a businessman with a zest for reading novels and whose preferences in literature I had hitherto shared, was startled to discover that I had spent the summer euphorically immersed in reading Lawrence's novels and stories. To him Lawrence was a bore, a clumsy bungler whose inflated rhetoric made him ineligible for the then fashionable hierarchy we had formerly agreed upon: James, Conrad, Flaubert, Joyce, Turgenev, Austen, and other respectable practitioners of the fictional art. He challenged me to account for this whoring after strange gods. Pressed by his cross-fire of questions, I found myself stumbling not from lack of conviction but because every item in my explanation seemed to depend upon an antecedent item. The only solution, as I told him, to develop a sustainable chain of argument that might justify what seemed to him my literary slumming would be to write a book.

That was eleven years ago. Distractions and diversions could be listed to account for such a long delay, yet the real cause for the postponement was my gradual realization that to write a book-length study of D. H. Lawrence offers special difficulties. Even so facile a commentator as Henry Miller found these difficulties to be insurmountable. After planning for several years a full-scale discussion of Lawrence, Miller finally abandoned this seemingly congenial task because, as Karl Shapiro explains discouragingly, Lawrence is one of those "Patagonian authors," like Rimbaud, and like Miller himself, about whom a book or "even a good essay" cannot be written.[1]

One obvious source for the block might be the strikingly uneven quality of Lawrence's achievements. Of his early critics, Lawrence observed witheringly: "They were always telling me I had got genius, as if to console me for not having their own incomparable advantages."[2] Every study of Lawrence could adopt the title used by Richard Aldington for his book (*Portrait of a Genius, But*), yet once this phase of his performance is confronted squarely and one learns, as with Dickens or Dostoevsky, how to work one's way through the different levels of his writings, unevenness is not really a formidable obstacle.[3]

A second source of blocking becomes evident when one reads not Lawrence but his critics. What is alarming is the discovery that Lawrence, much more markedly than other writers, seems frequently to lead the critic into exposing himself (or herself) rather than to providing a helpful account of the fiction under discussion. Katherine Anne Porter's complaint, that Mellors and Constance Chatterley would have nothing to say to each other or do with each other in between their occasional bouts of sex, does not tell us very much about *Lady Chatterley's Lover* but may illustrate a distinguished writer's set of intellectual values. These values may be admirable in their own right but they seriously hamper an appreciation of Lawrence's fictional world. Lawrence himself, as Aldous Huxley reports, was a man who was never bored.[4] The trifles of the daily round, even the shared washing of dishes, were to him exhilarating. His critic, who seems to detect nothing but monotony in the unintellectual sharing of such trifles which make up the daily lives of some of Lawrence's characters, is apparently responsive to what is finally a more restricted band in the wave-lengths of human experience than that taken for granted in the novel.

A more striking example is provided by Dr. Leavis. Every admirer of Lawrence will be permanently indebted to the pioneering studies of the novels and stories by this major literary critic, especially for his brilliant and energetic analyses of individual scenes or passages, yet how often we encounter pages in which our attention has been shifted away from Lawrence to the critic himself, pages devoted to an airing of Dr. Leavis's likes and dislikes in religion, or in academic and literary politics. In the pejorative sense of the verb (as Lawrence himself employed it) the artist in such pages is being *used*.

I shall, of course, fall into the same trap myself, yet I hope with some reluctance. Reticence is not the issue. If an understanding of *The Rainbow* were really to be fostered by the critic's parading his idiosyncrasies, none of us should hesitate to move into the spotlight, but the performance does not really serve the cause. Although happily sharing Northrop Frye's convictions about the crucially important role of literary criticism in our century, I am suggesting that the critic helps us most when he tries to get himself out of the way as much as he can.

Swift's prose style has been recommended as an ideal for its plateglass-like quality, a medium through which we can see the object rather than being distracted by the medium itself. Effective criticism is not anonymous but should function similarly. Although there is no such perfectly undistorted medium in prose style or in discussions of literature, and although Lawrence's own medium as a literary critic (a medium which suited him like his beard) was, itself, one of the most highly colored in the annals of criticism, it seems evident that we do his novels a disservice if in writing about them we merely follow his example. Early in his career, after remarking to Jessie Chambers that most authors write "out of their own personality," Lawrence added ruefully: "But I'm not sure that I have a big enough personality to write out of."[5] From a later perspective the remark is one of the funniest he ever made. He had enough personality for fifty writers, a surplus which makes it all the more necessary, in the presence of such a novelist, that the critic's autobiography ought preferably to be subordinated.

This obstacle would probably not have troubled Henry Miller whose critical essays are in the highly personal mode favored by Baudelaire, Shaw, and Lawrence himself. The chief obstacle, I suspect, to any sustained discussion, is that Lawrence's writings are extremely difficult. The difficulties of *Finnegans Wake* are immediately evident from the first page, and an impressive amount of scholastic energy has been successfully devoted to cracking its intricate code.

Women in Love is much less obviously difficult, but the more closely the novel is studied, the more does one become aware that it is equally as challenging as the Joycean puzzle books.[6] Under expert guidance, even the sophomore of today seems equipped to follow Leopold Bloom through Dublin's labyrinth, but he has been less well equipped to follow Gerald Crich's strange peregrinations from Gudrun's bedroom to the death scene in the icy Tyrolean peaks.

In 1954 the novelist, Walter Allen, noted that Lawrence and Joyce belong together in posing a problem "the solution to which is probably vital to the future of the novel as a serious literary form. Their technical innovations, which were a result of their view of man's nature, were such that they wrecked the whole structure of the novel as we have normally conceived it."[7] Joyce's discoveries, I suggest, have been clearly defined for us; Lawrence's less so. And their importance is not restricted to later novelists but is of crucial significance to critical readers as well. As Robert Langbaum says in his admirable book, *The Poetry of Experience:*

> The work of counting up the cultural treasure of the nineteenth and twentieth centuries and formulating from it a modern tradition may well fall upon the now emerging literary generation—a generation already recognizable as more critical than creative just because we of that generation have, I think, been

> rendered silent by our reverence for the immediate past, by our sense of having inherited a modern tradition, of having to master an impressive canon of modern 'classics' before we can speak out in our own right.[8]

I do not know whether Mr. Langbaum would agree to squeeze some older members into his club, but he has precisely described the spirit in which one "modern classic" needs to be treated and also indicated the root of the difficulties in writing about this achievement.

II

Throughout this eleven year period, and earlier, other critics and biographers do not seem to have suffered from the block experienced by Henry Miller. By 1958, seventy books and over a thousand articles had been published on Lawrence,[9] and the tempo of publication has subsequently increased, with a book-length study appearing, it seems, every three months. In 1961 Harry T. Moore announced, with satisfaction, that Lawrence had for the first time nosed out James Joyce in the number of books and articles written about him during the year.

Such satisfaction is not always shared. It is fashionable to deplore the quantity of commentary and to protest that an author's work is smothered by it. I suspect on the contrary that works of literature are, as it has been nicely said, like furniture in that they "gain a patina from much handling."[10] Certainly his sales have not suffered as can be determined in America by the rough-and-ready test of inspecting book counters in any drug store. A recent *Times Literary Supplement* article noted that Lawrence "commands a wider public than any serious modern writer for more than a generation, perhaps since Shaw."[11] Nor has his reputation among the critics suffered. In *The Georgian Literary Scene* a gloomy prediction about Lawrence's future status was offered by Frank Swinnerton:

> My belief is that the reputation of this author will decline. As men and women learn more and more about their own minds,

> his remarkable pioneer work will fall in importance . . . We shall be forced back upon his books as literature; and this test, without considerable reservation, they will not pass.[12]

This was in 1935. From a later perspective one can point out that while Mr. Swinnerton's assumptions were sound enough his prediction was wrong. We *have* been "forced back upon his books as literature," as the present study (among others) indicates, but Lawrence's stories and novels can pass the test. The respect, almost reverence, with which he is treated by many critics, despite occasional cat-calls from Kingsley Amis, Colin Wilson, and others making up the unconverted minority in the gallery, is a remarkable tribute. In Europe he is regarded as one of our major twentieth-century authors and has attracted attention from scholars and critics in France, Germany, and Italy.

What may give one pause is not the quantity of publications about Lawrence but the generally high quality of some of the critical writing (despite violent disagreements about what the right approach should be in discussing his work) in books by Eliseo Vivas, Graham Hough, Mark Spilka, F. R. Leavis, H. T. Moore, William Tiverton, Julian Moynahan and others. To elbow one's way into such a company, all of whom have valiantly wrestled to extract the sword from the stone, would give even Galahad pause. But the venture must be made.

When Graham Hough's *The Dark Sun* was published, V. S. Pritchett remarked that the book "has said all that needs to be said about Lawrence for a long time." This compliment to Mr. Hough's valuable book is certainly not undeserved. What is undeserved is the assumption that for a writer of Lawrence's stature any book (including what follows) will say the so-called last word. Browning's Grammarian settled Hoti's business (whatever it was), but no one has settled Lear's business, or Ivan Karamazov's business, or the business of a white whale. If this great romantic writer is becoming a comparable classic, there is certainly room for further attempts by any of us who have made a protracted study of his writings to indicate their distinctive qualities for other readers.

As for the advantages of close reading, the following observation sounds as if it had been delivered by a Professor of Classics but was offered by Lawrence himself in *Apocalypse:*

> It is far, far better to read one book six times, at intervals, than to read six several books. Because if a certain book can call you to read it six times, it will be a deeper and deeper experience each time . . . Whereas six books read only once are merely an accumulation of superficial interest.[13]

Lawrence's own fiction can be similarly tested. The best of it can be found inexhaustibly satisfying. Like Keats' urn, it can tease us out of thought.

III

What is meant when we call a novelist a poet is not always clear to me, although I have often done so myself. That we can expect to encounter some intensification of language, different from the plodding style of naturalistic novelists such as Dreiser, is probably what is implied, and the term has its uses provided that it does not obscure, in Lawrence's case, that his principal achievement is in the province with which the following study is exclusively concerned: prose fiction. I have drawn from his verse at several points and also from his essays and his delightful travel books, but the focus remains on the novels and stories. I have also drawn extensively from his letters, and to mention this source leads to confronting the question of what use is to be made of an author's biography.

I began this study as a textual purist, convinced by the then already greying New Critics, that it was improper in discussions of literature to introduce any evidence from outside the work itself. It gradually became evident that there was something foolishly rigid in this once usefully-corrective formula, and although my focus is on the work, not the man, I have derived a considerable amount of assistance from his biographers, as indicated in the fourth chapter.

I also began with a marked distaste for literary pilgrimages whether to Stratford on Avon, Stoke Poges, the so-called Old

Curiosity Shop, or to the Lawrence birthplace in Eastwood. Yet here again I was to discover that some typical twentieth-century prejudices can be merely crotchety.

To Australia I did not get, but I did follow Lawrence's trail elsewhere, with visits to Nottingham and to Eastwood with its collieries and pubs, the nearby Chambers farm of *Sons and Lovers*, Felley Mill of *The White Peacock*, and the hayfield of "Love Among the Haystacks." Also visited were Cossall (the setting for *The Rainbow*), Quorn (the setting for parts of *Women in Love*), and the Taos ranch, of course, including talks there, and elsewhere, with those who knew him as a man.

What effect such visits may have on one's reading of the novels I cannot say, but I have a hazy impression of its being helpful. The spirit of place being so characteristically a feature of his writings, one can visit such a village as Cossall and use his novel virtually as a guidebook.

Also, as the Acknowledgments section indicates, I have drawn from collections of manuscripts and typescripts of his writings on both sides of the Atlantic. It will take a generation of textual scholars to make an adequate study of Lawrence's revisions, and in view of the remarkable dispersion of his manuscripts in Texas, Toronto, California and Buckinghamshire, such scholars must be prepared to cover distances undreamed of even by the energetic members of Mr. Pickwick's Corresponding Society. Meanwhile, even if he can nibble only into the edges of these textual problems, a critic proposing to make an extensive study of novels such as *Women in Love* ought to derive what help he can from the available manuscripts.

IV

Two other limits of the study remain to be indicated. Not only was it necessary to pass over the poems and essays in order to concentrate on the novels and stories but among these latter a selection had also to be made. Out of the more than sixty shorter fictions, some eight are discussed at reasonable length, and several others in passing, but many remain unmentioned. These necessary omissions I especially regret.

That Lawrence was the most outstanding master of the short story in English seems to me evident, yet at present writing only one book devoted entirely to his shorter fiction has been published.[14] Of the nine or ten full-scale novels, I have discussed two (*The Rainbow* and *Women in Love*) extensively, and three others (*The White Peacock, The Trespasser, Sons and Lovers*) at reasonable length. Others, including the challenging *Plumed Serpent* which some consider to be Lawrence's greatest work,[15] appear primarily as supplementary illustrations. To be forced into selections of this kind was painful, and there were occasions when I was tempted to turn the study into a Cook's Tour, chronologically arranged, with a paragraph or so for each item of the itinerary, a mode once favored by French literary historians (*D. H. Lawrence: sa vie, ses oeuvres*). Selection, whatever its drawbacks, is preferable. One has to work on the hopeful assumption that readings suggested for the novels and stories which are discussed would make sense for those which were excluded.

In particular I hope this assumption may be valid for both *The Plumed Serpent* and for *Lady Chatterley's Lover*, two major works about which a further word of explanation needs to be inserted. Lawrence himself described his *Plumed Serpent*, at the time of its publication, as his most "important" novel, yet in a letter written the following day, he admitted that his own favorites—and most of us today would share his preferences—were *Sons and Lovers, The Rainbow*, and *Women in Love*.[16]

That parts of *The Plumed Serpent* show Lawrence in his best vein is evident. His uncanny power (fully displayed in the brilliant opening scene at the bullfight) to convey the smell of death in a land is memorable. Despite its many virtues, however, this novel seems his most labored production, and some of his own exhaustion in writing it is communicated to the reader. I find myself rereading parts of it with admiration but without the full measure of enjoyment that *Women in Love* provides. W. Y. Tindal, who regards *The Plumed Serpent* as "by far his best novel," likened it to Flaubert's *Salammbô*, an excellent comparison, I think, for Flaubert's near masterpiece can produce, at least for me, a similar sense of exhaustion.

As for *Lady Chatterley's Lover*, presumably no admirer of Lawrence would have any hesitations about appearing in a censorship court to defend the book vigorously on moral grounds. In a critical court, however, I should have to offer a more complex accounting. The love story itself seems moving and beautiful, and from it I have tried to weave some illustrative passages into discussions of other stories and novels. The background, on the other hand, is too often tedious in its effect, and whether or not Lawrence intended it to appear tedious seems irrelevant. The decadent world of the Pussum, Halliday, and the Pompadour crowd from which the lovers in *Women in Love* make their hard-won escape, may be horrifying, but unlike Sir Clifford's world out of which Connie and Mellors fight their way, it is never tedious. A dance of death, perhaps, but at least a dance.[17]

In most instances quality had some bearing on the choice of novels or stories, although a few of the early and less successful experiments (such as *The White Peacock*) were selected as providing adaptable and useful illustrations of recurring themes and techniques.

Considerations of quality also led to one other sort of selectivity, or more specifically, a form of emphasis. Lawrence is a major social critic occupying a role in the twentieth century comparable to Carlyle's in the Victorian age. In his well-known statement about *Lady Chatterley's Lover*, he indicated nicely how literature (in particular the novel) may operate to educate the emotions of the individual reader in such a way as to transform the course of a society's development, as Wordsworth's poetry affected the emotional life of John Stuart Mill:

> It can inform and lead into new places the flow of our sympathetic consciousness, and it can lead our sympathy away in recoil from things gone dead.

One may admire Lawrence's achievement in this role and give full weight to it without having to admire equally his use of some of the weapons in his social critic's arsenal.

In an important letter to Edward Garnett (April 22, 1914)

about *The Sisters,* Lawrence himself agreed that his writings had often displayed "the vulgarity and disagreeableness of the common people, as you say Cockney." "When the deep feeling doesn't find its way out," he noted, "a sort of jeer comes instead."

What angered him about his hitherto helpful editor and prompted him to break off relations with him was that Garnett wanted him to *cultivate* his "Cockneyism and commonness" instead of suppressing them. "Those are the things to criticise in me, not to rest your belief on," Lawrence said bitterly. Surely this reasonable request is worth heeding. The obstacle is that some readers seemingly well-disposed to Lawrence are unwilling, as Garnett was unwilling, to minimize the occasional jeering note in his writings, because it is one of his notes they relish most.

Although righteous indignation is said to be the principal emotional satisfaction of the middle classes, it is not restricted to that group. It seems to satisfy the needs of any of us who feel more than normally insecure in the social structure of English-speaking countries, perhaps especially in the intricately arranged levels of the Welfare State.[18] These satisfactions Lawrence's fiction can provide, but they seem to me of subordinate interest.

Of his hair-raising sense of the possible doom in store for mankind, a good deal will be said in what follows, and also of his intense awareness of human loneliness, an awareness verging at times into misanthropy itself. But of the cocky commentator airing his exasperations about an army doctor who performed a routine inspection of his rectum (in *Kangaroo*), or about a wealthy host who invited him into his house for dinner (in *Aaron's Rod*), or of a clergyman described by a character in "Daughters of the Vicar" as "a little abortion," I have not, myself, shared the pleasure such passages have provided for some other readers, and I have consequently given them much less attention.

Lawrence can, of course, be gloriously funny in his jeering vein. His portrait of Franklin in *Studies in Classic American Literature* consists of what George Orwell would call a "chorus of raspberries," [19] the kind of heckling to be heard at a lively union meeting but raised here to the nth by genius. Often in his fiction, however, the jeering is obtrusively high pitched (as in "St. Mawr") or else his commentary is flatly redundant.

In his essay on Dickens, Graham Greene speaks of the flat prose style into which an author falls in his least inspired moments as being similar to the brown paper used by shop-keepers to wrap up their commodities.[20] When Lawrence is airing his exasperations, whether in the mild or intense vein, elements of the brown wrapping paper prose style are too often in evidence. The following passage describing Harriett Somers' impressions of her fellow-passengers on an Australian bus is an example of commentary of the mild rather than high-pitched variety:

> An elderly man with bright, friendly, elderly eyes and careless hair and careless clothing. He was Joe, and the other was Alf. Real careless Australians, careless of their appearance, careless of their speech, of their money, of everything—except of their happy-go-lucky, democratic friendliness. Really nice, with bright, quick, willing eyes. Then a young man, perhaps a commercial traveller, with a suit-case. He was quite smartly dressed, and had fancy socks.

This is the brown wrapping paper prose. The passage tells us nothing relevant concerning Harriett, and even as a record of a traveler's impressions of an unfamiliar country it is so casual as to be almost flabby.

The other variety, especially evident in some of the later writings, is similarly unbuttoned but jarringly insistent rather than tired, as in "The Two Blue Birds":

> When a man has an adoring secretary, and you are the man's wife, what are you to do? Not that there was anything 'wrong' —if you know what I mean!—between them. Nothing you could call adultery, to come down to brass tacks. No, no! They were just the young master and his secretary. He dictated to her, she slaved for him and adored him, and the whole thing went on wheels. He didn't 'adore' her. A man doesn't need to adore his secretary.

To pay less attention to the jeering social critic or to the casual commentator does not require whitewashing or radical surgery. Nor does it involve condescension. It is merely to conform to a critical principle formulated earlier in our century by W. P. Ker and one worth reviving: "The best one can do, and it is no dishonourable office, is to get to the right point of view, to *praise* in the right way." [21]

2 Double Rhythms

> For it is as if life were a double cycle, of men
> and women, facing opposite ways, travelling opposite
> ways, revolving upon each other, man
> reaching forward with outstretched hand, woman
> reaching forward with outstretched hand, and
> neither able to move till their hands have
> grasped each other, when they draw towards each
> other from opposite directions, draw nearer and
> nearer, each travelling in his separate cycle,
> till the two are abreast, and side by side,
> until even they pass on again, away from each
> other, travelling their opposite ways to the
> same infinite goal.
>
> —*Study of Thomas Hardy,* Chapter VII

In Lawrence's last story, "The Man Who Died," the heroine is a twenty-seven year old priestess who has dedicated herself to Isis in Search, a goddess represented as striding through the world in "the tormented ecstasy of seeking." This striding figure embodies an emblem of Lawrence's own life with its eager seeking of experience from continent to continent, and more especially embodies an ever-recurring situation in his fiction. To this same goddess almost all his principal characters are dedicated.[1]

Like the picaresque hero of 18th century novels, his men and women are seekers. What they seek, unlike the Smollett-style picaro's pursuit of adventure for its own sake—whether it be Tom Brangwen and his granddaughter Ursula, Aaron Sisson and Kate Leslie, Gerald Crich and Alvina Houghton—is to establish some transforming relationship which will rouse them to life. Often they never find what they are seeking, or, having found it, they cannot sustain it. Yet the searching persists, for in Lawrence's writings the drive to love and be loved is the chief preoccupation of mankind, and not to love or be loved is the most destructive of life's frustrations as illustrated in "The Rocking-Horse-

Winner" with its eerie presentation of a household in which the mother "could not feel love, no, not for anybody." Like his hero, Rupert Birkin, Lawrence would have preferred a word less shopworn than *love* to describe these relationships,• but he was obliged to resort to it in the very title of his best novel.

Of drives other than the search for love he was, of course, aware. A coal miner's son, growing up in a household in which the halfpennies were scrupulously counted, he was intimately familiar with the economic pressures described by other novelists, especially by the Naturalists. It was also a household in which the mother urged the sons up the clerical or professional ladder away from the pit, an experience which contributed to his insights into the role played by class in human relationships. For the most part, however, the scramble for wealth and social prestige which fascinated Balzac, or the drive for professional prestige analyzed so skillfully by George Eliot in her portrait of Dr. Lydgate in *Middlemarch,* are peripheral in Lawrence's fiction. Even the drive inspiring the achievement of an artist is made subordinate. Despite a few discussions of painting in *Sons and Lovers,* this novel is closer to *David Copperfield,* a *Bildungsroman* in which the hero happens to be an artist, than to *A Portrait of the Artist as a Young Man,* a *Kunstlerroman in* which the role of the artist is the central topic of the book.

Again in *The Rainbow,* for example, we rarely see Tom Brangwen at work on the Marsh farm and we never see Will Brangwen at his lace-designing in the Ilkeston factory or Anton Skrebensky with his regiment. The omissions are not from ignorance. Farm scenes in "Love Among the Haystacks," factory scenes in *Sons and Lovers,* and even army scenes in "The Thorn in the Flesh" display a more than adequate familiarity with such occupations and thicken the texture of his fiction. Not from ignorance but from choice he focuses attention elsewhere.

Of Will Brangwen he writes: "During the day, at his work in the office, he kept himself suspended. He did not exist. He

• To his Buddhistic friends, the Brewsters, Lawrence wrote in 1921 that "the word *love* has for me gone pop." (*Letters,* II, 653.) And Lionel Trilling has noted that for Lawrence "'love' was anathema." (*Encounter,* LXI, 1958, p. 17.)

worked automatically till it was time to go home." And home, with its loves and hates, is the setting of most of Lawrence's novels, as it is in almost all the novels of Jane Austen.

What he said of Hardy's heroes and heroines applies even more fittingly to his own. None of them, he notes, "care very much for money, or immediate self-preservation, and all of them are struggling hard to come into being." And "to come into being" meant "the struggle into love and the struggle with love."

It may be objected that this generalization about the search for love is not applicable to three of his novels: *Aaron's Rod, Kangaroo,* and *The Plumed Serpent.* Written during the middle period of his career (1920-25), these three novels, it is true, do represent a deviation from the typical preoccupations of the rest of his fiction in which he had explored relations between lovers, husbands and wives, mothers and sons, fathers and daughters, or varieties of friendship between men, or, more rarely, between women.

In these three novels he seems preoccupied, instead, with problems of leadership and the drive for political power, a shift which may account for their being regarded, by many readers, as less successful than his other writings. One might, nevertheless, put up a case that the shift was less clear-cut than it appears. For one thing there is a continued recurrence of domestic scenes (as in *Kangaroo*), and as for the politics, it is evident that less attention is given to the leader's relations with the mass of his followers than to the various stages of his friendship with another man, sometimes his potential disciple: Lilly with Aaron, Somers with Kangaroo, Don Ramón with Cipriano, a continuation, in effect, of the studies of relations between men already presented in *The White Peacock, Women in Love,* and such stories as "The Blind Man."

The persistence of these preoccupations, even in novels treating of politics, may have added to the low regard in which Lawrence was held in the 1930's. During a decade when political considerations dominated literary judgments, his reputation suffered, not only because of his supposed leanings towards fascism, but because man as a political animal had not really engaged the full measure of his interest. "I'm afraid I don't know much about

Wobblies or I.W.W.'s," he admitted to Mabel Luhan late in 1923. "I don't know much about societies and groups anywhere."

By 1926 he had turned back, one suspects with a sense of release, to what had fascinated him from the beginning of his career as a novelist: human relations. On January 9 he wrote to Murry: "I don't care much about having my own way any more, even with myself." And two years later he recommended *Lady Chatterley's Lover* as "a good novel—love as usual—and very nice too."

II

"*Love as usual*"—Thus characterized, Lawrence's scope as a novelist seems curiously traditional, almost old-fashioned, an impression worth pausing over. His striking innovations must be confronted as well, but it is important first to note that even if he behaves, at times, like a bull in the novel shop, his fiction also very properly belongs in that shop despite his sometimes aspiring to settle instead in the chapel round the corner from it. In his concern for human relations, his fiction is fast rooted in the traditional novels of the 18th and 19th centuries, in Fielding, George Eliot, Dickens, and Hardy. Although exposed as well to the literatures of France, Germany, Russia, and Italy, his principal literary ancestry is English.

Marvin Mudrick in his dazzling discussion of *The Rainbow* tries to pay Lawrence a compliment by arguing that this achievement consisted in cutting himself off from the English tradition of novel writing, whose qualities Mr. Mudrick finds limited, and acquiring the virtues of the continental novelists.[2] Although the compliment is well intended, Lawrence himself would not have welcomed it. Speaking of Dostoevsky, Flaubert, Maupassant, and Tolstoy, he remarked: "It amazes me that we have bowed down and worshipped these foreigners as we have. Their art is so clumsy, really, and clayey, compared with our own." This judgment was passed in 1916, as he was completing *Women in Love*. The writings of Turgenev, he adds, are "so very *obvious* and coarse, beside the lovely, mature and sensitive art of Fenimore

Cooper or Hardy. It seems to me that our English art, at its best, is by far the subtlest and loveliest and most perfect in the world." [3]

That he may have surpassed his English predecessors can be legitimately contended. Most readers understand what Mark Schorer meant when he remarked that the last fifty pages of *Women in Love* have the "real Russian bang." [4] But to try to sever his firm connections with his 19th century English predecessors, perhaps because the critic does not share Lawrence's admiration for them, is a disservice to the novelist and to literary history. "You see, it was really George Eliot who started it all," he remarked to Jessie Chambers. "And how wild they all were with her for doing it. It was she who started putting all the action inside. Before, you know, with Fielding and the others, it had been outside. Now I wonder which is right?" [5]

Lawrence's innovations in *The Rainbow* stem from his wrestling to find a combination of the two modes, but his remark defines his own point of departure. Richard Aldington, who shared his generation's dislike for George Eliot, was faintly amused to detect in *The Rainbow* signs that Lawrence had been affected by reading the author of *The Mill on the Floss.* Whether or not one shares the amusement, Aldington's impression is surely accurately founded.

As for Hardy, it is commonly noted that Lawrence's descriptions of English landscape resemble those of Hardy, yet the real affinity is a more significant one. In his perceptive (although garrulous) essay on his much admired predecessor, Lawrence's analysis of Hardy's view of human relationships often seems to be an analysis of his own novels, as in his stressing the role of the search to which the principal characters are dedicated and for which they suffer:

> It is urged against Thomas Hardy's characters that they do unreasonable things. . . . That is quite true, and the charge is amusing. These people of Wessex are always bursting suddenly out of bud and taking a wild flight into flower, . . . Nowhere, except perhaps in Jude, is there the slightest development of personal action in the characters: it is all explosive. . . . The

> rest explode out of the convention. They are people each with a real, vital, potential self, . . . and this self suddenly bursts the shell of manner and convention and commonplace opinion, and acts independently, absurdly, without mental knowledge or acquiescence.

To stress Lawrence's affinities with earlier English novelists leads on to the related question of his modernity. The role of traditionalism in his concept of the novel may actually have contributed to his reputation as a radical experimenter, a paradox not so absurd as it sounds. His by-passing of the efforts of his immediate predecessors such as Henry James, whose principles of the well-made novel are still invoked to show where Lawrence went wrong, put him out of step. What was old-fashioned (and the same point is applicable to the work of several recent English novelists who have by-passed their predecessors such as Virginia Woolf) seems new-fashioned. I touch on this paradox because it relates to a second mode of categorizing Lawrence's status as a novelist.

Just as he is complimented for being un-English, so is he complimented for being "modern." The term seems unavoidable, and I shall certainly fall into using it, although one may wish sometimes that a fifteen-year moratorium could be declared after which the term might be meaningfully reinstated.

Lawrence has been dead for over thirty years, and his first novel was published more than fifty years ago. Yet in 1963 he is the subject of a chapter (and incidentally a good chapter) in a book by J. I. M. Stewart entitled *Eight Modern Writers* together with other "moderns" such as Conrad and Kipling. It is chilling, by comparison, to encounter an essay by Harry Levin entitled "What Was Modernism?" [6] the past tense accurately reminding us that the term, historically considered, is no longer necessarily a compliment in all quarters. In general, of course, we know what the tag is meant to connote. It is a way of saying that we approve of an author, whether it be Angus Wilson or Euripides, because we find his vision of life corresponds to our recent experience. Albert Guerard's book on Hardy, for example, urged his novels upon our attention on these grounds, and, so used, the term *mod-*

ern is certainly applicable to Lawrence. Yet a fairer test is offered by one of Lawrence's own critical dicta: "Only a first-rate book escapes its date." [7]

III

If his characters' search for love links Lawrence with the traditional English novelists, his impression of the nature of such relationships constitutes his distinctive trademark. Whatever innovations he made in fictional techniques were contrived to convey his view that men and women are attracted to or repelled from each other in ways for which no reasonable explanation seems to exist, that they respond to each other on an instinctual level which lacks a language, and that a vast Newfoundland of frictional conflicts and resolutions of conflict was, therefore, open for a novelist to explore and exploit. Also, and related to this awareness of frictions, Lawrence saw the establishment of relations as usually a stage rather than as a finality. Marriage in many novels is an end; the curtain comes down. In Lawrence it is often only another beginning. Being subject to the fluctuations which characterize, in his view, all experience, the seeming resolution of conflict dissolves. As in Wordsworth's ode, if the rainbow fades into the light of common day, the search resumes.

This distinctive view of the nature of human relations suggests the possibility of detecting a figure in Lawrence's fictional carpet. In the presence of an author's collective works, Henry James says, the first duty of a critic is "to seek out some key" to the author's method, "some utterance of his literary convictions, some indication of his ruling theory."

In 1922, a visitor in Taos, Maurice Lesemann, reported a conversation with Lawrence which provides hints of such a "ruling theory." Lesemann shrewdly noted that for many readers the value of Lawrence's writings consisted in the "exultation" aroused by his descriptions of flowers and animals but that Lawrence himself regarded this aspect of his work as of relatively minor consequence, involving little creative effort. Instead, "he is concerned for the most part with certain human relationships. . . . He is concerned with finding a philosophy which shall show him a rhythm running through the inconsistent truths of experience." [8]

The word *rhythm,* when applied to discussions of fiction, offers problems of definition. As used by E. M. Forster and also by E. K. Brown (whose *Rhythm in the Novel* is primarily concerned with Forster's practice) it refers to a device of linking the parts of a long narrative together by introducing recurring allusions or motifs and by variations on these motifs (such as the repeated and cumulatively expanding references to the echoing caves in *A Passage to India*).

Of this device Lawrence is himself a master, especially in *Women in Love,* but when he uses the term *rhythm* it is not in this special sense of a fictional technique. Instead, in his remark to Lesemann about the rhythm "running through" experience and also in his essay on Poe (if we can understand him there) he adapts a musical or prosodic term as a figure to signify universal forces. The force pictured in Dylan Thomas' poem (*The force that through the green fuse drives the flower/Drives my green age*) is rhythmic in its measured but compelling flow in time, like the force of the tides or the pulsing circulation of blood through our arteries. The figure is familiar enough.

What is characteristic of Lawrence is that one pulsing rhythm does not figuratively embody his own impression of life's forces. Instead, in his world, one such force is dramatically pitted against another in what he calls, in his essay on Poe, a double rhythm: "In true art there is always the double rhythm of creating and destroying."

In art at least then there is Death Against Life as well as what N. O. Brown has celebrated under the title *Life Against Death.* In his last letter to the painter, Mark Gertler, Lawrence spoke of the "painful depression" men suffer under a "*spiritual* change of life" or what the mystics call, he said, "the little death." "Then, in the end," he added, "you come out of it with a new sort of rhythm, a new psychic rhythm: a sort of re-birth."

In the essay on Poe the opposition described is not only between life and death forces, but between two contrary drives in human relations, the one impelling men towards isolation, the other towards union. To each of these contrarieties I have devoted a chapter: on being alone and on being together. Lawrence writes:

> The central law of all organic life is that each organism is intrinsically isolate and single in itself. . . . But the secondary law of all organic life is that each organism only lives through contact with other matter, assimilation, and contact with other life, which means assimilation of new vibrations, nonmaterial.

Each of these statements may be, by itself, commonplace, almost platitudinous. It is the combination of them that is significant and also that Lawrence here is not urging one at the expense of the other. What he recommends in Poe's art is, in effect, his perversity,[9] the denial or challenge to values which we expect Lawrence to recommend in his familiar role as advocate of vitalism.

His role as advocate is, in fact, perhaps too familiar. It monopolizes critical arguments about his therapeutic contributions to twentieth-century life or his contributions as a corrupter of youth, as was certainly evident in the extraordinary spate of articles following the trial of *Lady Chatterley's Lover* in 1960. To overlook its importance would be fatuous, and I have no proposals for trying to deck Lawrence in the incongruous garb of a Pateresque aesthete. I am merely stressing that his best fiction portrays conflicts, one force pitted against another, in which a dramatic testing is more significant than a simplified evaluation, especially a consistently righteous evaluation, of the protagonists.

In *The Romantic Image,* Frank Kermode touches on a useful contrast between the mode of "discourse" and of "image." Discourse, with its direct advocacy of a position, is obviously an essential feature of Lawrence's fiction, but image, which works by indirection and a semblance of detachment or suspended judgment, is equally an essential feature. It is on these grounds that the terms *double rhythm* or *double measure* do suggest an appropriate figure for what James called the "ruling theory" in Lawrence's novels and stories.

"A novel is an impression not an argument," said Hardy, although, as his later novels show, he did not, himself, always follow his own prescription. There were times when Lawrence, likewise, became impatient with the novel. Explosive expressions of his dissatisfaction in his letters are cited to prove that he was not, properly speaking, a novelist at all.

It is reassuring to encounter some of his letters of 1915 written during a period when he was so frantically obsessed with saving the world from the madness of war that he sometimes regarded art as impotent and proposed to Bertrand Russell, as well as to Murry, various kinds of direct action. As *The Rainbow* was about to be published, however, he recommended a friend to read it as "something new in the art of the novel, I think." [10]

A striking contrast is provided by his comment on the little magazine he and Murry were organizing in which he hoped to express his "essential beliefs." "This is my first try at direct approach to the public:" he writes, "art after all is indirect and ultimate." [11] At a time when he had every reason to prefer the direct mode of discourse over the indirect and more devious mode of his novels, this tribute to the art of fiction, with its contrarieties, its testings of human relationships, its lack of direct contribution to what was called the war effort, or to the anti-war effort, is a moving reminder of how Lawrence's fiction may most effectively be read.

3 The "S" Curve: Persephone to Pluto

SONS AND LOVERS

THE LOVELY LADY

THE WHITE PEACOCK

> No woman will give to a stranger that which she gives to her son, her father or her brother: that beautiful and glamorous submission which is truly the wife-submission. To a stranger, a husband, a woman insists on being queen, goddess, . . . the one and only.
>
> —*Fantasia of the Unconscious*

It has been said that the literature of love is concerned with three stages of the relationship, and that different writers emphasize different stages: the before, the during, and the after. The first, characteristically represented by the eager anticipatory stand-on-tiptoe effect in many poems by Keats, is abundantly represented in Lawrence's accounts of his characters in search of fulfillment. As an example on the smaller scale, Gudrun in *Women in Love* breaks away from Gerald's first passionate embrace even though she is "eager" to have more of him. "And even he was glad to be checked, rebuked, held back. For to desire is better than to possess, the finality of the end was dreaded as deeply as it was desired."

As for the second stage, the during, it is the mistaken impression of the man on the street that Lawrence wrote about nothing else. If the during means the act of sexual union itself, there are, of course, only a scattering of pages among the thousands Lawrence wrote. This scantiness could be accounted for simply because about the act there is finally not much to elaborate upon, despite the gallant attempts made in *Lady Chatterley's Lover* to satisfy Edward Garnett's request for a full-scale account of the experience.[1]

More important, however, is the fact that if the tensions engendered by the searching are resolved, permanently resolved that is, whether through sexual consummation or some other mutual recognition constituting a resolution, the search is over and the story is at an end. Again Lawrence's comment on Hardy's practice provides a precise description of one phase of his own narrative method:

> Having achieved and accomplished love, then the man passes into the unknown. He has become himself, his tale is told. Of anything that is complete there is no more tale to tell. The tale is about becoming complete, or about the failure to become complete.

Several of Lawrence's stories picture such a completed relationship as in "Love Among the Haystacks" or "The Horse Dealer's Daughter." Also similarly completed, but with less finality, is the relationship between Birkin and Ursula in *Women in Love.* These will be discussed in a later chapter under the heading "On Being Together."

Scenes picturing the harmonic resolutions of conflict constitute some of the high points of Lawrence's writing, and they also serve as a kind of value scale against which the comparative failures of other lovers can be established. Yet it is obvious that the bulk of Lawrence's fiction does not deal with the during leading to completion; his more typical subject is the after, "the failure to become complete," or, to extend his comment, the failure to prevent the dissolution of what had seemed to be a resolution. The search, that is, is resumed, but often in a different direction. The goal becomes isolation rather than union, as in the bitter stories which I have grouped in the succeeding chapter under the heading: "On Being Alone." Or, more typically in the novels, an uneasy partnership of contrarieties is precariously maintained in which violent discords lead to the spiritual destruction of one or both the partners, and, as *Sons and Lovers* demonstrates, to the destruction or near destruction of their children as well.

II

Autobiographical novels seem to be the easiest kind to write (most of us have one, or parts of one, in a back drawer of a desk), but they are very hard to write well.[2] As the thick volumes of Thomas Wolfe's sprawling novels illustrate, the temptation to throw in almost any experience which occurred in the author's own life, whether or not it contributes to his hero's development, is almost irresistible.

Joyce's solution in his *Portrait* was to exclude ruthlessly any incident or character that did not focus the reader's attention upon Stephen. The style and organization of *Sons and Lovers* is much more casual, much less "engineered" (to use a term of one of Joyce's admirers).[3] Lawrence insisted defensively in a letter that the novel "*is* a unified whole" even though it may be "a bit difficult to grip as a whole, at first." And he added that he hated "the dodge of putting a thick black line round the figures to throw out the composition." [4] Readers, however, are entitled to try imposing such thick black lines, and when they do, it is evident that the structuring of this novel is skillfully devised towards one end, the revelation of "the long and half-secret process" (as Lawrence calls it in his essay on Franklin) of a son's development away from his parents. The organization consists of a sequence of interlocking triangles such as mother-father-son; mother-elder son-girl; mother-son-spiritual girl; mother-son-physical girl. The attention given to William's affair with Gipsy Western may seem, on first reading, carelessly squandered, yet the linking of this triangle to those triangles in which Paul is more immediately connected is crucial, providing the needed preview, the play within the play, of Paul's doomed relationships with Miriam and Clara. And behind the crippled affairs of both sons, and accounting for both, is the crippled marriage of the Morels.

One must beware of the academic fondness for the blackboard

diagram, or the easy reduction of Lawrence's subtle complexities into the simplified formula, the pap for the undergraduate palates, yet the formula is there.

Zola, in his sometimes fatuously cocky manifesto, *Le roman experimental,* had urged the need for novelists to establish that under such and such conditions of heredity and environment such and such actions and character would inevitably eventuate. It is odd that Lawrence who, like Joyce, was to transform naturalistic techniques beyond recognition, has wittingly or unwittingly followed Zola's prescription in *Sons and Lovers.* The trials and errors of Paul Morel's affairs with Miriam and Clara derived, with the inevitability of cause and effect we expect in naturalistic fiction, from the nature of his parents' marriage.[5]

The married life of the Morels is perhaps the most vivid of Lawrence's many accounts of human conflict. Of their life before marriage we learn little, but there is enough information about their courtship to predict that such a coupling of opposites will result in strenuous tensions. Gertrude Coppard, "a Puritan" and "intellectual" is fascinated by "the dusky, golden softness of this man's sensuous flame of life, that flowed off his flesh like the flame from a candle, not baffled and gripped into incandescence of thought and spirit as her life was." We also learn at the outset, and it is a significant touch, of the miner's proposal at their first meeting, that she should go down with him under the earth. "But tha mun let me ta'e thee down some time, an' tha can see for thysen." Gertrude Morel never did take up the invitation literally, yet the early months of her marriage represent her figurative descent into darkness until she began to fight her way out from it. Later she persuades her children to join her in her ascent and in her repudiation of what her dark mate stood for.

From this matching of opposites derives Paul's crippled love affairs just as from the temptation and fall derived the later events of the Biblical narrative. If we seek such parallels, however, we can in this instance turn not to the Bible, which is usually Lawrence's principal storehouse for analogies, but to a variation of the classical myth of Persephone, to which he makes frequent allusion.

In his version the rape and marriage are the center of interest;

the traditional role of the bride's mother, Demeter, is subordinated. It is the tale of a dark man emerging from a cavern in the earth who discovered a fair princess gathering flowers in a field and persuaded her to be carried off to the underworld where he was a king and where she would reign as his queen. For many months the fair woman was happy in the realms of darkness, but after a time she began to feel she had been taken out of one state of trance only to enter another. And she yearned to return to the land of light where there were white-walled temples, and books, and learned priests. Bewildered by the dissatisfaction of his wife the dark king fought hard to prevent her from brooding, but he had to give in and allow her and their children to return to the land above the underground darkness.

The narrative is a variant of a familiar classical myth and has analogies also to the Danish legend of a merman's marriage to a mortal, a legend on which Matthew Arnold drew for his poem, *The Foresaken Merman,* with its haunting refrain:

> And alone dwell for ever
> The kings of the sea.

In the classical version, the fair woman was called Persephone (the name, according to Robert Graves, signifies "she who brings destruction"), and the dark man was Pluto or Hades. In the Lawrentian version, both in prose and poetry, references to the classical myth are sometimes made directly. In "The Ladybird," for example, the dark Count Dionys Psanek reflects upon his affair with Lady Daphne:

> Take her into the underworld. Take her into the dark Hades with him, like Francesca and Paolo. And in hell hold her fast, queen of the underworld, himself master of the underworld.

In one of the poems, *Bavarian Gentians,* the dark blue of these "hellish flowers" stimulated the poet to wish that he could witness the marriage of Persephone and Pluto "as he ravishes her once again/and pierces her once more." [6] More often the analogy is only indirect, and the names are remote enough. In the novels the woman is Gertrude Coppard and the man Walter Morel, or Anna Lensky and Will Brangwen, or Alvina Houghton and an Italian named Cicio, or Kate Leslie and Cipriano, a Mexican general, or the virgin Yvette, a clergyman's daughter, and a gipsy who is finally discovered to be named Joe Boswell.

The contrast of worlds is especially evident in *The Lost Girl,* a novel which Lawrence had originally entitled *Mixed Marriage.* Alvina's relations with Cicio occur first in the "pitch dark," and she tries to fight her way back to light. "Her mind remained distinctly clear. She could criticize him, find fault with him, the things he did." Yet she is "swept away." "Now Alvina felt herself swept . . . into a dusky region where men had dark faces and translucent yellow eyes, where all speech was foreign, and life was not her life. It was as if she had fallen from her own world onto another darker star."

In the short stories are also many instances of the Pluto-Persephone combination as in "The Blind Man," "The Ladybird," and "The Princess." One of the finest of the stories, "Fanny and Annie," pictures the reluctant return to an industrial town of a haughtily beautiful woman who is steeling herself to marry a foundry workman whom she has regarded as alternately attractive and repulsive. From the brilliantly effective opening paragraph describing her arrival in the railway station, one senses that the woman is re-entering Hell itself:

> Flame-lurid his face as he turned among the throng of flame-lit and dark faces upon the platform. In the light of the furnace she caught sight of his drifting countenance, like a piece of floating fire. And the nostalgia, the doom of home-coming went through her veins like a drug. His eternal face, flame-lit now! The pulse and darkness of red fire from the furnace towers in the sky, lighting the desultory, industrial crowd on the wayside station, lit him and went out. Of course he did not see her. Flame-lit and unseeing! Always the same.

The possible variations of a classic myth, which Lawrence saw re-enacted daily in his own home in Eastwood, provided him with a seemingly inexhaustible source of inspiration for fiction.

It was suggested earlier that Lawrence's basic narrative consists of an account of his characters' pursuing a search. The situation in the Persephone story is often represented as a crucial stage in such a search, emblematic of the impossibility of a union between opposites and the consequent loneliness of strangers sharing a bed for a lifetime, strangers who remain strangers.

At other times (and the paradox must later be confronted) such a pairing is treated as an ideal, as in the final scenes of a story such as "Daughters of the Vicar." In one of the best of his early essays, *The Spinner and the Monks,* the world of light and darkness are contrasted, and Lawrence concludes that the ideal "meeting point" is represented by "Persephone embraced by Pluto." "The two in consummation" he writes, "are perfect, beyond the range of loneliness or solitude." Above all, however, whether such a relationship is presented as a crippling one or as ideal, it provided Lawrence with the kind of dramatic tensions and juxtaposition of opposites which are at the core of his distinctive manner of writing fiction and which affect not only his construction of scenes but his prose style itself. Of *Women in Love* he noted that fault had been found with his style because of "the continual, slightly modified repetition." In reply he argued that "every natural crisis in emotion or passion or understanding comes from this pulsing, frictional to-and-fro which works up to culmination."

III

How did Lawrence regard the conflict between Walter and Gertrude Morel? And how did he expect us, as readers, to regard them? Was the Persephone figure "right" in her repudiation of her dark mate, or is the subject of right and wrong inappropriate in this instance? So phrased, such questions sound schoolmistressly simple, yet to attempt to answer them can lead into some of the principal problems that confront us in discussing Lawrence's writings.

One such problem is that of heroes and villains. The role of the hero in literature has become almost obsessively topical in recent literary criticism, and it is therefore of interest to have George

Orwell's report on what surprised him when he first read Lawrence's fiction.

> When I first read D. H. Lawrence's novels, at the age of about twenty, I was puzzled by the fact that there did not seem to be any classification of the characters into 'good' and 'bad.' Lawrence seemed to sympathise with all of them about equally and this was so unusual as to give me the feeling of having lost my bearings. Today no one would think of looking for heroes and villains in a serious novel.[7]

Orwell's statement may appear to be mere nonsense. As a man, Lawrence was as dogmatic and intensely opinionated as his Victorian predecessor, John Ruskin, and his opinions took in as many subjects as Ruskin had embraced.[8] How could such a man create a world without villains and heroes?

When he portrays the managing-engineer, Uncle Tom Brangwen, in *The Rainbow*, it is evident that the writer's loathing of industrialism has produced a hatefully villainous figure. Descriptions such as the following seethe with dislike:

> The fine beauty of his skin and his complexion, some almost waxen quality, hid the strange, repellent grossness of him, the slight sense of putrescence, the commonness which revealed itself in his rather fat thighs and loins.

Moreover, if Uncle Tom Brangwen is a villain it is also evident that other characters have been distinctly cast in heroic mold: Don Ramón in *The Plumed Serpent*, for example, or other leaders who bear a resemblance to Lawrence himself. It would be remarkable if the twentieth-century descendent of Carlyle, the author of *Heroes and Hero-Worship*, had written novels in which heroes have been eclipsed.

Yet despite all the qualifying clauses that my objections suggest, Orwell's observation is ultimately a sound one. It provides a helpful corrective against the kind of reader who salivates his way through Lawrence's books as if they were stories of infallible heroes righteously disposing of wicked industrialists or other categories of the unredeemed. Carlyle and Ruskin wrote tracts and essays, and made very few excursions into fiction; Lawrence wrote fiction and occasionally tried his hand at tracts and essays. Especially in his later work, the tracts and essays ("pollyanalytics" he called them) do get into the fiction inevitably, for as was suggested earlier Lawrence is certainly not the fastidious aesthetic novelist. A mixture of discourse and image is usually present, and from novels such as *Women in Love* we can distill the discourse to our satisfaction and conclude that we then have the book adequately bottled and labeled. But the distillation process has captured a vapor; the novel that Lawrence wrote is not to be thus confined. For the characteristic rhythm in his fiction is double: thesis thrusting against antithesis, lion against unicorn, darkness against light. Gertrude Morel, that is, is not a good force struggling against a bad force, but simply one kind of force, and her husband another kind. It is this sort of balancing that accounts for Orwell's impression of there being no villains or heroes in the novels.

Arthur Mizener once noted that in "all mediocre fiction which deals with serious moral issues, the author and the reader are Christ harrowing a hell full of all the people who disagree with them." Lawrence's writings can certainly offer adrenal stimulation of this variety. Portraits of inadequate males such as Rico in "St. Mawr" provide especially fine opportunities for such indulgences.* Yet most of his work conforms, instead, to Mizener's account of the effect of great fiction, which is "the nearest thing we have to the moral effect of experience itself under the ideal conditions which experience never provides, when we can understand it fully and face all its moral implications." [9]

* Brett's report of Lawrence's reading aloud from "St. Mawr" at the time he was writing the story is revealing. When the horse kicks Rico in the face "You [i.e. Lawrence] read it with such keen joy and pleasure at the final downfall of Rico and the terrible revenge of the horse, that Frieda is horrified; she says you are cruel . . . with great relish and giggling, you describe Rico's plight. You hate Rico so, that for a moment you are the horse." Dorothy Brett, *Lawrence and Brett, A Friendship* (Philadelphia, 1933), pp. 137-139.

IV

When Walter Morel gets up at dawn to prepare his own breakfast, Lawrence observes that "he preferred to keep the blinds down and the candle lit even when it was daylight." What is meant by associating "darkness" with the father in *Sons and Lovers* and "light" with the mother ought to be generally clear to most readers of Lawrence. The terms are intended to signify contrasting kinds of experience (unconscious or conscious); contrasting ways of acquiring knowledge (through the senses or through reason); contrasting concepts of social structure (static and traditional as in a primitive tribe or dynamic and progressive as in an expanding urban society). Of Lawrence's many attempts to describe these contrasting states, perhaps the most effective is his description of the Marsh Farm in the magnificent opening pages of *The Rainbow*. For generations the Brangwen farmers have lived in a happy state of darkness:

> They felt the rush of the sap in spring, they knew the wave which cannot halt, but every year throws forward the seed to begetting, and, falling back, leaves the young-born on the earth. . . . Their life and interrelations were such; feeling the pulse and body of the soil, that opened to their furrow for the grain, and became smooth and supple after their ploughing, and clung to their feet with a weight that pulled like desire.

I select this passage rather than a description of an underground scene to emphasize that darkness is a figurative state which may exist in what is literally bright daylight. The blonde-haired Brangwen men move about above the earth's surface, yet they live in a darkness like that of the miners or of the hero of "The Blind Man" who moves in a pitch-dark stable with uncanny confidence.

The wives and daughters of the Brangwens are not always satisfied with such a life of instinct, with men whose "brains were inert." If the Marsh Farm is Eden, the wives and daughters are the Eves who would taste of the Tree of Knowledge. Their eyes lift up from the earth to the spires on the distant hill sides, spires that remind them of a world of culture, "the far-off world of cities and governments and the active scope of man," different from the "blood intimacy" of the farm.

The world of light involves conscious awareness in place of instinctive knowledge. When Ursula Brangwen receives a proposal of marriage from Anthony Schofield, she is attracted physically to the young farmer, but recognizes sadly that his inner world is altogether different from her own:

> He was an animal that knows it is subdued. Her heart flamed with sensation of him, of the fascinating thing he offered her, and with sorrow, and with an inconsolable sense of loneliness. Her soul was an infant crying in the night. He had no soul. Oh, and why had she?

In *The White Peacock* the same distinction is made more playfully by Lettie when she teases the farmer, George Saxton: "You are blind; you are only half born; you are gross with good living and heavy sleeping . . . Sunset is nothing to you—it merely happens anywhere."

Furthermore, light may be associated with change of social status. Among the Brangwen women, as with Mrs. Morel, there is a desire not only for intellectual development but for an advancement of their sons from one social class to another. Their sense of time is what the sociologists call "future-oriented" whereas their husbands enjoy instead a relatively "future-ignoring present." [10]

A coal miner may be proud of his work, but as Richard Hoggart emphasizes in his study of working-class attitudes, *The Uses of Literacy*, he has no illusions about the possibility of changing his status and hence very little sense of competitiveness. Light is usually a middle-class attribute, Persephone a middle-class goddess. Finally, light is more often associated with women than with men, but the division is not always so neat. The clergyman, emancipated from the soil and mine, belongs to the world of light as does the industrialist Gerald Crich in *Women in Love.* Most complex of all are men such as Rupert Birkin in the same novel who is related to light but has some intellectual commitment to the values of darkness which at times he seems to be advocating. As stated in the *Last Poems* volume:

> Hell is the home of souls lost in darkness,
> even as heaven is the home of souls lost in light.

And the poet adds: "there are souls that are at home in both homes."[11] Discussion of such complex types can be postponed until later. Also to be postponed is how the values of light and darkness apply to the vexed question of Lawrence's treatment of primitivism and its opposites where again it can be shown, I think, the rhythm is once more a double one.•

V

These preliminaries serve to clear the ground for the question previously raised: how did Lawrence regard the elder Morels? Is *Sons and Lovers* an exposé, like Butler's *The Way of All Flesh* or Aldington's *Death of a Hero,* of a hateful paternal tyranny? In later life Lawrence himself asserted ruefully that he had loaded his dice in *Sons and Lovers* because his portrait of Walter Morel, he then believed, had been harsh and unkind. And from additional evidence concerning his early feelings towards his own father, the model for Walter Morel, we should be led to expect a savage cartoon. "I have to hate him for Mother's sake," the young

• The historian of ideas can demonstrate how Lawrence's awareness of double rhythms may derive from a long tradition evident in such writers as Paracelsus, Schelling, and Hegel, which in England became especially prominent in the 19th century. In Madame H. P. Blavatsky's *Isis Unveiled,* a book which Lawrence encountered early in his career, Paracelsus' principle is cited with approval: "Everything is double in nature; magnetism is positive and negative, active and passive, male and female . . . When the mesmerizer will have learned the grand secret of polarizing the action and endowing his fluid with a bisexual force he will have become the greatest magician living." (Pasadena, 1950, I, p. xxv). And with less of the electrical paraphernalia, Coleridge, in his discussion of Sir Walter Scott's having portrayed the conflict between social groups who value the past and those who value the future, refers to the "two great moving principles of social humanity; religious adherence to the past . . . on the one hand, and the passion for increase of knowledge . . . on the other. In all subjects of deep and lasting interest, you will detect a struggle between the opposites, two polar forces, both of which are alike necessary to human well being." (Quoted by J. H. Raleigh, *Victorian Studies,* VII, 1963, p. 31.) John Stuart Mill, in turn, in his essays on Coleridge and Bentham, developed Coleridge's point at full-length.

Bert Lawrence told May Chambers, and the intensity of his hatred astonished her:

> Bert seemed to send out jagged waves of hate and loathing that made me shudder. The father was hungry after his day's work in the pit and ate heartily as he talked—evidently so used to the atmosphere of animosity that he did not feel it.[12]

In October, 1910, he assured one correspondent that he had "never had but one parent," and in the following February, three months after the death of his mother, he exclaimed in a letter that he wished his father were in Hell, and added: "I shivered with horror when he touched me." [13] What remains remarkable is that in rewriting *Sons and Lovers* during the following year, Lawrence was able so largely to master his private hatreds and to create, in Walter Morel, not only a vivid portrait (one of the most vividly *presented* characters in all his fiction) but also a portrait of a man with whom the reader can sympathize. "Paul hated his father so," says the novelist, and under the unflinching spotlight we see the father as we might expect to see him:

> The collier's small, mean head . . . lay on the bare arms, and the face, dirty and inflamed, with a fleshy nose . . . was turned sideways, asleep with beer and weariness and nasty temper.

The spotlight focuses not only upon Walter Morel's physical grossness but upon his ultimate ineffectuality, his blustering threats to leave home and his ignominious return. Yet the portrait remains a portrait and not a cartoon because of the man's vitality and because of his isolation. The picture of his solitary breakfast is unforgettable, concluding as it does with these two sentences:

> He loved the early morning, and the walk across the fields. So he appeared at the pit-top, often with a stalk from the hedge between his teeth, which he chewed all day to keep his mouth moist, down the mine, feeling quite as happy as when he was in the field.

That wonderful touch of the hedge stalk, which endows the collier with the dimensions of an earth spirit, is the kind of detail that cancels out scenes in which he seems merely "despicable." Most of all, however, to achieve balance, Lawrence shows Morel as a man to be pitied. He becomes, in his own home, an "outsider" as Lawrence calls him (an epithet which gained notoriety through Colin Wilson, author of *The Outsider,* and also, oddly enough, a severe critic of Lawrence). Morel's isolation is emphasized by his blackness as he roars in out of the dark night and by his dialect. Like a first-generation immigrant in the United States, his every sentence puts a gulf between himself and his children, who speak a different language. His total isolation, at the end, when his wife is dying, is pictured in scenes that impressed Ada Lawrence as "too deep for tears." [14] One need not have been a member of the Lawrence family to endorse her tribute.

The balancing achieved in the presentation of Mrs. Morel is of a different order. As we close the book, with the death scenes in mind, our impression may be that the whole novel has been in the tender elegiac vein of the poems Lawrence wrote after his own mother died. Most readers would agree with Walter Allen when he notes that the novelist is distinctly on the side of the mother.[15] *Sons and Lovers* was written by Persephone's son, yet its portrait of the Persephone figure is much more inclusive than elegiac conventions allow. The spotlight is as unflinchingly turned on Mrs. Morel as it was upon her husband, only in her case, it is the destructiveness of her love in her relationship with others that is exposed.

In recent years, in fact, it has been my experience to encounter readers who argue that Mrs. Morel is a villainous woman, totally incapable of arousing sympathy on the part of any observant reader. She was responsible, they point out, for driving her husband to drink and isolation, for driving one son to death and

• In some of the love scenes Paul uses dialect as it is used by Mellors in *Lady Chatterley's Lover* as a kind of lovers' shorthand, a shift into the language of tenderness. The comic possibilities of dialect are also evident, although one suspects Lawrence eliminated some of the broader touches, on Garnett's advice, when he revised *Sons and Lovers.* In his play, *A Collier's Friday Night,* when the miner's daughter refuses to hang up the father's wet pit-trousers to dry, he comments: "I wonder how er'd like to clep 'er arse into wet breeches." In the novel this is toned down to "Should thee like to clap thysen into britches as cowd as a tub o' water?"

another to the point of death. The indictment leaves out of account the tenderness of tone—that indefinable quality in drama or fiction—with which Lawrence surrounds his portrait, and with which, in the film version, a distinguished and beautiful actress, Wendy Hiller, was able to endow the role. And yet the indictment is accurate enough. The facts are all there in the novel, but it takes a shift of attitudes, in a later generation, to force the inferences to be made.

Freud is popularly supposed to have changed our attitudes towards sexual restrictions. His more important influence has been to change our attitudes towards the relations of parents and children. Incest itself has always been subject to universal taboo, but it seems that it is only since Freud's theories have filtered into the general consciousness that one can say of a young man: "Poor fellow. He's *sick*. He loves his mother." What Philip Wylie in his *Generation of Vipers* categorized as Momism is by no means extinct, but it is no longer exalted as the highest of virtues. That Lawrence's portrait of the dedicated and energetic Mrs. Morel could be taken by earlier readers (including Jessie Chambers) as an idealization of motherhood and by some later readers as an exposé of motherhood is, in itself, testimony to the balancing which I am suggesting is characteristic of his best work. In 1913 Lawrence wrote to Garnett:

> I had a devil of a time getting a bit weaned from my mother, at the age of 22. She suffered, and I suffered, and it seemed all for nothing, just waste cruelty. It's funny. I suppose it's the final breaking away to independence.

Here is the main subject of *Sons and Lovers*, a subject with kinetic potential. That the novel has affected attitudes of readers is probable, but if we are to classify Lawrence as a kinetic writer (as he is usually classified in contrast to Joyce) it should be with the reservation suggested here.

Butler's *The Way of All Flesh*, a typical publication of the post-Victorian era, is a frontal attack on what seemed to its author to be a tyrannical institution, the family. Butler, like Harriet Beecher Stowe in *Uncle Tom's Cabin*, did his work well but not well enough to keep his novel truly fresh.[16]

Sons and Lovers is not an attack against fathers, or mothers, or families. It is a record of a family and of the pathos of its complex interrelationships. Or, to shift the terminology, Karl Menninger's praise of the novel in *Love Against Hate* may be cited. *Sons and Lovers,* says Dr. Menninger, is a classic study of "mother fixation" in which the son's real hostility to the mother has been skillfully concealed.[17]

VI

One reason that Lawrence was able to achieve variety in presenting his basic drama of the dark man and fair woman was that his own attitude towards the protagonists gradually changed.

When Mrs. Lawrence was dying of cancer in 1910, she finally recognized the futility of her long struggle against her husband. As Lawrence says in his essay, "Women Are So Cocksure".

> And at fifty, when the best part of life was gone, she realized it. And then what would she not have given to have her life again, her young children, her tipsy husband, and a proper natural insouciance, to get the best out of it all. When woman tries to be too much mistress of fate, particularly of other people's fates what a tragedy!

The significance of Mrs. Lawrence's admission does not seem to have made its full impact on her son in 1910; his own realization of it came later. I suspect that the incident accounts for a curious shift of tone that occurs in *The Lost Girl.* The first part of this novel, written early in 1913,* seems to have been infected by

* The "analytical" novel which Lawrence began writing in January, 1913, is commonly assumed to have been *The Sisters,* but was *The Lost Girl. The Sisters,* which he regarded at first as a pot-boiler, was not begun until the spring. Discussions of both novels get off to bad starts when a critic reverses Lawrence's terms and describes *The Lost Girl* as his "pot-boiler" and *Women in Love* as "all analytical—quite unlike *Sons and Lovers,* not a bit visualised." (See *Letters,* I, pp. 183, 193, 197, 200, and, *e.g.,* Eliseo Vivas, *D. H. Lawrence,* p. 21). By April 5, 1913, he had abandoned *The Lost Girl* temporarily, after completing 200 pages. After the war this batch of manuscript was finally retrieved from Germany where it had been in the keeping of Frieda's family, and by May, 1920, Lawrence was preparing the final version for

his reading of Arnold Bennett, especially the mockingly jocular tone Bennett used to describe life in a small Midlands town.[17] The opening pages of *The Lost Girl* sustain this jocular tone effectively, but in one early scene there is a sudden shift into a different key as Lawrence recalls what his mother had said on her deathbed. When the fifty-two-year-old Miss Frost breaks down into tears before Alvina, her crying is described as "the terrible crying of a woman with a loving heart, whose heart has never been able to relax."

> The terrible sound of "Never now, never now—it is too late," which seemed to ring in the curious, indrawn cries of the elder woman, filled the girl with a deep wisdom. She knew the same would ring in her mother's dying cry. Married or unmarried, it was the same—the same anguish, realised in all its pain after the age of fifty—the loss in never having been able to relax, to submit.

This passage, written after *Sons and Lovers* had been completed, suggests that Lawrence was moving away from the stage of hatred for his father to a stage of understanding his father. In the autumn of 1914 he grew a beard.

The main line of Lawrence's development from this time forward follows what psychoanalysts sometimes describe as an "S" curve. Many of us, in our early years, exhibit a passionate preference for one parent, and his or her standards, and then gradually shift allegiance later. The boy who dotes upon his mother

---

publication. Not having seen the manuscript I am only guessing when I suggest that the early parts of the published version were not extensively revised. It is significant, however, that during the war and immediately afterwards Lawrence often wished he could resume writing *The Lost Girl* but never attempted to do so until the 1913 manuscript was back in his hands. In January, 1916, he did speak of having written 150 pages of a novel "as blameless as Cranford," a phrase which Dr. Leavis tentatively assumed must refer to *The Lost Girl* but which is actually a reference to an early version of *Aaron's Rod.* (See *Letters,* Huxley, p. 427, and F. R. Leavis, *D. H. Lawrence: Novelist,* p. 21n.) In any event, until the tangled chronology of composition is unraveled, it is obviously risky to praise Lawrence, as Middleton Murry did, for the "improvement" displayed in his writing between *Women in Love* and *The Lost Girl.* (See *Son of Woman,* 1931, p. 125.)

and despises his father can become a man who realizes that his mother's standards were inadequate or stultifying and that what his father had stood for is what the son now recognizes as valid.

The "S" curve may be detected in Mark Twain's jest about reaching the age of twenty-one and being astonished to realize how much his father had learned in the preceding five years. Lawrence had to be much older than twenty-one before the discovery grew upon him.

In 1926 when he was forty-one years old, he told Barbara Weekley that he had "formerly hated his drunken father, but at this time had swung his sympathy towards him, away from his mother." [18] And in a late autobiographical sketch, as yet unpublished, he is even more explicit about his switch of allegiance:

> My mother fought with deadly hostility against my father, all her life. He was not hostile, till provoked, then he too was a devil. But my mother began it. She seemed to begrudge his very existence. She begrudged him and hated her own love for him, she fought against his natural charm, vindictively. And by the time she died, at the age of fifty-five, she neither loved nor hated him any more. She had got over her feeling for him, and was 'Free.' So she died of cancer. Her feeling for us, also was divided. We were her own, therefore she loved us. But we were his, so she despised us a little. I was the most delicate . . . She loved me tenderly . . . But now, in the after years, I realize that she had decided I was going to die, and that was a great deal to her.[19]

This realization may have been crystallized in 1924 when Lawrence's father died. The event, which Freudians in particular regard as one of the principal turning points in a man's life, was rarely mentioned by Lawrence. Like James Joyce, whose love for his improvident father was the principal love of his life (according to his brother's testimony), Lawrence had seemingly broken all ties with the man himself.• Joyce treated his father to an oc-

• See Stanislaus Joyce, *My Brother's Keeper* (New York, 1958), p. 238. When his father died Joyce wrote one of his best known poems, which ends with an appeal: "O, father forsaken, Forgive your son!" The poem is of the same date, 1931, as a short story by Kay Boyle, "Rest Cure," which portrays Lawrence's dying. The story has a perceptive scene of his confronting his

casional postcard; Lawrence, whose father could scarcely read, may not have managed even that token of contact. What mattered to both writers was not the actual aging parent but what each had stood for in earlier years. To this image both novelists returned in their writings.

If the "S" curve signifies the main line of Lawrence's development, it should be noted that the line cannot be represented as an unbroken progress. There are many points of turning back. Yet in his characteristic fictional mode of balancing one set of forces against an opposite set of forces, we can readily detect a change of emphasis between his early and late writings. A change of values, implied or explicitly stated, tips the balance from Persephone's side to Pluto's.

In his later years, as was mentioned, Lawrence affirmed that if he could rewrite *Sons and Lovers* he would recreate Walter Morel into a more sympathetic figure than he believed he had originally made him. Actually there was no need for Lawrence to rewrite the novel, because in other novels and stories he had already provided the corrections. Several instances can be cited of his returning to scenes in *Sons and Lovers* and recasting them in accordance with his later preferences. In *Aaron's Rod* (1922), for example, the hero, a married man who works as a checkweighman at the coal mines, begins to feel suffocated by the chill rigidities of his home in a small mining town. Like the hero of Bunyan's *Pilgrim's Progress,* he resolves to set out on a journey of self-discovery to distant cities, and his first step, like Christian's, involves his cutting himself off from the demands of his wife and children (although he continues to provide them with financial support).

This incident has been severely criticized by M. H. Abrams in a lively essay. According to Mr. Abrams, the incident demonstrates an artist requiring "our consent" to a position which by its eccentricity or perversity arouses "counterbeliefs" in the reader.[20]

Objections to Lawrence on such grounds involve a problem of

---

father's spirit which is evoked grotesquely by a bewildered red lobster. "I got on very well without you," the son says, but at the end he calls out: "Father, help me." See her *Thirty Stories* (New York, 1946), pp. 23-24.

literary criticism which will often come up in the present study but which must be only circumvented at this point. How do we detect, with certainty, an author's set of values, or, for that matter, a reader's set of values? One can readily say that Mr. Abrams approves of domestic responsibilities, but one cannot affirm, with comparable certainty, that Lawrence is *recommending* the abandoning of wives and children by their restless husbands. What is evident, in this part of *Aaron's Rod*, is that Lawrence was recasting those scenes in *Sons and Lovers* in which Mr. Morel had been shown vowing loudly of his intention to leave home and of his slinking back again, an absurd figure, with domestic responsibilities intact and triumphant.

A similar recasting can be seen in the short story, "Jimmy and the Desperate Woman" (written 1924). An early scene in *Sons and Lovers* had concerned a clergyman who, during a visit with Mrs. Morel, confronts her husband as he comes home from the mines. Morel's irritability and self-pity are stressed in the scene; he appears in his worst light. In the later version, however, Jimmy, an Oxford-trained editor of a literary magazine, confronts the miner-husband of Emily Pinnegar (a woman who writes verses) and on this occasion it is the miner who is endowed with force and dignity. It is the intellectual visitor (one of Lawrence's many later caricatures of Middleton Murry) who this time seems absurd.

But the most striking example of recasting occurs in another short satiric tale, "The Lovely Lady" (published 1927), a late story that illustrates how far along the "S" curve Lawrence's development extended. The lovely lady is a seventy-two-year-old widow who seems thirty in a good light. She is the mother of two sons. The first son, Henry, a handsome young man, had fallen in love with an actress and died "after an awful struggle" because "his mother had humorously despised him for the attachment. So he had caught some sudden ordinary disease." Her second son, Robert, now thirty-two years old, has been as "fascinated" by his mother as his brother had been. On him the effect of his attachment is that he cannot be a "lover of women." His Miriam-like cousin, who loves him despite his frigidity, recognizes that his mother was "going to kill Robert as she had killed Henry. It was clear murder: a mother murdering her sensitive sons, who were fascinated by her: the Circe!" The story, which involves the mother's exposure and death, is an effective horror story in its own right.

As in "The Rocking-Horse Winner" and in some stories of Henry James, what inspires horror is the spectacle of the perverse imposition of will. But to anyone familiar with Lawrence's life and writings "The Lovely Lady" takes on an additionally hair-raising dimension. Had Mrs. Lawrence lived until 1927, she would have been seventy-four years old (the Lovely Lady was seventy-two). Her son, William Ernest Lawrence, had died at twenty-three under identical circumstances as his counterpart in the story who died at twenty-two. And there is a further parallel, which although purely fanciful and not biographical in this instance, provides a final twist of the knife.

In *Sons and Lovers* the attachment between Mrs. Morel and the Congregational clergyman is of minor significance, not constituting a significant triangle, but in the original version of the novel, *Paul Morel,* the clergyman was a more prominent figure, a serious rival for Mrs. Morel's affections.[21] In "The Lovely Lady," the younger son is the offspring of an affair between the mother and her lover, a Jesuit priest.

In this late story, under the guise of fiction, we are witnessing the spectacle of the mature Lawrence, like Hamlet in the closet, confronting his mother, Gertrude, and reassuring his father's ghost. In the story, Cecilia asks Robert what it was his mother had wanted from life. "'She didn't even *love* herself,' said Ciss. 'It was something else—what was it?'" And Robert answers: "'Power to feed on other lives . . . She has fed on me as she fed on Henry.'"

It is startling to put beside this a passage from the recently discovered Chambers papers in which May Chambers records what Lawrence himself had said seventeen years earlier, in 1910, as his own mother was dying:

> "Strange, isn't it, that I couldn't please her?"
> "What *did* she want?" . . .
> "Me," he said softly. "Just me."

And the shift from *Sons and Lovers* is represented not only by a modification of values but by a marked shift of tones and method to which the form of a short story is more readily adapted than is a full-length novel. The tense balancing of forces characteristic of Lawrence's more typical fiction tends to break down when the central character is so incontestably villainous as is the lovely lady. When Persephone becomes Circe we can expect that Pluto is apt to become a somewhat righteous hero, a dark Perseus or a St. George, a figure who still carries off maidens to his regions of darkness, but more especially now as their saviour and protector rather than as their mate.

VII

"Hullo, Proserpine—had visitors?" The speaker here is the gamekeeper, Annable, in *The White Peacock,* greeting his second wife. Applied to this poor female drudge who lives in quarters almost as squalid as those of the brickmakers in Dickens' *Bleak House,* the classical name is incongruously humorous. It is as incongruous as the name the Saxtons use for their greedy sow who devours her offspring: she is called Circe. Incongruities aside, *The White Peacock* raises some interesting challenges for the interpreting of Lawrence's fiction, and I propose to round out this discussion of his contrasting rhythms by shifting away from his later stories back to this early novel, his first, written between 1906 and 1910, and published in 1911.

Our initial impression might be that the conflict is not yet there, for the action seems less important than the loving evocation of a pastoral setting,—the brooks, hayfields, and wild flowers which the characters observe in their walks—and it is further obscured by the quantity of their precious conversations about books and paintings. Moreover the narrative method is hardly conducive to clarity of focus. Despite the pains taken by the neophyte novelist, his handling of the first person point of view remains excruciatingly clumsy.

In *Wuthering Heights* (a novel strikingly similar to *The White Peacock* in its story and its ranking of characters) Emily Brontë sometimes got into difficulties in contriving to keep her narrator, Nellie Dean, on hand to report upon intimate exchanges between Cathy and Heathcliff. Nevertheless her method was almost always under control. Lawrence loses control after only a few pages. When Lettie Beardsall sets out to visit her lover, Leslie Tempest, her brother Cyril, the narrator, remains at home and yet continues to record the whole of their conversation.

On such grounds one can recognize why Elisio Vivas, in his study of Lawrence, refuses to discuss *The White Peacock* at all. It is, however, worth discussing, like an early Shakespearian play or Hardy novel, both for its charm in its own right and for its interest as forecasting Lawrence's characteristic preoccupations as a writer of fiction.

Near the end of the novel, George Saxton talks wistfully with Lettie, the woman he has always loved, and looking back over his fruitless pursuit of her he remarks: "I was only a warmth . . . to you. So you could do without me. But you were like the light to me, and otherwise it was dark and aimless." And earlier he exclaims: "I couldn't endure complete darkness, I couldn't. It's the solitariness."

Although this familiar image of light and darkness does not appear often in *The White Peacock,* the division it stands for is at the core of the book. In one category is the young farmer, Tom Renshaw. "He was exceedingly manly," says Lawrence, and then helpfully defines this quality: "that is to say, he did not dream of questioning or analyzing anything." At the end of the novel Renshaw is like the simpler characters in Hardy's novels, his Wessex peasants or Gabriel Oaks or Diggory Venn. He towers erect and happy in the midst of more complex characters who have fallen.

On the opposite side of the line is Cyril, the narrator, who is reputed to have a highly analytical mind. His occasional reflections and generalizations in the manner of George Eliot's authorial comments are perhaps meant to demonstrate his intellectual enlightenment, but in his case the light disappointingly washes out all color from Cyril's character. He is the man whose "soul" and consciousness are fully developed; the adjective "souly" is used in the novel to apply to characters who are emancipated or at times emancipated from the level of bodily pleasures. Of Annable, Leslie comments: "Splendidly built fellow, but callous —no soul."

All of the characters in *The White Peacock* could, in fact, be grouped along a spectrum of darkness and light.

Annable	Tom Renshaw	Saxton farmers	George	|	Lettie	Leslie	Emily	Mrs. Beardsall	Cyril

The important point to note about this spectrum is that it is a horizontal bar, not a scale of values arranged vertically. Tilting the bar so that the dark side appears to be on top is the commonest mistake in interpretations of *The White Peacock.*

The two characters at the center of the spectrum, George and Lettie, try in various ways to cross over to each other's side. Lettie is alternately attracted and repelled by the bulging biceps, masculine independence, and exuberant polka dancing of the young farmer, and he, in turn, is attracted away from his own set of values by the dazzling talk of this elegant bluestocking. Electrical vibrations, such as we encounter in Lawrence's later writing, indicate the intensity of their attraction:•

> They gazed at each other for a moment before they hid their faces again. It was a torture to each of them to look thus nakedly at the other, a dazzled shrinking pain that they forced themselves to undergo for a moment, that they might the moment after tremble with a fierce sensation that filled their veins with fluid, fiery electricity. She sought almost in panic, for something to say.

• Similar references to electrical contacts and energies, a prominent feature of Lawrence's imagery, appear in one of his earliest letters. On December 15, 1908, he was speculating about the "positive electricity" generated when two lovers kiss on the mouth. This body of imagery was apparently derived from a wide variety of sources as W. Y. Tindall shows in his *D. H. Lawrence and Susan his Cow,* pp. 66-67, 152. Another writer who would seem to have anticipated Lawrence most closely, Gerard Manley Hopkins, was virtually unpublished in 1908 and would not have been known to him. As J. Hillis Miller notes: "The world in Hopkins is a vast network of electrical discharges given and received by objects which are an inexhaustible source of the divine energy." ("The Creation of Self in Gerard Manley Hopkins." *ELH,* XXII, 1955, p. 304.)

But in this novel, unlike *Sons and Lovers,* Persephone does not get carried off by Pluto. Instead, in the manner of the frustrated lovers in Browning's *The Statue and the Bust,* they maim each other without union. George lacks confidence in his attempts to cross the line, and Lettie, like Cathy in *Wuthering Heights,* decides to marry a man of higher social status. She persists in going through with the marriage despite her discovery, before the ceremony, that Leslie is an unsatisfactory lover. The latter scene is, incidentally, a curiously indirect presentation, almost Jamesian, for the narrator, on this occasion, does not get inside the bedroom to report on the conversation between the lovers. In the original version of *The White Peacock* the scene may have been more explicit, for Lettie, made pregnant by Leslie, marries George. Whether Mrs. Lawrence ever read the novel is a disputed question, but she seems to have known of this scene, in its original form, and to have been disgusted by it. To compare the scene with the vivid account of Gerald's visit to Gudrun's bedroom (*Women in Love,* ch. XXIV) is instructive.

For the remainder of the novel we watch Lettie's frustrations as a society wife, and George's deterioration into a hopeless drunkard, a decline accelerated by his marriage to a curvaceous barmaid whose later concern for refinement is represented satirically and serves as a foil for Lettie's standards.

Similarities between *The White Peacock* and the novels of Hardy are obvious, but what seems to be a significant difference needs to be pointed out. The President of the Immortals is conspicuous by his absence; Lawrence does not follow Hardy's bent of attributing human sufferings to Fate, a subject to which, in fact, he seldom refers. Yet his characters, certainly in these early novels, are fated simply because they act out their own natures. Their combined self-assertions, like the voices in Hopkins' poem, make up the noise, sometimes harmonious, sometimes (as here) discordant, of his compositions:

> each hung bell's
> Bow swung finds tongue to fling out broad its name;
> Each mortal thing does one thing and the same:
> Deals out that being indoors each one dwells;

> Selves—goes itself; *myself* it speaks and spells;
> Crying *What I do is me: for that I came.*

To what extent is Lettie to blame for the unhappy sequence of events in *The White Peacock?* Her role (like Gertrude Morel's in *Sons and Lovers*) is the most difficult one to assess in the novel. The best way of approaching it is a roundabout one. Annable's role should be considered first.

The "dark figure" of Annable comes to fascinate Cyril as it has fascinated many readers. In the midst of the effeminate chatter of some of the other characters, the gamekeeper's blunt exclamation seems to be the voice of reality. "Do as th' animals do," he says, taking his gospel, oddly enough, from Herbert Spencer. His children "can be like birds, or weasels, or vipers, or squirrels, so long as they ain't human rot."

But is this really the voice of Lawrence's raisonneur? Surely the man is almost as sick, in his way, as George Saxton after he has become a drunkard, and for similar reasons of disillusionment. Cyril is warmly attracted to Annable as if he were an "affectionate father" for him, yet he recognizes that the man "was fundamentally very unhappy—and he made me also wretched." It should be noted that Annable was not born to be a happy farmer like Tom Renshaw. His tirades against "civilization" and "culture" are not native woodnotes wild, but the outbursts of someone who had been exposed to civilization at Cambridge. Soured because his first wife, the daughter of a peer, had become "souly," he consciously chose to repudiate everything on the light side of the spectrum, and his repudiation has something of the hysteria of the convert. That his break with his wife had been incomplete is indicated by his sudden death after he learns of her death.

It has been suggested by Graham Hough that Annable's role is extraneous. I should argue that it is effectively integrated, and that it operates in a way similar to the triangle of William-Gipsy-Mrs. Morel in *Sons and Lovers*. The sequence of Annable's relations with Lady Crystabel constitute a comparable play within the play. Of his resemblance to George Saxton we get various reminders. To his first wife Annable became, he says, "her animal—son animal—son boeuf." He describes himself elsewhere as a "bull." Lettie often refers to George as "Mon Taureau," and in such passages the two men become doubles, secret sharers. Cyril, watching George's rippling muscles after they have swum together, thinks back to the fate of the dead gamekeeper. "I remembered the story of Annable," he says. The reader is likewise expected to remember it, for Annable's early marriage provides a preview of what marriage between Lettie and George might have been like. Married or unmarried, this pair of lovers would, it seems, suffer.

Of Lettie's resemblance to Lady Crystabel we also have reminders, but the technique of suggested doubling, in this case, is less direct than for the two men. It derives from using an image (anticipating a method used in some scenes in *Women in Love*) as a kind of lens which brings various actions and characters into focus. The image here is the White Peacock.

According to Richard Aldington, *The White Peacock* was misnamed for it "has nothing to do with peacocks, white or blue-green, and everything to do with English people of the soil and of the mine half a century ago." [22] From a critic who is elsewhere frequently perceptive in his discussions of Lawrence this obtuse observation suggests a temporary amnesia. Lawrence's choice of title was as appropriate as was Shakespeare's for *The Taming of the Shrew*. For the image of the peacock, as some later critics have become more aware, is of crucial significance, even though the bird is not directly encountered until Part II of the novel, when it is identified by Annable with the "very soul of a lady." Pedants incidentally might object that Lawrence should have pictured a peahen rather than a peacock, but he took care of the difficulty, when revising his text, by using the possessive pronoun *its* rather than *her*.•

• In George Moore's *Evelyn Innes* the heroine walks through an art gallery with a man: "She followed attentive as a peahen, he spreading a gorgeous tail of accumulated information." Lawrence could hardly have used such a female bird to represent the arrogant female spirit he was portraying. The male peacock, he said in a later essay, is the final perfection of visual beauty and has such "assuredness" that it makes men angry. (*Phoenix*, p. 41.) In the earliest editions of *The White Peacock* Annable exclaims that the bird

The scene in the churchyard is an effective one. Cyril has never seen the gamekeeper in such a "state of perturbation" as is provoked by the gorgeous bird, with "its voluptuous neck," perched on the statue of an angel. The implication is that the bird in effect is the reincarnation of the wife who has just died. The manuscript version makes the identification more explicit by describing it as "the great ghoul of a bird." Like Swift, with his verses on Celia, Annable eases his resentment by linking the beautiful and the excremental: "A woman to the end, I tell you, all vanity and screech and defilement." Again the manuscript version is more explicit: "that's how a woman does defile this young angel in you—with her dirty screeching pride and show."

The linking of Lettie with the white peacock is most subtly handled in the subsequent chapter of the novel, and is made explicit throughout the rest of the book, especially after her marriage.

> As she turned laughing to the two men, she let her cloak slide over her white shoulders and fall with silk splendour of a peacock's gorgeous blue over the arm of the large settee. There she stood, with her white hand upon the peacock of her cloak, where it tumbled against her dull orange dress. She knew her own splendour, and she drew up her throat laughing and brilliant with triumph.

In rereading the novel, we may also note how often this comparison was anticipated in the earlier parts, in Lettie's preference for white clothing and even in the distinctive (and not always attractive) voice she assumes in her more flirtatious vein (the peacock's screech).

A chapter entitled "The Irony of Inspired Moments," which follows the scene of Annable and the peacock, might be described as the climax of the action. It also illustrates that if Lawrence's narrative-method is clumsy in this early novel his handling of evocative imagery is already masterful. George

---

had "run *her* filthy muck over that angel." In the second issue this was changed to "the miserable brute has dirtied that angel." In the manuscript Annable also refers to the bird as "the proud bitch!" which Lawrence corrected (in manuscript) to read: "the proud fool!"

looks at a copy of the illustrations Beardsley had drawn for Wilde's *Salomé*, and he suddenly resolves that he must have Lettie. At nightfall, after sending her some white violets which, he says, also remind him of her, he proposes to her, but it is too late.

If we open up the book that so excited George's desire for Lettie, we become aware of how subtly Lawrence has used his image. In the cover design, and in scene after scene, Beardsley shows Salomé, the prophet-slayer, dressed in peacock skirts or surrounded by groups of peacocks. And the immensely long torso, the towering height of the princess provides an explanation for Lawrence's having represented Lettie herself as almost six feet tall. Even George Meredith would have hesitated to picture one of his strapping heroines on such a scale. The young Lawrence, saturated in the art of the Pre-Raphaelites and of the 1890's, took the risk and relied upon his readers to surround his heroine with a cluster of associations: peacocks and tall princesses and what George Saxton calls the "naked lines" of Beardsley's provocative drawings. The sexual impact of these illustrations upon George is evident in the novel, but again a passage in the manuscript, later suppressed, underlines what his reaction was:

> I was thinking how she'd look, and I couldn't imagine. I wish she wasn't such a toff—I wish she'd come with no clothes on at all—like the drawings—and me as well: then she'd want me.

Cyril remarks sarcastically after this outburst: "Draw it mild do." And in later life Lawrence himself would speak of the Beardsley decade as "now a little ridiculous."[23] At the time of writing *The White Peacock*, however, he was much less detached from it.

Violet Hunt records that when she first knew Lawrence, he was "more conversant with decadent poetry" than herself or Ford. "And that," she added, "is saying a great deal, in fact, I think he had studied it too deeply."[24]

These associations are worth resurrecting as a reminder that Lettie, thus linked with Salomé and peacocks, could be viewed as representing what Salomé, according to Frank Kermode, represented to Wilde: "an innocent, totally destructive malice;

beauty inhumanly immature and careless cruelty."[25] Yet Lettie, like her colorful successor Gudrun Brangwen in *Women in Love,* is much more than a period figure, an 1890's belle dame sans merci. The complexity of the portraiture is evident in the image of the peacock itself. Why is the peacock a *white* peacock? The final interview between Annable and Cyril concludes as follows:

> "So she's dead—your poor peacock!" I murmured . . .
> "I suppose," he said, "it wasn't all her fault."
> "A white peacock, we will say," I suggested.

Annable laughs, and Cyril extends his hand in farewell, startled "by the white sympathy it seemed to express, extended towards him in the moonlight." The exchange is so brief that we can miss its significance. Whiteness evokes not merely Lettie's favorite color of dress but indicates how her character itself is to be estimated. It is her nature to dazzle by beauty, but she is distinctly not evil. Whiteness here is an evaluative test of character more than a color. Like Mrs. Morel, Lettie herself suffers from the relationships which cause others to suffer. What George Eliot said of her *Mill on the Floss* (in a letter of April 4, 1861) could have been repeated by the author of *The White Peacock.* "The very soul of my intention in the story," Eliot wrote, was "the exhibition of *the right on both sides* [on Tom Tulliver's, that is, and on Maggie's]."

In this connection it is interesting to consider Lawrence's comments on Sue Bridehead in Hardy's *Jude the Obscure.* Sue is another heroine whose relations with men end in destruction. An Oxford student who lived with her died of frustration; Jude is likewise destroyed, and her husband, Phillotson, suffers painfully from her amatory fluctuations. Desmond Hawkins labeled her bluntly: "the nastiest little bitch in English literature." Lawrence, by contrast, writes about her with warm understanding and sympathy. If Sue is like a bird it would be a dove rather than a peacock, but in any event for Lawrence she is, like Lettie, a creature of whiteness. "But as she was formed she was formed, and there was no altering it."[26]

VIII

This discussion of the Persephone-Pluto figures in Lawrence's earlier novels, and his methods of balancing one set of forces against another, has involved evaluating the characters and asserting whether or not each is sympathetically portrayed. Despite objections by purists, who would like to confine all criticism of fiction to the level of whether a novel has some prescribed shape and form, it is evident that most discussions of novels and plays inevitably swing back into the disputed and perhaps aesthetically disreputable territory of characters and their values. The really disturbing objection to such discussions is one rarely enough confronted. It concerns the extent to which the evaluations are affected by the critic's experience, age, sex, and political or religious preferences.

Despite the pioneer work of I. A. Richards in related areas, we know more about how an artist creates a novel than how a reader recreates it in his own mind. *Fiction and the Unconscious* by Simon Lesser does offer some helpful data, and approaching the issue from an altogether different direction is Wayne C. Booth's brilliant study, *The Rhetoric of Fiction,* which honestly confronts some of the problems of how an author's values, or implied values, may affect the responses of a reader. Yet about the predispositions of readers we need to know still more, not to eliminate or neuter the predispositions but to be aware of how they may sometimes contribute to incomplete or misleading interpretations of a writer's work.

The commonest misreading of Lawrence's novels derives, I suggest, from a special kind of reader, usually a male reader, who *wants* Lawrence to preach a gospel of darkness and to scorn the light instead of setting up the two forces in balance. Consciously or unconsciously such a reader may be an anti-intellectual, bored by the restraints and confinements of civilization, especially of the academy or establishment. Consciously or unconsciously he may perhaps be a misogynist, alarmed at the growing matriarchal tendencies in modern society. In either case, he is disposed to find in Annable's speeches about the rottenness of civilization and the destructiveness of women not one of the voices in *The White Peacock* but *the* voice of the novel, and having discovered the voice he applauds it exclusively.

The Persephone-Pluto drama arouses partisan spirit in the reader by touching upon values which he may never have examined but to which he adheres with passion and conviction. Given the state of contemporary society it may be that these values are admirable and wise. I am not concerned, at this point, in criticizing them but rather, by describing them, to suggest their effect on how Lawrence's stories and novels are read or misread.

Those who praise Lawrence by making over all his fiction into tracts advocating darkness may be responsible for the hostility of other sorts of readers, including, in particular, women readers.

One of the most remarkable ironies of Lawrence's reputation is that the living man was idolized by women (he himself regretted that he had less success with men) whereas his writings have subsequently suffered some of their severest drubbings at the hands of women critics. During his lifetime, aside from those in the inner circle, such as the Honorable Dorothy Brett, Catherine Carswell, or even Lady Cynthia Asquith, he was able to attract the affectionate devotion of others who saw him less often, including Hilda Doolittle in whose *Bid Me to Live* published in 1960, he is most enthusiastically portrayed. Even Katherine Mansfield, despite their abusive quarrels, found his spell uncannily irresistible. That one of the few women critics to defend *Lady Chatterley's Lover*, Dame Rebecca West, had also encountered him as a man is again an indication of his living magnetism.[27]

His writings, on the other hand, seem, with some exceptions, to have grated on feminine sensibilities as is evident in the critical comments of Katherine Anne Porter, Virginia Woolf, Gertrude Stein, Kathleen Nott, Simone de Beauvoir, and Dame Edith Sitwell. Dame Edith, in fact, was unimpressed by the man as well as by his writings which in her verdict (expressed in 1960) are doomed to shrink with time. In a more specifically damaging comment, Kathleen Nott assures us that "Lawrence, as we know, had no present use for love and personal relationship." [28]

One may wonder whether there is some quality of excessive

masculinity in Lawrence's fiction that might account for these repulsions, although it is always difficult to isolate masculine or feminine qualities in such a context. Virginia Woolf herself made an interesting sally into the subject arguing that the most satisfactory writers are neither masculine nor feminine but, like Jung's redeemer heroes, androgynous.[29] Oddly enough, on such reasoning, Lawrence ought to have been entitled to a high rank in Mrs. Woolf's hierarchy. Few writers are more strikingly androgynous. He had the same experience as Evelyn Waugh of having his first novel reviewed as if the author were a woman, and in Lawrence's case, the mistake is a readily understandable one ("She," said the prim reviewer in the *Athenaeum* of 1911, "is needlessly frank to a fastidious mind.").

I am suggesting that the protests of some feminine critics may have been aroused not by what Lawrence's fiction is, but by what some masculine critics say it is. Later stories such as "The Lovely Lady" present, as we have seen, their own problems of balance, but for the early fiction the bar of the spectrum is not tilted from its horizontal position.

The White Peacock provides, as I was indicating, an early test case. In what is probably the most informative and otherwise satisfactory study so far made of *The White Peacock*, Robert Gadjusek sets out to make Annable into Lawrence's spokesman.[30] I dispute this reading primarily on the basis of the analysis of the novel already elaborated in the present chapter. In addition, a few items of evidence beyond the text may also buttress the argument. According to Jessie Chambers, for example, the youthful Lawrence was preoccupied with the light side of the spectrum, not with the dark. "As for me," he told her, "I trust entirely to the intellect." [31] Later, however, about the time he was completing *The White Peacock*, he began to distrust such exclusive reliance upon intellect and spoke to his Eastwood friend Hopkins of "premental" consciousness. The two ways to knowledge were, at the time, both held.

The emergence of his philosophical position is also indicative. In an unpublished letter to one of his professors at Nottingham, he mentions how he had developed from monism, through pragmatism, to pluralism, a position which, in his case, meant not only his affirming the existence of different kinds of reality but of different modes of perceiving reality.

Of Annable's role in *The White Peacock* the most significant comment is Lawrence's own statement to Jessie Chambers who had protested about the introduction of his "cynically brutal" speeches into the revised version of the novel.• "He *has* to be there," Lawrence replied. "Don't you see why? He makes a sort of balance. Otherwise it's too much one thing, too much *me*."

Lawrence's statement is extremely helpful. It illustrates his conscious concern with double rhythm, and it reminds us that the young Lawrence, the Lawrence before the beard, was similar to Cyril, the young intellectual, and to Lettie herself (Jessie Chambers notes that both the brother and the sister represent aspects of Lawrence).

In *The White Peacock* the novelist is observing the dark Plutonic figure of Annable. Later in life, having rounded his "S" curve, he sometimes tried to become the dark figure, but at this stage he was the young artist in search, an observer of contrasting values, deeply fascinated by the world of darkness while still committed to the world of light.

One effect of these divided allegiances on Lawrence's character was noted by Henry Miller. In a letter to Lawrence Durrell, Miller recommended a study of both *Aaron's Rod* and Dostoevsky's *The Double* for their insights into the problems of double awareness. "Lawrence suffered from it too. And he knew it. . . . Not accepting oneself in toto. Not integrating." [32]

Jessie Chambers also lamented that Lawrence's character be-

• See "E.T.," *D. H. Lawrence,* pp. 117-18. Miss Chambers provides data concerning Lawrence's own early encounter with a gamekeeper, and of his first writing the scene of Annable and the angel when he was 22. Lawrence continued to irritate her with the gamekeeper, not only in *Lady Chatterley's Lover* but in his story "The Shades of Spring." In this story, the hero, a Paul Morel figure, returns from London to revisit the farm of Hilda, a heroine similar to Miriam in *Sons and Lovers.* He is astonished to find that she is enjoying a love affair with a young gamekeeper whom she visits in a fur-lined hut in the woods. Jessie Chambers was deeply upset by this story and affirmed the author was so split in his personality that he must be mad. What is especially interesting about the story (written perhaps in 1914) is that in this version Lawrence casts his Lawrence-like hero in the role not of Mellors but of Sir Clifford Chatterley.

come violently split. She speaks sadly of his "two selves" which, she says, were constantly fighting each other.[33] It might have been some consolation to her if she had realized that what cost her the affections of the man she loved gained for the world an artist whose distinctive vision of human relationships derived from these "two selves."

4 On Being Alone

THE BOY IN THE BUSH

ODOUR OF CHRYSANTHEMUMS

A FRAGMENT OF STAINED GLASS

THE TRESPASSER

THE PRUSSIAN OFFICER

THE MAN WHO LOVED ISLANDS

> He who is with himself dissatisfied,
> Though all the world find satisfaction in him,
> Is like a rainbow-coloured bird gone blind,
> That gives delight it shares not.
>
> —Hardy's *The Dynasts* II
> (Admiral Nelson the speaker)

"Nobody can be more clownish, more clumsy and sententiously in bad taste . . . He preaches and holds forth because he's not sure of himself. . . . The artist was so *much* greater than the man. . . . But he was a deep, great artist, even if he was rather a sententious man. . . . When he . . . gives us his sheer apprehension of the world, then he is wonderful, his book commands a stillness in the soul, an awe." This was D. H. Lawrence's verdict on Herman Melville as man and artist.

In the margin, beside the verdict, many of us have surely penciled a comment: *D.H.L. himself*. The artist was so *much* greater than the man. The man was a brilliant conversationalist whose lively talk could charm the sweetness out of a bear. Much of the time he was a wise man, and always he was a brave man. Sir Richard Rees's portrait of him in his *Brave Men, A Study of D. H. Lawrence and Simone Weil* (1958) rightly stressed this Lawrentian virtue. His death he confronted with an occasional snarl but without a whimper. The kind of courage which he valued in the

Italians of the Renaissance he himself embodied: "The courage of life is splendid in them. We badly need some of it today, in this self-pitying age when we are so sorry for ourselves that we have to be soothed by art as by candy." [1]

Everyone who met this man found him fascinating; some found him lovable. He was also at times, as his wife among others called him, a cad (in America the word is rarely used but we have the thing). The artist in him was often possessed by what he called a demon; the man was occasionally possessed by a devil. To do this man a favor was to risk courting his devil, as some of his friends and acquaintances learned to their cost. To Katherine Mansfield, dying of the same disease which ten years later was to kill him in turn, this man wrote: "You are a loathsome reptile—I hope you will die." •

Frieda's explanation of this side of her husband's character, in her *Memoirs,* is shrewdly observant and also suggests his similarity in this respect to Shelley: "Lawrence approaches all people (women especially) as if they were Gothic cathedrals, then he finds they are little houses and hates them for it!" [2]

In an age which regards heroics with suspicion Lawrence's combination of charm and occasional caddishness makes him an ideal subject for biography. It is, perhaps, because the man provides readers the pleasures of feeling superior that many more books have been written about him than about the artist. For not only does he reveal himself at times as devilish but even more nakedly as foolish. When we read about the frail shrill-voiced husband smashing victrola records over his sturdy wife's head, we may merely smile. But when we read some of the really fatuous

• See *Encounter,* LXXVI (1960), p. 76, and *Letters,* I, p. 620.—To be unoffended by such savage outbursts is surely no kindness to Lawrence and certainly not reassuring as an indication of a critic's view of human relations. Yet even here Dr. Leavis rushes in to defend his man in his " 'Lawrence Scholarship' and Lawrence." (*Sewanee Review,* LXXI, 1963, pp. 29-31.) It might be more helpful to recognize uncontrolled hostility for what it is and to save one's applause for Lawrence's real qualities of greatness, with which as a man he was abundantly endowed. As Dr. Erik Erikson notes in his *Young Man Luther:* "Religiously and artistically creative men often seem to be suffering from a barely compensated psychosis, and yet later prove superhumanly gifted in conveying a total meaning for man's life." (1958, p. 255.)

letters he wrote to Bertrand Russell we must, if we admire Lawrence, wince. "He preaches and holds forth because he's not sure of himself," as he said of Melville, and the biographers and editors provide us with all the information we need to trim the man down not merely to our own small size, it seems, but below it.

Because the present study is concerned primarily with the artist rather than the man, it would seem best to ignore the vast accumulation of information, whether favorable or unfavorable, that the biographers have provided. To ignore it would also accord with what used to be a generally established axiom of twentieth-century literary criticism: that biography should have nothing to do with our reading of literature.

"Isn't the individuality of the writer important?" an interviewer asked William Faulkner. "Very important to himself," he replied. "Everybody else should be too busy with the work to care about the individuality." [3]

The advantages of this approach to literature are manifest; the kind of teacher or literary columnist who used to deal with *Paradise Lost* by reciting anecdotes of Milton's love life without ever examining the poem itself has been happily driven into a corner. Not the elopement with Frieda but *The Rainbow* itself is then the proper subject.

A further attraction of this restrictive method is that in his reading of Lawrence, the critic will be spared the toil of working his way through mountains of memoirs. Yet the total divorce of literary criticism from biography is not, in Lawrence's case, a clear gain. If some comment buried in the amiable gushings of Dorothy Brett's recollections helps to explain "The Man Who Loved Islands" or if some reported conversation provides a key-piece for a puzzling scene in *The Rainbow,* the critic who ignores such aids on the theory that nothing outside the text itself is relevant must reconsider his theory.

The biographers and memoir writers sometimes provide data needed for an understanding not only of the man but of the artist and his work. And as the following discussion may show, when we are trying to draw together some of the recurring themes and situations in Lawrence's fiction, it is informative to track them back to the character of the man who created them.

II

"A great longing for solitude accompanies these characters of Lawrence," André Malraux writes. "In fact it may be said that for this 'couple advocate,' the 'other party' scarcely seems to count at all." [4]

Like most of the best observations about Lawrence's fiction, Malraux's insight represents a half-truth. In Lawrence's world such men and women as Tom Brangwen or Ursula Brangwen do not seek solitude initially. The first stage of his narrative, as I suggested earlier, portrays men or women as alone yet searching for release from loneliness. Of Mellors and Constance Chatterley, Yeats wrote: "These two lovers . . . are poignant in their loneliness, and the coarse language of the one, accepted by both, becomes a forlorn poetry uniting their solitudes, something ancient, humble and terrible." [5] Often, however, the relationship, as it develops, fails to resolve the needs of the seekers. Pluto and Persephone instead of maintaining a union of their "solitudes" can be driven apart into a state even more solitary than before they met. It is to this stage of Lawrence's narrative sequence that Malraux's observation more aptly applies. The failure of relationships leads to a "great longing for solitude." Lawrence himself used the term "aloneness" to describe this stage. Because it is one of the most recurrent situations in his novels and stories it deserves to be separately examined.

That the state of "aloneness" should recur so often in the writings of Lawrence may seem strange, for the man himself appears to have been exceptionally gregarious. He is a rare instance of a literary man who could write his books in a room full of people. Throughout his travels he contrived to surround himself with bands of men and women, and from his wife's presence he was rarely absent at any time. Why should a man of this order be so engrossed, as an artist, with what he called our "overmastering sense of separateness and aloneness"?

Hints for an answer can be drawn from his autobiographical sketches and his letters, and there is an especially helpful account in one of his novels, *The Boy in the Bush,* written in collaboration with the Australian novelist, M. L. Skinner. At what point autobiography ends and fiction takes over makes rough work for both biographers and critics of Lawrence, and one must exercise the usual saving clauses. Yet a remarkable feature of *The Boy in the Bush* is that even here, where the story was conceived and written by another person, Lawrence was able to impose upon the book the strong stamp of his own attitudes and experiences. His impress is especially evident, of course, in the final two chapters which, we know now, were rewritten by him in a way so drastic that his collaborator wept.[6]

In these chapters the hero is represented analyzing his own character and estimating the effect he has on others. Jack, like Lawrence, a man who had almost died, has married a tawny-eyed woman, Monica, who had had children by other men. Now he wants to move out into the bush country, establish farms, and have other wives in addition to Monica—to become a kind of patriarchal Abraham. When Mary, a Miriam-like girl, refuses to participate in his plan, Jack indignantly rides off on his red stallion alone. The sights of nature soothe him, and reflecting on the incident of Mary's refusal he realizes that he likes people well enough as long as the relationship remains casual rather than intimate:

> And, casually, they all liked him. It was only when he approached nearer, into intimacy, that he had a revulsion. . . . In intimate life he was quiet and unyielding often oppressive. In the casual way he was most yielding and agreeable. Therefore it was his friends who suffered most from him. He knew this. . . . So friendly with everybody, he was. And at the centre not really friendly even with his wife and his dearest friends.

This passage of character-analysis is also an author's self-analysis (its substance is repeated in one of his autobiographical sketches).[7] Regarded as self-analysis it provides a likely clue to one of the principal puzzles about Lawrence's character. In the thousands of pages making up Nehls' record of the impact the man had upon those who met him, a reader becomes baffled by the remarkable variety of responses he evoked. Those who knew him casually were almost invariably charmed; others who knew him more intimately, like Witter Bynner, found him "oppressive" as Jack had said. Lawrence knew this:

> Always
> in the eyes of those who loved me
> I have seen at last the image of him they loved
> and took for me
> mistook for me.[8]

At the core of Lawrence's character, despite his mask of charm and friendliness, was a keen sense of isolation, a consciousness that each of us dies alone and lives alone, a consciousness that Martin Heidegger and his school have considered to be the distinguishing mark of the human experience.

"We are such transitory little dots, it is no wonder we are sometimes lonely," Lawrence remarked in a letter at the age of 22, a passage he was to expand for his final scene of Paul's isolation in *Sons and Lovers*. Later, after reading Beethoven's letters and noting the musician's helpless search for "contacts," he commented memorably on our "crucifixion into isolate individuality—*poveri noi.*"[9]

At the time of writing *The Boy in the Bush* (September-November, 1923) Lawrence's sense of aloneness was most acutely awakened. After severe quarrelings, Frieda had sailed for Europe to visit her children. She refused to rejoin her husband in America where he was wandering across the continent alone. In this state of low spirits, his sense of alienation was as intense as Gulliver's after the fourth voyage. Lawrence pictures his hero, Jack, preferring to sleep in the stable with the horses rather than in a household where he would encounter people. "Perhaps his horse was the only creature with which he had the right relation," he reflects. This Gulliver-like repudiation of a stinking mankind reappears in some of the late poems as in *Lonely, Lonesome, Loney-O!*:

> But what is lovelier than to be alone?
> escaping the petrol fumes of human conversation
> and the exhaust-smell of people
> and be alone!

Exasperated explosions into misanthropy can be written off as inconsequential, yet for Lawrence they seem a significant outcrop of an important vein of his character.

It is necessary, of course, to distinguish between solitude, which *may* be pleasurable, and loneliness, which is always painful. Huxley's saying of Lawrence that here was a man who was never bored (which does not mean he was never irritable or dissatisfied) may recall Coleridge's awe-struck reaction to his friend Wordsworth: "He is a man of whom it might have been said, 'It is good for him to be alone.'"

For Lawrence, too, to be alone did not always mean to be lonely. But the Pleasures of Solitude, gently celebrated by essayists and writers of verse in the eighteenth century, represent something altogether different in spirit from the exasperated frustration evident in *Lonely, Lonesome, Loney-O!*.

Even more than most men, Lawrence had hungered for love, friendship, and loyal disciples. He spent a lifetime seeking them and losing them. Biographers may demonstrate that his disappointments were attributable to the inadequacies of his friends, both women and men, or to the class structure, but Lawrence himself seems to have sometimes recognized that one of the rhythms of his own character impelled him away from the people he wanted to love. The pain of the "crucifixion into isolate individuality" has been expressed by other writers as in the love lyrics of Matthew Arnold:

> A God, a God their severance ruled!
> And bade betwixt their shores to be
> The unplumbed, salt, estranging sea.

Although Lawrence too can protest against isolation in similar elegiac tone, he differs from Arnold in his almost fierce insistence that despite his need for love the individual is some sort of untouchable entity, ultimately separate from all mankind.

Major novels such as *Women in Love* can be misread for the same reason that Lawrence's character was misunderstood. The fiction of this "couple advocate" portrays unions but not unities; the individual particles never fully fuse. And the man who stirred the affections of men and women in almost every continent of the world was often as alone as the Pied Piper of Hamlin.

As Richard Somers reflects in *Kangaroo:* "Man's isolation was always a supreme truth and fact, not to be forsworn. And the mystery of apartness." When Lawrence's friends forswore the fact and tried, like Kangaroo with Somers, to penetrate the mystery, they usually encountered a hard shell of resistance, repelling if not repellent. In the strange character of his contemporary and namesake, T. E. Lawrence, a similar streak of untouchability can be detected and likewise in uneasy combination with a deep desire that the barriers might be broken down.[10] As artist, D. H. Lawrence confronted this "fact" he had experienced in his personal relations as a man and incorporated it prominently into his fiction.

III

In his *Rehearsals of Discomposure* Nathan Scott has reviewed the variety of ways in which modern artists such as Kafka and Proust have portrayed alienation. In this context, he groups Lawrence appropriately with Thomas Wolfe. "Naked and alone we came into exile. . . . Which of us has not remained forever prison-pent? Which of us is not forever a stranger and alone?" Although the tone of Wolfe's epigraph for his *Look Homeward, Angel* is more indulgently nostalgic than Lawrence's, there remains an interesting similarity in that both writers, growing up in crowded households, discovered early that family life may leave the individual isolated and apart. To illustrate Lawrence's presentation of this characteristic situation, his early story, "Odour of Chrysanthemums," provides an effective example.

"Odour of Chrysanthemums," one of the first of his stories to appear in the *English Review,* was published in 1911 and revised in 1914. In its original form, completed when Lawrence was twenty-three years old, it came into the hands of Ford Madox Ford who affirms that after reading only the opening paragraph of the manuscript he at once accepted the story for publication and anounced that he had discovered a genius.

Whether we believe Ford's colorful recollections of his discovery is of little consequence. What is more consequential is his detailed analysis of the qualities of that opening paragraph, a model analysis of what constitutes great narrative. Every detail, every phrase, as Ford shows, enables the reader to take in the scene, without "ratiocination" as he says, and with "practically none of the tiresome thing called descriptive nature, of which the English writer is as a rule so lugubriously lavish." [11]

The details contribute even more than Ford says. They are not merely atmospheric—items of local color that bring before us a community of miners returning to their waiting wives and families after a day's work in the pits. They contribute to reinforcing the theme, a theme which becomes explicit in the final scene when the wife is washing the body of her dead husband as he lies on the floor of their cold parlor. What overcomes her is not ordinary grief; such grief is expressed here by the mother as in *Riders to the Sea* after the drowning of the son, Michael.[12] What overcomes the wife is a terrifying recognition that she has been living intimately, for years, with a stranger. "The utter isolation of the human soul" appalls her. She kisses the body, "trying to get some connection. But she could not. She was driven away. He was impregnable." These insights into her marriage were added by Lawrence when he revised the story in 1914 to make the theme explicit, as in this striking addition:

> In her womb was ice of fear, because of this separate stranger with whom she had been living as one flesh. Was this what it all meant—utter, intact separateness, obscured by heat of living? . . . There had been nothing between them, and yet they had come together, exchanging their nakedness repeatedly. Each time he had taken her, they had been two isolated beings, far apart as now.

As in Joyce's best short story, "The Dead" (written in the same year as "Odour of Chrysanthemums" was first published), the final discovery scene involves a confrontation of the leading character with his true self, which Joyce represents by having Gabriel Conroy see himself in a mirror of the hotel bedroom he is sharing with his wife. Moreover, the insight gained takes in not only the plight of the leading character, in both stories, but widens out in circles that involve everyone else who has appeared earlier in the story, and, by extension, includes the general condition of mankind.*

In the opening paragraph Lawrence mentions a woman walking along the railway-line who steps aside to let the train go by: "she stood insignificantly trapped between the jolting black waggons and the hedge." This is a small touch but suggests a relationship which the story will expand. When Mrs. Bates herself talks to her father, a widower of whose remarriage she disapproves, he remarks: "Well, what's a man to do? It's no sort of life for a man of my years, to sit at my own hearth like a stranger." What becomes evident, through detail after detail, is that everyone in Mrs. Bates' household does sit by the hearth a stranger. Even the little boy, who complains (like his father) of having to consume his tea in darkness, is a stranger. "She saw herself in his silence and pertinacity; she saw the father in her child's indifference to all but himself." At tea, we learn, "their faces were hidden from each other." The flowers, too, contribute to the impression of bleakness, with their "cold, deathly smell." The flower in Mrs. Bates' apron links the unborn child with the autumnal and funereal.

If we seek to assign responsibility for this cheerless hearth, the story could be read as an indictment of a woman's failure to love, a failure that had driven her husband to drink (he had not been a drunkard before marriage). But such a reading seems superfluous. As has already been indicated in discussing *Sons and Lovers,* Lawrence had a lifetime of writing ahead of him in which to discover the faults of this kind of Persephone. Here he concentrates our interest upon the isolation itself, not upon who might be responsible for the condition. It is notable that when he cast the

* Another early Lawrence story resembling Joyce's "The Dead" is "The Shadow in the Rose Garden," a story that influenced *Burnt Norton* as Louis Martz points out in an article on T. S. Eliot's later poetry (*Sewanee Review,* Winter, 1947). In this other Lawrence story, the wife revisits the scene of an earlier love affair and encounters her former lover who is now insane. In the final scene, in a resort room, she is goaded into telling her present husband of her past, and he, like Gabriel Conroy, has at last to confront "the width of the breach between them." Despite these closer similarities of situation "The Shadow in the Rose Garden" lacks the final expanding effect that links "Odour of Chrysanthemums" with "The Dead."

same story into the form of a play, *The Widowing of Mrs. Holroyd,* he chose to emphasize the domestic discord and the woman's failure to love her husband. The discovery scene itself is absent from the play, a radical modification that points up a difference not only in intention but in medium. Stage drama, whatever its advantages, does not lend itself to some of the insights of narrative.

IV

Lawrence's early preoccupation with isolation is also demonstrable in an even earlier story, "A Fragment of Stained Glass." In this instance his skill in revision cannot conceal adequately the clumsiness of the original version, which had been written in 1907. The framework for the narrative, having the story told by the vicar, seems superfluous. Perhaps the scars on his face are supposed to relate his past to the serf's experiences, but the connection, if any, is tenuous and undeveloped. Moreover, at first glance, this curious story seems totally unrelated to the rest of Lawrence's fiction, a dead-end experiment never followed further. About the historic past he wrote only two stories, this one, probably his first story, and, oddly enough, "The Man Who Died," his last. Yet if we overlook the archaic stylistic mannerisms and examine the basic pattern, it becomes evident that "A Fragment of Stained Glass" can be read as a preview of several of his later stories and novels.

"A Fragment of Stained Glass" is the story of a man becoming an outcast. Prodded by harsh treatment, a serf retaliates by burning down his master's house. He then flees to the wintry woods where he is driven mad by his loneliness and fears. Unlike the soldier in "The Prussian Officer," the serf does find a companion. The miller's daughter ("the fox" she is called) joins him in his wild flight, which ends with their waking in the woods to the sound of wolves.

The most obvious example of retelling this story is "The Prussian Officer," but it is interesting to observe how often Lawrence reverts to variants of it, as for example his picturing the death of

Gerald in the wintry mountains in *Women in Love,* one of the most powerfully moving chapters in his fiction. In particular the scene of the serf's confronting the abbey wall and its Christ figure is a remarkable forecast of the scene of Gerald's terror when he stumbles upon the snow-covered crucifix near the mountain top.

I have used the term *outcast* rather than criminal as more generally applicable. The soldier has strangled his officer, and Gerald has almost strangled Gudrun to death, but in other instances no criminal act prompts the flight. In *The Trespasser* a moral code was broken; in *The Lost Girl* (as in E. M. Forster's Italian novels) only a set of small-town conventions, and in "The Man Who Loved Islands" no code is at issue.

Stories of outcasts, especially criminals, are of course the common stock of prose fiction. What is distinctive in Lawrence's narratives is his shifting our attention away from the expected excitements of the chase and concentrating upon something else.

In children's stories as in the novels of Graham Greene or in the pursuit of Sikes in *Oliver Twist* we are absorbed by the ever-popular spectacle of hunter and hunted. Lawrence reduces our share of this kind of basic pleasure; the pursuit, as such, rarely interests him. In "The Thorn in the Flesh" he comes closer than usual to rousing a kind of Graham Greene-like suspense; the bugles sounding from the barracks, audible to the hunted lovers hiding in the bedroom, are like the sound of a huntsman's horn. But even in this story we are not primarily concerned whether the outcast will be caught or will escape.

Instead of the suspense of the hunt Lawrence focuses upon the progressive stages of the outcast's alienation. The narrative pattern might be likened to a peeling off of protective layers, a shedding of skins, as when the hunted outcast Romero heaves the Princess's saddle and their riding-clothes into the icy tarn in front of their remote hideout in the mountains. Again and again he shows us his men and women in circumstances which force them to slough off contacts with friends, families, all past associations, until they stand alone, confronting their fates, like Macbeth at the end of the play with all his flimsy props pulled from under him.

Paul Morel, in *Sons and Lovers,* may seem untypical of the outcast, yet his situation at the end of the novel is the same. From

Miriam, his contact with the spiritual, he has cut himself off irrevocably, and from Clara, his contact with the flesh, he has likewise broken, and from his mother he is forever parted by death. In the final scene he is like the speaker in Robert Frost's poem, "one acquainted with the night." He stands alone, under the night sky, watching the stars with the terror of which Pascal wrote:

> Whatever spot he stood on, there he stood alone. . . . The people hurrying along the streets offered no obstruction to the void in which he found himself. . . . Where was he?—one tiny upright speck of flesh, less than an ear of wheat lost in the field. He could not bear it.

Paul's dilemma is resolved in the final paragraph, for *Sons and Lovers* (although some readers fail to see it) does have what is called a happy ending.[13] *The Lost Girl* is similar, despite the bleakness of the setting and the separation of the lovers by war. In other novels and stories, however, the outcast dies after his experience of being stripped of human contacts as in such stories as "England, My England" or "The Woman Who Rode Away."

Among the novels the most sustained treatment of the situation of alienation is *The Trespasser,* a work held in high regard by neither his critics nor by Lawrence himself, who feared the book revealed too much of his own "naked self." Perhaps the failings of this "rotten work of genius,"[14] as Ford Madox Ford styled it, may be attributed to its oppressively Wagnerian atmosphere which is unrelieved throughout except in moments of the hero's enjoyment of sea and sky. Siegmund's alienation is evident from the beginning; he cannot establish contact with Helena and he cannot reestablish contact with his wife and children. The mistress is a Sue Bridehead figure "with whom passion exhausts itself at the mouth." Despite her efforts to love him she only drains him. In scene after exhausting scene we watch the isolation of his lovemaking. "He had Helena in his arms, which was sweet company, but in spirit he was quite alone." Although she is ten years younger than Siegmund, all he can do is to call out to her hopelessly: "Hawwa—Eve—Mother!" From his scolding wife Siegmund is even more emphatically estranged. After returning to her household (a household described with a vivid grimness which Zola or Gissing might have envied) and finding that his last supporting prop, his children, have been turned against him, the outcast is confronting his final wall.

Unlike the isolated Walter Morel in *Sons and Lovers,* Siegmund does not think of drink as adequately obliterating. Instead, after a night of agony and sweat he hangs himself by a suitcase-strap on the door of his bedroom. His wife, who like Mrs. Bates in "Odour of Chrysanthemums" has been storing up a flood of rage to vent upon her husband, discovers, instead, his corpse. Unlike Mrs. Bates, however, Siegmund's wife never confronts the nature of their mutual isolation. More in the manner of George Eliot's Bulstrode in *Middlemarch,* "when the event summoned her to stand before the bench of her own soul's understanding, she fled, leaving the verdict upon herself eternally suspended." And again: "whenever her thoughts wandered towards a consideration of how he must have felt, what his inner life must have been, during the past six years, she felt herself dilate with terror, and she hastened to invoke protection."

A similar self-inflicted pre-frontal lobotomy is seemingly suffered by the heroine of the late story, "The Princess," although in her case the evasion is not analyzed. After Romero is shot we learn only that the Princess became "slightly crazy."

The Trespasser, one of Lawrence's most bitter stories of aloneness, is also, like the stories, so far considered, an early work. To account for this early bent we can assume that the spectacle of the alienation of his own parents provided all the impetus needed, although his reading of Hardy may perhaps have reinforced it. The typical heroes and heroines of Hardy, Lawrence believed, were likewise outcasts who were driven to die in the wilderness from "the isolation and the exposure." [15]

V

To illustrate the variety of ways in which Lawrence develops this particular basic theme and situation, two of his best short stories, "The Prussian Officer" and "The Man Who Loved Islands," deserve to be considered more extensively.

In June, 1913, Lawrence advised Garnett in a letter: "I have written the best short story I have ever done—about a German officer in the army and his orderly."

In the year following he made it an even better story by extensive revisions and additions (any reader still under the widespread illusion that Lawrence did not know how to polish his fiction by traditional methods of revision, not merely by rewriting afresh, should compare the two published versions of this story).[16] In its final form "The Prussian Officer" demonstrates a brilliantly successful rendering of a situation which had been clumsily handled in "A Fragment of Stained Glass."

The story may be divided into two parts. The first and longer section portrays the orderly being goaded by the captain's sadistic treatment and culminates with the murder. The second section portrays the murderer's feverish state of mind as he stumbles through the woods alone, cut off from all contacts, until his death. Because the first part pictures the establishment of a relationship rather than a disintegration of a relationship it would seem not to belong to the present discussion. I should nevertheless like to consider the story as a whole before discussing the finale.

Not all readers seem to share Lawrence's high regard for this story. Virginia Woolf affirmed that her only impression from reading it was of "starting muscles and forced obscenity." [17] Perhaps Mrs. Woolf should have reread the story before publishing her verdict, for "The Prussian Officer" contains no word remotely close to obscenity that I can see—unless the word *loins* was offensive to her exquisite ear.

Other complainants include Dr. Leavis, who rarely joins forces with Mrs. Woolf's Bloomsbury, and also Eliseo Vivas who, in turn, seems only rarely in agreement with Dr. Leavis about anything. Leavis finds "The Prussian Officer" unrepresentative of Lawrence because it is "sultrily overcharged, sensuously and emotionally," and that whatever power it may have is "unpleasant." [18] The present chapter will indicate, I hope, how representative the story is. The unpleasantness, to which he and Vivas object, raises other considerations. Of *Death in Venice* Lawrence commented (in a review completed at the time he wrote "The Prussian Officer") that Thomas Mann's story was "unwholesome."

The subject of his own story is likewise unwholesome, perhaps more unwholesome than *Death in Venice*. The tenderness of homosexual love is pictured by Mann; the violence and brutality of such a relationship is pictured by Lawrence, a violence heightened by the Captain's very ignorance of the sources of the pleasure he derives in inflicting pain upon the youth. Harry T. Moore calls it a story of "homosexual-sadistic frenzy," and Graham Hough calls it a "repulsively powerful story of a sadistic, quasi-homosexual relation." *The Prussian Officer* is also a story of violent anger; scene after scene crackles with this ugly passion. It is the kind of totally absorbing anger experienced by Lord Cardigan, the British cavalry commander who led the charge of the Light Brigade in the Crimea. The interference of another officer, Captain Nolan, so infuriated Cardigan that he galloped through the Russian batteries unscathed without thinking about the situation at all, his attention being totally taken up, as he later reported, by his rage against Nolan.

That the subject is both unpleasant and unwholesome is undeniable, but is unpleasantness in itself an adequate criterion for judging works of literature? What then are we supposed to do with *Othello* or with *Oedipus Rex*? I suggested earlier that discussions of Lawrence sometimes tell us more of the critic than of the work, as Professor Vivas' book—one of the best critical studies of Lawrence we have—will illustrate. From the judgments passed in his book it is apparent he disapproves strongly of violence and he believes in tenderness and understanding. But qualities that would make Professor Vivas an admirable friend, citizen, or neighbor are not always an asset in the literary critic if they seriously limit his range of appreciation, as for example when he deplores Lawrence's having pictured the domestic quarrels of Mr. and Mrs. Morel in *Sons and Lovers*.[19]

Lawrence himself said of *Death in Venice* that even though the story is unwholesome "it does not strike me as morbid, for all that, it is too well done." So is "The Prussian Officer."

Some of the few critical analyses of this fine story have grappled with the problem of Lawrence's emphasis upon the setting, the background of mountains—a kind of lost Eden which the fallen Adam longs for.[20] Yet the main line of "The Prussian Officer" does not stand out clearly in any of the essays devoted to it that I have encountered. Perhaps the most helpful lead is provided in a less likely source, Frieda Lawrence's *Not I, But the Wind:*

> The strange struggle of those two opposite natures, the officer and his servant, seems to me particularly significant for Lawrence. He wrote it before the war but as if he had sensed it. The unhappy, conscious man, the superior in authority envying the other man his simple, satisfied nature. I felt as if he himself was both these people. They seemed to represent the split in his soul, the split between the conscious and the unconscious man.

Frieda's remarks are a reminder that we misread this story if we confine our response to the kinetic level and classify it simply as an exposé of abuses of power in a military organization.

If we are looking for a satirical sketch of a German officer, it is instructive to read the account of the captain in *Ship of Fools* by Katherine Anne Porter, especially the scene of his watching the steerage passengers dancing to guitar rhythms "that moved the blood even against all efforts of the will." The contempt of this ship's officer for these representatives of un-Germanic "forces of darkness" is amusingly pictured by Miss Porter.[21]

Lawrence's captain is never treated satirically, and Frieda's comment on the story indicates why. Her remark also explains her husband's outburst of displeasure when his editor changed the title of the story from "Honour and Arms" to "The Prussian Officer." "Garnett was a devil to call my book of stories *The Prussian Officer*—what Prussian Officer?" he asked.

The new title, that is, has connotations prompting us to prejudge the Captain, a character with whom his creator had a good deal in common. In real life we might derive satisfaction from kicking the man who kicked his servant. In the story, however, the man is presented, throughout, with remarkable understanding. That the youth suffers is obvious; that the Captain also suffers must also be noted. He does not want "to be touched into life" by the youth; he struggles hard to control his fascination and is painfully overcome by forces he has denied.

In the recently published *Prologue* chapter for *Women in Love* there are some perceptive and moving passages describing Birkin's dilemma in his encounters with young soldiers like the orderly. His realization that he prefers their bodies to the bodies of women distresses him and he has to fight down his instinctive preference:

> It was for men that he felt the hot, flushing, roused attraction which a man is supposed to feel for the other sex. . . . And this was a new torture to him. Why did not the face of a woman move him in the same manner . . . as the face of a man? Why was a man's beauty . . . so vivid and intoxicating a thing to him, whilst female beauty was something quite unsubstantial . . . ? Every now and again, would come over him the same passionate desire to have near him some man he saw, to exchange intimacy, to unburden himself of love to this new beloved. It might be any man, a policeman who suddenly looked up at him, as he inquired the way, or a soldier who sat next to him in a railway carriage. How vividly, months afterwards, he would recall the soldier who had sat pressed up close to him on a journey from Charing Cross to Westerham; the shapely, motionless body, the large, dumb, coarsely-beautiful hands that rested helpless upon the strong knees, the dark brown eyes, vulnerable in the erect body.[22]

"The Prussian Officer," like most of Lawrence's fiction, explores a human relationship by dramatizing the effects of two individuals brought into contact. The structure of the first part might be likened to an *X*. As a result of the relationship, each, in effect, crosses over to become something of the opposite of what he was at the outset, in part to exchange roles.

In his *Aspects of the Novel,* E. M. Forster has analyzed Anatole France's novel, *Thaïs,* as a precise example of such a structure. Paphnuce, a saintly ascetic, meets Thaïs, an Alexandrian courtesan, and succeeds in influencing her to abandon her sinful life and to enter a convent. But the effect she has upon Paphnuce is catastrophic: the two characters change roles.

In "The Prussian Officer," after the climactic kicking scene, the young orderly leaves the room "looking old, and walking heavily." And the Captain, who has hitherto prided himself upon his conscious self-control, drinks himself into a stupor to obliterate conscious thought about his actions. "He had prevented his mind from taking it in, had suppressed it along with his instincts, and the conscious man had nothing to do with it." The unconscious man, which he had both envied and despised in the character of his servant, and suppressed in his own character, takes violent control of him.

The servant's painful awakening is of a different order for he is aroused not into full consciousness but out of innocence. Like Melville's Billy Budd, his innocent unawareness provokes his own downfall. The "strong flame" that burns in him as he seizes the Captain's throat had not been self-generated. It was lit, early in the story, by the "bluey" "cold fire" in the eyes of his officer. (This detail of eyes of cold blue fire reappears in "The Rocking-Horse Winner" where it is used repeatedly to describe the boy's gaze after his corruption—a symptom, in both stories, of the repressed and perverse.) At the outset, the orderly has "dark, expressionless eyes, that seemed never to have thought, only to have received life direct through his senses." But the Captain's flinging a glove into his face produces an explosion: "Then he had the satisfaction of seeing the black eyes flare up into his own, like a blaze when straw is thrown on a fire."

The incident of flinging the glove is significantly similar to an incident in *Sons and Lovers* and once again suggests why Lawrence understands his Captain. In trying to tutor the dreamy Miriam in algebra, Paul is overcome with rage at her stolid slow-wittedness:

> In spite of himself, his blood began to boil with her. It was strange that no one else made him in such fury. He flared against her. Once he threw the pencil in her face.

The effect of the relationship in the story is to isolate both men as a pair before one of them is left, of course, in total isolation. After the incident of the kicking, the orderly resolves (and it strikes the reader as plausible) that he will never tell anyone what had happened to him. "There were only the two people in the world now—himself and the Captain." In the instance of the Captain, the new alienation is less evident. As the solitary figure on horseback in a company of infantry he is accustomed to being alone. The orderly, however, had been a friendly, gregarious soldier until under the Captain's spell he found himself cut off from the "good fellows" in his Company. The peeling off of layers is once more characteristic of Lawrence's narrative. The "sweetheart" whom the orderly loved is never mentioned in the later sections of the story as having come to his mind. After the murder, when he sees a woman, he feels completely cut off from contact with her. "He had no language with which to speak to her. She was the bright, solid unreality."

Fourteen years after publishing "The Prussian Officer," in reviewing a book by the psychoanalyst Dr. Trigant Burrow, Lawrence stated his agreement with the author that the basis of most neuroses is not in the Oedipal relationships of childhood, where Freud found it, but in our "inward sense of 'separateness'" or "cut-offness" which, Lawrence believed, developed as man evolved from the animal stage into consciousness and awareness. When man became "aware," says Lawrence, he stood "for the first time, *alone.*"[23] The orderly in "The Prussian Officer," lured from his Eden into a state of groping awareness, might have served as a lively illustration for Lawrence's argument.

VI

As a final example of Lawrence's stories of aloneness there remains "The Man Who Loved Islands." This late story is the most fully developed illustration of the recurring fictional pattern we have been considering in which the leading character sheds a succession of protective layers until he stands absolutely alone.

Like several of Lawrence's later stories, "The Man Who Loved Islands" is a fable, and in this vein we learn little of the hero's past or his motives. "There was a man who loved islands," the opening sentence tells us, and it is enough. At thirty-five years of age the hero has sufficient private income to acquire an island somewhere off the coast of England and to set about enjoying himself on it. He is happy in being cut off from the mainland and in having a place which he can "fill" with his "own personality." He gradually realizes, however, that he cannot fill it. The seemingly congenial island is both too empty for his present purposes and, oddly enough, too full of historic or prehistoric associations. Druids, Gauls, and Vikings, who had once inhabited it, haunt his imagination at night.

His second stage of shedding protective layers is to cut himself off from his haunted sense of man's past. To this end he imports to the same island a battery of servants, farmers, and fishermen, with whose aid he hopes to establish a utopian community, "to regain Paradise." After five years the hero discovers that his utopian experiment must be abandoned. His servants call him Master, but he has not mastered them or established any satisfactory relation with them. "He knew quite well that his people didn't love him at all. He knew that their spirits were secretly against him, malicious, jeering, envious . . . He became just as wary and secretive with regard to them." Nor had he mastered the economies of island life.

The hero's next break is to move to a much smaller island with a modest staff of faithful servants, a "refuge" rather than a utopian community this time. Now he is cut off from "the race of progress." In this lotos-land the hero seems happy in his comparative isolation, in his "new stillness of desirelessness"—like the gamekeeper in *Lady Chatterley's Lover* before his affair with Connie.

But his housekeeper's daughter, his typist Flora, yearns for him, and he takes her, out of pity. This resumption of human intimacies appals him, and he begins to make preparations for his final break. Because Flora is pregnant he marries her, provides an income for her, but also abandons her to escape to his third and final island, a tiny treeless rock inhabited only by sheep and his cat, of which he soon disposes. For unlike Gulliver or Jack, the Lawrence-like hero of *The Boy in the Bush,* when the man who loved islands discovered mankind to be nauseating, he found no compensation in sleeping in a stable with horses. "What repulsive god invented animals and evil-smelling men? To his nostrils, the fishermen and the sheep alike smelled foul." His only satisfaction was in "being alone, absolutely alone, with the space soaking into him."

All these breaks he has made have been of the outcast's own volition. The final cutting-off is by nature itself. In an eerie finale the outcast hero watches the snow rolling in over the sea to blanket his island forever. If not the end of the world, it is the end of his world as in Robert Frost's anthology piece:

> I think I know enough of hate
> To say that for destruction ice
> Is also great
> And would suffice.

I have summarized "The Man Who Loved Islands" because, although it was one of Lawrence's own favorites among his stories, it is not so well-known as the others we have considered. Anthony West ranks it among his greatest, although without any full explanation of his choice, and some good critical articles have been devoted to it.[24] That other readers, including Graham Hough, have not found it to be a masterpiece is understandable.

On first readings it seems to be merely flippant, an example of the tired manner into which Lawrence sometimes fell in his last years when he dashed off his brittle and sarcastic sketches of friends in "Smile," or "Things," or "Two Blue Birds." A closer reading, however, may give us pause. Harry Moore calls it "a simple story." In structure it is simple, in the manner of Dickens's *Christmas Carol.* Yet it is actually one of the most puzzling stories Lawrence ever wrote. The difficulty resides, as so often in fiction, in identifying the tone and in observing how the tone functions —a difficulty much more evident here than in "The Prussian Officer." Is it entirely a satirical sketch, an exposé of a fatuous man's pernicious idealism, as most studies of the story assert? Or, is it, to a large degree, a portrait of Lawrence himself?

To answer these questions it will be necessary to come back to them in a large circle by reviewing the circumstances under which the story was written.

"The Man Who Loved Islands" was first published in an American magazine in July, 1927, and in an English magazine in August. It was republished in America in a collection of Lawrence's stories, but in England republication was blocked for several years (an advance payment of £300 had to be returned to his publisher by Lawrence in 1929). The obstacle to publication in England was provided by the novelist, Compton Mackenzie (later Sir Compton), who contended that the story contained libelous references to his own life. As Lawrence remarked in a letter: "Compton Mackenzie, after swallowing one story ["Two Blue Birds"] in which he appeared as a character was mortally offended by another more recent one in which I used him, and Secker wants me not to print it in a book."

If we review some of the items in Sir Compton Mackenzie's life, one can readily appreciate why he was offended. He had been a lifelong islander. In 1914 he settled on the isle of Capri where Lawrence later visited him in 1919. In 1920 he acquired two Channel Islands, Herm and Jethou, where he resided until 1928 when he moved to one of the Outer Hebrides (the popular film of 1947, known as *Tight Little Island,* was based on one of his books).

His late wife in her autobiography reports that when he was living on one of his Channel Islands he brought with him a girl from London, Nellie Boyte, who learned typing and shorthand and became his secretary. His wife, who had herself begun the study of shorthand, gave it up. "Fortunately Nellie was on Herm by this time, so I abandoned shorthand . . . for ever. Nellie and her parents were to share the island life for many years." [25] This information about Mackenzie's domestic arrangements was made known to Lawrence and used by him.

Lady Mackenzie also seems to have told Lawrence about the past history of the island. It seemed to her an "abode of ghosts"—an impression that he exploited with great skill. And as was his usual habit, Lawrence used several small details of Mackenzie's appearance and habits in his portrait of Cathcart such as the islander's fondness for cats and his intimate knowledge of the flowers which he had struggled to cultivate on his wind-swept retreats.

Oddly enough, when Mackenzie's novel, *Sinister Street* was published, he was, himself, accused of having drawn portraits of living people. He replied in a Postscript that he saw no reason for making exemptions "from the privilege of public men to be sometimes caricatured."

Thirteen years later, when Lawrence's story appeared, it must have been embarrassing for Mackenzie to test his own theory, for the element of caricature in the story is painfully evident. By 1950 he could be charitable enough to explain to Harry Moore that Lawrence "had a trick of describing a person's setting or background vividly, and then putting into the setting an ectoplasm entirely of his own creation."

This suggestion is worth following up, for I suspect we have in "The Man Who Loved Islands" an instance typical of Lawrence's methods of writing. Sometimes, inevitably, he never got much further than his raw materials (as Graham Hough has shown to be true of "The Border Line," an inept tale). But "The Man Who Loved Islands" is a created work, contrived from a variety of sources of which Mackenzie's experiences as an islander constitute only a part of the "ectoplasm."

The story seems to have been conceived, but not written, about a year before it was published. In March, 1926, Lawrence revisited the island of Capri where he had an intimate talk with Faith Compton Mackenzie who disclosed to him some domestic secrets concerning her islander husband. The result, she reports, was the "malicious caricature" of her husband and the "monstrous perversion of facts" in a story of Lawrence's not identified by her but which was probably "Two Blue Birds" (completed by May, 1926). Information from the same conversation was to be stored up by Lawrence and used for his island story.

At the time of his visit to Capri, Lawrence was at the bottom of one of the deepest troughs of depression he ever experienced. As when he wrote the bitter chapters of *The Boy in the Bush,* he was once more parted from Frieda, with whom he had quarreled so intensely that final separation seemed inevitable. This time he was not entirely alone; he had Dorothy Brett for company, a thirty-four year old woman as devoted to him as the thirty-three year old Flora who with her "bright, brown, curiously vacant eyes" idolized the hero of "The Man Who Loved Islands" and "submissively" followed him on his walks although "gloating on him from behind."

Until Lawrence broke with her for the last time, two weeks later, Brett had the privilege of walking about the island with him, and later reporting his "hopeless" moods in which he exclaimed: "I am so tired of it all, Brett, Oh, so tired! . . . I would like to buy a sailing ship and sail among the Greek Islands and be free." [26]

This dream of the Greek islands, like the dream of Rananim in 1915, also appears frequently in the letters of this period. In any event, whether or not Cathcart's "jangled" feelings on his second island reflect a state of mind experienced by Compton Mackenzie they do seem to reflect a state of mind experienced by D. H. Lawrence in 1926. "His desire, whatever it was, died in him with nauseous finality." Years before Sartre's novel was to establish Nausea as a favorite field for modern literary explorations Lawrence was already treating it with telling effect.

In 1928 Lawrence still recalled his experiences two years earlier as the time when he had himself fully experienced isolation. Brigit Patmore reports that when he told her of his feelings "he was away in a loneliness where nothing but what he desired could be of use to him." [27] In the summer of 1926 he complained to Rolf Gardiner of our "meaningless isolation," and added: "I have always been very much alone."

When writing of the man whose sense of nausea was so intense that he finally wanted to be cut off completely from human contacts, once again Lawrence did not have to rely on the islander he had heard about. As the Romantics had recommended, he could look in his own heart and write. In August, 1926, he took a trip to the Isle of Skye, off Scotland, and like Cathcart, found it "most refreshing to get outside the made world, if only for a day—like to Skye. . . . The made world is too deadening—and too dead." [28]

A further indication of his marked interest at this time in studying the desire for alienation is a fragment called "The Man Who Was Through With the World." Written late in 1926 or early 1927,[29] this story appears to be a preliminary sketch for "The Man Who Loved Islands." The hermit in this story takes to a mountain cabin (rather like Lawrence's establishment at Taos) instead of to the islands, and like Cathcart he arrives at a stage when his fellow-men seem to him "smelly." The interesting point is that this alternative version has impressed readers such as Lawrence Powell as "an amusing satire on the profession of 'hermiting.'" The comment brings us back to the problem of tone in the final version. The author of "The Man Who Loved Islands" was the man who remarked in a letter (March 12, 1918): "The one thing I don't seem able to stand is the presence of anybody else—barring Frieda, sometimes." The author was also the poet who affirmed sadly:

> So now I have no desire any more
> Except to be left, in the last resort, alone, quite alone.[30]

Why then should this same author strive to make a pure butt of a hero who followed such a desire to its logical conclusion? The word *hero* is deliberately chosen here, for a recent article argues that Cathcart is a "villain"—"a composite of everything Lawrence hated." [31] Another study, less emphatically, treats him as Lawrence's "most concentrated image of the disease of human idealism," although the critic notes perceptively that "in his final cold agonies there is something magnificent about Cathcart." [32] A third article, even more perceptively, notes without developing the point, that there is something Lawrentian about Cathcart in his attitude towards sex and his love of flowers, and that the story hence contains some "self-mockery." [33] If Cathcart is Lawrentian, can we label him villain? Again we come back to George Orwell's observation that Lawrence's fiction does not feature either heroes or villains.

Biographical information then may lead us to reconsider what Lawrence was about in this exceptionally fine story. That much of it is satirical is beyond question. A believer in the fundamental importance of warm human relations (as indicated in the succeeding chapter) Lawrence had to expose the "hermiting" of his self-centered and seemingly cold-blooded islander. The gregarious Lawrence is after what he calls his hero's "egoism" with a satirical club. But because Lawrence was himself powerfully moved, at times, by a sense of nausea in face of human contacts, and by an intense desire to be alone, he cannot simply demolish Cathcart. The "ectoplasm" Mackenzie spoke of was the product here of strongly divided feelings on the part of Cathcart's creator. One result is that the reader may be bewildered by the variety of tone used by the narrator. There is the heavy sarcasm of passage such as the following:

> There, take that, island which didn't know when it was well off. Now to be a honeymoon-and-golf island!

This is succeeded by soaring descriptions such as this:

> But once isolate yourself on a little island in the sea of space, and the moment begins to heave and expand in great circles, the solid earth is gone, and your slippery, naked dark soul finds herself out in the timeless world, where the chariots of the so-called dead dash down the old streets of centuries, and souls crowd on the footways that we, in the moment, call bygone years. The souls of all the dead are alive again, and pulsating actively around you. . . . Men of Gaul, with big mustaches, who had been on his island, and had vanished from the face of it . . . were there still, hurtling their big, violent, unseen bodies through the night. And there were priests, with golden knives and mistletoe; then other priests with a crucifix; then pirates with murder on the sea.

Some air of detachment may be present here but not of sarcasm. Lawrence, of course, is no repudiator of ghosts. In the mode of *The Road to Xanadu* it may be noted that eleven years earlier, in 1915, he himself had undergone a similar vision as he watched the ocean. "I cannot tell you why, but I am afraid. I am afraid of the ghosts of the dead. They seem to come marching home in legions over the white silent sea, breaking in on us with a roar and a white iciness." [34] The combination of ghostly legions and icy-white seas anticipates the scenes on the third island as well as those on the first island. It could be argued that "The Man Who Loved Islands" is one of Lawrence's best ghost stories even though the ghosts are disposed of early in the fable. It is a story of a man's being haunted, in successive stages, stages which Lawrence knew well.

In these terms we can appreciate more fully why such stories as

"Smile," or "Things," or "Two Blue Birds" are inferior. Each of these is merely sardonic; the author has no commitment. When he impales his victims he never impales himself. In "The Man Who Loved Islands," on the other hand, he is like Swift in *Gulliver.* "Did Swift hate or love mankind?" Examiners can usually be counted on to ask the question every year. That this old chestnut never can be cracked with a final answer is one reason that Swift's masterpiece, as well as the question itself, remains a favorite.

To be aware of the mixed bag out of which Lawrence was drawing for his story may help to account for the odd effect of such passages as the following:

> Amazing what he knew about Jersey cows, and cheese-making, ditching and fencing, flowers and gardening, ships and the sailing of ships. He was a fount of knowledge about everything, and this knowledge he imparted . . . as if he really belonged to the quaint, half-real world of the gods.

Again, this ironic description may evoke Mackenzie but it also applies to Lawrence, himself, at his New Mexican ranch.

Cathcart's difficulties on his first island may often remind us of Lawrence's struggles at Taos (of which he had earlier provided an effective account in "St. Mawr"). Other scenes evoke his sojourn in Italy where "Il Signor Lorenzo" distributed presents among the peasants on his estate in 1926.[35] The harvest supper on the first island, where the Master shares toasts with his disciples, seems almost a travesty of the Last Supper.[36] The sly butler plays the role of Judas to his Master who is likened to "Our Saviour Himself" by one of the women. So was Lawrence, of course, among others by Brett, who had painted him as a crucified Christ during their stay on the isle of Capri. "It's much too like me—much too like," Lawrence complained of Brett's painting.[37] In his story, the resemblances between himself and his hero are artfully blurred, and the detachment maintained by irony, yet that the resemblances do exist suggests why the author's intimate sense of aloneness helped to elevate a mocking sketch of an acquaintance into a great fable involving himself and involving his readers.

In his *Autobiography,* John Stuart Mill paid high tribute to Coleridge as the poet who had the most profound insight into human loneliness. And it is true that if we are looking for a literary work with which to link Lawrence's tale it is Coleridge's *Ancient Mariner* that seems most suitable, although William Golding's novel, *Pincher Martin,* which treats of a solitary islander's hallucinations, would also provide comparisons of interest. The fables of both Coleridge and Lawrence present, through a sequence of symbols, the haunted states of mind of men who have cut themselves off from contact with mankind and with nature. Coleridge, however, represents his hero's redemption, whereas the albatross remains suspended from Cathcart's neck until the end. It is appropriate that although *The Ancient Mariner* has its own kind of complexities, its tone is straightforward. The author expects us to pity his outcast. Lawrence's presentation demands more from us. A satirical exposé of the hermit is combined with insight into the hermit's sufferings, the latter derived, like Coleridge's, from the author's self-knowledge. On March 8, 1927, Lawrence wrote to Brett: "For me the human world becomes more and more unreal, more and more wearisome. I am really happiest when I don't see people."

VII

Two months before publishing "The Man Who Loved Islands" Lawrence began writing another long story of an outcast, in which as he said in a letter, "Jesus gets up [from the grave] and feels very sick about everything, and can't stand the old crowd any more—so cuts out." [38] This story, which eventually became "The Man Who Died," is strikingly different in tone from "The Man Who Loved Islands" because it is a story of a resurrection in which an isolated hero finds salvation and affirmation.

Many admirers of Lawrence prefer to regard all of his writings as simply affirmatives and to overlook the kind of stories I have been discussing here. They point to the magnificent passage in *Apocalypse* in which the dying novelist affirmed his faith in life itself:

> For man, the vast marvel is to be alive. . . . Whatever the unborn and the dead may know, they cannot know the beauty, the

marvel of being alive in the flesh. . . . We ought to dance with rapture that we should be alive and in the flesh, and part of the living, incarnate cosmos. I am part of the sun as my eye is part of me. . . . My soul knows that I am part of the human race. . . . There is nothing of me that is alone and absolute except my mind, and . . . the mind has no existence by itself, it is only a glitter of the sun on the surface of the waters.

The passage is, of course, a key one. Yet the recurring situation traced out in the present discussion is as important in his work as are the affirmations with which the succeeding chapters will be concerned. Indeed the affirmations are reinforced by the negations, as the double measures of *Women in Love*, his finest novel, can show. The Everlasting Yea from a ruddy-faced Rabbi Ben Ezra has little force to move us. From a writer who plumbed the depths of aloneness, who often suffered a Swiftian sense of nausea from human contacts, the passage from *Apocalypse* has a different and more significant impact.

5 On Being Together

THE HORSE DEALER'S DAUGHTER

LOVE AMONG THE HAYSTACKS

THE MAN WHO DIED

The climax or end, if end there be, of the search, the resolution of the state of aloneness occurs, in the Laurentian dialectic, when there is established a "connection between the vigorous flow of two lives." The phrase quoted is from a letter written when Lawrence was 23 years old. In later writings he shortened it to a single word: *togetherness,*[1] but because this term has subsequently been appropriated by popular magazines to signify a state of cosy clubbiness it now makes us shudder and can no longer be used as Lawrence intended. For him it was to signify a blessed state of discovery to which a few of his pilgrims arrived—usually after long and painful searchings.

To describe this state, rather than attempting to define it, examples from a selection of the short stories can be especially helpful. Some of the difficulties encountered in reading the full-length novels, especially *The Rainbow* and *Women in Love,* can be reduced by first considering comparable situations as presented on the more readily encompassed scale of his shorter fiction. Each of the stages of Ursula Brangwen's progress from a state of aloneness to a state of transfiguration following her discovery of Rupert Birkin can be traced out in the short stories, in particular the final stage of established connection.

In "The Horse Dealer's Daughter" we encounter a typical story of this variety in which two lonely people discover in each other a release. A twenty-seven year old woman, who tries to drown herself in a pond, is rescued by a doctor who reluctantly realizes that he loves her and wants to marry her. The overworked young doctor is unwell. He has few friends in the dreary colliery town, and he seems consciously resolved not to become intimate with anyone. The woman, Mabel Pervin, is much more drastically isolated. For her brothers she has kept house, but she has had no contact with anyone for years, her only concern being the memory of her dead mother. Like Paul Morel and like Lawrence himself after his mother's death,[2] Mabel Pervin thinks of suicide as a "fulfilment," a "glorification" which will enable her to approach her dead mother. This initial perversion of terms by which death is exalted above life is made evident later in the story.

At the outset the woman seems herself a part of a dreary landscape of "sloping, dank, winter-dark fields" and of a town "clustered like smouldering ash" in which the house of the dead is preferable to the house of the living. In the opening scene, the prancing dray-horses, so lushly described, are a touch of life in the depressing scene of penury, cold, mist, and marsh mud, but their lively presence is soon blurred by the grayness of death. Lawrence's power to make his setting function—to make us feel death's presence in our eyes and nostrils—is especially apparent in the later parts of the tale when the foul smell of the stagnant pond water in the woman's hair serves not only as a reminder of what has passed but as a threat of what might happen again if release is not secure and if the newly-found life-rhythm does not drown out the sound of its sinister opposite:

> She had gone suddenly very still. He looked down at her. Her eyes were now wide with fear, with doubt, the light was dying from her face, a shadow of terrible greyness was returning.

The scene of the release from loneliness is preceded by the rescue itself in which the man undergoes a kind of deathly baptism—a total immersion in "the foul earthy water." The experience becomes for him, in Pauline terms, a stage of his dying into life. Knowing death he is ready to absorb life.

It should be noted that in portraying the release of the two lovers, Lawrence uses a different technique for each. The woman's changes of feelings and her character itself are rarely analyzed. They are presented to us almost entirely by glances. It is extraordinary how often Lawrence relies upon the expression in a character's eyes to convey states of feeling. Scenes from many of the novels and stories could be cited, as for example in "The Fox" (which made a very good film) when March confronts the eyes of the fox itself. In *The White Peacock,* after she has sung *Drink to Me Only with Thine Eyes,* Lettie teases George Saxton by saying that he has no wine in his eyes to pledge with. And she adds: "I always think people who are worth much, talk with their eyes. That's why you are forced to respect many quite uneducated people."• This device may account in part for his novels and stories being so readily adaptable to film presentation rather than to stage presentation. The storyteller seems to be operating a close-up camera, focusing on one face or the other so as to enable the reader to see the scene and recreate the exchange of feelings between the characters.

Early in "The Horse Dealer's Daughter" the woman's inarticulate hostility is conveyed in a sentence: "Mabel looked at him with her steady, dangerous eyes, that always made him uncomfortable, unsettling his superficial ease." Later, after the rescue, there is this film-style scene:

> She shuffled forward on her knees . . . clutching him with strange, convulsive certainty . . . as she looked up at him with flaring, humble eyes of transfiguration, triumphant in first possession.

With the man, on the other hand, whose struggle is a much more complex one, Lawrence relies upon analyses of motives and feelings instead of upon visual presentation. The analysis includes the kind of small-scale insights we expect in good fiction, as for example the recognition of the difference between a doctor's response to a naked patient and to the women he has come to love. "He tried to remember her as she was when he had wrapped her in the blanket. But then he didn't want to remember, because she

• For sustained use of the eyes to convey situations in a story, "Jimmy and the Desperate Woman" offers the most striking demonstration. In the final 16 pages of this story there are at least 50 references to glances. Again the man's character is analyzed and the woman's is presented; we have to infer what she is like from her eyes. Cf. also J. P. Sartre's discussion of "le regard" in his *L'Etre et le néant* (Paris, 1948), pp. 310-64.

had been nothing to him then, and his nature revolted from remembering her as she was when she was nothing to him." The effect of the woman's eyes upon the doctor is here the main subject. Even before the rescue, her gaze has, as we say, sunk into him although the conscious mind does not yet recognize what the unconscious has experienced. When he meets her steady gaze as she is sponging her mother's gravestone in the cemetery, he feels that her eyes "laid hold of his whole being, as if he had drunk some powerful drug. He had been feeling weak and done before. Now the life came back into him, he felt delivered from his own fretted, daily self."

The expressions *transfiguration* or *delivered from self* in these passages are crucial, for the experience pictured is the turning point in the lives of both characters. Their discovery of each other is also a self-discovery, a major epiphany in which a brief moment of time expands into great circles. "He remained motionless, suspended through one of man's eternities."

II

Because the term *epiphany* has become excessively popular since James Joyce's artist-hero canonized it for secular purposes, critics may be inclined to banish it as too shopworn for further use in discussions of literature. To banish the term (or even to seek a substitute for it) is a temptation but also an evasion. And because the literary method it represents—the recording of what is called in *Stephen Hero* "a sudden spiritual manifestation"—provides especially useful insights into Lawrence's mode of writing, the term still deserves to be paused over. Strictly speaking, epiphany refers to the showing forth of a god,* but as a counter for literary criti-

* In this sense "The Last Laugh" (a story reminiscent of E. M. Forster's shorter fiction), in which the god Pan shows himself to each of the characters, is the most clear-cut example of an epiphany in Lawrence's stories. Much less explicitly "Tickets, Please" hints at the presence of the god among the women, the parallels with Euripides' *Bacchae* (a play Lawrence knew intimately) being especially interesting. Among the novels some of the scenes in *The Plumed Serpent* are likewise epiphanies in this sense, as when Quetzalcoatl seems to manifest himself to Don Ramón and to Cipriano.

cism it seems to have come to refer instead, however improperly, to the effect of the showing forth upon the beholder (as in T. S. Eliot's poem, *Journey of the Magi*). Hence an account in literature of any transforming experience has come to be described as an epiphany. Stephen Dedalus recognized that trivial and unpromising objects might stimulate such a response, and some of the most scalp-tingling passages in Wordsworth's *Prelude* record the overwhelming effect on the hero of seemingly commonplace incidents: the theft of a boat or the spectacle of a summer dawn after a dance. Or from Forster's *A Passage to India* the incident of Mrs. Moore's hearing an echo in a cave might be cited, trivial enough on the surface but overwhelming in its effects on her and others.

Triviality of stimulus is not, however, the crucial test for determining whether an epiphany is being represented. The "transfiguration" of the heroine in "The Horse Dealer's Daughter" has its trivial, essentially comical opening when she discovers that the doctor has undressed her while she was unconscious and she exclaims naively: "Do you love me, then?" But the rest of the scene is of a different dimension, as the story's original title, "Miracle," suggests.

In his lyrical essay of April, 1919, in celebration of the coming of spring after the Armistice, Lawrence wrote:

> The transit from the grip of death into new being is a death from death, in its sheer metempsychosis a dizzy agony. But only for a second, the moment of trajectory, the passage from one state to the other, from the grip of death to the liberty of newness.

Whether stimulated by a trifling catalyst, or by the significant, experiences of this kind are portrayed again and again in Lawrence's fiction. Epiphanies, as thus loosely described, are the very stuff of his writings. They would include major full-length scenes such as Ursula's encounter with the horses in *The Rainbow* as well as the succession of smaller-scale incidents in almost every chapter of his novels.

The following passage from *The Lost Girl* portrays Alvina's feelings in visiting a coal-mine and emerging afterwards from darkness into light. This incident, unlike Mrs. Moore's visit to the caves in *A Passage to India,* is not crucial. It is simply one of many affecting Alvina's development:

> There was a thickness in the air, a sense of dark, fluid presence in the thick atmosphere, the dark, fluid viscous voice of the collier making a broad-vowelled, clapping sound in her ear. He seemed to linger near her as if he knew—as if he knew—what? Something forever unknowable and inadmissible, something that belonged purely to the underground. . . . Her lungs felt thick and slow, her mind dissolved, she felt she could cling like a bat in the long swoon of the crannied, underworld darkness. . . . When she was up on the earth again she blinked and peered at the world in amazement. . . . Never had the common ugliness of Woodhouse seemed so entrancing. She thought she had never seen such beauty—a lovely luminous majolica, living and palpitating, . . . It was like a vision.

Similarly, in the fragmentary novel *The Flying Fish,* the hero is overcome with delight as he peers down into a world different from his own. Watching a school of porpoises from the bow of a ship, Gethin Day, who has been on the point of death, feels restored by the "swift laughing togetherness" of these "warm-bodied fish." [3]

A distinctive feature of the epiphany method as Lawrence uses it is that such experiences usually involve contrasts, especially (as in "The Horse Dealer's Daughter") the contrast of life and death. "The excellence of every art," Keats said, "is its intensity, capable of making all disagreeables evaporate, from their being in close relationship with Beauty and Truth. Examine 'King Lear,' and you will find this exemplified throughout."

Lawrence like his romantic predecessor knew that intensification is achieved by juxtaposition of light and darkness, love and hate, life and death. During the 1914-18 war, when he felt that his "soul lay in a tomb," he noted also "the amazing, vivid, visionary beauty of everything, heightened by the immense pain everywhere"—and after a sunny day in an English village, with "such quantities of light beating and throbbing all round," he felt "like

Persephone coming up from hell."[4] This was the double perspective he was to embody in *Women in Love.* The source of his distinctive vision, like Keats', may be traced to illnesses from which he early suffered.

In the *Fear of Death* Hazlitt observes that "no young man ever thinks he shall die," and Freud speaks of the switchover occurring at thirty-five after which no day passed without his thinking at some point of death. Lawrence, again with Keats, belies the generalizations. The pneumonia which attacked him when he was 17 and again when he was 26 was so severe that on both occasions he was almost given up for dead. He early became the man who almost died.

Medical explanations of literary achievements impress one usually as boring or irrelevant, yet in Lawrence's case it is evident that these severe illnesses permanently affected his appreciation of daily living, just as Dostoevsky's writing was affected by his early experience of fronting death before a firing squad. As Aldous Huxley noted: "For Lawrence, existence was one continuous convalescence; it was as though he were newly reborn from a mortal illness every day of his life. . . . A walk with him in the country was a walk through that marvellously rich and significant landscape which is at once the background and the principal personage of all his novels."[5]

It is the man who almost died who can see a world in a grain of sand and Heaven in a wild flower. The strength of the best celebrative epiphanies of his fiction, which are poignant without mere self-pity, derives from these early confrontations with death in his youth. "Teach me to live this day as 'twere my last,'"[6] a line from one of his favorite hymns as a boy, remained a favorite with the man. In this respect the man sometimes fulfilled the same role as the artist.

Helen Corke, in her recently published autobiography, records how Lawrence's vitality rescued her from a state of suicidal depression. Without destroying her desire for "aloneness," as she called it, "he lured me back among the living."[7]

III

As in Joyce's fiction there are many scenes in Lawrence such as Alvina Houghton's emerging from the coal mine, or Ursula Brangwen's encountering the horses, in which only one character is involved in the transforming experience. In other stories, Lawrence describes a mutual involvement, a kind of two-fold epiphany in effect, the united experience transforming both characters.

"Love Among the Haystacks" is a good example. This story in fact involves four persons. Two brothers, Maurice and Geoffrey, who have been "fiercely shy of women," discover love for the first time during a rainy summer night. That this beautifully told story remained unpublished during Lawrence's lifetime seems fantastic. One can only surmise that his editor in 1912 detected in its night scenes the ingredients for some kind of old-fashioned traveling salesman's tale and was reluctant to risk publication. Indeed recently published paper-back editions of the story, with luridly illustrated covers, are now featured on the drug-store counters beside editions of Erskine Caldwell and Mickey Spillane. The traveling salesman ingredient, featuring surprise encounters in the darkness, is certainly present just as melodrama is present in *Macbeth*. But purchasers are probably disappointed.

The dominant effect in "Love Among the Haystacks" is neither erotic nor Rabelaisian. The emphasis is on tenderness and understanding as in the best scenes of *Lady Chatterley's Lover* such as Connie's crying over the newborn chick, the kind of scene which justified the title originally chosen for that novel, *Tenderness*.

In the "ghastly" whitening air of a rain-soaked dawn, Geoffrey looks down at the woman who has spent the night in his arms:

> She was open-eyed, watching him; she had golden-brown, calm eyes, that immediately smiled into his.

The principal two-fold epiphany scene in "Love Among the Haystacks" involves this pair. Geoffrey's warming of the chilled feet of Lydia, the trampwoman, thaws the ice-jammed emotions of each until a conjoined flow of warmth is established. Surrounding this scene of the feet-warming there is almost an air of ritual with which Lawrence contrives to surround common acts in this and other stories. Here the Breughel-like opening scenes of the rhythmical pitching of hay, the noon dinner with its insistently formal white tablecloth near the shimmering golden field, and the evening scene of Maurice washing himself before his meeting with Paula have a quality that transcends the pastoral.[8]

The intensity of the scene in which the lovers discover each other, unlike the similar scene in "The Horse Dealer's Daughter," does not depend upon the presence of death. Only occasionally is death mentioned in the story as when Geoffrey fears that the dense black night is like death in which he might be "extinguished," and the trampwoman admits she had wished death would strike her ("But we're not that handy at dying," she says). In a setting of dazzlingly bright summer fields, death as such would perhaps be out of place. As a substitute here, the contrast is between life fulfilled and a life of frustration and loneliness. At 22, Geoffrey is "coiled up within himself in morbid self-consciousness, always lonely, surly, and a misery." In the intense heat of the morning, his jealousy of his younger brother's successful lovemaking is like a thundercloud that bursts when he pushes Maurice off the stack.

One may be reminded of Middleton Murry's rather naive discovery, in later years, that Lawrence had correctly understood human tensions and their release. In his *Autobiography*, writing 20 years after having watched a quarrel and reconciliation between Lawrence and Frieda, Murry admits:

> I was [then] very far from understanding, as I now dimly do, that the murderous frenzy is, in the pre-mental realm to which these happenings belong, a kind of electrical discharge that establishes a completer contact than before.[9]

For Geoffrey, the relief from tension derived from assaulting his brother is only temporary. By nightfall, when he discovers that Maurice and Paula are together on the stack, his feeling of despair is more acute than ever. At this point Lawrence shifts our attention fully upon him and Lydia. Unlike the quartet in *Women in Love,* where the pairings of each couple of lovers is described, we can only infer here, because of their unhappy appearance in the morning, that the younger lovers have not had a good night together. It is Maurice now, not Geoffrey, who cannot look others straight in the eyes. Geoffrey's new sense of assurance, despite the chill light of dawn, derives from the epiphany scene in the shed already referred to. The woman's tears are from her "loneliness," and of her Lawrence adds:

> Her bitter disillusionment with life, her unalleviated shame and degradation during the last four years, had driven her into loneliness, and hardened her till a large part of her nature was caked and sterile. Now she softened again, and her spring might be beautiful.

"Love Among the Haystacks" may thus remind us of Paddy Chayefsky's highly successful television play and film, *Marty,* which portrayed the mutual discovery of two lonely misfits. Also similar is the scene in "Daughters of the Vicar" when Louisa loses "her feeling of separateness" and like one of Shakespeare's heroines virtually proposes to the young miner. In Lawrence's fiction, as the story of Birkin and Ursula illustrates, the lovers do not have to be misfits, but those who experience the two-fold transformation to the full are invariably seekers who have been hitherto isolated. The "swoon" which occurs in almost all such scenes is dependent upon what has gone before:

> He turned and looked for a chair, and keeping her still in his arms, sat down with her close to him, to his breast. Then, for a few seconds, he went utterly to sleep, asleep and sealed in the darkest sleep, utter, extreme oblivion. . . . He returned gradually, but newly created, as after a gestation, a new birth, in the womb of darkness. Aerial and light everything was, new as a morning, fresh and newly-begun.

This passage describes the effect of their first kiss upon Tom Brangwen and Lydia Lensky in *The Rainbow,* but it could have been used to describe the coming together of any of these pairs of lovers. The language is strained with the effort of picturing an experience so intense that words can hardly bear the weight of it, but taken in the context of Tom's long and unhappy search, it is appropriate. The exultation is in the vein of Lawrence's poems, *Look! We Have Come Through!*, for in such epiphanies, as the speaker has it in Browning's *The Last Ride Together*, "the instant becomes eternity." •

IV

One disadvantage of such a grouping together of a number of similar scenes in Lawrence's fiction is that *any* coming together of men and women would seem to be endowed with the mutually supercharged effects that have been so far described.

It is a useful corrective to consider another group of novels and stories in which the man is what Lawrence himself called with derision, in later years, "the conquering hero,"[10] rather than the man in search. In stories such as "Glad Ghosts," or "The Virgin and the Gipsy," and to a lesser extent "The Fox," the male is presented as a kind of hunter. The epiphany, involving the release of the woman, is single rather than two-fold. Lawrence's uncanny insight into states of feeling remains impressive in these tales, especially his vivid account of March's response to the fox-like Canadian soldier, but the effect differs from the other stories so far examined because the man is an agent of release from isolation rather than himself released.

The fairy tale of the sleeping princess, as Harry T. Moore observes, is often retold in Lawrence's fiction.[11] Had not Lawrence himself rescued a sleeping baroness in Nottingham, just as Robert Browning had foiled the dragon of Wimpole Street? In later life, I suspect, Lawrence also seems to have wondered about the possi-

• In *The Tightrope Walkers* (1956), Georgio Melchiori points out T. S. Eliot's recognition of Lawrence's capacity "to communicate, in visionary flashes, the sensuous fulness of 'the moment.'" (pp. 89-102.) In the *Four Quartets*, "the moment in the rose garden" would seem to correspond to the two-fold epiphany in Lawrence's fiction. In his essays Lawrence himself tried to describe what he called "the instant moment," the "great mystery of time that has yet to be conquered." (*Phoenix*, pp. 220-23, and 306-07.)

bility of rescuing sleeping princesses other than Frieda Richthofen-Weekley. Stories such as "Glad Ghosts" were the result.

Lawrence's fidelity or even his effectuality as a husband are tempting topics for biographers to speculate about, and his overlooked short story, "The Overtone" might provide clues in view of the silence or unreliability of witnesses. This opportunity I must forego, but I will venture a guess about his inner life, an area of experience in which speculation can never be anything better than a guess. This will be merely to suggest that in his Leopold Bloom-like daydreams, shared by most of mankind, Lawrence was prone to imagine himself in the role of a St. George, or Perseus, or Caponsacchi. Especially in his middle years (1920-26), when a desire for leadership and power afflicted him, he would seem to have imagined himself as cast to rescue various women from states of unhappiness—sometimes women who were unhappily married—and thereafter to have shaped the wish or dream into fiction in which his hero plays such a role.

The circumstances of his writing "The Fox" (1918-21) can be readily followed in documents gathered together in Nehls' biography. "The Virgin and the Gipsy" seems to have been written in 1926 shortly after he had spent considerable time with a young girl from England whom he found attractive and for whose sufferings in a dull middle-class English household he felt some compassion.• This was Barbara Weekley, whose mother, Frieda, had escaped the same household, and Lawrence imagined in his story how a girl like her daughter might likewise be rescued.

"Glad Ghosts" (1925) in which the "sansculottist" hero restores peace to an aristocratic household by spending the night with his ladyship hostess seems to have been similarly inspired.[12]

Again in 1921 he met some Italian aristocrats, and in *Aaron's Rod* (1922) he has his hero encounter an unhappy Marchesa for

• Her English world, as it appears in "The Virgin and the Gipsy," was one of "roast beef and wet cabbage, cold mutton and mashed potatoes, sour pickles, inexcusable puddings." The last phrase would be worthy of Dickens. Lawrence's wit was often exercised at the expense of English dampness, especially after he had himself lived in sunnier lands. In 1923, in the vein of Dickens' Mr. Jingle, he described revisiting London: "Here I am. London —gloom—yellow air—bad cold—bed—old house—Morris wall-paper—visitors—English voices—tea in old cups—poor D.H.L. perfectly miserable." (*Letters*, II, 765.)

whom Aaron performs some restorative feats with his magic rod, the latter a Biblical symbol which Lawrence adapts to his own purposes.[13] The husband in this instance, as in "Glad Ghosts," "The Ladybird," and even *Kangaroo,* gives a kind of curious blessing to the intervention by the dark and potent outsider as if a healer had been summoned to improve his wife's condition of body and spirit.

The self-satisfying nature of the daydreaming out of which these stories or scenes seem to derive may help to explain why some of them are less effective, certainly less moving, than the more typical love scenes in Lawrence's fiction. In them a shared connection is not really achieved.

V

The importance in Lawrence's set of values of the more complete coming together of the searching lovers is evident in the following passage from his essay *We Need One Another:*

> A man who has never had a vital relationship to any other human being doesn't really have a soul. We cannot feel that Immanuel Kant ever had a soul. A soul is something that forms and fulfils itself in my contacts, my living touch with people I have loved or hated or truly known. I am born with the clue to my soul. The wholeness of my soul I must achieve.

To view the soul as something earned is comparable to Keats' conception (derived from Wordsworth) of the world as a "vale of Soul-making." [14] What is evident in Lawrence's view is that soul-making is rarely achieved in isolation; it depends upon relationships. As he told Dorothy Brett:

> My idea of Eternity, I can best illustrate by the rainbow: it is the meeting half way of two elements. . . . And that is eternal . . . the Nirvana . . . just that moment of the meeting of two elements. No one person could reach it alone without that meeting.[15]

Like most twentieth-century writers, Lawrence rarely speaks of immortality of spirit. Death is for him a finality. Instead he affirms that "immortality is in the vividness of life,"[16] a statement that may be dismissed as a mere play on words, yet it is a characteristic example of Lawrence's lifelong tendency to transpose traditional religious terms into a new context.

In *The Rainbow*, the 60-year-old widow, Lydia Brangwen, thinking back over her life with her two husbands, reflects that the first one is really dead but that Tom "had made himself immortal in his knowledge with her."

Terms such as transfiguration from "The Horse Dealer's Daughter" have already been cited, but perhaps the most daring stroke he ever attempted in this vein was to have the hero in "The Man Who Died" exclaim in the temple, as his frigidity melts: "I am risen." The example is extreme, but it may suggest why these high-pitched two-fold epiphany scenes are so important in Lawrence's fiction. In his view of the world, the coming together of lovers can be a resurrection, the most significant kind of resurrection that man will ever experience. Marlowe's regal hyperbole "make me immortal with a kiss" becomes domesticated.

VI

As a final and summarizing example of such stories there remains Lawrence's late work, "The Man Who Died." Written between 1927-29, this story presumably embodied Lawrence's final sermon, although the hero of the story affirms that he has given up preaching. "A sermon," he reflects, "is so much more likely to cake into mud, and to close the fountains, than is a psalm or a song." Many readers nevertheless find that the sermon here is louder than the song, and they construct from it a philosophy, as for example in Dorothea Krook's engaging but misleading appraisal in her book, *Three Traditions of Moral Thought*.[17]

That "The Man Who Died" was written by an author with a message is obvious enough. It is more pertinent to indicate first how this story is significantly representative, not of Lawrence's preaching, but of his fiction. The same story that he had been retelling throughout his career is here re-embodied with a striking finality of effect. At the end of his life he wrote his archetypal story.

The point may be disputed. It may be urged that "The Man Who Died" differs from the rest of Lawrence's fiction in being set in the past. As indicated above, the only other example of historical fiction in his work was his first story, "A Fragment of Stained Glass." And being set in Biblical times, the mannered style of "The Man Who Died" does mark it off from most of his other prose. Yet in its action and in its overall effect, the story is certainly archetypal.

The "dark-faced" black-bearded stranger is represented, like the blonde priestess, as pursuing a painful search for an ideal relationship. Both characters have experienced, heretofore, imperfect relationships with mankind, and these have been shed, in his case through his own near-dying. Both have learned to appreciate the necessity of being alone: "And perhaps one evening, I shall meet a woman who can lure my risen body, yet leave me my aloneness." Both are transformed by the epiphany scene. The man is healed into a resolve to live and to love: "Ah, tenderness!" he exclaims, "More terrible and lovely than the death I died." The woman is transformed by the satisfactions of conceiving a child. And it is an epiphany scene in both senses of the word, for the participants are changed—resurrected—and the god is made manifest. Each of the stages of Lawrence's basic narrative pattern are thus distinctly illustrated in this story.

At one point the man comments on the difference between himself and the priestess, her "soft strange courage of life, so different from my courage of death." The association of the man with death is constantly reinforced in the first part of the story; the peasants fear him as "a dead king, from the region of terrors."

Is the Pluto figure in Lawrence thus normally to be linked with death? In an earlier chapter when discussing the union of Pluto and Persephone, I deliberately avoided this complicating aspect of the myth, postponing it for the present chapter where it is more relevant. The complication is that Lawrence represents a descent into darkness under the earth in two very different ways. The dark underworld kingdom usually tokens, in his writings, the forces of unconscious life, potent and fertile, the forces sought out by the

Indians in their corn dance as Lawrence pictured it in one of the high points of his prose. At times, however, the dark underworld tokens instead the kingdom of death.

According to W. K. C. Guthrie's study, *The Greeks and Their Gods*, the same confusion (or what seems to be confusion) was common in Greece itself, as is evident in the two Greek words for earth, *ge*, referring to the fruitful earth in which furrows are ploughed, and *chthon*, the dead cold earth in which graves are dug.[18] Pluto, that is, would usually be the king of darkness but might also be the king of death. It may be comforting to know that the Greeks encountered difficulties of this order as Lawrence sometimes did, as for example in the Cathedral chapter of *The Rainbow*.

It is, nevertheless, possible to bring the two seemingly opposed clusters of associations into a unit in which the Plutonic figure may be king both in the world of the dead and in the world of potent darkness and his wife, Persephone, be Queen of death and yet also a force for life's renewal. The combination appears in Lawrence's letter to Katherine Mansfield after her brother was killed in the war:

> I knew you would have to die with your brother; you also, go down into death and be extinguished. But for us there is a rising from the grave, there is a resurrection. . . . You have gone further into your death than Murry has. . . . But one day . . . he will dare to go down, and be killed, to die in this self which he is. Then he will become a man; not till.

Like Dostoevsky, Lawrence often cited Christ's paradox: "Except a corn of wheat fall into the ground and die, it abideth alone: but if it die, it bringeth forth much fruit." One of his persistently recurring symbols is of the acorn or grain, seemingly dead in the cold earth, which bursts through its hard shell into a renewal of life. Without the descent into earth, the seeming death, there would be no resurrection as such. At the end of *The Rainbow* Ursula Brangwen recognizes that she must break out of the chill crust of her past, "like a nut from its shell which is an unreality."

> She was the naked, clear kernel thrusting forth the clear, powerful shoot, and the world was a bygone winter, discarded, her

> mother and father and Anton, and college and all her friends, all cast off like a year that has gone by, whilst the kernel was . . . striving to take new root.

This casting-off stage, in the progress of a typical Laurentian narrative, involves first a descent, a figurative dying (like the doctor's submersion in the foul pond-water in "The Horse Dealer's Daughter"), and afterwards an ascent or resurrection in which the man and woman discover a new strength and a fresh appreciation of life's joys. The descent has exposed them, that is, not only to death but to some unseen forces of renewal urging their return to life.

In the eighth chapter of *Lady Chatterley's Lover* Connie's return to life is prepared for in a beautifully rendered scene of her wandering into the woods on a cold and windy day in March. Without resorting to the sometimes excessive contrivances of the stream of consciousness technique the novelist enables us to witness how contrasting instincts affect the heroine's thoughts. Snatches of quotations from the English poets float through her mind, quotations reflecting her numbness of spirit, her desire for death. "Pale beyond porch and portal,//Crowned with calm leaves she stands"—the line from Swinburne's hypnotically rhythmic celebration of Proserpine as the goddess of death conveys to us the unhappy woman's death-wish. The very flowers of early spring seem, in their pallor, to be growths of Proserpine's hellish garden, and for Connie they prompt another line from Swinburne to float up into her mind, this from his other poem about Proserpine: "The world has grown pale with thy breath"—an allusion to Christ as the death-bringer. But there is a contrary current affecting her, represented by snatches of quotations suggesting rebirth, including Christ's words about the grain of wheat bringing forth fruit. The roaring March wind is a token not of the deathly goddess with her hushed garden and its "dead winds" of Swinburne's poem but of the goddess in her other role as inspiring fertility and the renewal of spring. "The wind of March," we are reminded, "was the breath of Persephone, this time; she was out of hell on a cold morning." [19]

A similar contrast is evident in the opening pages of "The Man

Who Died," but it is here even more typical in that darkness itself is represented in its double aspect of death and life.

> He woke numb and cold, inside a carved hole in the rock. . . . A deep, deep nausea stirred in him, at the premonition of movement. He resented already the fact of the strange, incalculable moving that had already taken place in him: the moving back into consciousness. He had not wished it. He had wanted to stay outside, in the place where even memory is stone dead. . . . Yet suddenly his hands moved. They lifted up, cold, heavy and sore.

This thrusting upward provides the main movement of "The Man Who Died" through to its almost exultant conclusion: "Tomorrow is another day." The contrary pull, back to the grave, is once again persuasively rendered, here by repeated references to the pain of unhealed wounds from the crucifixion, the nausea, the reluctance to establish contact with those who fetter the leg of the bird with a string. The affinities between the man and the bird are effectively suggested by this symbol of the string, yet the affinities must not be extended too far. The cock crows lustily simply because he is a cock. The man in the story has to *learn* how to crow. His dying was a stage in his learning, his cry a defiance not so much against other creatures but against death itself. " 'Great is Isis!' he said. 'In her search she is greater than death.' "

Fourteen years before writing "The Man Who Died" Lawrence had referred to the myth of Osiris and Isis. In a letter of 1915 concerning war and resurrection, he remarked: "My heart is quartered into a thousand fragments, and I shall never have the energy to collect the bits—like Osiris—or Isis." In fact in one of his earliest surviving letters (Oct. 26, 1908) he refers to Isis' role as restorer. His interest in what he called this "wild Egyptology" was probably impressed upon him by reading Madame Blavatsky's *Isis Unveiled,* a source which has provided amusement for some critics of Lawrence (and of Yeats) as is evident in the early researches of William York Tindall. Yet the novelist's controlled use of this myth may subdue the amusement. Belief in the historical existence of a particular god—the nineteenth-century preoccupation—is not an issue in "The Man Who Died." The priestess has need to think of the man as Osiris; the man himself does not consider the identification important.

How myth and history are used by Lawrence will be more fully discussed later. For the moment what may be noted is his practice of superimposing one set of religious associations upon another. As in Eliot's *The Waste Land* it is a method which can prompt an awakened response to accounts of a resurrection which may have become complacently accepted through excessive familiarity. The cycles passed through by Christ, Osiris, and presumably Dionysus, are made identical. Such an identification may be used to demonstrate the absurdity of the religious sense.

For some readers, the crucial passage in "The Man Who Died" is the man's discovery that his mission, as previously conceived, was a mistake. The "message" of the story could thus be made to serve as a text for the atheist or for anyone engaged in sloughing off traditional religion. Yet such readers should not gain much comfort from a story which, in its totality, is a re-enactment and reconfirmation of a basic religious narrative.

In her *Studies of Type-Images in Poetry, Religion, and Philosophy,* Maud Bodkin writes of the two chief aspects of Divinity that mankind has worshipped: the "pattern of a world-ruler essentially 'other' than ourselves, and that of a suffering hero and Saviour with whose sufferings and triumph over death we have intimate communion." In Dionysus, as in Jesus, she finds the suffering hero, the god with whose "ritual drama of death and rebirth, the temporal aspect of nature and human life finds expression." [20]

Lawrence's version may impose a startling, even shocking reading of the story of the suffering hero, but the essential basic pattern of death and renewal (antecedent to and incorporated into the Christian version) is never being ridiculed in "The Man Who Died." It is the heart, or if the word must be dragged back in, the real message of the tale.

Father Tiverton has affirmed that Lawrence can be an improving author for Christians,[21] and it is evident (his recommendation not being an exclusive one) that Lawrence may be allowed to be an improving author for others as well.

Like many readers I must admit that when a writer is solemnly recommended for his improving power, I am inclined to become restless, yet for this summarizing discussion I shall risk the word. As it relates to the release from isolation, "The Man Who Died" suggests an explanation of the sources of this improving power. If this story is a kind of archetypal example of Lawrence's fiction, and if here we have a retelling of one of the oldest accounts of man's connections with God and nature, it is evident that in all of Lawrence's characteristic fiction, not merely in a story set in Biblical times, we are being exposed to a religious sense that colors the whole narrative.

In addition to the correspondence between his basic story of the descent and renewal by the searcher with traditional stories of the life-cycle of a god, there is also present a unifying sense of the miraculous quality of ordinary experience:

> In the dooryard fronting an old farm-house near the
> white-wash'd palings,
> Stands the lilac-bush tall-growing with heart-shaped
> leaves of rich green,
> With many a pointed blossom rising delicate, with
> the perfume strong I love,
> With every leaf a miracle.

These lines from Whitman indicate why Lawrence, after showing how fatuous are the chuff-a-chuff elements in Whitman's poetry, ultimately hails him with some of the warmest praise he ever bestowed on another author.* Whitman too, in his role of the celebrator, was an improving author.

From Lawrence's writings, examples of the miraculous leaf crowd in upon one from every chapter of his work. As a small-scale example here is a sentence from the story "Second Best" describing a mole in the sunlight as observed by a girl:

* Dr. Leavis assures us that "it would be difficult to think of a writer more radically unlike Lawrence" than Whitman, and that Lawrence's essay on Whitman "should alone have been enough to warn anyone off the assimilation." (*D. H. Lawrence: Novelist*, pp. 12-13.) Admirers of Dr. Leavis discover when he is most emphatic he is sometimes most misinformed. For the plain fact is (to adopt one of Dr. Leavis's recurring phrases) that, in the essay to which he refers, Lawrence addresses Whitman in these terms: "Whitman, the great poet, has meant so much to me. Whitman, the one man breaking a way ahead. Whitman the one pioneer. . . . No English pioneers, no French." *Studies in Classic American Literature* (New York, 1923), p. 253. See also Karl Shapiro's essay on Lawrence and Whitman in *In Defence of Ignorance* (1960), 187-203.

> She watched the little brute paddling, snuffing, touching things to discover them, running in blindness, delighted to ecstasy by the sunlight and the hot, strange things that caressed its belly and its nose.

Or again, in "The Man Who Died," there is this more emphatic passage describing a cock covering a hen:

> And the man who had died watched the unsteady, rocky vibration of the bent bird, and it was not the bird he saw, but one wave-tip of life overlapping for a minute another, in the tide of the swaying ocean of life. And the destiny of life seemed more fierce and compulsive to him even than the destiny of death.

This capacity to convey the significance of such everyday details as the miracle of the leaf is developed to its highest point in Lawrence's two-fold epiphany scenes. By no means do all the love scenes in his writings take on this almost sacramental dimension. "One must learn to love, and go through a good deal of suffering to get to it, like any knight of the grail," he advised Sir Thomas Dunlop in 1914.

Only the select among Arthur's knights ever saw the Grail distinctly, and many of Lawrence's men and women never win through to the end of the obstacle course of which their relationship is made up. When achieved, however, the coming together of loving men and women, the shedding of loneliness and frustration, is portrayed by Lawrence with an aura to which the term *religious* is not incongruously applied. In such encounters the Grail is seen.

Of the sexual encounters in *Lady Chatterley's Lover* an elderly farmwoman remarked to her grandson: "'E makes a lot of fuss and lah-de-dah about it."[22] The old woman's response was reassuringly normal and predictable. It may remind us of Leopold Bloom's inner monologue commenting on the Roman Catholic burial ceremony during the funeral of Paddy Dignam, or of Theodore Gumbril's reflections on morning prayer in the opening section of Aldous Huxley's *Antic Hay*.

When a religious service, like the embrace of lovers, is stripped of its expected aura, and seen in its ordinariness, it will be greeted with the Orwellian chorus of raspberries to which I referred earlier. To treat an embrace as a religious gesture, to portray love in such serious terms, is to risk the snigger, as Lawrence himself was aware. An important scene in *Lady Chatterley's Lover* (Ch. XII) shows what he calls Connie's "double consciousness" when her sexual union with Mellors is unsatisfactory:

> . . . the butting of his haunches seemed ridiculous to her, and the sort of anxiety of his penis to come to its little evacuating crisis seemed farcical. . . . It was quite true, as some poets said, that the God who created man must have had a sinister sense of humour, creating him a reasonable being, yet forcing him to take this ridiculous posture, and driving him with blind craving for this ridiculous performance. Even a Maupassant found it a humiliating anti-climax.

Despite this awareness, Lawrence was prepared to run the risk. Sometimes he has to pay heavily for it as when he portrays a flower ritual in *Lady Chatterley's Lover* in scenes that even well-disposed readers find absurd. Usually he gets away with it. I suggest that his success resides, in considerable degree, in his surrounding the act of love with the fact of death. Instead of an erotic titillation—the kind of affair he himself savagely satirized in his clumsy novel, *Mr. Noon,**—the act becomes a creative gesture, assertive as the Easter ritual is assertive.

What J. D. Chambers said of Lawrence as a man is certainly applicable to him as an artist and to the role of double rhythms in his fiction: "He imparted some of his own intensity of living to the rest of us; later . . . he contributed to an abiding apprehension of tragedy behind the gayest, brightest exterior which has stayed with me ever since." [23]

*Eliseo Vivas argues persuasively that "St. Mawr" is the worst story Lawrence ever wrote. An even stronger case could be made for *Mr. Noon.* Lawrence himself recommended the story to his publisher as "very comical I think" and there are a few scenes that seem to anticipate the kind of fun displayed in Kingsley Amis' *Lucky Jim,* but *Mr. Noon* is on the whole a dreary production, an exhibition of jaded sarcastic commentary in Lawrence's worst vein.

Part Two
Two Major Novels

"I shall do a novel about Love Triumphant one day. I shall do my work for women, better than the Suffrage."

—Letter to Mrs. Hopkin, December 23, 1912

"That which is not partial, but whole . . . is the music which comes when the cymbals clash one upon the other: this is absolute and timeless. . . . It is that which comes when night clashes on day, the rainbow . . . which leaps out of the breaking of light upon darkness, of darkness upon light . . . the two-in-one; the crown that binds them both."

—*The Crown*

"Life makes its own great gestures, of which men are the substance. History repeats the gesture, so we live it once more, and are fulfilled in the past. Whoever misses his education in history misses his fulfilment in the past."

—*Movements in European History*, by D. H. Lawrence

"The most essential characteristic of the inner movement documented in Russian realism is the unqualified, unlimited, and passionate intensity of experience in the characters portrayed . . . It seems that the Russians have preserved an immediacy of experience which had become a rare phenomenon in western civilization of the nineteenth century. . . . The pendulum of their vitality, of their actions, thoughts, and emotions seems to oscillate further than elsewhere in Europe. . . . There is something truly monstrous—especially in Dostoevski . . . in the change from love to hatred, from humble devotion to animal brutality . . . from pious simplicity to the most cruel cynicism. Such changes often occur in one person—almost without transition—in tremendous and unpredictable oscillations."

—Erich Auerbach, *Mimesis*

6 *The Rainbow* as Bible

In the study of Shakespeare it seems at times that anyone anxious to make his voice heard in the crowded critical market place is led to argue that *Love's Labours Lost,* let us say, is the greatest of tragedies. No doubt the time will come when the critic of Lawrence will be able to attract attention to his wares only by arguing that *Kangaroo* or *Aaron's Rod* is his finest piece of full-length fiction.

Fortunately such eccentricity is not yet called for, and no apologies are needed for sharing the prevailing verdict that *The Rainbow* and *Women in Love* are Lawrence's masterpieces. Nor are apologies called for if some of the problems aired by the battery of recent critics who have devoted chapters to these two works are aired again here; to dismiss such problems as supererogatory would be to settle for *Hamlet* without the Prince.

The fact is that *The Rainbow* and *Women in Love* are not only Lawrence's most satisfying novels but his most difficult. So challenging are these puzzling masterpieces that discussions by the most skillful critics seem sometimes on target and sometimes disconcertingly off in the woods. What Lawrence said of the book of Revelation aptly applies to his own best novels and reminds us of the dangers of critical righteousness in reading them: "Gradually we realize the book has no one meaning. It has meanings. Not meaning *within* meaning: but rather, meaning against meaning." [1]

On a large scale *The Rainbow* and *Women in Love* feature the same recurring situation and narrative patterns that have been examined in previous chapters. Each is the story of characters in search of fulfilment, but here the searches are prolonged and intensified by being worked out in an enlarged social context.

In *Women in Love* the setting is of crumbling contemporary civilizations, Cities of the Plain from which the hero and heroine must make their hard-won escape. In *The Rainbow,* despite the intrusion of industrialism in the later sections, the setting is predominantly one of farm and village, a world of the past whose unchanging cycles represent the way mankind has lived from his beginnings.

Because I shall be stressing some of the mythic dimensions of *The Rainbow* in this chapter, it is useful first to point out that the story of the Brangwens is rooted in observed realities. When Lawrence was casting about for a locale for this novel, he happily hit upon one he had, himself, known intimately but not yet written about.

Instead of the raw mining village of Eastwood and the adjacent farms that had served him for *The White Peacock, Sons and Lovers,* and *The Lost Girl,* he shifted his scene to Cossall, a picturesque village on a hilltop near the border of Derbyshire, with its church and row of old almshouses overlooking a valley of marsh and farmlands.

Adjacent to "the old, little church, with its small spire on a square tower," as described in *The Rainbow,* was the home of Louise Burrows (who died in 1962) to whom Lawrence proposed marriage in 1910. During the four years of their protracted and somewhat sporadic courtship, Lawrence had abundant opportunity to soak himself in the atmosphere of the village and its surrounding landscapes and to observe the life of the Burrows family.

Somewhat curiously the role played by Louise Burrows in Lawrence's life and writings has been made light of by his biographers, perhaps because of Frieda's insistence that she, not Louise, was the model for Ursula Brangwen. According to her, the affair with Louise was merely "an escape from Miriam" and of very short duration.[2]

Whatever the role Louise herself may have played in Lawrence's life, however, there is no doubt of the impact on him of her household and family. Her mother, who died in 1954, like Ursula's mother was named Ann. Like her fictional counterpart Ann Burrows was the mother of eight children (six girls and two boys) several of whom provided the names Lawrence used for the Brangwen brood in *The Rainbow* and *Women in Love.*[3]

Her father Alfred Burrows clearly provided the model for Ursula's father, Will Brangwen. At the time of his death in 1948, at

Quorn in Leicestershire, his career was summarized in an obituary notice:

> The death took place at Quorn on August 5th, 1948, in his 84th year, of Mr. Alfred Burrows, who achieved a considerable reputation as a craftsman in wood and metal. Many fine examples of the ecclesiastical carvings which he loved to create beautify churches in this and other counties. He designed and carved much of the interior of the church at Cossall, Notts., his native place, and some carving in Quorn Church is also his work.
>
> At first a lace designer, Mr. Burrows gave up this career and for many years he visited grammar schools in the county of Leicester as a master of arts and crafts. He will be remembered at L.G.S. [Loughborough Grammar School] by those of a generation ago. He was also a connoisseur of antique furniture and an experienced church musician.•

Indeed a visitor to Cossall today can have the disconcerting experience which occurs when fact and fiction have been blurred by a novelist so that a character and his model are no longer distinguishable. The carved reredos in the church is the handiwork of the man, Alfred Burrows, but for anyone who knows *The Rainbow* it was carved by the character, Will Brangwen. The "high, stone, barn-like, ecclesiastical building" where Will Brangwen established his workshop in the adjacent almshouses is exactly as Lawrence described it. However elaborate the mythical mode in *The Rainbow,* the book is solidly grounded on recollections of an actual scene and an actual family. And sixty years after Law-

• From the *Loughborough Grammar School Magazine* as reported through the kindness of the Reverend S. A. Jackson of Quorn.—After the Burrows family moved from Cossall to Quorn about 1908, Lawrence continued to visit them in the new locale which he used as his setting for the Beldover scenes in *Women in Love* but blending it with scenes from Eastwood. The Moorgreen reservoir near Eastwood is usually assumed to have provided the sole model for the water-party scenes in *Women in Love,* but the reservoir adjacent to Quorn fits Lawrence's account more exactly. Swithland Hall, one of the two estates fronting the lake at Quorn, may have suggested to Lawrence the name of the Crich estate, Shortlands, which in an earlier version of the novel he called Shortland.

rence first saw it, the Cossall environment seems untouched by time and change.

Within walking distance of Cossall is the manufacturing town of Ilkeston, a reminder, like the railroad crossing the valley, of changes in a long established way of life. The village, with associations of a feudal past, the farm, with its traditional cycle of planting and harvest, remain a pocket in which time stands still. Lawrence needed a teeming Eden from which his searchers could launch out, and in this countryside he happily found what he wanted.

> It was enough for the men, that the earth heaved and opened its furrow to them, that the wind blew to dry the wet wheat, and set the young ears of corn wheeling freshly round about . . . they lived full and surcharged, their senses full fed.

This Eden-like plenitude remains a reference point, but not the only reference point, for the rest of the novel. As applied to the life of the Brangwen farmers, the word *Eden* is not used, so far as I have noted, until halfway through the book, but it is constantly implied from the opening pages.

In this Eden, however, as was suggested earlier, there are Eves. The Brangwen women look out to "the spoken world beyond," the world of the vicar symbolized by the church towers on the nearby hillsides.

According to Graham Hough, the theme announced in the opening chapter "disappears" thereafter, yet surely this is a misreading, for the opening chapter sets up the two contrasting rhythms which will be heard (sometimes, admittedly, with puzzling variations) throughout the duration of his long saga. Mankind has been moved, is moved, and will be moved by two forces.

The first, generally but not exclusively associated with men, and generally, but not exclusively associated with darkness, is here embodied in the cycle of rural life, a force representing warmth, mindlessness, with some instinctive awareness of cosmic powers, an awareness comparable to the religious sense supposedly characteristic of man in the primitive stages of his development. The pull towards the earth felt by the early Brangwen men is the same pull that Lawrence was later to describe in his justly celebrated account of the ritual corn dances of the Indians in *Mornings in Mexico*.

The other force, generally but not exclusively associated with women, and generally but not consistently associated with light, is embodied in those who look beyond "the teeming life of creation" to the world of the critical intellect, of science and literature, the civilized world which has emerged from centuries of human effort to dispel the darkness.

One of the most prevalent misreadings of *The Rainbow* derives from the common assumption that women, especially in Roman Catholic countries, are supposed to be obsessed with religion and are thus pillars of the church whereas men are indifferent. In *The Rainbow*, as the opening chapter indicates, the women may admire the church and its clergy as civilizing agents, but it is the men who are instinctively responsive to what Lawrence considers to be our religious needs, needs in which the light of theological argument bears no part.

In previously discussing the myth of Pluto and Persephone as representing a recurring situation in Lawrence's fiction, I raised a question which confronts us in every chapter of *The Rainbow:* how are we to judge between these two forces? Is light a token of evil, and darkness of virtuous masculinity? Unlike many readers of Lawrence, I argued that in his best writings we are usually being asked not to judge but to witness these conflicting forces. Like fire and water each can, under certain circumstances, destroy an individual or a society, but in itself each is simply a force.

R. W. B. Lewis, in *The American Adam,* argues that the best American writings, until recent years, embodied neither nostalgia for the past nor hope for the future, but both. "All genuine fiction," he contends, "is, by nature, ironic. For fiction . . . dramatizes the interplay of compelling opposites."[4] It is this kind of irony that we encounter in the great Cathedral scene in *The Rainbow* which will be discussed below. Or as Lawrence himself says: "Myth is never an argument, it never has a didactic nor a moral purpose, you can draw no conclusion from it."[5]

The first Mrs. Brangwen described in *The Rainbow* is anxious to have her sons push out from the valley of their ancestors by means of education. The effect on the boy, Tom Brangwen, of being exposed to the world of light seems not extensive. He ventures only to nibble the rind of the apple, not to swallow it. Yet the taste is enough to leave him with a sense of vague dissatisfaction that comes to the surface when he talks with a foreign aristocrat at an inn or later when he meets his brother Alfred's mistress and marvels that his brother can discuss with her the writings of Herbert Spencer and Robert Browning. And finally, Tom's choice of a somewhat exotic foreign wife is related to his brief exposure to values other than those of the Marsh farm.

Tom's step-daughter Anna is not an intellectual, but she is far more advanced than Tom because she has a critical intelligence that aligns her with the force of light. It is typical of her that, on the first day she meets the young man who will become her husband, she is overcome with an hysterical laughing-fit in church. To laugh in church is a recurring tactic used by the Brangwen women to let the light of critical intelligence flood in upon dark religious mysteries. Anna resorts to it again, in a shatteringly effective way, during the Cathedral scene.

And in the third generation, with her daughter Ursula, who is to be educated at University, the emancipation goes further. Old Testament narratives, which her grandfather embodied and her father revered, and which Ursula herself had sometimes admired, become, in the light of her enquiring mind, ridiculously quaint. At 17 she listens in church to Biblical passages evocative of her grandfather's teeming valley: "And you, be ye fruitful and multiply;" provoked her to mockery: "every cow becoming two cows, every turnip ten turnips." And as for Noah, Ursula reflects that she wishes she had herself been a nymph. "She would have laughed through the window of the ark, and flicked drops of the flood at Noah, before she drifted away to people who were less important in their Proprietor and their Flood."

Anna, without her daughter's education, has the same enlightened capacity to mock her husband's stubborn adherence to traditional religious mysteries. "She seemed to have sunlight inside her," Lawrence tells us, and under the glare of her sunlight Will Brangwen's religious enthusiasms wither. "Who do you pretend you are praying to?" she asks as he kneels beside their bed. Will, we are told, "preferred things he could not understand with the mind." The miracle of the water turned into wine, for example, he cherished brooding upon, but Anna forces him, like a German critic of the Bible, to examine the evidence "with the clear eyes of the mind" and thus to spoil the miracle for him just as Aldous Huxley, many years later, tried to make Lawrence himself see life through the clear eyes of Darwin.

Anna's role in their arguments, like Ursula's with Skrebensky (a lesser opponent) is that of a balloon-pricker. In the church at Cossethay she momentarily shares Will's "dark emotional experience" as he watches the glowing stained glass picture of the lamb, but she quickly resists "the power of tradition" and punctures the balloon. "Again she poufed with mockery."

Meredith, an author well-known to Lawrence, argues in his *Essay on Comedy* that two tests of a mature civilization are the capacity to enjoy comedy and the recognition of the importance of the intelligence of women—a test which, as he shows, found the German civilization of the 1870's wanting.

Lawrence's emphasis on the capacity for comic deflation displayed by his heroines makes them especially appropriate representatives of civilizing light. His emphasis on this aspect of their role was probably reinforced by his own experiences with Frieda, whose scornful laughter, as Mabel Dodge Luhan discovered with chagrin, could puncture the intensely earnest religious conversations which the American woman longed to have with Lawrence.

Birkin in *Women in Love* was "very earnest," but to Ursula "earnestness was always ridiculous, commonplace." Among his early heroines, only Lettie in *The White Peacock* exhibits this trait. Helena in *The Trespasser* or Miriam in *Sons and Lovers* are humorless, and Mrs. Morel is strongly attached to her church.

Later (post Frieda) heroines such as Harriett Somers in *Kangaroo* are in the same mold as Anna and Ursula, the most striking example being Kate in *The Plumed Serpent*. Only rarely has *The Plumed Serpent* been given a fair reading in this regard,[6] one which pays adequate heed to the ironic juxtaposition of the religious solemnities with Kate's mocking intelligence, her sense of absurdity, her capacity to laugh in church.

It can be argued that in these later novels the balancing of opposites breaks down and that the single beat of Quetzalcoatl's drum finally drowns out the sound of Kate's irreverent laughter just as Constance Chatterley's temporary awareness of the "farcical" aspects of the sexual act, as she experiences it with Mellors, is obliterated by his successfully overpowering love-making.

In *The Rainbow,* however, double rhythms are still predominant. On the "S" curve of his own development from viewing his mother as reference point to his viewing his father as reference point Lawrence was in 1915 at mid stage. Of Will Brangwen he notes, with an insight derived, one suspects, from self-knowledge: "Sometimes, he talked of his father, whom he hated with a hatred that was burningly close to love, of his mother, whom he loved, with a love that was keenly close to hatred, or to revolt."

It was about this same time, in fact, that Lawrence struggled to formulate his views of ideal personal and social relations into a theory of balanced opposites in his essay, *The Crown,* where the lion of darkness and the unicorn of light are ideally locked in conflicts. *The Rainbow* dramatizes the essential conflict and balancing of forces which are described in the pollyanalytics of the essay.

The noises made by lions are more impressive than whatever noises unicorns make, and it is therefore understandable why readers can invent confident summaries of Lawrence's religious position based exclusively on what the lion stands for.[7] Here is Will Brangwen entering Lincoln Cathedral:

> Then he pushed open the door, and the great, pillared gloom was before him, in which his soul shuddered and rose from her nest. His soul leapt, soared up into the great church. . . . She too was overcome with wonder and awe. She followed him in his progress. Here, the twilight was the very essence of life, the coloured darkness was the embryo of all light, and the day. Here, the very first dawn was breaking, the very last sunset sinking, and the immemorial darkness, whereof life's day would blossom and fall away again, re-echoed peace and profound immemorial silence. Away from time, always outside of time! Between east and west, between dawn and sunset, the church lay like a seed in silence, dark before germination, silenced after death. Containing birth and death, potential with all the noise

and transitation of life, the cathedral remained hushed, a great, involved seed, whereof the flower would be radiant life inconceivable, but whose beginning and whose end were the circle of silence.

Such soaring prose, as lush and open-stopped as Ruskin's in *The Stones of Venice,* can sweep us off our critical feet to the point where we forget that the Cathedral scene is a drama. Moreover, to reinforce the lion's voice, there is the commonly held assumption that Lawrence was unequivocally a primitivist and anti-intellectual. That his response to primitivism was a mixed one can be demonstrated and as for the anti-intellectualism, it is a comforting corrective to encounter at least one critic, John Bayley in *The Characters of Love,* who seriously contends that Lawrence's principal fault as a writer is his excessive intellectualism.[8]

When Anna struggles in the Cathedral not to be smothered by the darkness in which her husband has been reveling, she breaks the spell finally by pointing out to him the carved faces of some imps on a stone pillar, and Lawrence remarks: "Brangwen looked unwillingly. This was the voice of the serpent in his Eden." The reference to Eden here provides one of the helpful unifying threads that knits the big book together, but it once more raises the question: are we to regard the comment as the author's description of a fact or as a value judgment, a condemning of the forces of light?

II

To the Cathedral scene itself we can work back by considering how Eden is treated in *The Rainbow.* The Brangwen farm is, of course, primarily the Brangwen farm, but, as suggested above, it provides also one of the gauges by which other ways of life will be measured. The changes wrought by industrialism are represented at Cossethay by the canals and railways after 1840 and later by the wretchedly ugly mining community where Ursula's uncle, a Gradgrind figure, lives in his Coketown-style house, and also by the depressing respectability of Will Brangwen's house in Beldover—"the little grey home in the west" as it pitiably becomes in *Women in Love*. In all such changes we are impelled to contrast the seemingly happy darkness of man's past with the deplorable decline following our so-called enlightened progress, and to conclude with Milton that the taste of that forbidden tree, with loss of Eden, is indeed the source of all our woe.

In the great nineteenth-century debate, which is still with us, over the thatched-roofed cottage revered by Southey and scorned by Macaulay—whether industrialism represents progress or decline—it is evident that the author of *The Rainbow* is on the side of Southey, Ruskin, Morris, and other romantic conservatives. "We shall never rest," he noted prophetically in 1915, "till we have . . . put up barb-wire fences on the moon."[9] And in a later essay he remarks bitingly that if the Promised Land is Pittsburgh, then Pisgah wasn't worth climbing.[10]

A nostalgia for a lost past, which is part of the consciousness of all of us, even perhaps of Macaulay and C. P. Snow, and a fear that having taken some wrong turning we are doomed to suffer a bleak future, is painfully evident in many parts of *The Rainbow* and also *Women in Love*.

If we shift our attention from industrialism to other aspects of human development, however, we get from the novel a more complex sense of history. A primitive and mindless Eden, despite its attractions, is seen as a stage of development, not as a way of life to which we can really return or ought to return. Paradise is lost, and if it is regained it would not be the same paradise. In one of the best of his sketches, Lawrence records his mixed response as he listened to an old Apache reciting to a group of Indians before a camp-fire:

> It was not for me, and I knew it. . . . The soul is as old as the oldest day, and has its own hushed echoes, its own far-off tribal understandings sunk and incorporated. . . . But me, the conscious me, I have gone a long road since then. . . . I never want to deny them or break with them. But there is no going back. Always onward, still further. . . . I stand on the far edge of their firelight, and am neither denied nor accepted. My way is my own, old red father; I can't cluster at the drum any more.[11]

A similar mixed response is experienced by Ursula in *The Rainbow* when she considers an offer of marriage from Anthony Schofield whose farm reminds her, she says, of the Garden of Eden. To reject the ancestral pull, to cut the cord linking her with a mindless past, is painful for her, but as "a traveller on the face of the earth" she knows she cannot return. The fall is not simply fortunate or unfortunate but both. Like Wordsworth longing for the lost contacts of childhood but accepting, in the same poem, the realities of maturity, Lawrence in his novel is not recommending that the ills of mankind can be solved by some mass denial of civilization. *The Rainbow* re-embodies some of the same tensions as Wordsworth's great ode, one of Lawrence's favorite poems.

The urge of the Brangwen women to thrust themselves and their men out of the happy valley of the past up the hillsides of the future, evident in the opening pages of *The Rainbow* and fully illustrated in the development of Ursula, is to be regarded, then, as a fact of the human condition not as a wicked falling away from perfection.

There were times, of course, when Lawrence resented what the critical intelligence had cost him in his own religious development. Yeats' celebrated statement about T. H. Huxley would have applied effectively to Lawrence's own experiences: "I am very religious, and deprived by Huxley and Tyndall, whom I detested, of the simple-minded religion of my childhood, I had made a new religion." [12] Carlyle's resentful attitude towards Hume, Gibbon and Voltaire, who had robbed him of the security of ancestral faith, is similar. But resentment is not repudiation. Neither Yeats nor Carlyle ever pretended that what had withered under the light of intelligence could be restored to life in its original form.

At one point in *The Rainbow* Lawrence has a word of praise for the traditional cycle of Christian festivals. The celebrations of Easters and Christmases at Cossethay provide, he says memorably, a "rhythm of eternity in a ragged, inconsequential life." But he goes on to comment, immediately afterwards, that the Hebrew Old Clothes, as Carlyle called them, are worn out and deadening. Ursula has to find her way, as her creator did, with the traditional routes blocked off.

One further aspect of the fortunate and unfortunate fall requires comment. For Lawrence, the loss through enlightenment could be not only of Christianity, but of the religious sense itself (as Lawrence, at least, conceived it), a pre-Christian or post-Christian sense of communion with cosmic forces for which the particular form is inconsequential. Will Brangwen whose eyes, as Anna says scornfully, are "in his chest" represents this sense. As a reformer and critic, it was Lawrence's role to point out that a civilization in which this dark sense is totally ignored will die of religious starvation. This reformer's urge, coupled with his resentment against what Arnold called the rigorous teachers who had trimmed his religious fire, doubtless add volume to the lion's voice in *The Rainbow.* Nevertheless the unicorn sustains her role in this book, and it is the novelist, not the religious reformer, who is ultimately in charge of the match.

III

Like the scene of Ursula's confronting the horses at the end of *The Rainbow,* the visit of Will and Anna Brangwen to Lincoln Cathedral is fitly regarded as a key scene in the novel. One of the many puzzles raised by this scene is why Lawrence chose to abandon the regular time sequence adhered to elsewhere in his chronicle. Chapter VI, "Anna Victrix," ends with an account of the static stage to which Will and Anna arrived some years *after* the cathedral incident. Apparently Lawrence wanted us to be aware throughout "The Cathedral" chapter of the way their dramatic conflict would be resolved.

A more significant feature of the presentation is that the visit to Lincoln is preceded by a visit to the vicarage of Baron Skrebensky whose cultivated wife despises the "uncritical, unironical nature" of Will Brangwen so that his limitations are evident to his bride. Exposed to this household of light, the young Anna is reminded of "how different her own life might have been," and she realizes that through marriage she has been lapsing away from the individual pilgrimage towards critical self-knowledge on which she once felt she had been launched. Before she enters the cathedral, therefore, her guard is up, yet so powerful is the lure of darkness within the building that she has to struggle desperately, as we have seen, to reassert her values, to laugh the walls and arches down so that light can get in. Specific phases of Christianity do come under her attack, but what she is really out to destroy is the religious sense itself.

For Will the ecstatic religious response he experiences within the dark interior is his "consummation," and every sentence of the lushly described ecstasy implies an analogy between religious union and sexual union—a blotting out of the mind and also of the whole world of time in which pilgrimages take place.

Lawrence's conception of what was, for him, the basic religious experience in the Edens of this world has nowhere been more finely rendered than here. How trite is the statement that a spire is a phallic symbol and how boring to be told that a church is a womb or tomb symbol. Lawrence does not talk about symbols; he creates the experience. Moreover, to reinforce his analogy between religious consummation and sexual consummation he relies not only on the cathedral scene itself but upon our remembering another scene fifty pages earlier.

> Inside the room was a great steadiness, a core of living eternity. Only far outside, at the rim, went on the noise and the destruction. Here at the centre the great wheel was motionless, centred upon itself. Here was a poised, unflawed stillness that was beyond time, because it remained the same, inexhaustible, unchanging, unexhausted.

This passage describing the bedroom of the cottage in which Will and Anna spend their honeymoon uses exactly the same terms as are used to describe the cathedral. E. M. Forster would call such a repetition and appeal to the reader's memory an example of the novelist's use of musical techniques. In the present instance it is exceptionally effective:

> He was with her, as remote from the world as if the two of them were buried like a seed in darkness. . . . As they lay close together, complete and beyond the touch of time or change, it was as if they were at the very centre of all the slow wheeling of space and the rapid agitation of life, deep, deep inside them all,

> at the centre where there is utter radiance, and eternal being, and the silence absorbed in praise: the steady core of all movements, the unawakened sleep of all wakefulness. They found themselves there, and they lay still, in each other's arms; for their moment they were at the heart of eternity, whilst time roared far off, forever far off, towards the rim.

It is noteworthy too that the scene in the bedroom ends in exactly the same way as the scene in the cathedral. When the lovers count the strokes of the clock the darkness begins to dissipate, and when Anna insists upon seeing friends for a party the sanctuary of the bedroom is violated:

> He was anxious with a deep desire and anxiety that she should stay with him when they were in the timeless universe of free, perfect limbs and immortal breast. . . . But no, he could not keep her. She wanted the dead world again—she wanted to walk on the outside once more.

In the cathedral, the same impulse leads Anna to repudiate her husband's passionate need for remaining forever in spirit in the dark womb of the roofed building. "There was the sky outside," she reflects, "a space where stars were wheeling in freedom," and so she forces Will to regard the impish carved faces, mocking reminders, like the goblins that E. M. Forster detected in Beethoven's Fifth Symphony, that the beautiful confined world of the marriage bed and of the cathedral is incomplete.

If this reading of the scene is an accurate one, we are still left with a puzzle to cope with—at least one puzzle. Is the cathedral with its arches to be identified with the arch of the rainbow? Throughout the novel, throughout Lawrence's writings in fact, rainbows are associated with the resolution of a stormy conflict between light and darkness, a token of hope for man's future.[13]

Each of the three narratives into which the novel is divided concludes with a rainbow scene. Tom Brangwen's state of loneliness when he is disunited from his wife is compared vividly to his feeling "like a broken arch thrust sickeningly out from support." Later when his lonely state is relieved and man and wife come together in the familiar pattern of a "baptism to another life" their union is likened to the forming of a rainbow arch. The child Anna now "played between the pillar of fire and the pillar of cloud in confidence . . . She was no longer called upon to uphold with her childish might the broken end of the arch. Her father and mother now met to the span of the heavens, and she, the child, was free to play in the space beneath, between."

When Anna is herself an adult, her own vision of the rainbow, as described at the end of Chapter VI, is as a token of hope. And Ursula, on the final page of the novel, after her vision of her own future and of mankind's future, discovers in the rainbow arch a resolution of her own stormy conflicts.

The arched cathedral, with its "jewelled gloom," can readily be identified with the traditional rainbow symbol, and Lawrence himself implies the comparison at several points. Yet he seems also to have realized that the identification as such can be misleading, and to have groped to suggest the differences between Will's response to the cathedral arch which shuts out the sky and Anna's response to the rainbow arch which is the sky. The dramatic conflict of forces in the cathedral scene concludes with both wife and husband "altered." The husband has discovered that the exclusively Dionysian darkness in which he reveled was half of life but no longer an absolute. The cathedrals, he realizes, do contain still, for him, "the dark mysterious world of reality," but he sees them now "as a world within a world . . . whereas before they had been as a world to him within a chaos . . . an absolute, within a meaningless confusion." •

•At a later stage in his marriage Will reverts to an "Absolute" again when he discovers that his wife's body is Absolute Beauty, the equivalent of the "absolute beauty of the round arch." Heretofore, we learn, he had preferred, like Ruskin, the pointed Gothic arches as emblematic of man's imperfection. The complexities introduced by this passage are excessive, for if we equate the rainbow arch with the classical arch a rich symbol becomes blurred and merely confusing. One can agree with Harry Levin's generalization in *The Power of Blackness* that the best symbols are indefinite in meaning, but we can draw the line when enrichment is simply misleading. The passage seems a kind of afterthought, but unfortunately it is one on which Mark Spilka leans hard in his discussion of *The Rainbow*. It misleads him, I suspect, to mix his arches with crosses. In his *Study of Thomas Hardy* (*Phoenix*, p. 454) Lawrence returns again to some assorted reflections on mediaeval cathedrals, but his most helpful discussion is an early letter contrasting Lincoln Cathedral with the commercial "temples" of London. The

IV

Anna Brangwen too was "altered" by her exposure to what her young husband stood for:

> She was willing now to postpone all adventure into unknown realities. She had the child, her palpable and immediate future was the child [Ursula]. If her soul had found no utterance, her womb had.

What are we to understand by this *adventure into unknown realities*? In an earlier passage, Lawrence tries to convey the nature of this woman's search by analogies from the Bible. Anna, we learn, has stopped on Pisgah mount, from whence she can see the rainbow, a symbol of "the promise," but herself no longer a "traveller surging forward." And then, most strikingly, we encounter this analogy:

> The child she might hold up, she might toss the child forward into the furnace, the child might walk there, amid the burning coals . . . as the three witnesses walked with the angel in the fire.

To bring this subject blatantly and clumsily into the open, it can be said that *The Rainbow* is the story of the ancestry, birth, development, suffering, trials and triumphs of a prophet, or, more accurately, a prophetess, Ursula Brangwen, whose mission it will be to show the way out of a wilderness into a Promised Land. The comparison of Ursula to several great Biblical figures is exploited in a remarkable variety of ways. Her resemblance in the above passage to one of God's witnesses who can survive the test of fire is

---

arches in London, he noted, "are round and complete; the domes high for the magnification of the voices," and the effect of these noisy buildings on the spectator is to make him feel cheerful and confident in the strength of human intelligence. The silence of the Gothic Cathedral, by contrast, is agitating, "mystical and wearying." Lincoln and Ely "set the soul a-quivering." (*Letters*, I, 29.)

repeated, 250 pages later, on the night when she annihilates her lover, Skrebensky, in their final sexual encounter on the moonlit sand dunes:

> There was a great whiteness confronting her, the moon was *incandescent as a round furnace door,* out of which came the high *blast* of moonlight . . . a dazzling, terrifying glare of white light. . . . He felt himself *fusing* down to nothingness, like a bead that rapidly disappears in an incandescent flame [italics mine].

Only when we recall the Biblical parallel does this passage make its full impact or even make sense. Skrebensky is like the soldiers who conducted Shadrach, Meshach, and Abednego to the door of the fiery furnace, who were themselves consumed by flames that left God's witnesses unharmed.

If Ursula reminds us of Biblical prophets, what is Anna's role? Evidently she is cast as a forerunner, a Moses, a John, or even a Mary. The scene of her dancing naked during her pregnancy "to the unseen Creator who had chosen her," a scene that ranked as the most offensive in the book to the censors who banned *The Rainbow* in 1915, is actually a modern Magnificat.[14]

Some readers will protest that such comparisons are offensive, and others that they are absurd or irrelevant. After all, Ursula Brangwen is an ordinary enough girl from a Nottinghamshire village, daughter of an inconsequential wood-carver and lace-designer, a girl who teaches school, attends college, and has an affair with an army officer.

Her mother's career is even more ordinary, and to imply that either woman's life has the significance we associate with the lives of the prophets is, such readers say, nonsense. The objection, though sound, can be met. On one dimension Lawrence is certainly presenting a prosy enough tale. His subject, as he said in a letter of 1914, was "woman becoming individual, self-responsible, taking her own initiative." [15] In this respect, *The Rainbow* (like *The Lost Girl* which he began to write at the same time) is concerned with a topic that used to be called Modern Woman, a topic that was being exploited, in a one-dimensional realistic and topical way in popular magazines and also by such writers as H. G. Wells and Arnold Bennett whose novels Lawrence had been reading and whose success he could not help but envy.[16]

The Rainbow could have been another *Ann Veronica* (which Lawrence had read in 1910 and pronounced to be not very good). It is fortunately a great deal more, yet much of the book can compete with Wells or Bennett on their own terms. Ursula's experiences as a schoolteacher in the blackboard jungle of Ilkeston, for example, are largely of this topical and documentary dimension. The very title of the chapter devoted to these experiences, "The Man's World," suggests a problem novel of the Edwardian or Georgian era. On this level, then, what Lawrence calls Anna Brangwen's *adventure into unknown realities,* which she abandons, would mean simply female emancipation. Three generations of women are pictured as emerging from the bondage of the dark past into the light of the emancipated modern world.

The fact that the above phrase, *female emancipation,* falls with a kind of dull thud and that *adventure into unknown realities* is not offensive is in itself a promising sign. *The Rainbow* can convey impressively a sense of sixty years or more of English social history from 1840 to 1905 let us say,• and yet convey even more impressively a sense of timelessness.

The pilgrimages pursued by each generation in *The Rainbow* have the effect of sagas, experiences that are recurrent in every age, in which topicality is of minor consequence. How is this achieved? In part it is because Lawrence had the good fortune or the good taste to recognize that woman's suffrage, for example, was not likely to prove a subject of lasting interest in a novel.

For Ursula "the liberty of woman meant something real and deep. She felt that . . . she was not free." But "the automatic

• There is some indication that Lawrence originally intended the action to end about 1913 instead of 1905, but his use of the Boer War obliged him to push the action back further. He seems to have had an eye out for possible anachronisms. When Ursula, a late Victorian heroine in *The Rainbow,* rides through the country in a "motor-car" (Chapter XI), it is evident that the experience is an unusual one for the 1890's whereas in *Women in Love,* the motor-car is part of the landscape. Even Birkin, unlike his creator, drives one. For an interesting analysis of how Lawrence gains the effect of timelessness in individual scenes see Roger Sale's brief essay "The Narrative Technique of *The Rainbow,*" *Modern Fiction Studies* V (1959), pp. 29-38.

system that contained the vote" is of little concern to her. Her search, instead, is in the areas of "religion and living." Rather than upon politics, or even the economic problem of competing with men for employment, Lawrence concentrates upon the personal and religious phases of life, a man's or woman's fulfillment in relations with other men and women, a topic most appropriate to the novelist. He also deals with the characters' relations with God, a topic most appropriately dealt with, if it is to be a literary subject, by the poet or poetic novelist.

The *adventure into unknown realities* is a timeless one partly because of the very imprecision of the phrase. What is it that Ursula, as a "traveller," really wants? On the same night when she tests her lover, Skrebensky, in the fiery furnace of the moonlight, we have this characteristic exchange:

> She stood on the edge of the water, at the edge of the solid, flashing body of the sea, and the wave rushed over her feet.
>
> 'I want to go,' she cried, in a strong, dominant voice, 'I want to go. . . .'
>
> 'Where?' he asked.
>
> 'I don't know.'

The concluding admission, "I don't know," is an almost comically lame one but it is not a period piece. Not being dependent on political movements, the undefined yearning and dissatisfaction expressed by Lawrence's heroines in such scenes are represented as perennial human urges.

In addition to his focusing attention on personal relations and his minimizing of topicality, Lawrence achieves his effect of timeless interest in *The Rainbow* even more by his ambitious scheme of Biblical analogy. On one dimension, which *The Rainbow* shares with the novels of Wells and Bennett, Ursula is the ordinary village girl whose struggle to find herself in the modern world is representatively commonplace. On a second dimension, however, a dimension rarely represented at all in the novels of Wells and Bennett, this ordinary girl is likened to a prophet from the Bible whose life-story is told as if it were of mythic or epic-scale significance.

The kind of reader, to whom I referred above, who finds the conception of Ursula as prophetess an absurd misreading will be well advised to devote himself to other novelists, for the Bible is not incidental decoration in *The Rainbow;* its mark is evident in the prose style, in the exalted pitch of scene, and in the underlying conception of the significance of each character's actions.[17]

Lawrence once described the Bible as "a great confused novel," and one is tempted, in the fashion of Oscar Wilde, to retort that *The Rainbow* is a great confused bible. The Bible, Lawrence adds, is not a book about God but about man alive: "Adam, Eve, Sarai, Abraham . . . Judas, Paul, Peter: what is it but man alive, from start to finish? . . . The Bible—but *all* the Bible—and Homer, and Shakespeare: these are the supreme old novels. These are all things to all men. Which means that in their wholeness they affect the whole man alive." [18]

We may be reminded of James Joyce's saying that Homer's *Odyssey* "embodies everything." Indeed there is considerable similarity between Joyce's use of Homeric parallels in *Ulysses* and Lawrence's use of Biblical parallels. Even though the apparent discrepancy between the large-scaled epic heroes and heroines of antiquity and their more ordinary modern-day equivalents is played up by Joyce for effects of comedy that are different from Lawrence's (especially when he is in Eastwood prophetic strain), the author of *Ulysses* is nevertheless using similar methods for similar ends. Both novelists, dissatisfied with the one-dimensional level of naturalistic fiction, create a second dimension by suggesting, through parallels, that human experience is constant rather than totally chaotic.

The sense of order a reader derives from these repetitive spectacles can be ultimately reassuring and consolatory. In connection with *Women in Love* more must be said, in a later chapter, of Lawrence's overall mythic method and his use of analogies other than Biblical ones. In *The Rainbow* what he is constantly trying to make us share is his sense that the Bible stories not only were but are. This goodly effort accords not only with the basic assumptions of his Protestant background, but with his conception of the function of literature.

Emma Bovary and her husband, Lawrence once noted, "are too

insignificant to carry the full weight of Gustave Flaubert's sense of tragedy"[19]—an Aristotelian observation that is also applicable to Arthur Miller's *Death of a Salesman*. "The great tragic soul of Shakespeare," Lawrence adds, "borrows the bodies of kings and princes—not out of snobbism, but out of natural affinity."

In *The Rainbow* he cannot portray Anna Brangwen *as* a princess, but by surrounding her ordinary life with Biblical counterparts, he does portray her as *like* a princess.

Northrop Frye, in one of his several gallant attempts to slice out new categories from the traditional literary pie, suggests a scale of five fictional modes extending from myth (in which the hero or heroine is a divine being) through romance, epic, and the novel to the "ironic" mode in which the hero or heroine is inferior in power or intelligence to ourselves. In fifteen centuries, Frye notes, European fiction "has steadily moved its center of gravity down the list," with the ironic mode dominant in twentieth-century fiction[20]—in Bennett, we might say, or later in Kingsley Amis.

Lawrence's distinction, I am suggesting, is his mixture of modes. Beginning with Bennett, at the novelistic or ironic level, he moves on to endow his heroine with dimensions appropriate to myth, romance, and epic. *The Rainbow* thereby eludes classification not only in the traditional terms of novel-criticism but in Frye's more distinctive categories as well.

Joyce's use of Homer has received so much attention from scholars that readers can readily see the Odyssean shadows looming as counterparts behind every scene in his novel.

The Rainbow oddly enough has received less attention of this kind, perhaps because the old assumption dies hard that all educated readers will be thoroughly familiar with the minutiae of every page of the Bible. Lawrence himself, "soaked" in Biblical reading to the saturation point (as he says in *Apocalypse*), certainly makes such an assumption in his writings. His allusiveness takes a great deal for granted. In *Aaron's Rod,* for example, where he returns to some of the same Biblical parallels used in *The Rainbow,* there is the incident of Lilly restoring the sick Aaron to health by rubbing his body with camphorated oil.

For readers such as myself, more readily familiar with all the biographies of Lawrence than with certain passages of Exodus and Leviticus and Numbers, this curious scene seemed significant only in what it tells of an incident in Lawrence's own life, with homosexual overtones, of which Middleton Murry has left an account.[21] Yet readers as familiar with the Bible as Lawrence expected us to be will readily recognize that allusion is being made to God's instructing Moses (Exodus XXIX, 7, and XL, 15), "Then shalt thou take the anointing oil, and pour it upon his head, and anoint him."

It is fascinating to speculate about Lawrence's preoccupations with incidents having homosexual overtones, but we miss the core of *Aaron's Rod* if we are sidetracked into overlooking the analogy to the prophet consecrating his chief priest who will fail at times to follow in his footsteps (Numbers XII and Exodus XXXII). Aaron Sisson's vacillating attitudes towards the leadership of Lilly, the main subject of the novel, are forecast in the scene of his anointing and consecration.*

In a useful study of the ways in which the Bible has affected twentieth-century novelists, *The Prophetic Voice in Modern Fiction* (1959), William Mueller discusses novels by Joyce, Camus, Kafka, Silone, Greene and Faulkner. It is curious that he says nothing of *Aaron's Rod* and other novels by a writer who, more than any of those named, reflects Biblical influences and correspondences on almost every page.

In *The Rainbow*, these correspondences occur in clusters. In many instances they are not worked out rigidly. They serve simply to evoke a general sense of resemblances. Thus Tom Brangwen is frequently associated with Noah, as in his drunken death and the exposure of his body to his children, but his death in a flood does not correspond to the Bible story.[22] What the novel is conveying to us effectively is a general sense that the early Brangwens are patriarchal. The stories about them which Ursula as a little girl hears

* The lapse from the Biblical level into bathos is painfully illustrated in the closing dialogue of *Aaron's Rod*. Of Lilly's advice to Aaron about what person he should submit to ("Your soul will tell you") Anthony West comments witheringly that this final exchange sounds like an anxious Victorian girl asking her Nannie: "But how shall I know if it is Mr. Right?" "Your heart will tell you, dear, you can't make a mistake when Mr. Right comes along." *D. H. Lawrence* (1950), p. 123.

in the Marsh bedroom from Lydia, her grandmother, "became a sort of Bible to the child."

Tom Brangwen is also, as I suggested earlier, associated with Eden, but as one who suffers at times from wondering what his role really is. At his daughter's wedding, he sees his life as a pilgrimage across a plain:

> He felt himself tiny, a little, upright figure on a plain circled round with the immense, roaring sky: he and his wife, two little, upright figures walking across this plain, whilst the heavens shimmered and roared about them.

In this figure we have the principal link between *The Rainbow* and the Bible as a whole. The movement of each generation, even for those who pause in the journey across the plain, is away from Eden towards the promised land and eventually towards the kind of far-reaching changes in man's state that are forecast in the Apocalyptic vision. Of such changes, as the last paragraph of the novel indicates with its rainbow symbol, Ursula Brangwen is to bear witness.

In *The Plumed Serpent* Kate actually becomes a priestess (admittedly a somewhat reluctant one) of a new cult, a situation that strained Lawrence's fictional resources to the breaking point. In *The Rainbow* Ursula's role is conveyed, instead, by an analogy which achieves the dimension desired without incongruity because of the very vagueness of her mission. The heightening gained by the effective use of the mythic method functions in this novel for prophecy as well as for history and fiction.

7 *The Rainbow* as Novel

In an earlier chapter it was suggested that the recurring situation in virtually all of Lawrence's fiction is of a pilgrim in search. In the preceding chapter, by emphasizing Lawrence's use of analogies, I have suggested that in *The Rainbow* the individual pilgrimages take on expanded dimensions by means of comparisons, both explicit or implicit, to Biblical histories.

To round off the discussion, I should like to return to the less exalted levels at which novels ordinarily find their scope and to examine a few scenes in *The Rainbow* which illustrate Lawrence's special skills on these levels. If, that is, the generations of Brangwens are seeking some indefinable connection with the cosmos, they establish it, or fail to establish it, through their contacts with other persons. As a study of personal relations, *The Rainbow* remains a novel as well as a bible. It is a study of pairings, perfect and imperfect, of violent attractions and repulsions, in which the novelist attempts to find new ways of portraying how men and women feel towards each other.

Such an objective suggests nothing new; it could apply to Tolstoy or Eliot or Austen. As far as scope is concerned, it is odd how Austen's famous formula for her tidy novels is applicable to *The Rainbow:* "3 or 4 Families in a Country Village is the very thing to work on." [1] To explore the impression one person in such families makes upon another, Austen relies on a well contrived succession of exchanges. Chapter XI of *Pride and Prejudice*, for example, after featuring at Netherfield a kind of verbal badminton match between Elizabeth and Darcy, concludes characteristically:

> "Do let us have a little music," cried Miss Bingley, tired of a conversation in which she had no share. "Louisa, you will not mind my waking Mr. Hurst?"
>
> Her sister made not the smallest objection, and the pianoforte was opened; and Darcy, after a few moments' recollection,

was not sorry for it. *He began to feel the danger of paying Elizabeth too much attention.*

The passage I have italicized prepares the reader for the scene, twenty-three chapters later, when Darcy makes his first proposal of marriage. We infer that he is susceptible to Elizabeth's attractions, and we make the inference long before she is made aware of his being susceptible. Moreover, we can try to imagine, in the interval, the nature of his passion for Elizabeth, but Austen is not concerned with representing it directly. Its current may, no doubt, be running violently, but it is underground where we cannot detect it.

Lawrence, of course, is preoccupied almost exclusively with a direct presentation of these feelings. "That's her," Tom Brangwen exclaims to himself the first time he sees Lydia Lensky on the road, and after their eyes meet briefly in passing, and a "pain of joy" runs through him, we have this paragraph:

> The feeling that they had exchanged recognition possessed him like a madness, like a torment. How could he be sure, what confirmation had he? The doubt was like a sense of infinite space, a nothingness, annihilating.

I have chosen this short passage almost at random, although after even a brief sample of Austen's elegant world this particular outburst may seem more than ordinarily violent. The sense of strain it conveys reflects Lawrence's problem in his pioneering explorations into basic levels of experience.

Darcy's feelings about Elizabeth, when he sees her again at Rosings, were presumably the same as those felt by Tom Brangwen on the night he was to make his proposal of marriage as he stood grasping his fistful of daffodils and watching Lydia Lensky through the kitchen window of the vicarage. If the two men were to converse together in a drawing room (could such an exchange be imagined) or even to converse in the Red Lion pub, Darcy and Tom Brangwen would seem not to belong to the same species. In their feelings as lovers, on the other hand, the two men are virtually identical.

This, I take it, is what Lawrence meant by his frequently quoted but rarely explained remark: "You mustn't look in my novel for the old stable *ego*—of the character. There is another *ego*, according to whose action the individual is unrecognisable, and passes through . . . states of the same single radically unchanged element." [2]

The remark is only a half-truth. Tom Brangwen is as vividly realized a character as Darcy is, for Lawrence in this instance does not abandon the kind of differentiation we expect from Austen or Dickens or Balzac. The novelty of his method consists in his exploring, at the same time, the areas in which the differentiation between the two men is minimal, the area in which all of us are approximately identical: the hourly round of attractions and repulsions of which most of our experience consists.

A critic who gleefully points out that paragraphs describing the feelings of Tom Brangwen could be inserted into other parts of *The Rainbow,* and applied equally well to describe the feelings of Will Brangwen, has not demolished the novel, but merely described what Lawrence was trying to show.

To discriminate between the values of such feelings, as experienced by different men and women, is another problem, one which Lawrence wrestled with as a moral critic and did not always solve. But to show the similarity of feelings shared by different men and women—to iron out their individual drawing-room idiosyncrasies—was his special objective as a novelist, and the source of much of his successful art. As his friend Catherine Carswell noted, however, it is what gives his novels their "peculiar flavour . . . which at first makes them so distasteful and so puzzling to many readers." [3]

In the first five chapters of *The Rainbow* the explorations of feelings center on one character, Tom Brangwen, in his role as son, husband and father. This section, which Lawrence was at work on late in 1914, was probably conceived and written at a later date than the rest of the novel, despite what has been sometimes affirmed by critics who consider these chapters to have been written in his early manner and the Ursula chapters as later.[4] These chapters make up the most readily satisfying of the three parts of *The Rainbow,* perhaps because the relationships represented are less complex than those in the stories of Will and Anna or of Ursula and Skrebensky.

As in "Love Among the Haystacks," two lonely strangers meet and, after a struggle, establish a happy marriage—the first to be described in Lawrence's novels.[5] During the courtship, the man wishes at times that he "could stand alone," but under the stars he knows that "without her he was nothing," with her "he would be real." The woman, for her part, experiences "the pain of a new birth in herself," a return to life. Part of the success of this love derives from their mutual recognition of separateness in union, a distinction also stressed by the theologian, Martin Buber, between *Thou* and *I* as objects of love.[6] Of their sexual relations, Lydia says when he asks her what he is to "remember" about her: "I want you to know there is somebody besides yourself." And Tom Brangwen learns to remember.

As for the objection that such lovers would have nothing to talk about when they were not engaged in the sexual act, it is clear that Lawrence is not glossing over something. He does not picture Tom Brangwen and his wife discussing socialized medicine or the paintings of G. F. Watts. On the Jane Austen drawing-room plane this pair remain what they were when they met: two strangers still gropingly trying to communicate with each other through barriers of language and class differences. It is on another plane that they discover each other ("She had felt Brangwen go by almost as if he had brushed her"), a plane only tenuously connected with the pleasures of rational discourse. "He knew her," Lawrence says, "without understanding." Yet to describe their final coming together his choice of Biblical language is altogether appropriate: "The house was finished, and the Lord took up his abode."

If the story of Tom Brangwen's role as lover and husband follows the typical pattern of Lawrence's fiction, the story of his role as a father is more distinctive. In a writer who himself had no children the sureness of touch in his portrayal of fathers and daughters is remarkable (although by the time he wrote *Lady Chatterley's Lover* he seems to have lost control of it); the trifling incidents as well as the major encounters of such relationships are presented with insight and tenderness. Will Brangwen, coming home from work, sees:

> a tiny, tottering, wind-blown little mite . . . running in tiny, wild, windmill fashion, lifting her arms up and down to him, down the steep hill. . . . Once she fell as she came flying to him. . . . and when he picked her up, her mouth was bleeding. He could never bear to think of it, he always wanted to cry, even when he was an old man and she had become a stranger to him.•

Even for a generation of readers almost obsessively ill-disposed towards accounts of little girls, a generation that is prepared to read about Lolitas but not about Little Nells, such passages may skirt the sea coasts of sentimentality but never quite land there.[7]

The relations between Tom Brangwen and his daughter similarly build up through a succession of trifling encounters, but they are most effectively memorialized in two full scale scenes. One takes place on the night when Lydia is giving birth to Tom's son, and her daughter Anna becomes hysterical with anxiety and terror. The other is Anna's wedding. In both our attention is focused on the feelings of the father. We see and hear Anna as the child or as the bride, but we see inside her father.

In the first scene the tensions are built up to the snapping point. After "I want my mother" is repeated nine times within two pages, the reader is as ready to scream with exasperation as is the father who has been listening helplessly to the moaning cry of the woman in labor, himself in terror at the prospect of reverting once more to isolation and loneliness. Characteristic techniques, such as these repetitions, which sometimes fail to function in Lawrence's fiction, are here triumphantly effective.

The violence of language functions likewise. As the father undresses the child in a rage, fumbling with the buttons, "she kept stiff, overpowered, violated." • The release from tensions, his own

• An interesting example of counterpointing occurs 51 pages later, after Ursula has grown up. Irritated by her not having taken care of his woodworking tools, Will flings a duster across his daughter's face, and Lawrence notes: "She did not forget, she never forgot."

• William Carlos Williams, an early admirer of Lawrence, centers his well-known story, *The Use of Force,* on a similar seemingly trifling incident. A doctor's action in forcing a sick child to open her mouth for medical examination is represented as a violation, almost a rape. See *Make Light of It* (New York, 1932), pp. 131-35.

as well as the child's, when he carries her out through the dark rainy night into the "softly illuminated stillness and calmness of the barn" is masterful. Whenever a reader has doubts of Lawrence's stature as a writer of fiction, as for example when confronted with the "Bits" chapter in *Kangaroo* or with a vulgar potboiler like *Mr. Noon,* he can readily dissolve his doubts and restore Lawrence to his proper stature by a rereading of such scenes as this.

Like many but not all of Lawrence's great scenes, as was suggested in discussing his short stories, this one seems ideally adapted to the medium of film. The cathedral scene, which is emphatically analytic, would tax the resources of a film producer, but this nativity sequence could be followed with the camera eye (and camera ear) almost exactly as Lawrence wrote it:

> There was the rhythmic sound of the shovel in the barn, then the man returned walking stiffly between the two weights, the face of the child peering out from the shawl. Then the next time, as he stooped, she freed her arm and put it round his neck, clinging soft and warm, making all easier.

The rhythmic movements here seem as if composed for camera treatment—and this at a time when novelists were not yet tempted by the lures of Hollywood to write fiction aimed eventually for the patrons of Houghton's Pleasure Palace, the moving picture theater amusingly described in *The Lost Girl.*

An even more striking example is the later courtship scene when Will and Anna gather sheaves of grain "coming and going, in a rhythm." Sergei Eisenstein showed that there are many scenes in Dickens which illustrate one of the principal techniques of montage in film, and the courtship scene of Will and Anna is similar. Varying tempo is established in the scene by extending or shortening the intervals between what are, in effect, shots. But although it might be interesting as well as topical to explore further the possible over-all affinities between Lawrence's fiction and what Alain Robbe-Grillet calls the *ciné-roman,* I must leave the subject as a promising sidetrack and return to *The Rainbow.*[8]

As for the wedding scene itself (of which Lawrence was justly proud), the harmony with which it concludes is arrived at characteristically out of a mounting succession of tensions which culminate in a happy climax. During the courtship, the household crackles with the tensions of desire and jealousy. When the grown girl, Anna, takes her lover out through the rainy night to the lantern-lit chicken loft, her father follows her and as he sees the pair standing in each other's arms "a black gloom of anger, and a tenderness of self-effacement, fought in his heart." "He thought again of the child he had carried out at night into the barn, whilst his wife was in labor. . . . Now she would say he was finished. . . . Almost he hated her. How dared she say he was old." After a struggle against this "clinging to the young," Tom, like the aging kings and chieftains in Frazer's *Golden Bough,* accepts his new role and gives up part of his domain to his younger rival.[9]

A more homely indication of the acuteness of Lawrence's insights than a comparison to *The Golden Bough* was provided for me by an acquaintance whose daughter was about to be married. Finding himself facing the prospect, without knowing why, as a fearsome ordeal, he asked whether some works of fiction portraying such a situation could be recommended to him. His request led to my discovery that at least within the range of my own reading, this universal situation has, surprisingly, been only rarely portrayed in fiction.[10] To recommend *The Rainbow* as a substitute for a Domestic Advice column in the newspapers seemed incongruous, but my paternal acquaintance was more than satisfied with it, even on these grounds. Its insights prepared him, he reported later, for his experiencing at the ceremony itself the same bewildered sense of time past blurring into time present that Tom Brangwen discovers. And in the finale at the honeymoon cottage, as one relationship ends and another begins, as the girl shifts from daughter to wife, this same reader found in the poignant ringing down of a curtain the resolution he had been seeking.

Lawrence's camera work in this final episode is once more extraordinarily skillful. We have been watching the whole scene through the eyes of the father, but on the last page our perspective shifts from the father and his group singing Christmas carols in the frosty air outside into the warm bedroom itself. The "burst of men's singing" frightens Anna momentarily. "It's Dad" she said in a low voice." . . .

> She sank down again into bed, into his arms. . . . The hymn rambled on outside, all the men singing their best. . . . The firelight glowed against the darkness in the room. Anna could hear her father singing with gusto. "Aren't they silly," she whispered. . . . And even as the hymn rolled on, they ceased to hear it.

In Keats' *Eve of St. Agnes* the warmth of the lovers in Madeline's bedroom is intensified by the contrast of the wintry cold, the family hatreds, and the figures of death and old age that surround them. Lawrence in this instance contrives instead to harmonize his opposing rhythms into a unity.

If *The Rainbow* were likened to a symphony in three movements, it is fitting that the first should have the most harmonious resolution of the three. Essentially it is a pastoral movement. Comparisons to Eden are, as we have seen, inescapable, but there is another association much less explicit throughout, but implicit in both of the scenes which have been here discussed: it is the promise of Christmas itself.

II

Ten or twelve years after the Christmas wedding scene, Lydia Brangwen, now a widow, seeks to find peace by avoiding being involved with the "dissatisfactions" of her sons. "She did not want her sons to force upon her any more *the old brutal story of desire and offerings and deep, deep-hidden rage of unsatisfied men against women.*" The bitter reflection on love and marriage which I have italicized suggests a further comparison with Austen's *Pride and Prejudice.* In the second chapter, after Mr. Bennet has played his witty game with his family about his visit to Netherfield Park, he leaves the room "fatigued with the raptures of his wife." In the light of this equally bitter (even though understated) phrase we can, if we are inclined, reconstruct what Mr.

Bennet's life as a husband must have been like, in particular the seething irritations of which it was probably made up. Of Anna's response to her husband, Lawrence tells us: "One day she thought she would go mad from his very presence, the sound of his drinking was detestable to her." Mr. Bennet must have suffered similarly, but Austen rarely represents these feelings. Just as we have to reconstruct Darcy's passionate response to Elizabeth—the very aspects of their relationship on which Lawrence would focus—so we should have to reconstruct the underlying tensions and discords which were the daily fare of the Bennet household.

In Part II of *The Rainbow* (chapters VI-IX), Lawrence presents vividly the feelings of a couple in such a situation. If Part I (constituting the first five chapters of the novel) is a moving tribute to the healing power of marriage and of family relationships, Part II is a revelation of the discords and irritations which may predominate in such relationships. This second generation of Brangwens have their briefly idyllic honeymoon, and, later, a renewed coming together after their struggle in the cathedral, and later still, when Will Brangwen is thirty years old, a further coming together after he makes some fresh discoveries of the sexual resources of his wife. Yet the principal impression left by these four chapters is that domestic discords have been sounded much more emphatically than domestic harmonies. Tensions dominate over the resolutions of tension.

Having referred earlier to an acquaintance who found consolation from the scene of Anna Brangwen's wedding, I should venture for Part II, another homely example, but in this instance a very different kind of response. A young man once solemnly reported in great distress that after reading about the marriage battles of Will and Anna, he had broken off his own engagement to be married.

Was this, we may ask, a response to these scenes that Lawrence would expect? Is this part of *The Rainbow* to be read as if it were an exposé of marriage like *Jude the Obscure*? Here is a representative episode:

> She turned to her sewing. Immediately the tea-things were cleared away, she fetched out the stuff and his soul rose in

rage. He hated beyond measure to hear the shriek of calico as she tore the web sharply, as if with pleasure. And the run of the sewing-machine gathered a frenzy in him at last.

"Aren't you going to stop that row?" he shouted. "Can't you do it in the daytime?"

She looked up sharply, hostile from her work.

"No, I can't do it in the daytime, I have other things to do. Besides, I like sewing, and you're not going to stop me doing it."

Whereupon she turned back to her arranging, fixing, stitching, his nerves jumped with anger as the sewing-machine started and stuttered and buzzed.

But she was enjoying herself, she was triumphant and happy as the darting needle danced ecstatically down a hem, drawing the stuff along under its vivid stabbing, irresistibly. She made the machine hum. She stopped it imperiously, her fingers were deft and swift and mistress.

If he sat behind her stiff with impotent rage it only made a trembling vividness come into her energy. On she worked. At last he went to bed in a rage, and lay stiff, away from her. And she turned her back on him. And in the morning they did not speak, except in mere cold civilities.

And when he came home at night, his heart relenting and growing hot for love of her, when he was just ready to feel he had been wrong, and when he was expecting her to feel the same, there she sat at the sewing-machine, the whole house was covered with clipped calico, the kettle was not even on the fire.

She started up, affecting concern.

"Is it so late?" she cried.

But his face had gone stiff with rage. He walked through to the parlour, then he walked back and out of the house again.

The intensity of feeling conveyed by this characteristic domestic exchange depends partly on the energetic verbs and partly on the choice of the mechanical object against which the irritation is expended, as in Yeats' famous comparison of G. B. Shaw to a smiling sewing machine. One suspects, too, that Lawrence was drawing on his own experience. At least we know that years after writing this scene he was, himself, to relive it. Mabel Dodge Luhan records that the first time she ever felt Lawrence's true power and was impressed to regard him as almost godlike was when he turned up at her house one morning "perfectly transfigured with rage." "'I can't stand it over there,'" he exploded. "'Frieda has got a woman there sewing! She has your sewing-machine going and there are yards and yards of stuff all over.' His irritation was discharging itself into power." [11]

Both in the scene from real life and in the scene from fiction there are the ingredients for traditional domestic comedy. The quarrels of marriage have been in all ages, from Aristophanes to the newspaper comic strips, a subject for laughter. One can readily picture how Ben Jonson or Dickens (with his gallery of shrewish wives) would have presented the same episode and have shown up the absurdity of such a violent response to trifles. Chaucer, too, exhibits the typical comic tone with which we expect to respond to such scenes. When his Wife of Bath reports with satisfaction of her finally successful efforts to subdue her young husband (her fifth) who used to infuriate her by reading stories aloud of the wickedness of women, one may be reminded of Anna Victrix. Will Brangwen is finally goaded into burning the wood panel on which he had been carving his picture of the creation of Eve (the much debated story of man's original supremacy over woman), and Alice of Bath's husband is likewise forced to burn his beloved book about the "wickednesse" of Eva and her successors. But how different is the tone:

> And made hym brenne his book anon right tho.
> And whan that I had getten unto me,
> By maistrie, al the soveraynetee,
> And that he seyde, 'Myn owene trewe wyf,
> Do as thee lust the terme of al thy lyf;
> Keep thyn honour, and keep eek myn estaat'—
> After that day we hadden never debaat.

The ingredients are, as I said, virtually identical, yet without raising the much disputed topic of Lawrence's own sense of humor I don't think anyone finds the quarreling between Will and Anna to be in the same comic vein of Chaucer or Jonson or Dickens. Anna's capacity for pricking balloons by mockery is, as previously suggested, an indication of her critical intelligence and her own comic sense. At times her sallies may prompt us to smile, yet for the most part a sense of comedy remains one of the weapons in *her* armory rather than a set of attitudes, shared by reader and writer, that would be the key to our enjoyment of the scenes if they were intended primarily to evoke laughter.

The revolutionary assumptions underlying *The Rainbow* are, according to Marvin Mudrick's excellent essay,

> that the relationship between husband and wife is the central fact of human existence, that the living nucleus of this relationship is the act of sexual union, that the act of sexual union is infinitely serious, complex, and difficult, and that an act of such radiant significance must be fairly treated by the honest novelist.[12]

One may be bothered by some of the adjectives in this passage, as though sexual relations were being compared to intricate ballroom-dancing techniques—for which we are recommended to take lessons at some School of the Dance—a possibility altogether abhorrent to Lawrence. Nevertheless, what Mr. Mudrick says in his solemn fashion here is well said and needs saying. The seriousness of the quarreling between Will and Anna derives from the seriousness of their search for an ideal sexual relationship, of which the daily frictions are a symptom.

We may ask, finally, do they find such a relationship? "She had thought him just the bright reflex of herself. As the weeks and months went by she realised that he was a dark opposite to her, that they were opposites, not complements." In novels by other writers, this dichotomy might be an insurmountable obstacle, but in novels by Lawrence it does not have to be. It leads to battles, which are represented simply as a part of human relationships, each person being on a different wave-length, in effect, which may coincide only rarely. But it need not lead to the divorce court; in fact, it can be a facet of an ideal marriage.

Although Will and Anna seem at times to approximate such an ideal union of light and darkness, their marriage really falls short of it. They successfully surmount one obstacle to such a relationship by rooting out whatever sense of shame might inhibit the varieties of sexual gratification open to them—a subject which may be more appropriately discussed in connection with Birkin and Ursula in *Women in Love.* Afterwards, Lawrence assures us hurriedly, the husband developed a "real purposive self," and here we encounter the first false note in *The Rainbow.* The novelist *tells* us; he does not show us.

Neither in the rest of *The Rainbow* nor in the Will and Anna scenes in *Women in Love* do we get any convincing demonstration of the husband's transformation.[13] For throughout the frenzied performance of their later sexual relations one continues to hear the ominous Wagnerian horn-call that sounded throughout *The Trespasser.* "It was all lust . . . a passion of death." Or again, "it was a duel; no love, no words, no kisses even."

That marriage may be a constant duel is not represented in *The Rainbow* as a matter for comedy or for tragedy. The dueling of the second generation of Brangwens is not the flaw in their relationship, despite the reactions of squeamish readers who are appalled by the scenes of friction. The flaw is nowhere precisely defined; instead it is sensed as a whiff of death that blights the full growth of their love. Yet once again, the great quality of this section is not evaluative but representational.

In addition to Lawrence's discovery, of which Mr. Mudrick has told us, that sexual relations (especially in England) should be important in marriage, this section of *The Rainbow* demonstrates his more unusual discovery that our daily lives consist largely of experiencing successive waves of attraction towards others and repudiations of others. In marriage, each partner's hypersensitive awareness of the other, hostile or affectionate, in the bedroom as well as out of the bedroom, and of the surrounding family is, in this part of *The Rainbow* family chronicle, memorably conveyed. To exploit such a discovery in fiction, tensions, conflicts, discords were as important as harmonious relationships.

The story of Will and Anna Brangwen is a study of imperfect sympathies, or, as Anna's mother more emphatically expressed it, the "story of desire . . . and deep, deep-hidden rage of unsatisfied men against women."

III

The story of Ursula, the representative of the third generation of Brangwens, is presented at much greater length than the two earlier stories. Even well-disposed critics have detected in these seven final chapters some falling away from the high level of the earlier sections of *The Rainbow*. Repetitive scenes, which function well elsewhere, remain here, sometimes, merely repetitive. And the ordinary brown paper language in which a writer wraps his packages in uninspired moments[14] is disappointingly in evidence in the flaccid style of such incidents as Ursula's entering the university (chapter XV).

When Lawrence's writing is below his best it usually irritates or exasperates; only rarely is it dull. The flatter parts of these later chapters of *The Rainbow* suffer, it must be admitted, from this unusual failing. Yet after we have granted the comparative inadequacy of such parts, it does not follow, as some critics contend, that the over-all conception of theme and character is lost to sight in this section.

As the previous chapter was concerned with showing, Ursula's search for adventure in "unknown realities" is a gathering together of all the strands of this big chronicle. One aspect of her search remains to be considered, her relations to her lover, and also one scene in some detail in which these relations culminate.

In this short scene, appearing a few pages before the end of the novel, Ursula crosses an open field in the rain where she is frightened by encountering a herd of horses. After finally evading them, she toils homewards uphill and resolves to abandon her plan to marry her lover, Anton Skrebensky.

As the scene is often read, the virile male horses are supposed to remind us of her virile male lover. Her act of successfully evading the horses is thus assumed to be emblematic of her successful evasion of the forces of darkness and her resumption of her true mission in life as a woman.

What this interpretation misses, in brief, is that the horses are to remind her and us, not of what Skrebensky is, but of what he is not. Yet if this remarkable scene is often misunderstood, one is hardly entitled to critical indignation. It is one of the most impressive scenes in Lawrence's fiction, exhibiting distinctive fictional trade-marks that are altogether his own, but it is also one of the most complex and difficult passages he ever composed. The complexity derives in part from the narrative method, to which we can return, and in part from the complexity of the antecedent relationship itself.

What were Skrebensky's inadequacies? What were Ursula's demands from life and from love? No relationship in Lawrence's fiction is more baffling than this one, not even that between Gerald and Gudrun in *Women in Love*. Yet I think that although the relationship may remain, ultimately, a mystery, it is not a mere muddle.[15]

Ursula's yearning for hilltops crowded with culture, as Browning calls them, a yearning inherited from generations of Brangwen women, is conjoined with her search for a partner worthy of her. From childhood her standards are almost fantastically high. Emma Bovary, with an imagination fed on the fare of the romances she had read, expected her lovers to conform to her storybook code. "Have you your pistols?" she asks her lover, Rodolphe, who is understandably startled by her question. Ursula's imagination has been fed, instead, on the Bible. Her favorite passage, and one for which she never loses appreciation, is the story of the Sons of God who chose wives among the "daughters of men."

> There were giants in the earth in those days; and also after that, when the Sons of God came in unto the daughters of men, and they bore children unto them, the same became mighty men which were of old, men of renown.

Throughout *The Rainbow* and also *Women in Love* this passage is recurrently invoked, not as when Flaubert exposes with comic irony the absurdity of romantic expectations, but as a seemingly legitimate measure of the adequacy of the mortal men with whom Ursula has relations. Although she is also aware of comparable Greek "myths" (as she calls them), such as the story of Jove and Europa, she prefers the Old Testament account of these Sons of God or angels* as her reference point.

At 16 she meets Skrebensky and assumes that her ideal has been realized. "She laid hold of him at once for her dreams. Here was one such as those Sons of God who saw the daughters of men . . . He was no son of Adam."

Six years later, when she is at the university, she clings to these high expectations of him even though she has had several occasions to find him a mere mortal, not a god. "He would have been her angel. He held the keys of the sunshine." And again, he would be the "doorway to her, into the . . . inexhaustible freedom which was the paradise of her soul."

Like Dorothea Brooke, in George Eliot's *Middlemarch*, who fondly believed before she married him that Mr. Casaubon was a second Milton or Hooker, Ursula convinces herself that this attractive young officer is the man who had come out of the Eternity "to which she herself belonged." Thus her two goals, the thrust towards an intelligent understanding of life, and her need for a superman worthy of her expectations, are combined. The success of their relationship is staked on these high expectations.

Her gamble seems, at first, much more reasonable than Dorothea Brooke's gamble on Casaubon where the reader can foresee, far in advance of the heroine, that the odds are hopeless. At the outset Lawrence presents Skrebensky through Ursula's eyes as a free spirit, full of vitality. The fact that his chosen branch of the Army service is the Engineers should be a preliminary hint to anyone aware of Lawrence's scale of values, but even as we see him later he is never presented as a mere villain. So attractive is he, in fact, that Hugh Kingsmill was foolishly lured into finding him identical with Tom Brangwen and with Lawrence himself.[16]

If we compare the subtlety of the way in which Skrebensky is presented with the comparative crudity and simplification of the portrait of Sir Clifford Chatterley, we recognize one of the reasons why *The Rainbow* is a better novel than the later one. Clifford,

* An example of recurring themes in *The Rainbow* is the speech of Ursula's grandfather at her mother's wedding, in which he gropingly tries to explain what angels are (chapter V).

paralyzed from the waist down, is an easy pawn readily relegated to his wheelchair. Skrebensky is distinctly not paralyzed, and potency as such is not the issue.

In the first period of their love affair, Ursula blissfully enters into "the pristine darkness of paradise," and the long passages devoted to their exultant love-making indicate that whatever is wrong with Skrebensky it is not his inadequacy as a bedroom companion. Instead of a cripple, this man, like Gerald in *Women in Love*, is apparently a sexual athlete. What then is the flaw? Why is it that during their excursion to the continent "the first sense of the death towards which they were wandering" soon becomes the dominant motif in their affair?

The easy way out is to conclude that the novelist changed his mind about his character and simply botched his story. Also suggestive of botching is that by the end of this affair it is the woman, more than the man, who is associated with darkness. Skrebensky resolves never to think of Ursula after she has annihilated him. "She was the darkness, the challenge, the horror." If the woman is here the darkness (and the Conradian phrasing of Lawrence's passage is impressive) it would seem that the basic dichotomy which was established on the opening page of *The Rainbow* has been abandoned by a clumsy artist. Yet a careful reading suggests that the latter change-over was, in fact, prepared for and that it is the basis on which this affair disintegrates.

The word *change-over* is not quite accurate. Maturity for Ursula consists in her discovery that her preoccupation with critical intelligence and the values of civilization had excluded half of life, and that any view of the world which fails to reckon with the dark jungle is false and inadequate. It is while she is at university that Lawrence tries to express this discovery explicitly.

> This world in which she lived was like a circle lighted by a lamp. This lighted area, lit up by man's completest consciousness, she thought was all the world: . . . Yet . . . this inner circle of light in which she lived and moved, wherein the trains rushed and the factories ground out their machine-produce and the plants and the animals worked by the light of science and knowledge, suddenly it seemed like the area under an arc-lamp, wherein the moths and children played in the security of blind-

> ing light, not even knowing there was any darkness, because they stayed in the light.
>
> But she could see the glimmer of dark movement just out of range, she saw the eyes of the wild beast gleaming from the darkness, . . .
>
> The darkness wheeled round about, with grey shadow-shapes of wild beasts, and also with dark shadow-shapes of the angels, whom the light fenced out, as it fenced out the more familiar beasts of darkness.[17]

Although this discovery, as the final paragraph of the whole novel tries to suggest, does not involve her abandoning her original search for light, it leads to her attempting to combine her previous set of values with an awareness of an opposite set. Two rhythms rather than one will be associated with her. The new awareness profoundly affects her demands from men. The Sons of God will come out of the darkness rather than out of the Corps of Engineers. Significantly, after the resounding trumpet call has been sounded in the paragraph quoted, Skrebensky reappears on stage as if in response to Ursula's challenging demands. Momentarily resplendent in her eyes, he later is exposed to this Brunhild as a Gunther not a Siegfried.

The paragraph quoted is one of the most explicit statements of Ursula's discovery of darkness, but there are many earlier incidents which anticipate it. In the early stage of the courtship, when she is seventeen, she was appalled to experience "a sudden lust. . . . to lay hold of him and tear him and make him into nothing." At this stage she tries to deny to herself that she has any affinities with the jungle. When her "daytime consciousness" reasserts itself, she dismisses her acts of destructive cruelty as a fit of momentary madness and insists that she is tender and loving.

We may be reminded here of comparable transitions in Dostoevsky's characters, memorably described by Erich Auerbach as sudden "monstrous" changes "from love to hatred," from "devotion" to "animal brutality," these changes occurring "in tremendous and unpredictable oscillations." [18]

With the girl, Ursula, the fits of madness keep returning. In scene after frantic scene, she is impelled to attack her lover at every point until she has destroyed him as a man. Not to copulate like an animal in the jungle, but to destroy like an animal in the jungle, is her driving urge. The traditional role of woman as a passive "beloved" she repudiates. Lambs, she reflects, cannot love; they can only be loved.

> Raging, destructive lovers, seeking the moment when fear is greatest, and triumph is greatest, the fear not greater than the triumph, the triumph not greater than the fear, these were no lambs nor doves. She stretched her own limbs like a lion or a *wild horse,* her heart was relentless in its desires. [Italics mine.]

This early passage offers a helpful lead into the later scene of the horses, but it also helps to clarify the real nature of the possible cruelty in love relations, as Lawrence presents them, which many readers find oppressive. Once again, as in the Will and Anna section, the struggle for supremacy is not represented as deplorable or necessarily conducive to suffering. It is when the struggle is between unequal contestants, when the lion is a cowardly lion or the unicorn has a broken horn, that real suffering is inflicted. If either partner is vulnerable, the other will freely attack there with beak and claw. The many references to the destructive beak of the woman effectively suggests her capacity, if the man is vulnerable, to castrate him. In *The Rainbow* this repeated allusion seems to be figurative, although elsewhere in Lawrence's writings it is more literal. Mellors in *Lady Chatterley's Lover* complains bitterly of "a woman's blind beakishness." Such women as his first wife "have beaks between their legs . . . all self! tearing and shouting!" In a less violent vein, there is a passage in the essay, *Pan in America,* in which the deer hunter asks his wife not to "turn the horns of the moon against me."

After Skrebensky's final encounter with the "fierce, beaked, harpy's kiss," he is destroyed as a man. The conventionality of his opinions and values had left him vulnerable to this woman's critical intelligence, and she had cut him down mercilessly in their conversations together. "Not on any side did he lead into the unknown," Ursula reflects. He may go to Africa or India, yet he is no "traveller" in her sense of the word. But his real vulnerability, despite his seemingly adequate sexual prowess, is that he is incapable of arousing in Ursula "the rich fear" that she demands a man to inspire.

Skrebensky is revealed as an attractive male lamb, a representative of a later generation of men whose contacts with darkness have been broken. As such he is doomed to be sacrificed at the altar of the white goddess, that "horrible figure that lay stretched in the moonlight on the sands with the tears gathering and travelling on the motionless, eternal face."

The brutality of Skrebensky's destruction may lead to our asking what has happened to the tenderness of the love relationship as pictured in such stories as "Love Among the Haystacks"? In *The Rainbow* and in *Women in Love*, real tenderness is possible only among equals. The destruction of the inadequate male may be distasteful or horrifying, but it is not unprepared for, nor is it a clumsy change of attitude on the part of the novelist. Nor is it merely operatic.

Visitors to English-speaking countries in the second half of the twentieth century have remarked often upon the matriarchal system in which the typical male is characterized like Skrebensky by what Lawrence calls a "self-effacing diffidence," a system in which a lion, whose mane is clipped, is unable to sustain the crown in equal combat with an overpowering partner. Prescience in forecasting future social relations is not the principal quality one seeks from a novelist, but the acuteness of Lawrence's diagnosis remains a noteworthy asset.

IV

If this version of the love affair with Skrebensky is accurate, the scene of Ursula's encounter with the horses will make sense. Before the encounter, having discovered that she is pregnant, Ursula comes to a crucial, if temporary, decision. She decides that her whole search for some indefinable goal and her fantastically high demands for a superman have been a mistake. "For what had a woman but to submit?" This kind of reflection of hers exemplifies a common problem in reading Lawrence's novels.

Readers who have decided that Lawrence is simply a proponent of the triumphant male will copy out Ursula's reflection as if it were an aphorism. Yet her decision to marry Skrebensky and to settle down humbly into the conventional world he represents, a decision formulated immediately after the scene in which he had been reduced by her to nothingness, is a betrayal of all her previous efforts. What is evident to the reader is not, of course, evident to her. She discovers it only after some "seething . . . madness" sends her out walking in the rain where she instinctively leaves the tempting protection of the forest trees with their "*martialled* silence" and plods defenselessly across the open fields heading once more "back to stability and security." "The ordered world of man," which married life with this officer in the Engineers would involve for her, is dramatically contrasted, throughout the scene, with a world of a different sort. The ordered world of man is not a bad place; she is fervently relieved when she regains it after her terrifying encounter, but it is, at best, half of life, and her rediscovery of its inadequacy leads her to abandon her resolution to marry Skrebensky, and leads also, shortly afterwards, to her losing, by miscarriage, Skrebensky's child.

The only excuse for formulating so prosaically what Lawrence has presented so vividly is that despite the vividness of the scene, the real nature of Ursula's experience is often unrecognized. Just as critics of Hopkins' *The Windhover* seem, at times, to have done everything possible to prepare themselves for understanding that difficult poem except to watch a bird in flight, so some critics of Lawrence's scene seem never to have had the fearsome experience of crossing an open field and encountering a herd of animals. What are Ursula's responses? She experiences, as we might expect, fear, but also admiration, and after she has escaped, a sense of pity for these powerful creatures. Each of these responses is worth pausing over.

In explaining the aims of Symbolist writing, Mallarmé formulated the following principle: "Describe not the object itself, but the effect it produces." [19] Lawrence contrives to do both. The horses in the scene are clearly before us; we see them and hear their thudding hoofs as if we were crossing the open field ourselves. As Harry T. Moore notes in his excellent brief discussion of the scene, the horses are presented with "shocking effectiveness."

At the same time we recognize the feelings they arouse in the heroine. Ursula's terror, intensified by the typical Laurentian touch of her sensing that "something" is there before she sees anything, is a "living seed of fear." Similarly on the first occasion on which Mellors is seen by Lady Chatterley he emerges from the woods "with such a swift menace" that she is frightened by him. If the effect is fear, and if Ursula has explicitly indicated earlier that one response Skrebensky never evoked in her was the "rich fear" she wanted, it is obviously an error to associate her lover with these animals merely because he is a male. The fear they arouse must be as old as man, that of the traveler who doth walk in fear and dread in lonely places where the god Pan manifests himself. And the panic fear Ursula experiences in this epiphany scene is "living" because, leading as it ultimately does to the loss of the child, it breaks the final link of a false connection. Her panic experience, painful as it may be, saves her.

Freud says that the dream of being pursued by horses is extremely common and is indicative of sexual anxiety.[20] Lawrence in his essays is more explicit. In *Apocalypse* he notes:

> Far back in our dark soul the horse prances. . . . And as a symbol he roams the dark underworld meadows of the soul. He stamps and threshes in the dark fields of your soul and of mine. The sons of God who came down and knew the daughters of men and begot the great Titans, they had 'the members of horses,' says Enoch. Within the last fifty years man has lost the horse. Now man is lost.[21]

In *Fantasia of the Unconscious* he analyzes at length what is meant by "a persistent passionate fear-dream about horses," although in this instance as a dream experienced by a man rather than a woman. Our response, he argues, is not only fear but admiration. The "emotional reference" is, he notes, "sensual" and not exclusively menacing.[22] In *The Rainbow* these pollyanalytics are once again concretely embodied into a fictional scene. Ursula's sensual response is conveyed not by analytic statement such as I am trying to formulate, but by the lush description itself of the animals and their movements.

It should be added that this is a scene from D. H. Lawrence not from Robinson Jeffers' *Roan Stallion* and that actual physical union with the animal, as contemplated by Jeffers' heroine, is not Lawrence's topic. The horse here remains a symbol of powerful masculinity not an object of desire in itself.

The final aspect of Ursula's response to her encounter is that, as she escapes from the open field back to the ordered world, she feels almost a sense of pity for having frustrated the horses. "They were almost pathetic, now."

If we reflect back over Ursula's previous development and inquire when it was that she had earlier experienced a combined sense of fear, admiration, and pity, we can appreciate how impressively Lawrence has prepared the ground for his final scene. This combination was exactly her response to Schofield, the farmer, and his Garden of Eden. More significantly, it is exactly the way she felt when she encountered the barge-keeper, early in the courtship with Skrebensky. In this scene, with Skrebensky diffidently present in person, we are led to make a contrast, as Ursula does, between one type of male and another, the one a force even though a "captive soul," the other a "nothing." More briefly, the same contrast is developed when Skrebensky suffers an outburst of tears and the young couple take a taxi to a London hotel.

> The driver saluted and drew up . . . She winced as the driver's dark, red face was thrust round upon her, a full-blooded, animal face with black eyebrows and a thick short-cut moustache.
> 'Where to, lady?' he said, his white teeth showing.

And again, when the driver lights his lamps, Ursula shudders as she watches his dark face. "It was the face almost of an animal, yet of a quick, strong, wary animal that had them within its knowledge, almost within its power. She clung closer to Skrebensky." At the hotel she gets another moment of panic when an Italian waiter comes to their room, and she senses his limited understanding, his mere animality.

Like the figure of the man run over in the railway station that haunted the memory of Tolstoy's Anna Karenina, the figure of the animal-like male keeps reappearing in Ursula's life and profoundly affects her development, just as the lobster-like moustached face and figure of his unrefined father kept reappearing in Lawrence's imagination and profoundly affected his own development. The inadequacies of the mere animal she knows, and she can escape him as she escaped the horses, but something of what he represents she must also find.

In *Women in Love,* when Ursula at last does find in a man who is worthy of her what she did not find in Skrebensky, there is a highly interesting flashback to the horses scene in *The Rainbow.* When Birkin calls at her house to propose marriage (which she refuses) she watches him afterwards with mixed feelings of superiority and fear. "He was ridiculous, but she was afraid of him. She was as if escaped from some danger."

To mention Birkin is a reminder that Lawrence had originally conceived Ursula's whole development as a story to be covered in one novel rather than split into two. In *The Sisters,* her unsatisfactory affair with Skrebensky (who was called, at that time, Templeman)• was to culminate happily in her discovery of Birkin, a man powerful enough to arouse fear, enlightened enough to meet her intellectual needs, even at times foolish enough to provide occasion for her triumphant laughter, yet the hero for whom she had long searched.

To end her quest in such a way would have been much easier for Lawrence to contrive than what confronted him when he decided to break her story into two parts. To make the break, he did choose a good place; Ursula's repudiation of the deathly conventional role, which marriage to Skrebensky would have involved, had led her out of the depths to a rebirth. Yet one detects in the last paragraphs a sense of strain because the account of the final

• On January 29, 1914, to justify "the Templeman episode" Lawrence wrote to Garnett: "In the scheme of the novel, however, I *must* have Ella [Ursula] get some experience before she meets her Mr. Birkin." He agreed to modify the Templeman episode, but insisted that some "significant" love episode was essential to an understanding of her later character. A fragment of the manuscript version of *The Sisters* which has survived provides some tantalizing glimpses of the original sequence. After Birkin proposes to her, and she has accepted him, Ursula reencounters Ben Templeman, as her previous lover is called, and her former feelings of love are momentarily revived. In the final versions of *Women in Love* or *The Rainbow,* after the horses scene, this episode would have been impossible.

stages of her development has to be postponed and, as a substitute, we have to be content with a kind of prophecy of the future union of darkness and light when the heroine will encounter one of the sons of God, and society itself will be regenerated. That a great poetic novel in which seemingly ordinary characters have been enlarged to Biblical dimensions should end on such a note is ultimately appropriate even though the straining crescendo is at times deafening.[23] One traveler has crossed the plains which her ancestors had struggled over, and after a near death has caught a glimpse of a promised land. The vision she catches of a future regeneration of man is not blueprinted from the workshops of the social planners. It is closer in spirit to the resolving affirmations with which Shelley characteristically ends his poems.[24] In the incantatory evocation of a new society "rising to the light" from the dead husks of the old, there recurs Shelley's favorite image and something too of Shelley's stridency:

> To defy Power, which seems omnipotent;
> To love, and bear; to hope till Hope creates
> From its own wreck the thing it contemplates; . . .
> This is alone Life, Joy, Empire and Victory.

If this stage of the heroine's progress is celebrated too stridently, it is some compensation to recall the painful discords of scenes that preceded her rebirth. And in *Women in Love,* the novel that followed *The Rainbow,* despite Ursula's final resolution of her own individual difficulties, the somber notes are much more persistently in evidence.

8 Dies Irae: *Women in Love*

"But the men of Sodom were wicked and sinners before the Lord exceedingly."
—*Genesis*, xiii, 13

Of the many good twentieth-century novels written in English about war, *Women in Love* seems outstanding. To propose such high ranking for a novel by a civilian and one in which the 1914-18 war is never so much as mentioned might be written off as mere whimsy, but I think it can be substantiated. Moreover, it may serve as one way of dramatizing, at the outset, a difference between this novel and its predecessor, *The Rainbow*, a difference we sense without always being able to identify precisely. Lawrence himself reminded one of his correspondents that the key to understanding his earlier novel was its title. *The Rainbow* evokes both destruction through flood but also salvation and restoration through God's covenent, the rainbow being the "sign that life will never be destroyed, or turn bad altogether." [1]

In 1917, however, after completing *Women in Love*, Lawrence could see, he said, "no Rainbow" in Europe. "I believe the deluge of iron rain will destroy the world here, utterly: no Ararat will rise above the subsiding iron waters." [2] The dominant tone of *Women in Love* is impressively conveyed by the song from which James Baldwin took the title for his book on the American Negro, *The Fire Next Time:*

God gave Noah the rainbow sign,
No more water, the fire next time.

Women in Love, because it contained "the results in one's soul of the war" was described by its author as "purely destructive, not like *The Rainbow*, destructive-consummating." [3] I shall dispute this reading. The double rhythms of destruction and creation are still present in *Women in Love* as they are present in *The Rainbow.* That the rhythm of destruction is here more insistent and compelling than the creative is, however, beyond dispute, and its prominence justifies Lawrence's own description of his book as "wonderful and terrifying," which it is. And again, when he had virtually finished writing it (November 7, 1916) he commented: "The book frightens me: it's so end-of-the-world."

II

As late as January, 1920, Lawrence was enthusiastically making plans to publish a huge two-decker novel in which *The Rainbow* (published but suppressed) would be combined with *Women in Love* (completed but unpublished). The two novels, he contended, do represent "an organic artistic whole." Although this ambitious scheme was abandoned, he liked to refer to *Women in Love* as a "sequel" to *The Rainbow,* sometimes admitting, however, that it was "very different." [4]

Those who attempt to read *Women in Love* without having read its predecessor will discover that Lawrence was right on the first count. They will be puzzled by occasional flashbacks as when Ursula recalls a character of whom they have never heard such as her grandmother, Lydia Lensky, or her lover, Skrebensky, or when they learn that her father, about whose past they are ignorant, is the same now at fifty as he was at twenty. What is more important, they are unprepared for the exultant note of some of the love scenes in which Ursula's long and arduous search is at last triumphantly resolved in her discovery of one of the "sons of God," the figure itself being one of several that continue to link the two novels. Yet those other readers who begin instead with *The Rainbow* will find that Lawrence was also right on the second count; *Women in Love* is "very different."

To reconstruct the circumstances under which the "second half of *The Rainbow*" became what it is will reinforce our impression of differences and continuity. Unlike many dusty textual reconstructions, this one could be a fascinating story in its own right and of a complexity so extraordinary that a book-length study would be required to cover it. What follows will be only an exploratory or capsuled account.

From March, 1913, when he began writing the first of several versions of the narrative of Ursula Brangwen and her sister, Lawrence kept assuring his correspondents that the novel he was about to write would be so impeccable that modest maidens could read it without a blush and also that it would be a short novel. Both resolutions kept breaking down. By January, 1915, a version which he had been calling *The Wedding Ring* had become so vast that he decided to split it into two novels. Two months later, when the surgical operation had been completed, he sent the first half of his narrative to the publishers with *The Rainbow* as its title.[5]

Remaining in his hands was a considerable heap of manuscripts and typescripts which he put aside for more than a year. It was not until late April in 1916 that he picked them up again and began to recompose them, as he said, into what we now know as *Women in Love*.[6] Working at a furious pace, he had completed a revision of 27 out of the 31 chapters by May 30th, a feat that dazzled Richard Aldington, who calculated that the rate of fresh composition was 3000 words a day for ten weeks. Lawrence's methods of rewriting and revision have been glamorously misrepresented, and the extent to which he virtually recopied parts of his earlier versions, instead of attempting to compose an altogether new version, needs to be recognized.[7] In the present instance we have the best of evidence for this. Lawrence himself reported as he was finishing *Women in Love* on November 7, 1916, "There was a lot of the original draft that I *couldn't* have bettered."[8]

What this review points up is that parts of *Women in Love* were written without being affected by the impact of war. They belong with *The Rainbow* of which Lawrence said (although he had "revised" it after the outbreak of 1914): "I don't think the war altered it, from its pre-war statement."[9]

It is a tribute to the artist's skill in his over-all revision that we do not *know* which parts of the original drafts of *Women in Love* were not revised, and his manuscripts do not enable such identifications to be made with certainty. One can simply venture guesses, as for example that the scene of Birkin's offering the rings to Ursula was one of the unrevised parts. I should also nominate the flight to the continent (chapter XXIX), some of the early school and courtship scenes, and perhaps the somewhat labored chapter on "The Industrial Magnate" (XVII).

On the other hand, when we come to consider which parts were written later than *The Rainbow,* we can occasionally venture something better than a guess when we know that a scene in the novel was affected by some event of 1916 to which a date may be assigned, as for example, that in the summer of 1916 Katherine Mansfield retrieved a volume of Lawrence's poems from a group of mockers at the Café Royal, an incident which clearly served to inspire chapter XXVIII, "Gudrun in the Pompadour." It also seems likely that the Halliday-Pussum scenes (chapters VI and VII) were freshly conceived in 1916 being modelled on Lawrence's impressions of the composer Philip Heseltine who had moved (on April 22, 1916) into a London flat in which an African statue was a prominent feature of the decor.[10]

In general all of the London scenes reflect the mood of 1916-17 whereas those located at Beldover are less insistently bitter. The Breadalby scenes seem to be a mixture and illustrate Lawrence's lifelong practice of incorporating recent personal experiences into novels as he rewrote them. An interesting example is provided by the vivid account of Hermione Roddice's murderous attack on Birkin when she tries to smash his skull with a piece of lapis held in her left hand. It is just possible that the second volume of the memoirs of Lady Ottoline Morrell (supposedly the model for Hermione) will disclose that in one of her quarrels with Lawrence she attacked him in some such manner, but the possibility seems remote. Instead, as Harry T. Moore has shown, the incident seems to have been derived from an experience in Cornwall when the left-handed Frieda Lawrence came close to cracking her husband's skull by smashing a stone dish over the back of his head. This incident occurred in the late summer of 1916.[11]

The mixture of early and late incidents and impressions is also evident in the characters. *Women in Love* is too often read as an uncomplicated *roman à clef.* Instead, as was demonstrated concerning "The Man Who Loved Islands," the technique of creating ectoplasms is very much in evidence in this novel.

That the creation of Gerald Crich owes something to Lawrence's deeply-felt friendship for John Middleton Murry is obvious, but we do less than justice to the subtlety of one of his most memorably created characters if we simply equate Gerald with this single model. When Murry failed to recognize himself in Gerald, he was not being more than ordinarily obtuse, for several living men seem to have influenced Lawrence's conception of Gerald, not merely one. Frieda reports somewhat mysteriously that he was modelled on a friend of Lawrence's youth whom she does not name. Harry T. Moore demonstrates that the experiences of an Eastwood mine owner, Major Thomas Philip Barber, contributed significantly to the story of Gerald.[12] I suspect, myself, that some elements might also have been inspired by Lawrence's friendship with the blond soldier, Richard Aldington, and more importantly with the handsome young David Garnett. Like Gerald Crich, an enthusiastic swimmer whose prowess in the water had impressed Lawrence, David Garnett had been his companion on an alpine walking-tour in 1912. An opening chapter for *Women in Love* entitled "Prologue" (which Lawrence decided not to publish) begins with an account of Gerald's friendship with Birkin as it developed on a similar alpine expedition. To thicken the mixture even further, we have W. W. Robson's suggestion that Gerald was done "from within," that he is Lawrence himself "in important ways."[13]

Gudrun Brangwen seems to have had a similarly complex ancestry. Before Katherine Mansfield sat for her portrait (Lawrence first met her in June, 1914) there were earlier models, perhaps one of the five sisters of Louise Burrows, and also Frieda's younger sister, Johanna von Richthofen, whom Lawrence described as "very beautiful, rather splendid in her deliberate worldliness."[14]

Just as early and late encounters contributed to the created ectoplasms of these complex characters so does the whole novel take its tone from a blending of pre-war and mid-war experiences and attitudes. That there remain elements of continuity linking *The Rainbow* and *Women in Love* is explicable in the light of the unusually prolonged stretch of time devoted to the composition of the later novel, and also of its having incorporated scenes once part of the whole *Wedding Ring* sequence. Yet it is obvious that Lawrence was deluding himself when he contended that the two novels make up an organic, artistic whole. They could not, and need not. Between the winter of 1914 and the summer of 1916, his war-time experiences and, to a lesser extent, his intensive study of books about the rise and fall of civilizations were so to color his view of life and love that a firm welding of the two novels into a unity had become an impossibility. The verb *color* requires stressing, for what differences there are between *The Rainbow* and *Women in Love* do not depend on a shift of values or even on modifications of technique, but simply on a change of palette from bright to somber.

III

In *Sodome et Gomorrhe* (1943), Jean Giraudoux's last play, the Archangel announces that the doomed city may be spared not by the discovery of ten just men within its walls but of one pair of truly loving men and women, "un couple parfait," two equal and complementary beings whose union represents God's ideal: "cette nature indivise, ces admirations et ces dégoûts indivis." [15] Because the Biblical story of Sodom also provided Lawrence with his principal analogue for *Women in Love,* the resemblances between his novel and Giraudoux's bitter drama, with its quartet of lovers and its indirect reflection of a war, are often striking. The differences, however, are even more striking, for in the play no such loving couple is ever found, and without redeemers, the city is doomed.

In Lawrence's novel, against a background of fetid corruption, a man and woman do discover each other, and their union establishes the possibility of hope and salvation. I deliberately introduce this point here even though it is out of place for the discussion that follows, because before we become totally immersed in this horror story, and it is a horror story, we must give due weight to what the whole novel takes in. Between 1916 and 1920, Lawrence was groping to find a suitable title for his novel. He sometimes called it *Noah's Ark.* On another occasion it became *The*

Latter Days. Most appropriately he struck upon *Dies Irae* or *Day of Wrath,* and he proposed that the lines from the mediaeval chorus should serve as his novel's epigraph:

> Dies irae, dies illa
> Solvet saeclum in favilla.

Dies Irae would certainly have been an excellent choice; it makes the title function by condensing into a phrase the dominant impression the whole novel imposes on us. Yet almost as if to counteract this dominant impression and to remind us of his novel's second rhythm, he chose a title without the apocalyptic connotations of his alternative choices, and one that is evocative, instead, of the possible escape from Sodom: *Women in Love.*

The subject indicated by the chosen title is picked up effectively in the opening scene of the two sisters discussing their prospects of love and marriage, a relatively quiet scene almost in the vein of opening chapters in novels by George Eliot or Jane Austen. Some bitterness is evident in the dialogue, but it is subdued, and only gradually does the somber quality of the novel make itself felt as we come to realize that Beldover is in the land of Sodom. The specific analogy is withheld until chapter V when Birkin is reflecting on what the world would be like "if mankind is destroyed, if our race is destroyed like Sodom." In the opening chapter itself the somber note is first struck in the encounter between Gudrun and the coal miner's wives who stare at her "with that long, unwearying stare of aborigines." When they jeer at her, she is overcome with a fit of anger "violent, and murderous. She would have liked them all annihilated." This misanthropy is picked up again in the second chapter when Birkin comments to Mrs. Crich on the colorless wedding-guests: "It would be much better if they were just wiped out. Essentially, they don't exist." As toasts are being proposed, Birkin, who has been "thinking about race or national death," beckons the footman to refill his champagne glass:

> And the hired footman came, with a silent step of cold servant-like disapprobation. Birkin decided that he detested . . . mankind altogether, in most of its aspects.

The servant here is not Mr. J. Alfred Prufrock's symbolical snickering Eternal Footman but a representative specimen of mankind, and merely as such is to be hated. "Social hatred" as Birkin later calls it when speaking of its embodiment in the decadent artist, Loerke, is one of the states of mind most repeatedly represented in *Women in Love*, and one of the principal components of its destructive rhythm. As such it needs, later, to be more closely examined. If we inquire first into the sources of this social hatred we are led on to Lawrence's view of the 1914-18 war.

IV

It would be fascinating to speculate on what sort of novels Lawrence might have written if his health had allowed him to be enlisted into the army and if he had survived the experience of four years of trench-warfare. Unlike almost all of those since 1914 who have written novels of war—Hemingway, Aldington, Graves, Dos Passos, Mailer, Waugh, to name a few among those writing in English—Lawrence was never in uniform, and his perspective of battle itself has the limitations one expects from a civilian. Only rarely did he attempt to picture front-line experiences as in "England, My England" and in Captain Herbertson's narrative in chapter X of *Aaron's Rod.* The latter account is vivid enough reporting, but other novelists including his former editor, Ford Madox Ford, have represented battle scenes much more memorably as *A Man Could Stand Up* will illustrate. Although he was certainly no pacifist, Lawrence exhibits some of the lack of sympathy for the sufferings of the active participants that seems to be characteristic of some civilians, especially those of age for military service who have been exempted.[16] The note of pity which Wilfred Owen strikes in his *Anthem for Doomed Youth*, embracing survivors as well as victims, is rarely expressed by Lawrence:

> The pallor of girls' brows shall be their pall;
> Their flowers the tenderness of silent minds,
> And each slow dusk a drawing-down of blinds.

A lack of sympathy is probably unconsciously engendered, especially during a white feather war such as 1914-18, to protect the non-participant from an unconfronted sense of guilt which on rational grounds he can repudiate as groundless but which nonetheless produces a recurrent gnaw. A revealing study might be made of the effect in their writings of their civilian status in wartime on such men as Lawrence and Aldous Huxley, or in the Second World War, on W. H. Auden whose position seems to be one that comes under repeated satirical attacks in the novels and sketches of Evelyn Waugh. Even G. B. Shaw, who was fifty-eight years of age in 1914, exhibits a little of the characteristic edginess when he asserts in his *Preface* to his play, *Heartbreak House* (1919):

> Only those who have lived through a first-class war, not in the field, but at home, and kept their heads, can possibly understand the bitterness of Shakespeare and Swift, who both went through this experience.

Up to this point some of the drawbacks evident in Lawrence's writings which derive from his lack of front-line experience have been touched on, yet it must also be recognized that Shaw's statement is not mere nonsense, and that to write a great novel about war in this century, there were some clear gains for Lawrence in his having experienced the event as a civilian rather than as a participant. The anxiety and fear of the man in a trench or foxhole as shells zero into range of his position were ones that Lawrence never knew, but there were other kinds of wartime terror that he did know intimately and of which he wrote with telling effectiveness: the fear that the world as we know it is doomed to extinction, and the fear (which Orwell was to portray as the most alarming aspect of life under the nightmarish regime of Big Brother) that behind the friendly smile of our neighbor is a man full of hate who is plotting to betray us into the hands of the authorities. The man in uniform also knows something of these anxieties, yet he is much less likely to be acutely aware of them because of the coating of numbness that often accompanies his more immediate experiences of war, a coating thickened (at least in the early phases of the 1914-18 conflict) by the attitude of such young men as Raymond Asquith who looked on the event as a kind of "glorious picnic." [17]

Moreover, from the point of view of later readers of *Women in Love*, historical circumstances in the twentieth century have contributed to the advantage the novel gains from its author's unusual perspective. As the 1939-45 war happened to shape itself in most countries, the impact of events on the state of mind of those not in uniform was as crucially important as the more special adventures of airman, soldier, or sailor. A fuller appreciation of Lawrence's record of such an impact, as embodied in *Women in Love*, was thus fostered by events occurring twenty-five or thirty years after the book was written.

V

On September 8, 1915, Lawrence witnessed a Zeppelin bombing raid on London and afterwards described his impressions of this new phenomenon of wartime:

> Then we saw the Zeppelin above us . . . And underneath it were splashes of fire as the shells fired from earth burst. Then there were flashes near the ground—and the shaking noise. It was like Milton—then there was war in heaven. But it was not angels . . . It seems as if the cosmic order were gone, as if there had come a new order. . . . So it seemed our cosmos has burst . . . the stars and moon blown away, the envelope of the sky burst out, and a new cosmos appeared; with a long ovate, gleaming central luminary . . . with its light bursting in flashes on the earth, to burst away the earth also. So it is the end—our world is gone, and we are like dust in the air.

Compared to the massive bombings inflicted on Rotterdam, Hamburg, or London, in the 1939-45 war, even without adding Hiroshima to the list, a Zeppelin raid of 1915 may seem quaintly out of place, yet the difference is only one of scale. The response of the spectator, if we may call him that, is the same. As a civilian Lawrence discovered in 1915 a sense which all men have subsequently had to live with, a sense acutely intensified in 1945 by the use of atomic weapons, but one which did not originate in that use, that our world may simply be wiped out. Near the end of *Women in Love,* this cataclysmic awareness is given voice in the conversations between the German sculptor, Loerke, and the English artist, Gudrun Brangwen:

> As for the future, that they never mentioned except one laughed out some mocking dream of the destruction of the world by a ridiculous catastrophe of man's invention: a man invented such a perfect explosive that it blew the earth in two, and the two halves set off in different directions through space, to the dismay of the inhabitants: or else the people of the world divided into two halves, and each half decided *it* was perfect and right, the other half was wrong and must be destroyed; so another end of the world. Or else, Loerke's dream of fear, the world went cold, and snow fell everywhere, and only white creatures, polar bears, white foxes, and men like awful white snow-birds, persisted in ice cruelty. Apart from these stories, they never talked of the future.

A sense of what modern war might mean, a sense now part of the consciousness of all of us, has seldom been more awesomely illustrated than in this passage. Yet the apocalyptic dimensions of *Women in Love* are not always so clearly related to the bomb raid of 1915 and to the possibilities of some specific explosive destruction. In a letter of April, 1917, Lawrence was prophesying: "There will fall a big fire on the city before long, as on Sodom and Gomorrah," and earlier he predicted: "I believe an end is coming: the war, a plague, a fire, God knows what."

It is this less specific sense of universal cataclysm, of which the war was the engendering agent, that is more characteristic of *Women in Love* than passages about "the perfect explosive that blew the earth in two." There are, for example, several references to the destructive possibilities of flood. After Gerald emerges from the icy cold underwater current where he has been searching for his sister's body, he exclaims bitterly: "There's room under that water there for thousands. . . . a whole universe under there." And he adds:

> When you are down there, it is so cold, actually, and so endless, so different really from what it is on top, so endless—you wonder how it is so many are alive, why we're up here.

Later, when Ursula is deserted by Birkin, her sense of isolation is pictured in terms of the Biblical flood:

> There seemed to be no hope in the world. One was a tiny little rock with the tide of nothingness rising higher and higher. She herself was real, and only herself—just like a rock in a wash of flood-water.[18]

The cataclysm of fire provides a further cluster of associations related to the war (without the relationship being explicitly stated) especially in the several allusions to the fate of Sodom. In chapter XI, when Birkin and Ursula argue about how the world will end, a world in which people "distil themselves with nitroglycerine," Birkin likens his contemporaries to "apples of Sodom." On the surface "they look very nice and rosy, your healthy young men and women. But they are . . . Dead Sea Fruit, gall-apples." •

Over three hundred pages later, this image is picked up again when the almost lusciously beautiful Gudrun Brangwen in her winter-resort hotel room is soliloquizing about her haunted awareness of clocks. She wonders if her hair might suddenly turn white overnight:

> She had *felt* it turning white so often, under the intolerable burden of her thoughts, and her sensations. Yet there it remained, brown as ever, and there she was herself, looking a picture of health.

The cunning intricacy with which *Women in Love* has been knitted together is nicely illustrated in this short passage. The deceptively rosy-looking apples of Sodom are not directly mentioned;

• In its preoccupation with the possible doom of mankind *Women in Love* can be grouped with other works of the same decade such as Oswald Spengler's *Der Untergang des Abendlandes* (1918-22), and the Kurt Pinthus' collection of expressionist works *Menschheitsdämmerung*. See Walter H. Sokel, *The Writer in Extremis* (Stanford, 1959), pp. 2-3. A film version, the classic *Lot in Sodom*, was produced by J. Sibley Watson in 1933.

the reader is expected to remember, and with them, mankind's possible destruction by fire—this in the midst of a section of the narrative which powerfully evokes another mode of destruction, the return to an age of ice. Of these different modes of destruction Loerke's "dream of fear" that "the world went cold" is the most vividly portrayed of them all and does not call for illustrations from the three chapters Lawrênce devoted to it.

Flood, fire, ice, or bomb—not one mode of sudden destruction (such as a documentary novel might present) but various modes combine to convey a civilian's response to war: "it is the end—our world is gone, and we are like dust in the air."

Several passages in the novel and many passages in the letters express a nostalgic sadness felt after 1914 that the established order of the past was being swept away:

> I am so sad, for my country, for this great wave of civilisation, 2000 years, which is now collapsing, that it is hard to live. So much beauty and pathos of old things passing away and no new things coming: this house of the Ottoline's—it is England —my God, it breaks my soul . . . the great past, crumbling down.•

Written from Garsington Manor, the model for Breadalby in the novel, this letter evokes the pace of what seemed in retrospect the relatively carefree pre-war world. In a post-war story, Lawrence evoked it again when picturing a couple in "The Captain's Doll" enjoying their luncheon in the mountain sunshine:

> It seemed lovely: almost like before the war: almost the same feeling of eternal holiday, as if the world was made for man's everlasting holiday.

• *Letters,* I, 378. To compare the similar wording which reappears in the novel is instructive. In chapter XXVI, Birkin is stirred by inspecting on old chair in the market which evokes for him Jane Austen's England: "So beautiful, so pure! It almost breaks my heart. My beloved country—it had something to express even when it made that chair." And in the "Breadalby" chapter, Birkin looks at the park in the morning and thinks: "how lovely, how sure . . . the things of the past were—the lovely accomplished past—this house, so still and golden, the park slumbering its centuries of peace."

Other writers, poets in particular, have expressed this nostalgia and gently lamented the end of the long weekends or of the tea parties at Rupert Brooke's Grantchester, and this note is struck from time-to-time in *Women in Love.* But the more distinctive note in Lawrence's novel is its sense of the dooms hanging over mankind which in their cumulative effects, as I have suggested, contribute most directly to the hair-raising impact the book can make on readers. Sherwood Anderson exclaimed after completing it: "It's tremendous . . . like a storm I once lived through." [19] My own comparison, on first reading it, was to a performance of Verdi's *Requiem* with its deafening battery of trumpet sounds ricochetting off the walls of the concert hall united with the full chorus chanting *Dies irae! Dies irae!*—this before I knew of Lawrence's having once proposed the phrase for his title.

VI

Shortly before her death Katherine Mansfield protested in a letter that some novels she had been reading had been written as if the war had not happened. "The novel can't just leave the war out," she said.[20] Lawrence would have agreed, but he was aware that there are different ways of getting the war in. There was the direct way, as in his own *Aaron's Rod,* and there was the indirect way which we have been examining in *Women in Love.* In his *Foreword* he, himself, remarked that his novel "took its final shape in the midst of the period of war, though it does not concern the war itself." And he then remarks, a little mysteriously:

> I should wish the time to remain unfixed, so that the bitterness of the war may be taken for granted in the characters.

The timelessness of the novel is devised with care. In the "Crème de Menthe" chapter, for example, when Halliday's mistress asks Gerald: "Are you a soldier?" he replies that he has resigned his commission, and Birkin adds: "He was in the last war." The typescript shows that what Birkin had originally said of his friend was: "He was a captain in the South African War." By striking out the precise reference, Lawrence sets his scene so that it could have taken place in 1910, 1920, 1950, 1965, or some future date to which the same general remark would be once again applicable. It is a world in which people drive automobiles yet go up to their bedrooms in country houses by candlelight, and through such small details one might be able to plot out a bracket of possible dates for the action, but the task would be more pointless than pedantic. *Women in Love,* as Lawrence wished, derived from a specific historical event and yet can be read as if it had just been published. Like the characters in Malcolm Lowry's novel, his men and women live Under the Volcano, a volcano which has been either erupting or threatening to erupt every year since 1914.

The indirect way of representing the effects of war developed in *Women in Love* may be contrasted with the almost nakedly direct method used in the "Nightmare" chapter of *Kangaroo.* Among the many discomforts and indignities he suffered as a civilian, including his expulsion from Cornwall as a suspected spy, the incident which affected Lawrence most profoundly was a medical examination to which he was subjected in September, 1918. Occurring too late to affect *Women in Love* the experience smoldered until 1922 when it was fanned back into full flame in a chapter about which no critical agreement seems to exist. The seething outburst of indignation and rage against the insensitivity of authorities has aroused an enthusiastic response in some readers. Others find "Nightmare" an embarrassing spectacle of childish hysteria, perhaps the most offensive chapter in all of the author's writings. That its "expression of outrage is vulgarly direct" has been justified because the sort of treatment against which the novelist is protesting is comparable to the treatment later meted out to the victims of Auschwitz.[21]

To point out that the "Nightmare" chapter does have prophetic virtues is worth doing but can obscure the fact that bad books may be written on behalf of excellent causes. It would seem to me that whatever Lawrence was trying to express in this segment from *Kangaroo* was more effectively expressed in *Women in Love.* No right-minded reader disputes the cause of individual freedom which the chapter supposedly celebrates, but if the chapter prompts many readers to find the champion himself somewhat absurd, then it is not only ineffective art but ineffective propaganda on behalf of a good cause.

One clue to the difficulty is that hardly anyone in discussing the chapter refers to the hero as Somers. More than for any other segment of Lawrence's fiction, here we call the hero by the author's name. The author's undiluted autobiography almost invites readers to become detached from his sufferings and to institute comparisons from life which can be damaging. Thus Olive Moore commented in 1932:

> More than his private parts would have been mishandled in France, in Germany, in America, had he lived there with an enemy-alien wife who [as Catherine Carswell said] 'was not only German but loudly provocative and indiscreet.' [22]

Much more damaging, and not a symptom of mere gentility, is that "Nightmare" forces into the open the question of Lawrence's civilian status as *Women in Love* does not.

For weighing and comparing different kinds of sufferings no scale of measurement has ever been devised, yet anyone who pauses during Lawrence's tirade to reflect that the self-pitying protest is from a man lucky enough to be spared the experiences of Mons, Ypres, Passchendale, and who reflects also that the speaker's less fortunate friends and contemporaries had been subjected several times to the same medical examination and would have regarded it as a minor irritant compared to their other experiences—such a reader will obviously be unmoved by an event which the novelist himself had found very moving. Self pity, as Shelley's best poems show, can be transformed into great art. In the "Nightmare" chapter, the transformation is not achieved. The direct method invites the reader to switch on overhead lights under which the spectacle of suffering pales, as it does not pale in *Women in Love.*

VII

The medical examination of 1918 was the culminating incident in a long series of wartime experiences which profoundly affected

Lawrence's attitudes not merely towards authorities but towards his fellow man. Feelings of misanthropy and aloneness about which he wrote some of his best short stories were intensified during the war years into a state described by the hero of *Women in Love* as that of "madness." And every major character is at different times infected with this madness, in particular Birkin in the earlier parts of the novel, and later, as Birkin is gradually cured of it, Gudrun.

When Lawrence said in his *Foreword* to this novel that "the bitterness of the war may be taken for granted in the characters," what did he mean? As we have seen, the novel impresses bitterness on us by its reminders of cataclysmic doom, an impression heightened also by the preoccupation with alternative ways of extinction through slow decline, which remain to be illustrated. Most of all, "the bitterness of the war" is incorporated into the relations of each character to the others, and especially to mankind in general.

A brief scene may be cited in which all these forms of bitterness are made manifest. Birkin and Gerald are traveling to London by train, and Birkin gets more and more alarmed and restless as they approach the vast city. "Don't you feel like one of the damned?" he asks as they reach the inferno.

> "I always feel doomed when the train is running into London. I feel such a despair, so hopeless, as if it were the end of the world."
>
> "Really!" said Gerald. "And does the end of the world frighten you?"
>
> Birkin lifted his shoulders in a slow shrug.
>
> "I don't know," he said. "It does while it hangs imminent and doesn't fall. But people give me a bad feeling—very bad."

As Lawrence said earlier of Birkin: "His dislike of mankind, of the mass of mankind, amounted almost to an illness."

What is the cause of Birkin's illness? Why do people give him a bad feeling? The novel does not tell us; his response we can write off, if we like, as simply irrational, a sense that the rat-like proletarian (as pictured in chapter XXVI) will inherit the earth. His creator's hatred of mankind is similarly irrational, but through his letters one can see some of the more specific sources of it in his wartime experiences, his discovery that the enemy is not necessarily just a man in the opposite trench but the neighbor, even the seeming friend, especially when more than two or three of them are gathered together.

Lawrence has often been classified as an anarchist; if he is, it is of a special breed. The anarchist hates authority but may admire and use the mob. Lawrence hated certain abuses of authority but his dread of people *en masse* was even stronger. In a letter of 1915, after seeing at Worthing a large gathering of soldiers, he observed grimly: "They will murder their officers one day." [23] The unwary reader may assume this to be something from Mailer's *Naked and the Dead* and that Lawrence the anarchist is applauding the possibility of a violent overthrow of authority, but if we read the whole passage, it is evident that the opposite is the case; he is appalled by the potential reversion to mob rule. As late as *The Plumed Serpent* he was looking back on his own wartime experiences in Cornwall when he pictures Kate reflecting on the nature of fear:

> In England, in Ireland, during the war and the revolution she had known *spiritual* fear. The ghastly fear of the rabble; and during the war, nations were nearly all rabble. . . . In those days, Kate had known the agony of cold social fear, as if a democracy were a huge, huge cold centipede which, if you resisted it, would dig every claw into you.

Social hatred is portrayed in *Women in Love* as an illness, as Lawrence calls it, but even more as a fact that must be faced in human relations. The most helpful lead into this aspect of his novel occurs in a passage about the war in his brilliantly-written Introduction to the Maurice Magnus *Memoirs*. Lawrence does not mention *Women in Love* here, yet his discussion of the necessity of using the light of knowledge to confront the horror of human iniquities, which war brings to the surface, is exceptionally pertinent:

> Humanity can only finally conquer by realizing. It is human destiny, since Man fell into consciousness and self-conscious-

> ness, that we can only go forward step by step through realization, full, bitter, conscious realization. . . . And we've got to know humanity's criminal tendency . . . Knowledge, true knowledge, is like vaccination. It prevents the continuing of ghastly moral disease. And so it is with war. . . . We all fell. . . . We fell into hideous depravity of hating the human soul; a purulent small-pox of the spirit we had. . . . The small-pox sores are running yet in the spirit of mankind. . . . Cleanse it not with blind love: ah . . . But with bitter and wincing realization.[24]

It will be noted that in this passage Lawrence uses the first person plural pronoun rather than the *he/they* pronouns of his "Nightmare" chapter or the *I/they* of many passages in his letters. In his own responses to others, not merely in observing the emotions of others, he discovered in wartime the full nature of hate and its importance on the personal as well as the national scale.

Although closely associated with a circle of pacifists such as Lady Ottoline Morrell and her husband, and Bertrand Russell, Lawrence himself had the good fortune not to be a pacifist. I do not wish to be misunderstood here; it might be more accurate to say, not his good fortune, but ours as readers of his novels. The pacifist may be an admirable man and a kindly lover of the human race. Alternatively, as subtle psychoanalytical explanations might demonstrate, he may be more full of hatreds than the next man, but the difference would not bear on the present argument. Whether or not he is full of concealed hatreds the pacifist must bend all efforts to a denial of such feelings; no professing pacifist could have written *Women in Love*. Lawrence was appalled by the war but never was under an illusion about his own capacities to hate. In 1915 he told Lady Ottoline: "Soon we in England shall go fully mad, with hate. . . . I am mad with rage myself. I would like to kill a million Germans—two millions." It was a hatred that took in more than Germans. In September, 1916, as he was typing a copy of *Women in Love*, he wrote from Cornwall to Koteliansky:

> When I see people in the distance, walking along the path through the fields to Zennor, I want to crouch in the bushes and

> shoot them silently with invisible arrows of death. I think truly the only righteousness is the destruction of mankind, as in Sodom. . . . But they creep in, the obstructions, the people, like bugs they creep insidiously in, and they are too many to crush. I see them—fat men in white flannel trousers—pères de familles—and the famille—passing along the field-path and looking at the scenery. Oh, if one could have but a great box of insect powder, and shake it over them.[25]

This awesome outburst, with its repulsive image of the human insect (which plays a prominent role in *Women in Love*) would indicate that if anyone were to be left in charge of a push button in wartime, it ought not to be D. H. Lawrence. It should also indicate, however, one of the author's most important qualifications to write a great novel about war. However repulsive the outburst would appear if read before a Peace Congress, it illustrates the kinds of insight and self-knowledge out of which *Women in Love* was written. What Marlow in Conrad's *Heart of Darkness* had finally to confront was that his forerunner, the idealistic Mr. Kurtz, a fellow "emissary of light," had ended his report on his humanitarian mission in the Congo with the exclamation: "Exterminate all the brutes!"

This, I take it, is what Lawrence meant in his *Introduction* to the Magnus memoir about the need for "realization" of the war. It is what distinguishes *Women in Love* from the "Nightmare" chapter in *Kangaroo.* When we read about the insensitive medical authorities, our liberal conditioned reflex juices flow, easily, almost pleasurably. But when we confront the pervasive universality of hate laid bare in the earlier novel, we wince away from the experience.

In his *Irrational Man* the philosopher William Barrett offers a helpful analysis of Nietzsche, William James, and some of the Existentialists, and although he makes only a few references to Lawrence it is evident that these could be expanded into a chapter, for it is with those writings in which the importance of irrationality in man's behaviour is stressed that *Women in Love* is in many ways most akin. Regions Bloomsbury never knew thy domain shall sway—not because Bloomsbury's civilized values were wrong, but because in view of the temper and events of the war years, this set of values was unrealistic and incomplete in its assumptions about man's nature. And novels which recognized only this otherwise admirable set of values would be similarly unrealistic and incomplete.

As a brief preliminary example, the scene of Hermione Roddice's attempt to murder Birkin may be cited. On occasion, in the novel, Hermione's role is comic. With her long-drawn out "Gooood-bye!" we are treated to the comic spectacle of the literary lion-huntress. This scene of the attempted murder, however, is played straight, and the emphasis is upon the difference between her set of consciously held values and the nature of her emotional life:

> Hermione was looking at him with leering eyes, along her cheeks. He could feel violent waves of hatred and loathing of all he said, coming out of her. It was dynamic hatred and loathing, coming strong and black out of the unconsciousness.

After the attack, in which she achieved "her voluptuous consummation," she responds like the Prussian officer after his attack on his orderly. She blots out the experience and denies to herself the "ecstasy" she has discovered in giving vent to her hatred.

On Birkin the effect of her attack is to intensify his sense of nausea at the prospect of human contact into a state of "madness" in which the only satisfactory contact is the touch of pine needles and wet grass on his naked flesh ("more beautiful than the touch of any woman"):

> What a dread he had of mankind, of other people! It amounted almost to horror, to a sort of dream terror—his horror of being observed by some other people. If he were on an island, like Alexander Selkirk, with only the creatures and the trees, he would be free and glad.

Ten years before he was to create the misanthropist and misogynist Cathcart, in "The Man Who Loved Islands," Lawrence was portraying a sick hero's desire for isolation on a lonely island and his fear and hatred of his fellow men.

It is suggestive to compare this scene with the quarrels between

Anna Brangwen and her husband in *The Rainbow*— the scene of the sewing machine for example. Once again Lawrence is about his special task as a novelist in representing the alternating attractions and repulsions making up a relationship between two individual characters. The difference is that in this scene in *The Rainbow*, the quarrel remains largely personal and domestic; whether or not Anna is *Victrix* does not lead her husband into formulating generalizations about mankind. In *Women in Love*, however, the quarrels tend to radiate out from the individual couples to involve relations with neighbors and with societies. Loving and hating are more emphatically social acts.

VIII

That *The Rainbow* also has dimensions beyond the level of naturalistic narrative was indicated in showing how extensively Lawrence established analogies between the experiences of the Brangwens and various incidents in the Bible. In this respect *Women in Love* has an even more elaborate frame of reference, for instead of the comparisons being restricted to the story of one people—the race of Israel—the comparisons this time are expanded to take in many peoples and nations. The analogy between London and Sodom is recurrently made in *Women in Love*, yet the Bible story of how a certain corrupt civilization was destroyed is, in this novel, only one of many stories and histories being drawn upon. How civilizations die, or might die, is the subject of *Women in Love*—not how the course of one civilization is like that of one other civilization—which was treated in *The Rainbow*. The differences between the two novels derive not only from the author's awareness of the war, but from his more extended use of history, prehistory, and myth in the later work. The history of Israel still provides parallels but expanded now by an awareness of other past civilizations: Rome, Carthage, Greece, Egypt, Babylon, the legendary Atlantis, and the lost city states of Africa.

One can readily understand why Virginia Woolf could have gained the impression that Lawrence "never looked back at the past" and also why a later critic, J. H. Raleigh, asserts that "Joyce stands for history, Lawrence for futurity," [26] yet both estimates are misleading. Man's past, or perhaps more precisely *his* impression of man's past, was crucially important to Lawrence. Murray's book on Greek religions annoyed him as did H. G. Wells' history by their assumptions about the inferiority of the past. As Achsah Brewster noted: "The old gods were as important to Lawrence as the new, different but not inferior." [27] Or as the leading character in his story "Glad Ghosts" says: "my desire to go onwards takes me back a little."

It must be recalled that like Dickens, with his pot-boiler production, *A Child's History of England,* Lawrence ventured into writing a volume of history, setting to work on it shortly after he had completed *Women in Love.* Published in 1921, his *Movements of European History* confirms what is evident elsewhere in his writing, that minute historical accuracies were of little concern to him. The "broken-pots of historical facts" bored him, he said, but in writing his history he deeply enjoyed trying to locate "the thread of the developing significance" of past events.[28] The past he treated in the same way as he treated countries such as Sardinia or New Mexico in his travel books; by its store of examples of cultures similar to our own, or different from our own, the past provided him with an opportunity for impressionistic speculations on the nature of man, and on man's probable fate. His keen interest in anthropological studies was similarly inspired. Hence in his reading he tended to prefer accounts of epochs or peoples about which our store of information is not altogether precise. Of the Etruscans he noted: "That which half emerges from the dim background of time is strangely stirring." [29]

This interest in the history and legends of past civilizations was keenly intensified during the years of the war. Shortly before its outbreak in 1914 he had planned to spend a month reading in the library at the British Museum in order to prepare for his "next novel." These proposed researches had to be postponed until moving to Cornwall in 1916, where in relative isolation, he settled down to an intensive course of reading which he was to pursue for many months until, and after, he began writing this "next novel" in late April, 1916. As a result *Women in Love* is, in the jargon of the social sciences, one of the more *researched* of English novels.

In view of his mood of wartime despair, one might expect Lawrence, at this time, to have sought anodynes in his reading. The reverse was true. In requesting friends to send books, he specified that he did not want to read novels or poetry or "belles lettres." [30] Instead of fiction he was soaking himself in works of history, anthropology, mythology, and ethnology. On January 21, 1916, he asked Koteliansky to bring him books on "Norse or Anglo Saxon or early Celtic" cultures, studies of "Orphic religions, or Egypt, or on anything really African." And by April 1, he reported to Kot that his head was now full of "Greek translations and Ethnology" rather than "stories."

More specifically, he read Frazer's *Golden Bough* and *Totemism and Exogamy,* and Sir Edward Tylor's *Primitive Culture* (these following an earlier reading of Jane Harrison's *Ancient Art and Ritual*—"you have no idea how much I got out of that . . . book," he reported). A *History of the East* with its account of the "crashing down of nations and empires" impressed him and led to his reading a history of early Egypt and also Niccolao Manucci's *History of the Mogul Dynasty in India* which made him realize that "these Hindus are horribly decadent and reverting to all forms of barbarism in all sorts of ugly ways." • He was also led (when he could bear it, he said) to Thucydides where he had to confront "the fact of these wars of a collapsing era." "It is too horrible to see a people . . . fling itself down the abyss of the past, and disappear." [31] His response to Thucydides (whom Birkin in the novel is represented as reading when Hermione tries to murder him) indicates the spirit in which Lawrence undertook his program of study. "The Peloponnesian war was the death agony of Greece." "*All* Greece died. It must not be so again." A knowledge of past civilizations and of cultures in other continents provided a Spenglerian perspective on the crumbling world of 1916, and in particular on what seemed to Birkin, in the novel, "the dying body" of English civilization itself:

• *Letters* I, 451-52. Cf. the account of Halliday's "aristocratic-looking" Hindu servant in *Women in Love:* "Birkin felt a slight sickness, looking at him, and feeling the slight greyness as an ash or a corruption."—It is also worth noting that even with his relatively small cast of characters Lawrence was able to introduce enough foreigners, Russian, German, Hindu, to suggest that the fate of man, rather than just the fate of England, is at stake.

> 'You think the English will have to disappear?' persisted Gudrun. It was strange, her pointed interest in his answer. It might have been her own fate she was inquiring after.

To know how Gudrun might die, how England and the western world might die, history and legend were helpfully informative, although not comforting.

How was this store of reading put to use in *Women in Love*? When Ibsen was asked what he had been reading he is reported to have replied that he read nothing; he was a writer. Lawrence would not have subscribed to such nonsense, but he was also aware that an author's reading can swamp his book if it is dumped there in its raw state. George Eliot's *Romola* is a painful example of what happens when laborious researches remain unincorporated into fiction, and Lawrence's own *Plumed Serpent* suffers, at times, from the same failing. In *Women in Love,* on the contrary, the information and insights gleaned by the author from Tylor and Thucydides become integrated components of a picture. Rarely discussed directly (like the war which is never mentioned) they add immeasurably to the scope of his story of a sick society.

IX

In chapter XI Ursula Brangwen listens to Birkin's thunderings on the degeneration of hate-filled modern man. At times she is impressed; at other times, like her mother in the solemnity of the cathedral in *The Rainbow,* she is amused. A crucial point in their argument occurs, however, when he is predicting a day of wrath in which humanity will be quickly wiped out. She disagrees. "She knew it could not disappear so cleanly and conveniently. It had a long way to go yet, a long and hideous way. Her subtle, feminine, demoniacal soul knew it well." If the many references to cataclysm in *Women in Love* suggest the impact of war, this reference to an alternative doom for mankind, the "long way," the slow decline into extinction, suggests in general the influence of the novelist's reading. But what is Ursula supposed to mean by her mysterious and fearsome reference to this "long and hideous way?" Does the novel ever explain what is meant or are we left, as Conrad leaves us in his *Heart of Darkness*, shuddering at the implications of Kurtz's famous phrase—"The horror! the horror!"—without our ever clearly knowing what the horror is?

I think we can come close to identifying what the horror is in Lawrence's book although his commentators seem rarely to have been concerned with the problem. It could, of course, be maintained that the inquiry should not be pushed, because readers may be more powerfully affected by something sensed, imprecisely, as elusively threatening, than by an identifiable threat. The poems of Coleridge, a master of the rhetoric of horror, could be cited to reinforce the objection:

> Behold! her bosom and half her side—
> A sight to dream of, not to tell!
> O shield her! shield sweet Christabel!

Nevertheless, because many of the misunderstandings of *Women in Love* originate in an inadequate recognition of what the horror, or horrors, might be, we must risk this not very significant loss and seek out a confrontation.

These remarks must serve as a preamble to a consideration of a scene in chapter XIX of major importance as embodying the climax of one of the two main plot lines. In one respect the scene resembles the "Nightmare" chapter in *Kangaroo* inasmuch as every study of Lawrence refers to it without any agreement having been arrived at. The problem here, however, is not one of liking or disliking (it is generally admired); the problem is one of interpretation and understanding. The scene embodies a kind of soliloquy in the third person, with Birkin confronting, in his mind's eye, an African carving he had contemplated many times at Halliday's flat in London. Like the scene of the doctor's descent into the pond-water in "The Horse Dealer's Daughter," it is climactic in that after the confrontation or descent the character reaches a major decision. Birkin's experience culminates immediately in his resolving to marry Ursula, and as he sets out for her house to make his proposal, the ugly town of Beldover seems to him radiantly beautiful. "It looked like Jerusalem to his fancy," as

Christminster ("the heavenly Jerusalem") looked to Hardy's Jude. Before the resolution is reached and the brief epiphany experienced, Birkin has to make a deep descent.

Among the African fetish statues he had seen in Halliday's London apartment, Birkin remembers one of a woman, a "slim, elegant figure from West Africa, in dark wood, glossy and suave. . . . He remembered her vividly: she was one of his soul's intimates." Why is it that the statue had haunted Birkin so persistently? Like many of his generation in the western world, Birkin enjoys African carving for its aesthetic satisfactions, yet it is obvious that his almost obsessive concern is not motivated by a search for beauty. It is what these statues tell him about the history of civilization and of his own future:

> He remembered her: her astonishing cultured elegance, her diminished, *beetle face,* the astounding long elegant body, on short, ugly legs, with such *protuberant buttocks,* so weighty and unexpected below her slim long loins. She knew *what he himself did not know.* She had thousands of years of purely sensual, purely unspiritual knowledge behind her. It must have been thousands of years since her race had died, mystically: that is, since the relation between the senses and the outspoken mind had broken, leaving the experience all in one sort, mystically sensual. Thousands of years ago, *that which was imminent in himself* must have taken place in these Africans: the goodness, the holiness, the desire for creation and productive happiness must have lapsed, leaving the single impulse for knowledge in one sort . . . in disintegration and dissolution, knowledge such as the beetles have. [Italics mine.]

Birkin's reflections serve as a flashback to the earlier scene in Halliday's apartment when another African statue was seen, this time through the eyes of Gerald. He, too, is disturbed by the statue (it is of a woman in labor), and although he finds no aesthetic pleasure he nevertheless senses what Birkin associated with it. It conveys to Gerald "the suggestion of the extreme of physical sensation, beyond the limits of mental consciousness." • The early scene

• In this discussion I am quoting from the original version of *Women in Love* (London, 1921) before Pussum was changed into Minette. The revisions

of the breakfast party is memorably staged with the four naked men standing round the statue and commenting on the "terrible face, void, peaked, abstracted almost into meaninglessness by the weight of sensation beneath." And the affair of the preceding night is also effectively incorporated by Gerald's significant discovery that the statue makes him think of the Pussum, the "violated slave" still asleep in the adjacent bedroom. But Gerald makes one blunder in his response to the statue. He thinks it is crude and savage. Birkin hastens to correct him:

> 'There are centuries and hundreds of centuries of development in a straight line, behind that carving; it is an awful pitch of culture, of a definite sort.'

Gerald's mistake is one often made by those readers of Lawrence who overlook what Birkin calls the "astonishing cultured elegance" of the statue and assume that he is evoking a work by a savage. Such a reading blurs the main point of his soliloquy. Lawrence had learned from his reading (and his subsequent study of Leo Frobenius' *The Voice of Africa* confirmed the point) that long before the coming of Europeans there had existed great city states in Africa which had produced highly sophisticated works of art and established a tradition of fine craftsmanship.[32] A slow decline, not a cataclysm, finished off this civilization, and it is the nature of this decline that Birkin tries to conjure up as he contemplates what the statue symbolizes for him.

Parenthetically it should be added that, so far as our apprecia-

---

which Lawrence introduced into his later edition were prompted by the threat of a libel suit, and although a few of them might reflect a more significant change of intention, most of them are mere insulators, and not being consistently changed, they also lead to confusion. Because Heseltine, who was threatening the libel suit, had African statues in his apartment, Lawrence obliged by changing the one referred to in chapters VI and VII into a statue from the West Pacific and by deleting the references to Negroes. But in chapter XIX he left these unchanged. See also his reference in an essay to "an African fetish idol of a woman pregnant" (*Reflections on the Death of a Porcupine,* pp. 140-41). At least from our present perspective, one detail of these revisions is an amusing example of Lawrence's humor. The name *Pussum* was changed to *Minette* presumably because Heseltine's mistress had been known as the Puma, but the name of Heseltine's wife, whom he married in December, 1916, was *Minnie* Channing.

tion of *Women in Love* is concerned, it does not matter fundamentally whether Birkin is right or wrong in his information about disputed points of Africa's past. Nor does it matter fundamentally whether his assumptions about one of the ways a civilization may decline are accurate or inaccurate. They are part of the given world of this novel and essential to an understanding of it. The basic assumption, and one developed in the parody scene at the Pompadour when Birkin's letter is read aloud by Halliday, is that a civilization having evolved out of its savage beginnings may lose its creative urge and lapse into decadence before becoming simply extinct. "There is a phase in every race— . . . when the desire for destruction overcomes every other desire." As intoned by the drunken Halliday for the amusement of London's Bohemia (this "menagerie of apish degraded souls"), the effect of the pronouncement is painfully comic—painful because no other direct statement in *Women in Love* is more significant or more serious—and astringently comic because of the setting in which it is framed. If the social process so conceived is unchecked a civilization declines to a stage which may have some resemblance to the original savage stage; it suffers a "reduction"—an abstract term upon which Lawrence leans often and hard in his fiction and letters.

Writing to his Jewish friend Mark Gertler, whose "obscene" painting seems to have inspired the account of Loerke's frieze of the drunken workers in the novel, Lawrence uses the same historical formula: "You are of an older race than I, and in these ultimate processes, you are beyond me. . . . At last your race is at an end—these pictures are its death-cry. And it will be left for the Jews to utter the final . . . death-cry of this epoch: the Christians are not *reduced* sufficiently." [33] And in "St. Mawr" he restates more explicitly the assumptions on which these gloomy predictions are based:

> Every new stroke of civilization has cost the lives of countless brave men, who have fallen . . . in their efforts to overcome the old, half-sordid savagery of the lower stages of creation, and win to the next stage. . . . And every civilization, when it loses its inward vision and its cleaner energy, falls into a new sort of

sordidness, more vast and more stupendous than the old savage sort.

During the composition of *Women in Love* Lawrence discovered some living illustrations much closer at hand than the Africans for his theory of cultural degeneration. His Cornish neighbors impressed him as a surviving pocket of a once impressive "pre-Christian Celtic civilisation" which had degenerated. In view of the beetle-like face of the African statue, the following description of the Cornish people (whose souls, he said, were like black beetles) is especially interesting:

> The aristocratic principle and the principle of magic, to which they belonged, these two have collapsed, and left only the most ugly, scaly, insect-like, unclean *selfishness*. . . . Nevertheless . . . there is left some of the old sensuousness of the darkness . . . something almost negroid, which is fascinating. But curse them, they are entirely mindless.[34]

This cluster associating the Celtic and African reappears in *Lady Chatterley's Lover* in a description of another Celt, the Irishman Michaelis:

> She saw in him that ancient motionlessness of a race that can't be disillusioned any more, an extreme, perhaps, of impurity that is pure, . . . he seemed pure, pure as an African ivory mask that dreams impurity into purity, in its ivory curves and planes.

That the African statues signify for Birkin a whole process of decline and fall, and that however aesthetically pleasing they evoke for him the impurity of a degenerated civilization, are points I have been laboring partly because of an extraordinary discussion of these statues by Horace Gregory in his *Pilgrim of the Apocalypse*. According to Gregory, Lawrence found his principal characters of less interest than the statue of the West African woman, "for him, perhaps the most important figure in the book."

> She is positive, concrete, the perfect representation of life as opposed to the imperfect human beings surrounding her. . . .

> What the statue is made to represent is the *normal* essence of Gudrun and Ursula combined—their deviation from the statue's norm . . . is the perversion imposed upon them by their individual existence. . . . In all four characters, male and female, the statue sets the standard, never fully realized by any of them.[35]

And Mr. Gregory concludes his analysis by asserting that "the image of the West African savage" was a fragment of hope in the midst of death. When a perceptive critic blunders into stating something so fantastically wrong as this (and other critics share his view) one is led to labor a point. Birkin's reflections in his soliloquy, developing like Keats, in his address to the Grecian urn, continues, and we may well ask what fragment of hope is there here:

> There is a long way we can travel, after the death-break; . . . We fall from the connection with life and hope, we lapse . . . into the long, long African process of purely sensual understanding . . . He realised now that this is a long process—thousands of years it takes, after the death of the creative spirit. He realised that there were great mysteries to be unsealed, sensual, mindless, dreadful mysteries, far beyond the phallic cult. How far, in their inverted culture, had these West Africans gone beyond phallic knowledge? Very, very far. Birkin recalled again the female figure: the elongated, long, long body, the curious unexpected heavy buttocks . . . the face with tiny features like a beetle's. This was far beyond any phallic knowledge.

Only when Birkin makes his resolution to repudiate the direction pointed by the statue does the rhythm of hope make itself felt.

This much is clear, but the passage of Birkin's reflections remains one of the most puzzling in the novel. What is meant by the repeated references to some kind of knowledge "beyond phallic knowledge"? What is it that the woman knew that Birkin does not yet know but dreads he will know? The horror for Birkin is not the state of mindlessness itself. The term *mindlessness* appears often in Lawrence's writings to describe the state of darkness in which the Brangwen farmers live or the coal miners in *Sons and*

Lovers. That a degenerating culture loses contact with the values of light and abandons the quest for intellectual effort (the quest portrayed in *The Rainbow*) may be deplorable but not terrifying and threatening, as in Birkin's reflections about the "dreadful mysteries far beyond the phallic cult." The latter seems to be the horror, the horror, in *Women in Love.* Whatever it is, three things may be said of it which call for more extended discussion. It involves some form (or rather forms) of sexual perversion; Birkin is strongly attracted to it (as the Pussum said of Birkin's sermon, "Oh, he was always talking about Corruption. He must be corrupt himself, to have it so much on his mind."). And thirdly, its culmination is death itself, or more specifically some form of suicide, individual and national.

The first point, about sexual perversions, is the most difficult to establish, and even raising the question is enough to rouse the ire of some brands of Laurentian admirers. The difficulty is that the novel itself is not explicit, could not be explicit, in this area, and we have to grope our way up a rickety ladder constructed of image-clusters and scraps of information. Halliday's mistress, the Pussum for example, is explicitly associated with the corruption when Lawrence says of her: "She was very handsome, flushed, and confident in dreadful knowledge." Less explicitly, a link is established by references to marsh flowers (she is "soft, unfolded like some red lotus in dreadful flowering nakedness,") and she is associated with the beetle-faced statue not so much by her fear of beetles but by her very appearance as in this remarkable passage:

> There was something curiously indecent, obscene, about her small, longish, dark skull, particularly when the ears showed.

Like many of the characters in *Women in Love* the Pussum is a vividly realized fictional creation yet at the same time, as representative of the corruption which the book treats, she is tagged by the novelist with evaluative terms such as *obscene.*

Gudrun Brangwen, a more highly complex character, is similarly presented. Her wood carvings were thought by Gerald to have been made by the same hands as those which created the African statues, and indeed Gudrun's affinities with what the statues suggested to Birkin are referred to many times. Most explicitly there is a passage near the end of the novel which is a kind of commentary on the earlier soliloquy. The passage consists of reflections (virtually a soliloquy again) on the difference between what Gerald offers as a lover of Gudrun and the kind of experience that Loerke could give her. Gerald's love-making has many qualities of perversity, but because he still has some "attachment" to moral virtues, "goodness" and "righteousness," he cannot provide the special sexual thrills that Loerke promises:

> Was it sheer blind force of passion that would satisfy her now? Not this, but the subtle thrills of extreme sensation in reduction. It was . . . the last subtle activities of . . . breaking down, carried out in the darkness of her.

She reflects further that she no longer wants a man such as Gerald but a "*creature*" like Loerke (who had been described by Birkin as a sewer rat and by Gerald as an insect):

> The world was finished now, for her. There was only the inner, individual darkness . . . the *obscene religious mystery* of ultimate reduction, the mystic frictional activities of diabolic reducing down, disintegrating the vital organic body of life. . . . She had . . . a further, slow exquisite experience to reap, unthinkable subtleties of sensation to know, before she was finished. [Italics mine.]

Before an attempt is made to explicate Gudrun's soliloquy a word should be interjected about Loerke himself. Better even than the Pussum and Gudrun, Loerke illustrates Lawrence's bold technique of creating characters who are fully alive and so eloquently self-assertive that they may engage our sympathies, and yet, in terms of the book's overall theme, of exposing them as appalling examples of social corruption. It is almost a tightrope-walking performance, and one can see why some of these creations have aroused divergent responses in his readers. Loerke was even described by Nathan Scott (who sees Lawrence through the spectacles of Denis de Rougemont) as a "Laurentian saint." And to Anaïs Nin also, simply because he is an artist, he is the man to be admired. Of the fact that at the end of the book Gerald is dead and Loerke alive, Miss Nin says:

> So it is Gerald who dies, not Loerke. It is the 'mindless sensuality' which dies. Yet it has been said that Lawrence in *Women in Love* had urged us to mindless sensuality and disintegration.[36]

The title of Miss Nin's book is *D. H. Lawrence: An Unprofessional Study,* and one wonders just how far the saving clause of her subtitle can be extended. Perhaps the most important equipment for a reader of Lawrence is just a nose. After his affair with the Pussum, Gerald admitted to Birkin:

> There's a certain smell about the skin of those women, that in the end is sickening beyond words—even if you like it at first.[37]

Lawrence surely expects us to be similarly responsive, and a reader who concludes that Loerke is a Laurentian saint would seem to be lacking in a sense of smell. "He lives like a rat, in the river of corruption, just where it falls over into the bottomless pit," says Birkin. Mankind, he adds, wants "to explore the sewers," and Loerke is "the wizard rat that swims ahead." His very name evokes his negativism, the Loki of the sagas and of William Morris's *Sigurd the Volsung:* "And Loki, the World's Begrudger, who maketh all labour vain."

What is it then that this ruthless little "creature" can provide that Gerald cannot offer? Both men have sadistic propensities and can presumably furnish the masochistic satisfactions that Gudrun craves. When she sees a picture of Loerke's nude statue of the young girl art-student on horseback (his preferences in girl-flesh anticipate those of the hero of Nabokov's *Lolita*), a girl who had to be subdued by his slapping her hard, "Gudrun went pale, and a darkness came over her eyes, like shame, she looked up with a certain supplication, *almost slave-like.*" The counterpointing here is extremely intricate, for we are reminded that perhaps the two high points of Gudrun's earlier appreciation of Gerald had been when she watched him subdue a rabbit by force or, more pertinently, when he drove his spurs into the flanks of his mare (scenes which will be discussed more extensively in my final chapter). And the phrase *almost slave-like* also flashes back to the Pussum whose submissive response to Gerald was similarly described.

Both men, then, have this capacity in common. What Loerke is capable of beyond it is the provision of some perverse pleasures, and the cluster of associations is consistently hinting at some exploitation of the anal and excremental areas. The recurring references to the abnormally prominent buttocks of the African statue and to sexual relations in which the connections with "creative life" are severed (anal intercourse has long been practised as a mode of avoiding conception), the traditional association of beetles with excrement, and the allusions to Loerke as a creature of the sewers all contribute towards some explication of both Birkin's soliloquy and that of Gudrun.

The hints concerning anal relations between men and women do not, however, indicate the full extent of the "further sensual experience" which Birkin contemplated. Gudrun's soliloquy, in particular, refers to some "obscene *religious* mystery of ultimate reduction." What is the term *religious* meant to suggest to us? Are we supposed to conjure up some Black Mass? Loerke, one might add, is well named to make a celebrant in such a rite, for in some Norse myths *Loki* is the devil. Perhaps it is merely the Bacchic festivals that are hinted at, or bestial erotic ceremonials,[38] or blood-sacrifice ceremonies such as the Druids had performed, or so Lawrence believed, in Cornwall. Somers in *Kangaroo* recalls his experience during 1916 in Cornwall of drifting into a "blood-darkness." "Human sacrifice!—he could feel his dark, blood-consciousness tingle to it again, the desire of it, the mystery of it." Again Conrad's *Heart of Darkness* provided a model (if a somewhat obscure one) in its allusions to Kurtz's participation in "certain midnight dances ending with unspeakable rites, which . . . were offered up to him." All that can be indicated about the introduction of the term *religious* into Lawrence's account of cultural degradation is that it reinforces a sense of the sinister without clarifying the nature of the corruption.

A further set of associations is less obscure but for Lawrence equally sinister, one that suggests that a declining society will revert to homosexuality. Loerke's perversities might include his love-hate relationship with his "companion" Leitner—they had for long shared a bedroom and "now reached the stage of loathing"—but this remains undeveloped. The problem of homosexuality takes us back from Gudrun and Loerke to Birkin's soliloquy and its expression of anxieties.

Unlike Proust, whose novels of this period also treat of the Cities of the Plain, Lawrence elected to avoid any direct representation in *Women in Love* of what Ezekiel calls the "abomination" of Sodom; he offers us no study of a M. de Charlus. The Bohemians are described as "degenerate," and there is some emphasis on the men being effeminate in manner with high-pitched squealing voices, but if London is to be likened to Sodom it is more because of its probable future fate than its present condition in this respect. If for the moment we shift from the novel to the novelist, however, we may detect a figure in this carpet. Lawrence's letters of 1915 and 1916 contain a remarkable number of references to his horror of beetles which is related, in most instances, to a horror of homosexual relations. In the Moore edition of the letters alone there are eighteen references to beetles and insects during the years 1915-16. On April 30, 1915, he reported his disgust after seeing an "obscene" crowd of soldiers:

> I like men to be beasts—but insects—one insect mounted on another—oh God! The soldiers at Worthing are like that—they remind me of lice or bugs.

Most revealing are passages referring to a visit paid by Francis Birrell to the Lawrences (in the company of David Garnett):

> These horrible little frowsty people, men lovers of men, they give me such a sense of corruption, almost putrescence, that I dream of beetles.[39]

On this particular occasion his revulsion took form in an incident that as reported by Garnett, seems fantastic. So wrought up was Lawrence by Birrell's visit that he struggled to cast a spell over him, and the young man actually woke up at night with his tongue swollen so abnormally that he was in great pain.[40] As Lawrence himself reported, such young men "are cased each in a hard little shell of his own," and "they made me dream of a beetle that bites like a scorpion. But I killed it." One may associate the incident with Kafka, but much more striking is a similarity to the situation in *Genesis* when the men of Sodom gather outside Lot's house and demand that his guests, two angels, be delivered to the crowd "that we may know them." The guests retaliate on the men of Sodom by striking them with blindness—this on the night before the destruction of their city.

Francis Birrell was not the only man to provoke the beetle nightmare in Lawrence at this time. For some reason his unhappy visit to Cambridge led to his associating Keynes and the whole group there with beetles and corruption, and also with Cambridge were linked such Bloomsbury figures as Duncan Grant.• In a letter to Henry Savage in December, 1913, in which he frankly aired his feelings about homosexual relations, Lawrence concluded:

> One is kept by all tradition and instinct from loving men, or a man—for it means just *extinction of all the purposive influences.*

It may be noted that the phrase which I have italicized is almost identical with the words used by Birkin in confronting the beetle-faced statue. As he contemplates the possible lapse from "the desire for creation and productive happiness," he speaks of the fall "from the connection with life and hope."

In this reconstruction of what is implied in Birkin's fearsome sense of the slow degeneration of western man, nothing so far has been said about machinery. So much has been written by others about Lawrence's vitalistic dislike of industrialism (and I shall add my mite in discussing Gerald Crich) that it is perhaps a useful corrective to see that the horror in *Women in Love* is not exclusively industrialism, against which Lawrence's nineteenth-century predecessors in this role, Carlyle, Ruskin, Morris, had al-

• See Nehls, I, 269, 301, 302.—The beetle image reappears in Lawrence's play *David.* King Saul, in a mood of black despair, prophesies that David's God will be devoured by a beetle which hides in the bottomless pit. *The Plays of D. H. Lawrence* (N.D.), p. 261.

ready expended themselves in valiant invectives. It is manifested rather in various forms of sexual corruption. The degeneration of the African civilization, or of Sodom, did not depend upon the discovery of power-operated lathes or steam shovels. Industrialism may accelerate and will certainly complicate the process, but from his study of history and legend, Lawrence was aware of patterns of human propensities that were independent of how coal and iron are worked, and the differences between what he calls the African process and the Arctic process are not crucial. The end of the slow process of degeneration of past societies was extinction, and a degenerate contemporary society would descend the same slope.

The image of the death-slope is Lawrence's of course rather than mine. It crops up in the novel and also in several of his wartime letters. In August, 1915, he commented brutally on the kind of young man who joins the Roman Catholic Church, or the army, in order to enjoy obeying orders as a "swine with cringing hindquarters." • "I dance with joy when I see him rushing down the Gadarene slope of the war." In the Biblical story (about which Gladstone and T. H. Huxley had had their celebrated controversy) a community infected with evil spirits gains some relief by Christ's intervention, the evil spirits being driven out and into a herd of their swine. The swine, like a horde of lemmings, plunge down a slope into the sea and perish.

For Lawrence's purposes in 1916-17, the story of the Gadarene swine was richly suggestive. Not only did it provide one more analogue for the annihilating plunges taking place between the trenches across the Channel but an image suggesting the combination of swinish sensual corruption with a herd madness, an inexplicable propulsion towards self-destruction. The degenerate society, after exhausting all the possibilities of perverse sensuality represented by Loerke, finds its final thrill, its "voluptuous satisfaction"—a phrase describing Gerald's sensations as his fingers tighten on Gudrun's soft throat—in death itself.

• *Letters,* I, 360. Cf. *Reflections on the Death of a Porcupine,* pp. 83-84. In a Leconte de Lisle-like passage about baboons and their "unthinkable loins," vultures and other creatures, Lawrence pictures the carrion-eating hyena with the same striking phrase: "his cringing, stricken loins."

In his wartime essay, *The Crown,* Lawrence tried to formulate the connections between what he calls "perversity, degradation and death," especially death in war:

> So that as the sex is exhausted, gradually, a keener desire, the desire for the touch of death follows on . . . Then come . . . fatal wars and revolutions which really create nothing at all, but destroy, and leave emptiness.

Those who prefer to lay the sources of war conveniently at the door of the munitions-makers will derive little satisfaction from Lawrence's recognition of destructive madness: "we go careering down the slope in our voluptuousness of death and horror . . . into oblivion, like Hippolytus trammelled up and borne away in the traces of his maddened horses." [41]

X

The most effective use of the image of the slope occurs during the coming together of Ursula and Birkin on the night before their marriage. After a violent quarrel with her father about her proposed marriage, she arrives at Birkin's cottage in tears:

> He went over to her and kissed her fine, fragile hair, touching her wet cheeks gently.
>
> 'Don't cry,' he repeated, 'don't cry any more.' He held her head close against him, very close and quiet.
>
> At last she was still. Then she looked up, her eyes wide and frightened.
>
> 'Don't you want me?' she asked.
>
> 'Want you?' His darkened, steady eyes puzzled her and did not give her play.

As in scenes from stories and novels already discussed, the exchange of feelings through the eyes is emphasized, and the ascent from the downward slope culminates in a poignantly rendered coming together:

'Do I look ugly?' she said. And she blew her nose again.

A small smile came round his eyes . . . And he went across to her, and gathered her like a belonging in his arms. She was so tenderly beautiful, he could not bear to see her, he could only bear to hide her against himself. Now, washed all clean by her tears, she was new and frail like a flower just unfolded . . . And he was so old, so steeped in heavy memories. Her soul was new, undefined and glimmering with the unseen. And his soul was dark and gloomy, it had only one grain of living hope, like a grain of mustard seed. But this one living grain in him matched the perfect youth in her.

'I love you,' he whispered as he kissed her, and trembled with pure hope, like a man who is born again to a wonderful, lively hope far exceeding the bounds of death. She could not know how much it meant to him, how much he meant by the few words . . . But the passion of gratitude with which he received her into his soul, the extreme, unthinkable gladness of knowing himself living and fit to unite with her, he, who was so nearly dead, who was so near to being *gone with the rest of his race down the slope of mechanical death,* could never be understood by her. He worshipped her as age worships youth, he gloried in her because, in his one grain of faith, he was young as she, he was her proper mate. This marriage with her was his resurrection and his life. [Italics mine.]

The poignancy of the release from loneliness is similar to the effect of scenes in "Love Among the Haystacks," *The Rainbow, Lady Chatterley's Lover,* and "The Man Who Died," but perhaps most moving of all in this novel because of the overpowering nature of the destructive rhythms and the variety of ways in which they have been made to sound throughout the action. The hero is not a mere visitor full of righteousness; he is himself a citizen of Sodom, infected with a society's hatreds, degeneracy, and desire for death. Whatever the African statue stood for, as I suggested above, attracts all the characters, even at times Ursula, who usually insisted that she was a "rose of happiness" and not one of the Baudelairian flowers. And for Birkin the attraction had been a powerful one. "You are a devil, you know, really," Ursula says to him early in their relationship. "You want to destroy our hope.

You *want* us to be deathly." And later: "You are so *perverse*, so death-eating."

The perversities associated with the statue take in more than being half in love, as Birkin was, with easeful death. What the "further sensual experience" might be which prompted him to his soliloquy, and which he decides to repudiate, has already been indicated. As for the "horror" of homosexuality, there have been readers, beginning with the early reviewers of the novel, who find the "Gladiatorial" and "Man to Man" chapters in this respect obscene. And if Lawrence had included the "Prologue" chapter with which he had originally opened the novel, with its account of Birkin's realization that he likes the bodies of men better than the bodies of women, such readers would have had even more cause for alarm. The problem is extraordinarily complex and (not in the mere squeamish sense) delicate, calling for a nice discrimination between an "abomination" and an ideal relation, a discrimination that some readers may be too impatient to make. In his 1918 essay on Whitman, Lawrence himself struggled to clarify the differentiation which had been assumed in his novel. For having sung of the "love between comrades" Whitman is highly praised by Lawrence as one who had made pioneering efforts on behalf of a great cause. Such a love, provided that it never acts "to destroy marriage" is recommended as healthy and life-giving. If it becomes an alternative to married love instead of a supplement, it is, on the contrary, deathly.[42] The *Blutbrüderschaft* that Birkin wanted to establish with Gerald was supposedly a life-giving relationship not to be confused with the deathly degeneracies evoked in his soliloquy.

With the help of the Whitman essay, this distinction can perhaps be grasped, although as the final page of the novel shows, Ursula herself adamantly refused to grasp it. "I wanted eternal union with a man too: another kind of love," Birkin says wistfully.

> 'I don't believe it,' she said. 'It's an obstinacy, a theory, a perversity.'

More difficult to grasp, however, is the parallel differentiation between some of the corruptive relations suggested by the statue and the innocence of exploratory relations between men and women as lovers. And here Ursula can, herself, be the spokeswoman for the innocence. At the ski-resort she reflects as she is going to sleep:

> They might do as they liked . . . How could anything that gave one satisfaction be excluded? What was degrading? . . . Why not be bestial, and go the whole round of experience? She exulted in it.

This passage is only slightly veiled and offers few problems. What was puzzling is the earlier scene at an English inn when Ursula discovers in Birkin's body "the source of the deepest life-force."

> She had thought there was no source deeper than the phallic source. And now, behold, from the smitten rock of the man's body, from the strange marvellous flanks and thighs, deeper, further in mystery than the phallic source, came the floods of ineffable darkness and ineffable riches.

In 1961, G. Wilson Knight set out to explain what Lawrence was picturing in this curious scene by citing lines from the love poems in which the woman "put her hand on my secret, darkest sources, the darkest outgoings." As might be expected, Knight's explanation prompted an outburst of angry articles in the magazines, most of them concerned with *Lady Chatterley's Lover*. Indeed the novel went on trial, in effect, for a second time. A lawyer, the Warden of All Souls at Oxford, discovered that in one of the several sexual encounters described in that novel, intercourse in the Italian style had been practised.[43] It had also been occasionally practised, it seems, by Will and Anna in *The Rainbow* and by Birkin and Ursula in the scene in the Tyrol referred to above.

For the present discussion I am not going to be concerned with the legal or even the aesthetic aspects of the practice beyond simply endorsing Mark Spilka's comment (made several years before the controversy became prominent) that Lawrence treats it as an act having a limited function which, as a Puritan, he seems to have thought can serve as a kind of "discovery and purification."[44] What is relevant here is not whether some sort of Ovidian

Ars amatoria could be compiled from Lawrence's writings, but whether the passages cited from *Women in Love* represent a serious artistic blunder on the part of the novelist, creating such a blur that the theme of the novel, and the drama of the hero's development, are both hopelessly obscured. More specifically, if the "dreadful mysteries, far beyond the phallic cult" associated with the beetle-faced statue are represented in one scene as degenerate and in another scene (with only a slight shift in terminology) as redemptive—when Ursula is transfigured by her discovery of a "source deeper than the phallic source"—how is a reader supposed to respond to what seems like a total contradiction?

Of the many critical discussions of *Women in Love,* the only one which I have encountered that even raises some of the questions that I have been trying to grapple with here is that by Eliseo Vivas. Vivas' conclusion is that Lawrence introduced a contradiction which is seemingly not resolved, because the novelist has pictured Birkin as rejecting "the African process" and then shown him as, in effect, succumbing to it.[45] On these grounds we might throw up our hands and say of Lawrence himself what Ursula, in a fit of pique, said of Birkin: "He says one thing one day, and another the next—and he always contradicts himself." What may be enjoyed as a colorful trait in a fictional character is not necessarily a commendable asset in the artist who created the fictional character. Fiction can be great when it is tentative and exploratory, making us aware of the puzzling complexities of choice confronting the characters, but if it is merely muddled it will not stand.

As when discussing the cathedral scene in *The Rainbow* I myself suggest again that although Lawrence may be asking too much of us in his account of Birkin's development, the sequence itself is not a muddled one. We are being expected to discriminate between sensual experiences enjoyed by a pair of loving men and women (which are regarded by the novelist as innocently enjoyed) on the one hand, and degenerate indulgences of a society which has cut all connections with spiritual values on the other. Perhaps like the comparable discrimination we were expected to make between a full-fledged homosexual relationship and *Blutbrüderschaft* we may, despite the cluster of horrors associated with the statue, find the distinction too fine, too naïve even, for the stretch of our patience. Yet if we are to understand the development of the characters as well as the social background against which their relations are worked out, the effort to establish the distinction is one worth making. Again, as with the discussion of Whitman, we can derive some help from one of Lawrence's essays. In *Pornography and Obscenity* he writes:

> The sex functions and the excrementory functions in the human body work so close together, yet they are, so to speak, utterly different in direction. Sex is a creative flow, the excrementory flow is towards dissolution, de-creation, if we may use such a word. In the really healthy human being the distinction between the two is instant, our profoundest instincts are perhaps our instincts of opposition between the two flows. But in the degraded human being the deep instincts have gone dead, and then the two flows become identical . . . It happens when the psyche deteriorates, and the profound controlling instincts collapse.[46]

The discriminatory effort required in this instance, it may be added, is called for in many other places of this story, for *Women in Love* is one of the most demanding of novels. The kind of complexities encountered in discussing the two soliloquies, Birkin's and Gudrun's, which I have been treating expansively here, could be demonstrated again in connection with what Vivas has called the "constitutive" symbols of which the novel is full—the great scene of Birkin stoning the moonlit water for example,[47] or the winter scenes in the mountains culminating in Gerald's confronting another statue, a Tyrolian Christ sticking up out of the snow "under a little sloping hood, at the top of a pole."

What I have been stressing myself is that the complexities derive much of their density from Lawrence's choosing to portray Birkin in particular not as a White Knight, incorrupt and incorruptible, but as a suffering character dramatically involved in extricating himself from a death-loving world to which he is deeply, almost fatally, attracted. Like Conrad in similar presentation of Kurtz and Marlow, Lawrence in this way perhaps doubles the difficulties confronting his readers, but the clear gain in the overall effectiveness of his novel as a novel is beyond measurement. In a society made up of "a herd of Gadarene swine, rushing possessed to extinction,"[48] Gerald Crich is clearly infected with the madness and perishes. Birkin himself is a near casualty. As Wilfred Owen says in his haunting late fragment, *Strange Meeting:* "Foreheads of men have bled where no wounds were." But these affinities (or lack of them) between Birkin and his industrialist friend can be more conveniently developed in a brief *Exeunt* chapter.

9 Escape from Sodom: The Dance of Life

"The war will go on for a very long time . . . I feel, that even if we are all going to be rushed down to extinction, one must . . . speak for life and growth, amid all this mass of destruction and disintegration."

—Letter to Harriet Monroe, September 18, 1915

In a lively critique appearing in *The Twentieth Century* Sir Herbert Read, after citing, with what seems to be amusement, the claim of Dr. Leavis that *The Rainbow* and *Women in Love* "are the greatest novels in the English language," adds this comment:

> And Angus Wilson, reviewing Dr. Leavis's book in *Encounter*, says that *Women in Love* 'has a form as strict as some court dance.' A *court* dance! Perhaps a folk dance, to the music of scrannel pipes—one cannot deny that there is some impulsive energy at play.[1]

While the sounds of *ho ho ho* are dying away—a *court* dance indeed—we may pause to inquire into the set of assumptions underlying Sir Herbert's joke. Perhaps because Lawrence was capable of clumsy bungling in such productions as *Kangaroo* (as indeed he was) it is assumed that in none of his books can we expect an artful construction. Assumptions of this sort may calcify the critical arteries to such a degree that the novel under discussion does not get the considerate examination it deserves. Subtle counterpointing, or whatever is its choreographic equivalent, *Women in Love* has in abundance. The intricate linking of scene to scene, the pairings, variations, crossings, repetitions, as the four lovers live out their parts, reinforced from time to time by further variations introduced by other characters, by Hermione and Loerke in particular, surely justify the analogy to an artfully designed and patterned dance. Yes, a court dance.

To say that the basic pattern of the novel features one pair of lovers representing a dance of life and the other pair a dance of death is, of course, a crude simplification which must be constantly corrected in what follows, yet it can stand as a point of departure. From the opening scenes in which Gudrun and Ursula discuss the possibilities of love and marriage, through the debates between Gerald and Birkin on the same subject, the four central characters are seen in the typical Laurentian role of seeking to establish relationships. One pair succeeds; the other fails. Ursula and Birkin escape from Sodom; Gudrun and Gerald remain caught up in it. Gerald in fact suffers a fate similar to Lot's wife who was transformed into a pillar of salt, he to a column of ice, his "shapely" face "frozen like an ice pebble."

How is the differentiation between the pairs indicated? Or is it indicated? Ever since the time of Middleton Murry's early review of the novel a criticism recurrently made is that the relationships are identical. The novelist, it is said, has neglected to provide clues to prepare us for the different fates encountered by the contrasted pairs of the quartet. In one respect, at least, the criticism is sound enough although irrelevant. As indicated earlier, passages from *The Rainbow* describing the sexual gratifications experienced by one pair of lovers could be transposed to describe the gratifications of another pair of lovers, without incongruity. And why not?

In *Women in Love* it is in the context of the act, not the act itself, that the differentiations are indicated. The first union of Birkin and Ursula occurs in Sherwood Forest—the name itself is effectively evocative—and the chapter concludes with their happy awakening in the morning light after their discovery of each other in the darkness. The following chapter, in which the first sexual union of Gerald and Gudrun occurs, opens with this sentence: "Thomas Crich died slowly, terribly slowly," and every detail—most strikingly the clay from his father's grave that clings to Gerald's boots as he enters Gudrun's bedroom—reinforces the linking of their kind of love with death.

Representationally there is no comparison between the effectiveness of the two scenes; the Sherwood Forest sequence is relatively undistinguished, especially in the unfortunate comparison of Birkin as a car-driver to an Egyptian Pharaoh, whereas the scene in Gudrun's bedroom is brilliantly rendered.

What we are concerned with at the moment, however, is not the effectiveness of the representation but rather whether the novelist has provided adequate indications of differences. And once again, surely, what is being required of the reader is simply to rely on his senses, including his sense of smell:

> Into her he poured all his pent-up darkness and corrosive death, and he was whole again. . . . The terrible frictional violence of death filled her, and she received it in an ecstasy of subjection, in throes of acute, violent sensation . . . And he was a child, so soothed and restored and full of gratitude.

As Gudrun lies awake afterwards listening for the striking of the hours on the church clock we are prepared for the later scenes of her haunted consciousness of time passing, "the terrible bondage of this tick-tack of time," accentuated by her awareness of her sister's happiness in marriage. The contrast culminates, of course, in the Tyrol where Ursula and Birkin, oppressed by the lifeless scene of ice and snow, elect to escape southwards to Italy with its growth and greenery, leaving the other pair in the icy setting which suits their kind of love, or love-hate.

Even before the incident in Gudrun's bedroom in Beldover, the contrast between the pairs of lovers is built up in other ways, often by pairs of scenes. One of the most vivid of these, the generally admired scene in which Gudrun and Gerald subdue a rabbit, is especially effective in making us sense the perverse quality of one relationship and in preparing us for the contrasting scene of the chapter succeeding it in which Ursula watches Birkin shattering the moon's image. On both occasions a vigorous conflict in the relationship between a man and a woman is brought before us, but one conflict ends in a friendly pact while the other with a pact Lawrence calls a "mutual hellish recognition."

The term *pact* may remind us of an earlier incident when Birkin, in a moment of happiness, had proposed to Gerald that they should swear a *Blutbrüderschaft*—without an actual mingling of blood from their arms but as an oath of love. Gerald had backed away from the suggestion. Now, in the later scene, after the rabbit has slashed Gerald's wrists and those of Gudrun, he commits himself to a different pact, this one literally sealed with blood. Their communion, conveyed again by what their eyes tell of their desires, is an initiation into a rite not of love but of "abhorrent mysteries."

> She lifted her arm and showed a deep red score down the silken white flesh.
>
> 'What a devil!' he exclaimed. But it was as if he had had knowledge of her in the long red rent of her forearm, so silken and soft . . . The long, shallow red rip seemed torn across his own brain, tearing the surface of his ultimate consciousness, letting through the forever unconscious, unthinkable red ether of the beyond, the obscene beyond.

Another extraordinarily effective detail in this scene is that Gerald is dressed for riding, and as he brings his hand down on the rabbit's neck to subdue its frantic struggles, with Gudrun watching him admiringly, we are reminded of the earlier recognition scene when she had watched him subdue his mare, forcing it to endure the sights and sounds of the noisy railway train—a kind of rape and blood-letting which produced in her what seems a kind of orgasm:

> 'And she's bleeding! She's bleeding!' cried Ursula, frantic with opposition and hatred of Gerald. She alone understood him perfectly, in pure opposition.
>
> Gudrun looked and saw the trickles of blood on the sides of the mare, and she turned white. And then on the very wound the bright spurs came down, pressing relentlessly. The world reeled and passed into nothingness for Gudrun, she could not know any more.

(An interesting comparison can be made to the scene of Vronsky's breaking the back of his mare during the race in *Anna*

Karenina, for in both scenes the man's handling of his mare forecasts for us the nature of his relationships with women.)

In both the rabbit and horse scenes it is worth noting that Lawrence is not writing as a member of the Humane Society. The kind of pity Hardy calls for in his accounts of suffering rabbits (a pity characteristic of much writing in England since the eighteenth century) is not Lawrence's concern. Bismark, his rabbit, may represent one of the forces of nature that Gerald enjoys subduing, a dangerous "black-and-white tempest," but there is no sentiment lavished on the creature. He is vividly, but hardly endearingly, brought to life before us. The emphasis is on how the characters feel, what attracts and repels them. A kind of triangulation is characteristic of the staging of both the horse and rabbit scenes; the animals serve the same purpose as the African statue when Birkin and Gerald are inspecting it, or Loerke's sculpture as seen by Ursula and Gudrun; in each instance the animal or the object is the apex of a triangle, a point of focus enabling us to recognize in particular what it is that the characters are thrilled by. As Lawrence said bitterly to Aldous Huxley after reading *Point Counter Point* (its portrait of a depraved society having appalled him):

> It is as you say—intellectual appreciation doesn't amount to so much, it's what you thrill to. And if murder, suicide, rape is what you thrill to, and nothing else, then it's your destiny . . . You live by what you thrill to.

The ultimate palpitating thrill, he added (perhaps thinking back to his own exposure of war in *Women in Love*), would be a "super-war" which would sweep away "the vast bulk of mankind."

When Richard Aldington complained that the "depravity" in the rabbit scene is "worked-up" he seems to have been overlooking how crucial such a scene is if we are to understand the violent drives that dominate the affair between Gerald and Gudrun. The tensions between them are such that their relationship culminates in the man being driven to death by the woman after he has half-strangled her with the same strong "sinewy" hands that she had admired subduing the tempestuous rabbit.

In December, 1915, Lawrence was delighted to inspect a recently published volume of illustrations, *Ajanta Frescoes*, many of the scenes featuring happy lovers in dance-like poses. These ancient paintings, representing a gracious pre-Hindu civilization which had flourished 1400 years ago, moved him deeply. "Botticelli is vulgar beside them," he noted.

> They are the zenith of a very lovely civilisation, the crest of a very perfect wave of human development. I love them beyond everything pictorial that I have ever seen—the perfect, perfect intimate relation between the men and the women; so simple and complete, such a very perfection of passion, a fulness, a whole blossom.[2]

Perhaps Lawrence's pleasure was aroused by his seeing in these illustrations a kind of pictorial equivalent of the ideal love relationship he would try to show between Ursula and Birkin, and, in addition, a contrast to the different kind of relationship that would exist between Gudrun and Gerald:

> That which we [in the western world] call passion is a very one-sided thing, based chiefly on hatred and *Wille zur Macht*. There is no Will to Power here—it is so lovely—in these frescoes.

Of this western kind of passion Gerald's affair with Gudrun is a compelling study. The significance of the relationship is enhanced effectively by the repeated linking of Gerald's role as a lover to his role as an industrial leader. With the ruthlessness of some of the generals on the Western Front he successfully imposes his will on his workmen, yoking them to his concept of mechanical efficiency, and persuading them, with telling effect, to share his values. Lawrence himself remains the realistic novelist in this account of industrial relations, for so far as I can see he himself has no solution to propose. The Cheeryble-like father of Gerald, who believed in a benevolent paternalism, is represented as hopelessly out of place in a society which finds its satisfactions in mechanical improvements; the workmen much prefer what Gerald stands for. What we do get is not a solution to a problem, but a study of the industrialist himself, and the pitiable sense of "nothingness" he experiences after he has got his machine running smoothly, and there seems no further outlet for the imposition of his will. As a lover he experiences a similar sense of nothingness after he has exerted in that role his "one-sided *Wille zur Macht*."

The possibility that all passion derives its pleasures from the imposition of will—a cynical theory abhorrent to Lawrence—was explored by the eighteenth-century French novelist, Choderlos de Laclos, in his *Les Liaisons dangereuses* (1782) and 175 years later by another French novelist, Roger Vailland, in *La Loi* (1957). As one of Vailland's characters remarks in that novel, the act of copulation is in itself only a minor pleasure and would be the same with a goat as with a woman; true pleasure consists in conquest, in the game of forcing the other party to accept the humiliating role the conqueror imposes (at the outset of their relationship, Gudrun announces confidently to Gerald that she has not only struck the first blow but will strike the last—as she does).

Gerald is, of course, much more complicatedly motivated than is Vailland's game-player. In his constant searching he *wants* to find love and affection, but as he himself admits, he never finds them. What he experiences instead is the thrill of sexual conquest and also, as the frenzied finale of his death dance illustrates, he discovers hate. At the end he is more lonely and isolated than was Walter Morel in his household in *Sons and Lovers*, more lonely than even Gudrun herself. His tragedy is not so much the emptiness of his economic role but his lack of inner fulfillment in relations with others. And his suicide is one of those rare instances of an effective finale which the reader feels is appropriate to the character's situation and state of mind.•

• On the level of *roman à clef* it may be pointed out that none of the men who seem to have served as models for the portrait of Gerald was led to suicide. On the other hand, Philip Heseltine, the model for Halliday in *Women in Love*, died of gas poisoning in 1930, and Mark Gertler, the painter who contributed to Lawrence's creation of Loerke, succeeded in committing suicide in 1939 after more than one earlier attempt. Others of the set who committed suicide, including Carrington, an art student with whom Gertler was in love, are listed in David Garnett's *The Familiar Faces* (1962), p. xv.

II

The trouble with stressing this basic contrasting pattern of death dance and life dance as I have so far been doing is readily apparent. The novel begins to sound as if it were retelling the parable of the Wise Virgins and the Foolish Virgins. Such a simplified contrast would have an unfortunate effect on our response to the book. As readers of fiction we should find only one pair of lovers interesting; the other pair would not fully engage our attention. Gerald, who had accidentally shot his brother, is likened by Lawrence more than once to Cain, and as fictional characters, the Cains are always more interesting than the Abels. Perhaps for this reason most of the best discussions of *Women in Love,* including those by Schorer and Leavis, have stressed Gerald's role at the expense of Birkin's. As Schorer concludes: "Gerald is not the saint, he is the sinner; he is—us." [3] This is well said, but a good word for Birkin needs to be got in as well.

Having emphasized for the moment the basic contrast, I should like to resume the line of argument developed in the previous chapter that by the intricate interplay of his double rhythms in this book Lawrence enables us to appreciate his leading character not as a saint but as a character.

At the end of the novel as Birkin is tearfully confronting the frozen corpse of his dead friend, he recalls the saying of some French religious teacher that God cannot do without man. And he reflects:

> But surely this is false. God can do without man. God could do without the ichthyosauri and the mastodon. These monsters failed creatively to develop, so God, the creative mystery, dispensed with them.

The reference to the dinosaurs here picks up a scene hundreds of pages earlier in the book in which the sociologist, Sir Joshua Malleson, and some other guests at a house party are pictured swimming in the pond at Breadalby:

'Aren't they really terrifying?' said Gudrun. 'Don't they look saurian? They are just like great lizards. Did you ever see anything like Sir Joshua? But really, Ursula, he belongs to the primeval world, when great lizards crawled about.'

Gudrun looked in dismay on Sir Joshua, who stood up to the breast in the water, his long, greyish hair washed down into his eyes, his neck set into thick, crude shoulders. He was talking to Miss Bradley, who, seated on the bank above, plump and big and wet, looked as if she might roll and slither in the water almost like one of the slithering sea-lions in the Zoo.

By introducing the vast stretches of geological time, the effect of both passages, one satiric and the other tragic, is to enlarge the dimensions even further than the references to extinct civilizations such as Sodom, and to make us aware that the novel treats not only of how civilizations may die but how species themselves may become extinct.

If we ask how man is to evade the fate of the saurians or of the Sodomites we may turn to a passage written by Lawrence after the war. Because it recapitulates the cataclysms and declines pictured in *Women in Love,* it is of special interest:

Floods and fire and convulsions and ice-arrest intervene between the great glamorous civilizations of mankind. But nothing will ever quench humanity and the human potentiality to evolve something magnificent out of a renewed chaos.[4]

This heart-lifting prediction, with its stress on *human* potentiality, is from *Fantasia of the Unconscious;* the novel is never quite so assertive. The happy discovery of the lovers is indeed consolatory, but the bleakness with which it is framed keeps the hope distinctly earth-bound. As they are resolving to flee London, Ursula asks Birkin about the rat-like proletarians they had talked with in the furniture market:

'And are they going to inherit the earth?' she said.

'Yes—they.'

'Then what are we going to do?' she asked. 'We're not like them—are we? We're not the meek?'

'No. We've got to live in the chinks they leave us.'

> 'How horrible!' cried Ursula. 'I don't want to live in chinks.'
> 'Don't worry,' he said. 'They . . . like market-places and street-corners best. That leaves plenty of chinks.'

This sort of passage demonstrates that when Lawrence said in his *Foreword* to *Women in Love* that the "bitterness of the war may be taken for granted in the characters," he meant *all* the characters. It is also the kind of passage that produces disappointment in many readers, for if all that the novel seems to propose is that lovers may escape from Sodom only to hide themselves in some remote "chinks" without further social responsibilities—in Taos or Taormina, let us say—the prospect is not, for such readers, an adequately encouraging one. Even Dr. Leavis, in one of his most candid evaluations of the novel, admitted that he was left "wondering" by Birkin and Ursula considered "as a norm." He concluded that at this point Lawrence "has been defeated by the difficulty of life: he hasn't *solved the problems of the civilization he analyses*." [5]

Often as I find myself in agreement with Dr. Leavis when he discusses *Women in Love* as a dramatic poem, I am left "wondering" by the comment I have italicized. Is a novel supposed to *solve* our problems for us? Or is it not enough that it should represent them for us? I do not raise this inquiry in any spirit of flippancy, for the question of whether or not a novel can be enjoyed in much the same way as concerts and ballets are enjoyed underlies most of the disagreements about the fiction we read.

In one of his short stories, James Baldwin pictures a night-club pianist and his band making music that was "not about anything very new" but the players were exerting themselves in the gloom "to find new ways to make us listen."

> For, while the tale of how we suffer, and how we are delighted, and how we may triumph is never new, it always has to be heard. There isn't any other tale to tell, it's the only light we've got in all this darkness.[6]

Would many readers accept this as a description of what they expect from a novel, or are they looking for something more specific? When Birkin reflects on the doom in store for men if they fail, like the saurians, "creatively to develop," are we to expect the novelist to have worked out a program of creative development for us? I can only conclude, lamely enough, that it is, as the academic phrase would have it, a matter of degree. If we demand too much of the novelist, even a novelist such as Lawrence who would welcome the burdensome role of providing solutions, we load his willing back to the breaking point. If what we want is a kind of specific Keynesian blueprinted policy to save a sagging economy, we might as well throw Lawrence back to the lions of the 1930's. And for the more immediate issue, if the author of *Women in Love* had reached a "solution" to the problems of the 1914-18 war period, one thing is clearly evident: the character of Birkin, and of Ursula too, would be so deficient of drama as to be without interest. Lawrence's failure, relatively speaking, to "solve" the problems of wartime civilization may have been the world's loss but it was his novel's gain.

III

By way of recapitulation a brief scene from the chapter titled "In the Train" may be helpful, and a convenient lead into the scene is provided by a passage from the letters. Despite his admiration of Conrad's early writings, Lawrence became exasperated by his predecessor's pessimism: "But why this giving in before you start, that pervades all Conrad and such folks—the Writers among the Ruins. I can't forgive Conrad for being so sad and for giving in." In a similar vein he complained of another predecessor, Arnold Bennett: "I hate England and its hopelessness. I hate Bennett's resignation. Tragedy ought really to be a great kick at misery."[7] In this comment we have one of the two voices that we encounter in Lawrence's fiction. It is a reassuringly vigorous voice, positive and assertive, a voice that to the ears of some commentators seems to be the only utterance he ever used. It may be noted, however, that his condemnation of Conrad as a Writer among the Ruins was delivered in 1912. Four years later, writing *Women in Love* in the mist of the frenzied tensions of war, he did not himself give in, but he certainly experienced what it was like to feel as Conrad had felt.

As Birkin and Gerald ride on the train from Beldover into London they are led into a discussion of the possible end of the world, a discussion cited in my preceding chapter. What prompts them on this occasion to air a topic that keeps reappearing throughout the novel is that Birkin's despair has brought to his mind Browning's poem, *Love Among the Ruins:*

> Birkin watched the country, and was filled with a sort of hopelessness. He always felt this, on approaching London. His dislike of mankind . . . amounted almost to an illness.
>
> 'Where the quiet coloured end of evening smiles
> Miles and miles—'
>
> he was murmuring to himself, like a man condemned to death. Gerald . . . leaned forward and asked smilingly:
>
> 'What were you saying?' Birkin glanced at him, laughed, and repeated:
>
> 'Where the quiet coloured end of evening smiles,
> Miles and miles,
> Over pastures where the something something sheep
> Half asleep—'

The irony that can be enjoyed when we put this passage beside the letter criticizing Conrad is of small consequence. What is of consequence is that this brief dialogue condenses into a few lines the main themes of the whole novel. Among the several alternative titles such as *Day of Wrath* that Lawrence considered for his novel, he might have added *Love Among the Ruins* as equally appropriate. The passage is, moreover, an excellent example of Lawrence's analogical method, or, more precisely, one of his analogical methods.

Of the absurdities into which injudicious symbol-hunting may involve critics of Lawrence we need continued reminders,* but

* What ought to be required reading for anyone proposing to discuss symbols in Lawrence's writings or, for that matter, symbols in any twentieth-century writings, is an essay by Patricia Abel and Robert Hogan, "D. H. Lawrence's

such a caution must not obscure how heavily he relies upon symbol or analogue to create the particular texture of his best novels. To demonstrate this general point, it is instructive to contrast the account of Gerald and Birkin journeying on the train and their further experiences in London with a comparable sequence in a novel by a chastely non-symbolic contemporary writer, Kingsley Amis.

Four chapters of Mr. Amis's novel, *Take a Girl Like You*, are devoted to recording a trip to London taken by two men. They visit London shows and cafés, and the hero, like Gerald, has a brief affair and then returns home. At no point in these four chapters does the novelist introduce even a hint of a comparison between his hero's activities and those of any other hero of any other place and time. The picaresque action remains exclusively on one level and fully engages our attention as such. If the hero were to encounter a West African statue at someone's apartment, it would be simply a piece of furniture or a prop, not something to set the characters (and readers) speculating about man's fate, present, past, and future. And if Mr. Amis's hero were to recite a snatch of lines from Browning (a less likely event) it would remain in the context of the dialogue and never require us to stretch our memories and imagination to relate the microcosm to an implied macrocosm. Let me hasten to add that I am not seeking to belittle Mr. Amis's novel and to demonstrate his inferiority in Lawrence's company. Unlike most of his reviewers, I found *Take a Girl Like You* to be engaging comedy. I am merely trying to emphasize the

---

Singing Birds," an essay ostensibly devoted to explaining a paragraph of *The Rainbow*. This solemn-faced parody of the prevailing critical clichés (especially those of the imitators of Northrop Frye) which loom large in our critical and scholarly journals, is so cleverly done that it often misfires. I have found that almost all graduate students will read it without a flicker of a smile, and the fact that it has been reprinted in collections of essays about Lawrence, seemingly as a serious contribution to scholarship, has sometimes made me fear for my own sanity in regarding it as a clever burlesque. Undergraduate readers, however, have been more reassuring in their response to it. Less corrupted by the mythological patter of our highbrow reviews, they soon recognize that a hoax is being perpetrated, a pile-driver being employed to crush a peanut almost in the manner of Pope's *Rape of the Lock*. The essay is reprinted in H. T. Moore's *Miscellany* of Lawrence criticism (1959), pp. 204-14.

differences between an eighteenth-century style of fast-paced and lively one-dimensional narrative and the highly-wrought multi-leveled scenes of which *Women in Love* is made up.

In his study of allegory, *Dark Conceit,* Edwin Honig notes:

> The primary function of the analogical or of any symbolic system is not properly to get at a philosophical truth but to employ the symbol in its simultaneous progressive and retrogressive direction, thereby making history and experience meaningful.[8]

This describes very well the function of Lawrence's analogical methods. By parallels with the Bible, with classical myth, with history and legend, he surrounds his characters with clusters of associations which endow their individual experiences with historical significance, or more importantly, general human significance. This feature of his writing has been abundantly illustrated in discussions both of *The Rainbow* and of *Women in Love.* Another closely related analogical method is represented by the passage from Browning's poem. As in the scene in *Lady Chatterley's Lover* in which snatches of Swinburne's poems about Proserpine float into Connie's consciousness,[9] here again the novelist assumes that the fragmentary quotation will evoke in his reader's mind the whole poem, and that the situation in which one despairing man finds himself as he watches London through the train window will thereby become more meaningful because of its repeating, with variations, the situation experienced by another.

The speaker in Browning's monologue is about to join the girl he loves who is waiting for him in the ruins of a tower of what was once the site "of a city great and gay." Throughout the poem, with its curiously halting movement, the speaker's anticipated happiness in love is repeatedly played off against his haunted awareness that great civilizations become extinct and disappear with scarcely a trace. In the wide plain, love is both celebrated and dwarfed by the immense backdrop of time and space. The contrasting rhythms culminate in the familiar final stanza:

> In one year they sent a million fighters forth
> South and North,
> And they built their gods a brazen pillar high
> As the sky,

Yet reserved a thousand chariots in full force—
Gold, of course.
Oh heart! oh blood that freezes, blood that burns!
Earth's returns
For whole centuries of folly, noise and sin!
Shut them in,
With their triumphs and their glories and the rest!
Love is best.

Against Browning's finale the same complaint can be leveled as was urged against Birkin's proposed resolution of his misanthropy and despair through love. In the train he says to Gerald:

> 'It seems to me there remains only this perfect union with a woman—sort of ultimate marriage—and there isn't anything else.'
> 'And you mean if there isn't the woman, there's nothing?' said Gerald.
> 'Pretty well that—seeing there's no God.'

Like "Love is best" Birkin's prescription hardly solves the problems of civilization, but in its very limitation it keeps Birkin alive in more senses than one. A more damaging criticism might be that the statement suffers because it is direct rather than oblique, and that it seems so simple a commonplace, so rigorously assertive, as virtually to invite our dissent. Extracted out of context "Love is best" becomes merely one of those formulae elaborately stitched on linen and framed for bedtime edification which now amuse us in old-fashioned boarding-house rooms. Within the grim context of both the novel and the poem, however, with the dramatically contrasting evocations of impermanence, corruption, and hate, it is not contemptible; it has force.

Frieda Lawrence, who had suffered painful experiences throughout the period in which *Women in Love* was written, was later able to look back over the war years with a new perspective and to recognize that something had been gained. "Life is life only when death is part of it," she wrote. "I think the great gain of the war is a new reincorporation of death into our lives." [10]

Notes and Index

Notes

ABBREVIATIONS

Letters: *The Collected Letters of D. H. Lawrence*, ed. Harry T. Moore (1962), 2 vols.
Letters (Huxley): *The Letters of D. H. Lawrence*, ed. Aldous Huxley (1932).
Nehls: *D. H. Lawrence: A Composite Biography*, ed. Edward Nehls (Madison, Wisconsin, 1957-59), 3 vols.
Miscellany: *A D. H. Lawrence Miscellany*, ed. Harry T. Moore (Carbondale, Illinois, 1959).
Phoenix: *Phoenix: The Posthumous Papers of D. H. Lawrence*, ed. Edward McDonald (1936).
Poems: *The Complete Poems of D. H. Lawrence*, ed. Vivian de Sola Pinto and Warren Roberts (New York, 1964), 2 vols.

CHAPTER 1

1 Karl Shapiro, Introduction to *The Tropic of Cancer* by Henry Miller (New York, 1961), p. v. Miller's book, *The World of Lawrence*, has not been published so far as I know. A fragment from it appears in his *Wisdom of the Heart* (1947), pp. 161-73. See also his *Sunday After The War* (1945), pp. 220-61.

2 *Assorted Articles* (1930), p. 150.

3 Resemblances between Lawrence and Dickens have rarely been commented on. A helpful lead for an essay is offered by Peter Coveney in his book on children in literature: "With both novelists there was indeed the tendency to ineffectual and often irresponsible outcry, the same ever-present danger of over-statement, of squandering emotion in self-pity and social recrimination. With both men there was an inability to exorcise, perhaps to forgive the past."—*Poor Monkey* (1957), p. 73. See also *Dickens and the Twentieth Century*, ed. John Gross and Gabriel Pearson (1962), pp. 62-63.

4 See K. A. Porter, "A Wreath for the Gamekeeper." *Encounter*, XIV (1960), 71-73. It is suggestive to set beside Huxley's report a remark by Joyce concerning his pleasure in talking with clerks and waiters. "I never met a bore," he said. See Richard Ellman, *James Joyce*, p. 5, and Huxley's Introduction to *The Letters of D. H. Lawrence* (1932), p. xxxi.

5 "E.T.," *D. H. Lawrence* (1935), p. 121.

6 Even admirers admit that some of Lawrence's best writings are almost repellent upon first reading. See e.g., Leavis' admission that to "get through" *Women in Love* requires "great determination," *For Continuity* (Cambridge, 1933), p. 120. Rebecca West noted that the images in the same novel "do not give up their meaning till the book has been read many times." *D. H. Lawrence* (1930), p. 39. Concerning similar difficul-

ties in *The Rainbow* see E. W. Tedlock, Jr., *D. H. Lawrence: Artist and Rebel* (Albuquerque, New Mexico, 1963), pp. 91-96.

7 Walter Allen, *The English Novel* (1954), pp. 328-29. R. P. Blackmur, who is much less well-disposed to Lawrence, also notes that his genius was such that he is "an obstacle that cannot be gotten round." *Anni Mirabiles: 1921-1925* (Washington, 1956), p. 16.

8 R. Langbaum, *The Poetry of Experience* (1957), p. 37n.

9 Armin Arnold, *D. H. Lawrence and America* (1958), p. 163.

10 Samuel Hynes, *The Pattern of Hardy's Poetry* (Chapel Hill, 1961), p. 3.

11 *TLS* (Jan. 5, 1961), p. 10.

12 Quoted by H. Coombes, "D. H. Lawrence Placed," *Scrutiny,* XVI (1949), 45.

13 *Apocalypse* (New York, 1932), p. 6. In a similar vein he reports in his essay, *The Crown,* that he could not reread Tolstoy's *War and Peace* because, for him, a single reading had exhausted all its meaning.

14 See Kingsley Widmer, *The Art of Perversity* (Seattle, 1962).

15 E.g., see William York Tindall, *Forces in Modern British Literature* (New York, 1956), p. 226, and *D. H. Lawrence and Susan his Cow* (New York, 1939), p. 113. Stephen Potter's early study of Lawrence also stresses the importance of *The Plumed Serpent* as the novel in which Lawrence reached a solution to his problems, a reading ably replied to by Paul de Reul in his *L'oeuvre de D. H. Lawrence* (Paris, 1937), pp. 8-9.

16 *Letters,* II, 859.

17 A further inducement to avoid a full-scale discussion of *Lady Chatterley's Lover* was offered by the publication in 1963 of Julian Moynahan's *Deed of Life.* His chapter on this novel seems to be the best estimate so far to have appeared. Also perceptive is Ian Gregor's critical chapter, "The Novel as Prophecy," in *The Moral and the Story* (1962), which sympathetically confronts the basic flaw in this novel.

18 In an essay generally unsympathetic to Lawrence and his readers, Sir Herbert Read says bluntly that "his novels exude some *ressentiment* of the little man, perhaps of the provincial little man . . . who imagines he is despised by women; so that people of this kind, who sense this strain in Lawrence, become his passionate advocate." *The Twentieth Century,* CLXV (June, 1959), 558.

19 George Orwell, *A Collection of Essays* (New York, 1954), p. 121.

20 Graham Greene, *The Lost Childhood* (New York, 1952), pp. 51-53.

21 W. P. Ker, *Browning.* In *Essays and Studies by Members of the English Association* (1910), p. 70.

CHAPTER 2

1 See W. B. Stanford, *The Ulysses Theme* (Oxford, 1954), especially chapters XIV, XV, XVI.

2 See Marvin Mudrick, "The Originality of *The Rainbow.*" In *Miscellany,* pp. 56-82.

3 *Letters,* I, 488.

4 Mark Schorer, "*Women in Love* and Death." In *D. H. Lawrence: A Collection of Critical Essays,* ed. Mark Spilka (Prentice-Hall, Inc., 1963), p. 60.

5 "E.T.," *D. H. Lawrence,* p. 105.

6 Levin's essay was first published in the *Massachusetts Review* (August, 1960), and reprinted in *Varieties of Literary Experience,* ed. Stanley Burnshaw (New York, 1962). See also John Holloway,

The Chartered Mirror (1962), pp. 143-45.

7 *Phoenix,* p. 327.

8 Nehls, II, 196.

9 Lawrence's insights into the role of darkness in American literature is referred to in *The Power of Blackness* by Harry Levin (1958), p. 154.

10 *Letters* (Huxley), p. 255.

11 *Letters,* I, 368.

CHAPTER 3

1 *Letters,* II, 1079. On the proportion of sexual descriptions see also Richard Hoggart's *Introduction* to the Penguin edition of *Lady Chatterley's Lover.*

2 See *The Dickens Critics,* ed. G. H. Ford and Lauriat Lane, Jr. (Ithaca, 1961), pp. 358-59.

3 J. V. Kelleher in *Portraits of an Artist,* ed. W. E. Morris and C. A. Nault (New York, 1962), p. 85.

4 *Letters,* I, 191.

5 Some distinguished critics, including Mark Schorer, would probably disagree with this reading. To them *Sons and Lovers* fails to account for the hero's frustrations. Their argument is summed up in Norman Friedman's article in *PMLA,* LXX (Dec. 1955), 1183-84. The case seems to me to lean too hard on Jessie Chambers' understandably disappointed reaction to the novel rather than on the novel itself. See "E.T.," *D. H. Lawrence,* pp. 201-04. A different kind of inquiry might be worth raising. If Paul is crippled as a lover of women, does the novelist explore the possibility that his hero might, therefore, be inclined to be a lover of men? Despite the strange relationship between Paul and the man he has cuckolded, Baxter Dawes, *Sons and Lovers* has less to say about male relationships than several other novels by Lawrence. According to Frank O'Connor, however, this relationship is of crucial importance because it interferes with our understanding of Paul's relations with Clara. The second half of *Sons and Lovers* is therefore a failure by comparison with the triumphant first half (the latter is ranked by O'Connor as "the greatest thing in English fiction."). *The Mirror in the Roadway* (1956), pp. 272-79.

6 *Poems,* p. 956.

7 Orwell, *A Collection of Essays,* p. 152.

8 According to Lawrence, Ruskin was likewise crippled by the same kind of mother-fixation from which he himself had suffered. See *Letters* (Huxley), p. 77.

9 Arthur Mizener, *Highlights of Modern Literature* (New York, 1949), p. 19. In Lawrence's self-parody scene in *Women in Love* (ch. XIX), he has Halliday use the same term as Mizener: "according to this letter . . . we're all flowers of mud . . . Birkin harrowing Hell—harrowing the Pompadour."

10 See F. R. Kluckhohn and F. L. Strodkbeck, *Variations in Value Orientations* (Evanston, Illinois, 1961), p. 14. The statistical analyses of this study of primitive and advanced cultures provide an interesting substantiation of Lawrence's more impressionistic account of contrasting values.

11 *Poems,* p. 711.

12 Nehls, III, 570.

13 *Letters,* I, 65; 69-70; and *Letters* (Huxley), p. 6.

14 Ada Lawrence, *Early Life of D. H. Lawrence* (1932), pp. 24-25.

15 See Walter Allen, *The English Novel,* p. 344. For another view of the mother-son relationship, see Alfred Kazin's perceptive analysis in *Partisan Review,* XXIX

(1962), 373-85, and also Lina Waterfield's autobiography, *Castle in Italy* (1961), pp. 139-40.

16 A contrary interpretation, arguing for the complexity and freshness of Butler's novel, is ably developed by Daniel Howard in his *Introduction* to the Houghton Mifflin edition of *The Way of All Flesh* (1963).

17 Karl Menninger, *Love Against Hate* (New York, 1942), p. 57. The similarly mixed attitude of Stendhal is described by Lionel Trilling in *The Liberal Imagination* (New York, 1950), p. 164n. On some of the connections between Freud and Lawrence, see F. J. Hoffman, *Freudianism and the Literary Mind* (Baton-Rouge, 1945), pp. 149-80; and for a more elaborated (but disappointing) study, see Daniel Weiss, *Oedipus in Nottingham* (Seattle, 1963). Concerning the psychoanalytic concept of ambivalence in human relations, "love and hatred directed toward the same person at the same time," there is a helpful summary in Franz Alexander's *Fundamentals of Psychoanalysis* (New York, 1948), pp. 106-108.

18 Nehls, III, 22-23, and 245.

19 *Getting On,* an unfinished autobiography in the collection of Lawrence papers of the University of Cincinnati Library.

20 M. H. Abrams, "Belief and Suspension of Disbelief." *English Institute Essays* (New York, 1958), pp. 28-30. See also Eliseo Vivas, *D. H. Lawrence* (Evanston, 1960), pp. 23-24 and 30-31.

21 See Nehls, I, 146. Some phase of the courtship of his parents was reportedly a source of embarrassment to Lawrence, but its nature is unknown. See Nehls, I, 26, 114.

22 Richard Aldington, *Introduction* to the Phoenix edition of *The White Peacock* (1955), p. viii.

23 *Phoenix,* p. 327.

24 Nehls, I, 127.

25 Frank Kermode, *Romantic Image* (New York, 1957), pp. 73-74.

26 *Phoenix,* p. 507.

27 Rebecca West's report of her meeting with Lawrence in Italy is in her *D. H. Lawrence* (1930), pp. 18-36.

28 Kathleen Nott, "Lawrence by Daylight." *The Observer,* Nov. 13, 1960. See also "A visit with D. H. Lawrence," by Edith Sitwell, *New York Herald Tribune,* Dec. 20, 1960, and *TLS,* Nov. 28, 1963, p. 993; Simone de Beauvoir, *Le Deuxième sexe* (Paris, 1949), I, 336-42. For Virginia Woolf and Miss Porter, see above pp. 4, 75. See also Willa Cather *On Writing* (New York, 1949), p. 42. More sympathetic critical studies of Lawrence by women writers include Anaïs Nin, *D. H. Lawrence: An Unprofessional Study* (Paris, 1932); Diana Trilling, Introduction to *The Viking Portable Lawrence,* and Mary Freeman, *D. H. Lawrence: A Basic Study of His Ideas* (University of Florida, 1955).

29 See C. J. Jung's *Psychology of the Unconscious* (New York, 1916), especially pp. 231-32, a discussion of the "strongly androgynous character of the dying and resurrected Redeemer," which provides helpful information about the kind of wandering heroes one encounters in Lawrence's novels.

30 Robert E. Gadjusek, "A reading of *The White Peacock.*" In *Miscellany,* pp. 188-203. See also Raney Stanford's "Thomas Hardy and Lawrence's *The White Peacock,*" *Modern Fiction Studies* V (1959), 19-28.

31 "E.T.," *D. H. Lawrence,* p. 131.

32 *Lawrence Durrell and Henry*

Miller, A Private Correspondence (New York, 1963), p. 108.

33 See "E.T.," *D. H. Lawrence,* p. 136.

CHAPTER 4

1 *Phoenix,* p. 277.

2 Frieda Lawrence, *The Memoirs and Correspondence* (1961), p. 192.

3 *Spectator* (Aug. 8, 1958), p. 202.

4 André Malraux, "Preface to the French Translation of *Lady Chatterley's Lover." The Criterion,* XXI (Jan. 1933), 218.

5 *The Letters of W. B. Yeats* (1954), p. 810.

6 See Nehls, II, 271-72.

7 In the sketch (*Assorted Articles,* pp. 151 ff.) Lawrence tries to account for his not having been "much of a human success" in his personal relationships. His explanation here is that he is not at home with the middle classes and cannot return to the working classes. *Kangaroo* (chapters I and II) includes a penetrating analysis of the effects on Somers of his having shifted from working class to gentleman. See also *Letters,* II, 993.

8 *Poems,* p. 601. In one of his late letters to Murry, Lawrence described their relationship as a "dissonance."

9 *Letters,* II, 1020, and I, 20.

10 See Robert Graves, *Goodbye to All That* (1957), p. 268.

11 Nehls, I, 109.

12 Lawrence's early admiration for Synge's play gives weight to the opinion that *Riders to the Sea* was Lawrence's model for "Odour of Chrysanthemums," but the differences between the two works seem to me much more marked than the similarities. See *Letters,* I, 57, 76.

13 The importance of Paul's turning towards the light at the end is emphasized by Anthony West, *D. H. Lawrence* (1950), pp. 114-15.

14 *Letters,* I, 86, 94. For a reasonable appraisal of the real merits as well as the flaws of this early novel, see Leo Gurko's essay in *College English* (Oct. 1962), pp. 29-35, and also Ethel F. Cornwell, *The Still Point* (New Brunswick, New Jersey, 1962), pp. 220-22.

15 *Phoenix,* p. 411.

16 The early version was published in *English Review,* XVIII (1914), 298-315.

17 *The Moment and Other Essays* (1947), p. 79 (the essay was originally published in 1931). For a defense of Mrs. Woolf as a reader of Lawrence, the following essay is a lively corrective: Robert Hogan, "D. H. Lawrence and his Critics." *Essays in Criticism,* IX (1959), 381-87.

18 F. R. Leavis, *D. H. Lawrence: Novelist* (1955), p. 246.

19 See Eliseo Vivas, *D. H. Lawrence,* pp. 193-94.

20 See Kingsley Widmer, "D. H. Lawrence and the Art of Nihilism." *Kenyon Review,* XX (Autumn 1958), 604-616. Also see Frank Amon, "D. H. Lawrence and the Short Story," in *The Achievement of D. H. Lawrence,* ed. F. J. Hoffman and H. T. Moore (1953), pp. 226-231.

21 See *Ship of Fools* (New York, 1962), p. 216 and also pp. 364-66.

22 *Prologue to Women in Love,* with an introduction by George H. Ford. *Texas Quarterly,* VI (Spring 1963), 107-09.

23 *Phoenix,* pp. 378-79, and *Nehls,* III, 683. Jung also has much to say on the painful isolation which results from "every step forward" from unconscious to conscious awareness. See *Psychological Reflections: An Anthology of the Writings of Carl G. Jung* (New

York, 1953), pp. 28-35. For a later study of the evolution of consciousness and isolation, see Charles Davy, *Towards a Third Culture* (1961).

24 See *Letters* (Huxley), p. 718, p. 735, and West, pp. 85-87, 94. In addition to the articles mentioned below, see also Julian Moynahan, *The Deed of Life* (Princeton, 1963), pp. 186-96.

25 Faith Compton Mackenzie, *Always Afternoon* (1943), pp. 121-22. See also her *More Than I Should* (1940), pp. 66, 89.

26 Dorothy Brett, *Lawrence and Brett* (Philadelphia, 1933), pp. 271-72.

27 Nehls, III, 258.

28 *Letters,* II, 931.

29 Because the story appears in a notebook containing jottings for the Etruscan studies, Lawrence Powell concluded that it must be a late work (*The Manuscripts of D. H. Lawrence,* 1937, p. 28). In August, 1926, Lawrence was studying books about Etruria with Aldington in London and might have begun the fragment at that time. John R. Elliot, Jr., in his *Introduction* to the published version of the story (*Essays in Criticism,* IX, July, 1959, 213-21) states that it was probably written in early spring of 1927, with March 8 a terminal date. The possibility that Lawrence began writing it after "The Man Who Loved Islands" in order to disguise the resemblance to Mackenzie might be considered but seems unlikely.

30 *Poems,* p. 602.

31 Frederic R. Karl, "Lawrence's *The Man Who Loved Islands*" in *Miscellany,* p. 269.

32 Julian Moynahan, "Lawrence's *The Man Who Loved Islands,*" *Modern Fiction Studies,* V (Spring 1959), 58-59.

33 Kingsley Widmer, "D. H. Lawrence and the Art of Nihilism," p. 615.

34 *Letters* (Huxley), p. 223.

35 See Nehls, III, 62, 64.

36 It would be tempting to push the Biblical analogies further. The old carpenter could be likened to Joseph and even the cow that fell off the cliff to the incident of the Gadarene swine. Often in Lawrence such exercises in analogy may be illuminating, but in this instance they do not add up.

37 *Lawrence and Brett,* p. 287.

38 H. T. Moore, *The Intelligent Heart* (New York, 1954), p. 364.

CHAPTER 5

1 E.g., *Letters,* II, 1231; *The Plumed Serpent,* Chapter XXV; *Reflections on the Death of a Porcupine* (Philadelphia, 1925), p. 173.

2 See Nehls, I, 72.

3 *Phoenix,* pp. 794-95.

4 Nehls, I, 238, and *Letters,* I, 337. On intensity in life and art see also *Death of a Porcupine,* p. 148: "Life does not mean length of days. Poor old Queen Victoria had length of days. But Emily Brontë had life. She died of it."

5 Huxley, *Introduction* to *The Letters,* p. xxx.

6 See Douglas Grant, "England's Phoenix." *University of Toronto Quarterly,* XXVII (1958), 223.

7 Helen Corke in *Texas Quarterly,* V (1962), 175.

8 To a former student, John Ades, who is preparing a study of affinities between Lawrence's writings and landscape paintings, I am indebted for helpful comments on this story.

9 *The Autobiography of John Middleton Murry* (New York, 1936), pp. 406-10.

10 *Phoenix,* p. 192.

11 H. T. Moore, *The Intelligent*

Heart (New York, 1954), p. 117.

12 Biographers suggest that Lawrence's story "The Thimble" and its later version "The Ladybird" derive from his acquaintance with Lady Cynthia Asquith and her husband. See *Letters*, I, p. 491n. "Glad Ghosts" is another story of this category and similarly inspired. For whatever the information is worth, I should myself record that Lady Cynthia assured me, in a conversation in 1956, that "The Ladybird" was modeled on the life of Lady Mendl.

13 In Joyce's *Ulysses* the flute is a female symbol (see Modern Library edition, p. 281). In *Aaron's Rod* it is distinctly male.

14 Letter to George Keats, April 15, 1819.

15 Dorothy Brett, *Lawrence and Brett*, pp. 279-80.

16 *Phoenix*, p. 369.

17 Dorothea Krook, *Three Traditions of Moral Thought* (Cambridge, 1959), pp. 255-92. For a more judicious appraisal see Eugene Goodheart's *The Utopian Vision of D. H. Lawrence* (Chicago, 1963), pp. 149-59, and also his general comments (pp. 35-37) on the nature of the "resistances" present in Lawrence's best writings.

18 W. K. C. Guthrie, *The Greeks and their Gods* (1950), pp. 218-219, 284.

19 See Julian Moynahan, "*Lady Chatterley's Lover:* The Deed of Life," in *D. H. Lawrence: A Collection of Critical Essays*, ed. Mark Spilka (1963), p. 89.

20 Maud Bodkin, *Studies of Type-Images* (Oxford, 1951), p. 10.

21 See William Tiverton, *D. H. Lawrence and Human Existence* (1951), p. x.

22 Richard Hoggart, *The Uses of Literacy* (Penguin edition), p. 14.

23 Nehls, I, 48.

CHAPTER 6

1 *Phoenix*, p. 295.

2 Frieda Lawrence, *The Memoirs and Correspondence*, pp. 296, 316. Frieda's letters to Koteliansky (unpublished) are even more emphatic on this point. One biography in which Louie's role is given proportionately more attention is Piero Nardi's *La Vita di D. H. Lawrence* (1947), pp. 122-26, 155, 195.

3 In the novel Anna has 9 children, but one dies in infancy. The names of the two eldest Burrows children, Louisa and Ethel, have no counterparts in Ursula and Gudrun, but the other names were useful. William Burrows appears as William Brangwen, Cissie as Cassie, Connie as Katie, Dora as Norah. See *The Rainbow*, chs. X, XIII; and *Women in Love*, ch. XV.

4 R. W. B. Lewis, *The American Adam* (Chicago, 1955), p. 91.

5 *Phoenix*, p. 296.

6 See Jascha Kessler, "Descent in Darkness: The Myth of *The Plumed Serpent.*" In *Miscellany*, pp. 239-61. See also Mark Schorer, "Fiction with a Great Burden." *Kenyon Review*, XIV (1952), 162-68.

7 See Eliseo Vivas, *D. H. Lawrence*, pp. 98-99; 139; 211-17.

8 John Bayley, *The Characters of Love* (1960), pp. 24-25.

9 *Reflections on the Death of a Porcupine*, p. 53.

10 *Phoenix*, p. 741.

11 *Phoenix*, p. 99. See also Arthur Lovejoy's classic essay on the paradox of the Fortunate Fall in his *Essays in the History of Ideas* (Baltimore, 1948), pp. 277-95.

12 W. B. Yeats, *Autobiographies* (1955), p. 115.

13 For other references to the rainbow, see *Letters*, I, 328; *Death of*

a *Porcupine*, p. 16; and Dorothy Brett, *Lawrence and Brett*, pp. 279-80. In *Kangaroo*, chapter VIII, Somers reflects: "The rainbow was always a symbol to him . . . a pledge of unbroken faith, between the universe and the innermost."

14 For this comparison and other suggestions in this chapter I am indebted to John Adamczyk, a former student of the Colgate Rochester Divinity School, whose participation in a seminar on Lawrence was for me a great help.

15 *Letters*, I, 273.

16 Lawrence read his immediate predecessors, Bennett, Wells, Galsworthy, with mixed feelings. An early admiration for Bennett's *Old Wives' Tale* and Wells' *Tono Bungay* gradually gave way to disappointment in *Anna of the Five Towns* and *Ann Veronica*, and by 1915 he was describing Bennett as "an old imitator." (*Letters*, I, 399). At the time he began planning *The Sisters*, however, in the spring of 1913, he was exceptionally anxious about the sales of his books. Of *Sons and Lovers* he said: "It's got to sell, I've got to live." (*Letters*, I, 193). In this mood, without in any sense losing his own independence as an experimenter, he seems to have been prepared to examine the requirements of popular fiction as exemplified by other novelists. "The woman problem," as it was called, had been and was to remain a leading topic for writers of fiction. It was commonly represented by stories of girls like Sophia Baines in *The Old Wives' Tale* who broke away from home to seek new and unconventional relationships. In addition to his reading of Bennett and Wells, Lawrence had read George Moore's *Evelyn Innes* and some novels by Compton Mackenzie whose *Carnival* (1912) is a typical story of a girl's revolt from conventions. *The Lost Girl* and *The Rainbow* and *Women in Love*, however distinctive, are also part of the Georgian literary scene. See *Letters*, I, 57, 60, 148, 150, 203, 226, 527; and Nehls, III, 614-15.

17 On Lawrence's Protestantism, see J. H. Raleigh's "Victorian Morals and the Modern Novel." *Partisan Review*, XXV (1958), 241-64. For Lawrence's own comments, see *Apocalypse* and also his essay, "Hymns in a Man's Life," in *Assorted Articles*, pp. 155-63. The Biblical influence on Lawrence's prose style has been analyzed by Frank Baldanza in *Modern Fiction Studies*, VII (1961), 106-14.

18 *Phoenix*, pp. 535-36.

19 *Ibid.*, p. 226.

20 Northrop Frye, *Anatomy of Criticism* (Princeton, 1957), pp. 33-34.

21 J. M. Murry, *Reminiscences of D. H. Lawrence* (1936), p. 53.

22 Similarly in the short story, "Samson and Delilah," the parallel extends only to the trapping and binding of the hero by the soldiers but does not otherwise relate to the Bible story.

CHAPTER 7

1 *Jane Austen's Letters*, ed. R. W. Chapman (Oxford, 1932), p. 401.

2 *Letters*, I, 282.

3 Catherine Carswell, *The Savage Pilgrimage* (1932), p. 71.

4 A helpful reconstruction of the order in which the parts may have been written is offered by Harry T. Moore (*The Intelligent Heart*, p. 189). For an analysis of the differences between the "early" and "late" styles in *The Rainbow*, see M. Wildi, "The Birth of Expressionism in the Works of D. H.

Lawrence." *English Studies,* XIX (1937), 241-59.

5 Tom and Emily Renshaw in *The White Peacock* are happily married, but their role in the novel is of minor consequence. In the manner of some of Hardy's characters, they serve as background figures.

6 Martin Buber, *I and Thou* (Edinburgh, 1937), p. 59. See also William Tiverton, *D. H. Lawrence and Human Existence,* pp. 105-06.

7 Although accused of almost every literary vice by his critics, Lawrence has usually been spared the charge of sentimentality. Exception would have to be made for the German philosopher, Ernst Bloch, who banished him as a "sentimental penis-poet." See *TLS* (March 31, 1961), p. 194.

8 See Sergei Eisenstein: *Notes of a Film Director* (1959), pp. 196-257, and Robbe-Grillet's introduction to *L'Immortelle* (Paris, 1963).

9 See e.g., J. G. Frazer, *The Golden Bough* (1955), IV, 191-92. Frazer's theories about the supplanting of aging leaders, which were well known to Lawrence, have been disputed by later anthropologists.

10 A long list could be made of novelists who have portrayed phases of the relations between fathers and daughters, such as Fielding, Austen, Balzac, Dickens, James, F. Scott Fitzgerald, Mann, Henry Green, Nathalie Sarraute—in fact almost any novelist's name could be added, but the particular phase portrayed by Lawrence of the father's sense of alienation seems rarely to have been given extended treatment.

11 Mabel Dodge Luhan, *Lorenzo in Taos* (1933), p. 93.

12 Marvin Mudrick, "The Originality of *The Rainbow.*" In *Miscellany,* p. 61.

13 In *Women in Love* Will Brangwen is described as a man "of nearly fifty, who was as unresolved now as he was at twenty, and as uncreated."

14 See above, Ch. I, note 20.

15 Cf. Graham Hough who contends that it "*ought* to be a mystery, but in fact it becomes a muddle." (*The Dark Sun,* p. 69). Julian Moynahan also comments on the difficulties: "Why do some of these characters succeed in saving themselves while others fail? This question is virtually impossible to answer." (*The Deed of Life,* Princeton, 1963, p. 47).

16 Hugh Kingsmill, *D. H. Lawrence* (1938), pp. 68-70.

17 Marlow's interview with Stein in Conrad's *Lord Jim* features a similar contrasting of reality as perceived under the lamplight and as perceived in the darkness.

18 Erich Auerbach, *Mimesis* (Princeton, 1953), p. 523.

19 Stephen Mallarmé, *Selected Prose,* translated by Bradford Cook (Baltimore, 1956), p. 83.

20 *The Basic Writings of Sigmund Freud* (Modern Library, 1938), p. 391.

21 *Apocalypse,* pp. 97-98. See also Cicio's remark in *The Lost Girl:* "In England railway-engines are alive, and horses go on wheels." See also *Etruscan Places,* p. 108; *Letters* (Huxley), p. 233, and "St. Mawr," *passim.*

22 *Fantasia of the Unconscious* (New York, 1922), p. 251.

23 For criticism of the finale of *The Rainbow* an article by S. L. Goldberg is well argued: *Essays in Criticism,* XI (1961), 418-34.

24 Early in his career Lawrence regarded Shelley as one of the greatest of writers (see e.g., *Letters,* I, 253 and the early play, *A Collier's Friday Night,* p. 44). Later his enthusiasm waned, and

Frieda, who regarded Shelley as a writer to be laughed at, liked to believe that her distaste had been responsible for her husband's shift of allegiance. What may be a kind of transcript of one of these literary debates appears in "The Border Line" in reference to Nietzsche, a writer "adored" by the wife but for whom the husband has only "contempt." That Lawrence had much in common with Nietzsche is nevertheless evident. [See Harry Steinhauer, "Eros and Psyche: A Nietzschean Motif in Anglo-American Literature." *Modern Language Notes,* LXIV (1949), 217-28.]

CHAPTER 8

1 Nehls, I, 412.
2 *Letters,* I, 519.
3 *Ibid.*
4 *Letters,* I, 495, 615.
5 For the book we now know as *The Rainbow* the earlier title, *The Wedding Ring,* would not have been suitable. There is a passing reference to Lydia Lensky's wedding ring but of insufficient importance to account for the title. On the other hand the second half of the long narrative could have used the title appropriately, for in the crucial proposal scene three rings figure prominently in Birkin's quarrel and reconciliation with Ursula (chapter XXIII of *Women in Love*). A typescript version of the chapter establishes the link more precisely by descriptions of one of the rings as a wedding ring. These were deleted before publication. A further indication of the suitability of the title is suggested by a fragmentary manuscript dealing with the other pair of lovers, Gerald and Gudrun. In this version (probably dating from 1913 and early 1914) Gerald returns to Shortlands from the Tyrol and proposes marriage to Gudrun (who is, like Lettie in the original version of *The White Peacock,* pregnant). The double weddings, only talked about as a possibility in the final version of *Women in Love,* seem at one point to have been considered to be part of the narrative. (The pages of this manuscript, part of the University of Texas collection, are numbered 291-96.)
6 On January 20, 1917, he told Pinker: "I recomposed all the first part on the typewriter."
7 See an essay by George H. Ford in *Texas Studies in Literature and Language* (Summer 1964), pp. 134-37.
8 *Letters,* I, 482.—Further corrections and revisions were made in 1917. In February, 1917, Lawrence's agent prepared typed copies of *Women in Love,* transcribing them from the author's typescript and manuscript. One of the typed copies was retained by Lawrence for inserting further corrections; the other circulated among his friends. Some striking modifications seem to have been made at this late stage, especially in chapter XXIII, "Excurse."
9 *Letters,* I, 519.
10 See Nehls, I, 350-51.
11 See H. T. Moore, *The Intelligent Heart,* p. 225, and Nehls, I, 395-96. Catherine Carswell reports that the Lawrences described the incident to her on September 3, 1916, as having occurred "shortly before."—In this same "Breadably" chapter is an account of a costume party similar to one at Garsington described in a letter of late November, 1915, but in view of the Morrells' fondness for frequently staging such diversions it would be unwise to try to link the scene to any specific

date. See *Letters* (Huxley), 283-84.

12 See Moore, *The Intelligent Heart,* pp. 24-26.

13 W. W. Robson, "D. H. Lawrence and *Women in Love.*" In *The Modern Age,* ed. Boris Ford (1961), p. 296. On Aldington, see Nehls, III, xiii. On Garnett, see George H. Ford's essay on Lawrence's *Prologue* chapter, *The Texas Quarterly* (Spring 1963), pp. 95-96.

14 *Letters,* I, 125. The likeness between Nusch and Gudrun was suggested by her niece, Frieda's daughter. See Nehls, III, 162.

15 Giraudoux, *Sodome et Gomorrhe* (Paris, 1951), pp. 17, 98.

16 See, e.g., Cynthia Asquith, *Remember and Be Glad* (1952), pp. 140, 145.

17 *The Early Memoirs of Lady Ottoline Morrell* (1963), p. 177.

18 Cf. Lawrence's outbursts in *Letters,* I, 339, 524: "It would be nice if the Lord sent another flood and drowned the world. Probably I should want to be Noah. I am not sure." On Sodom see *ibid.,* pp. 373, 510.

19 Quoted by Armin Arnold, *D. H. Lawrence and America,* p. 173.

20 See also John McCormick's *Catastrophe and Imagination* (1957) which has a helpful chapter on war novels (pp. 204-37). His regard for Lawrence is very slim (see his chapter VIII).

21 Neil Myers, "Lawrence and the War." *Criticism,* IV (1962), p. 48.

22 Olive Moore, *Further Reflections on the Death of a Porcupine* (1932), p. 23.

23 *Letters,* I, 338. In some of Lawrence's post-war stories the hero, sympathetically portrayed, is an infantry officer such as Captain Anstruther in "The Border Line": "a ceaseless born fighter, a sword not to be sheathed."

24 *Introduction* to *Memoirs of the Foreign Legion* (1924), pp. 89-90.

25 *Encounter,* III (1953), 31. See also K. W. Gransden, "Ranaim." *The Twentieth Century* (Jan. 1956), p. 26.

26 Virginia Woolf, *The Moment and other Essays,* p. 82, and J. H. Raleigh in *Partisan Review* (1958), p. 260.

27 Nehls, III, 403.

28 *Letters* (Huxley), p. 466. See also Philip Rieff's essay "A Modern Mythmaker" in *Myth and Mythmaking,* ed. Henry A. Murray (New York, 1960), pp. 240-75.

29 *Etruscan Places* (1932), p. 44.

30 *Letters,* I, 416. The only fiction he seems to have read during this period was Melville's *Moby Dick,* about which he was enthusiastic, and some novels of Dostoevsky, which he professed to find distasteful (perhaps in part to deflate John Middleton Murry's reverential attitude to the Russian master).

31 *Letters,* I, 249, 416, 424, 425, 436, 451, 454, 466, 468.

32 On April 18, 1918, Lawrence wrote that he had read "two ponderous tomes on Africa" by Frobenius, and in *Aaron's Rod* he pictures Lilly reading the same author.—See also Basil Davidson, *The Lost Cities of Africa* (Boston, 1959), and André Malraux, *The Voices of Silence* (New York, 1953), p. 132.

33 *Letters,* I, 477-78. (Italics mine.)

34 *Letters,* I, 418, and *Letters* (Huxley), pp. 303, 329.

35 Horace Gregory, *D. H. Lawrence: Pilgrim of the Apocalypse* (New York, 1933), pp. 45-46, 49.

36 Anaïs Nin, *D. H. Lawrence* (Paris, 1932), p. 110. See also Nathan A. Scott, Jr., *Rehearsals of Discomposure* (1952), p. 157.

37 Cf. a reference to the women of the South Sea Islands whose skin he could not conceive of touching: "flesh like warm mud. Nearer the reptile, the Saurian age."—*Studies in Classic American Literature* (New York, 1923), pp. 202-03.

38 So far as I know there is no record of Lawrence's being exposed to some library of erotic literature such as Swinburne was exposed to under the guidance of R. M. Milnes. His distaste for such writers as Casanova ("he smells") is well known. *Letters* (Huxley), p. 523.

39 *Letters*, I, 333.

40 Nehls, I, 269, 301.

41 *Reflections on the Death of a Porcupine*, pp. 66-67, 80.

42 D. H. Lawrence, *The Symbolic Meaning*, ed. Armin Arnold (1962), p. 263.

43 See John Sparrow in *Encounter* (Feb., 1962), pp. 35-43, and June, 1962, pp. 83-88, and replies by Colin MacInnes and Stephen Potter in *Encounter* (March, 1962), pp. 63-65, 94-96. See also Wilson Knight in *Essays in Criticism* (Oct., 1961), pp. 403-17, and Andrew Shonfield in *Encounter* (Sept., 1961), pp. 63-64, and letter to the editor, *TLS* (August 4, 1961). An earlier controversy provoked by Colin Welch's accusing Lawrence of witchcraft can also be found in *Encounter* (Feb., 1961), pp. 75-79, and March, 1961, pp. 52-55. Also relevant are Middleton Murry's comments in his *Reminiscences of D. H. Lawrence* (1933), pp. 223-27.

44 Mark Spilka, *The Love Ethic of D. H. Lawrence*, p. 100.

45 Vivas, *D. H. Lawrence*, pp. 261-67.

46 *Phoenix*, p. 176.

47 Again Vivas' account (pp. 257-61) is especially helpful. For a contrasting interpretation of the scene, see Murray Krieger, *The Tragic Vision* (1960), pp. 37-49.

48 *Letters*, I, 520.

CHAPTER 9

1 Herbert Read, "On D. H. Lawrence." *The Twentieth Century*, CLXV (1959), p. 558. Cf. Angus Wilson, "At the Heart of Lawrence." *Encounter* (Dec., 1955), pp. 83-85.

2 *Letters*, I, 404. For Lawrence's critical comments on later Indian civilizations, see above p. 124.

3 *D. H. Lawrence: A Collection of Critical Essays* (ed. Mark Spilka), p. 60.

4 *Fantasia of the Unconscious*, p. 9.

5 F. R. Leavis, *D. H. Lawrence: Novelist*, p. 28.

6 *Fiction of the Fifties*, selected by Herbert Gold (New York, Doubleday Doran, 1959), p. 63.

7 *Letters*, I, 150, 152.

8 Edwin Honig, *Dark Conceit* (Evanston, Illinois, 1959), p. 61.

9 See above p. 107.

10 Frieda Lawrence, *Not I, But the Wind* (1935), p. 140.

Index

In the Norton Library

LITERATURE

Austen, Jane *Persuasion* Intro. by David Daiches N163
Brace, Gerald Warner *The Garretson Chronicle* N272
Browning, Robert *The Ring and the Book* Introduction by Wylie Sypher N433
Burgess, Anthony *A Clockwork Orange* Afterword by Stanley Edgar Hyman N224
Burgess, Anthony *Tremor of Intent* N416
Burney, Fanny *Evelina* N294
Conrad, Joseph *The Arrow of Gold* N458
Conrad, Joseph *Chance* N456
Conrad, Joseph *The Rescue* N457
Edgeworth, Maria *Castle Rackrent* N288
Fielding, Henry *Joseph Andrews* Introduction by Mary Ellen Chase N274
Gaskell, Mrs. Elizabeth *Mary Barton* Introduction by Myron F. Brightfield N245
Gogol, Nicolai V. *"The Overcoat" and Other Tales of Good and Evil* N304
Golding, Arthur, TR. *Shakespeare's Ovid* N336
Gosse, Edmund *Father and Son* N195
Hamilton, Edith, TR. AND ED. *Three Greek Plays* N203
Harrier, Richard C., ED. *Jacobean Drama: An Anthology* Edited with Introduction, Notes, and Variants (Norton Library Seventeenth-Century Series) N434a (Vol. I) and N434b (Vol. II)
Hawthorne, Nathaniel *The Blithedale Romance* Introduction by Arlin Turner N164
Herrick, Robert *The Complete Poetry of Robert Herrick* Edited with Introduction and Notes by J. Max Patrick (Norton Library Seventeenth-Century Series) N435
Homer *The Iliad* A Shortened Version translated and edited by I. A. Richards N101
James, Henry *The Awkward Age* N285
James, Henry *"In the Cage" and Other Tales* N286
Jonson, Ben *The Complete Poetry of Ben Jonson* Edited with Introduction, Notes and Variants by William B. Hunter, Jr. (Norton Library Seventeenth-Century Series) N436
Lawrence, T. E. *The Mint* N196
Lederer, William J. and Eugene Burdick *The Ugly American* N305
Lucian *Selected Satires of Lucian* Edited and Translated by Lionel Casson N443

Lynn, Kenneth S., ED. *The Comic Tradition in America: An Anthology of American Humor* N447

Mackenzie, Henry *The Man of Feeling* Introduction by Kenneth C. Slagle N214

Mish, Charles C., ED. *Short Fiction of the Seventeenth Century* (Norton Library Seventeenth-Century Series) N437

Peacock, Thomas Love *Nightmare Abbey* N283

Reeves, James, ED. *The Idiom of the People* N289

Richardson, Samuel *Pamela* Introduction by William M. Sale, Jr. N166

Rilke, Rainer Maria *Duino Elegies* N155

Rilke, Rainer Maria *The Lay of the Love and Death of Cornet Christopher Rilke* N159

Rilke, Rainer Maria *Letters of Rainer Maria Rilke, 1892-1910* N476

Rilke, Rainer Maria *Letters of Rainer Maria Rilke, 1910-1926* N477

Rilke, Rainer Maria *Letters to a Young Poet* N158

Rilke, Rainer Maria *The Notebooks of Malte Laurids Brigge* N267

Rilke, Rainer Maria *Sonnets to Orpheus* N157

Rilke, Rainer Maria *Stories of God* N154

Rilke, Rainer Maria *Translations from the Poetry* by M. D. Herter Norton N156

Rilke, Rainer Maria *Wartime Letters of Rainer Maria Rilke* N160

Rizal, José *The Lost Eden (Noli Me Tangere)* Translated by Leon Ma. Guerrero N222

Rizal, José *The Subversive (El Filibusterismo)* Translated by Leon Ma. Guerrero N449

Seneca *The Stoic Philosophy of Seneca* Essays and Letters, translated and with an introduction by Moses Hadas N459

Stendhal *The Private Diaries of Stendhal* N175

Tolstoy, Leo *Anna Karenina* The Maude Translation, with an introduction by George Gibian N326

Tolstoy, Leo *Resurrection* The Maude Translation, with an introduction by George Gibian N325

Trollope, Anthony *The Last Chronicle of Barset* Introduction by Gerald Warner Brace N291

Turgenev, Ivan *"First Love" and Other Tales* N444

Whitman, Walt *Leaves of Grass* The Comprehensive Reader's Edition, edited by Harold W. Blodgett and Sculley Bradley N430

Wollstonecraft, Mary *A Vindication of the Rights of Woman* Introduction, Chronology, and Bibliography by Charles W. Hagelman, Jr. N373